If only she'd come an hour later this morning . . . if only she hadn't come at all.

Because of a stupid little key, Molly was now a major player in a murder investigation. Eyeing the cluster of police huddled around the body in the driveway, she turned away from the patrol car and stole a glance at the growing crowd beyond the yellow tape. Mumbling ever so politely above the sounds of the surf behind them, the residents of Carmel's Scenic Road were soon joined by beach joggers and tourists drawn to the pulsing lights of the three patrol cars blocking the village's most traveled and expensive residential street. The magnificent view of Carmel Bay, and its famous white sand beach, took second place to the horrible scene before them.

Molly pulled the brim of her cap down, sucked in her breath, and pounded her fist against the car. She should have left after calling 911. The natural instinct to be a good citizen was going to kill her chance to start over. Ordered by the first cop on the scene not to leave, she knew it was the beginning of the end.

The minute the cops checked her out, as she knew they would, she'd have to leave Carmel. . . .

DEALING IN MURDER

ELAINE FLINN

AVON BOOKS
An Imprint of HarperCollinsPublishers

This book is a work of fiction. References to real people, events, establishments, organizations, or locales are intended only to provide a sense of authenticity, and are used fictitiously. All other characters, and all incidents and dialogue, are drawn from the author's imagination and are not to be construed as real.

AVON BOOKS
An Imprint of HarperCollins*Publishers*
10 East 53rd Street
New York, New York 10022-5299

Copyright © 2003 by Elaine Flinn
ISBN: 0-06-054579-8
www.avonmystery.com

First Avon Books paperback printing: November 2003

Avon Trademark Reg. U.S. Pat. Off. and in Other Countries, Marca Registrada, Hecho en U.S.A.
HarperCollins® is a registered trademark of HarperCollins Publishers Inc.

Printed in the U.S.A.

10 9 8 7 6 5 4 3 2 1

*To all the hardworking antique and collectable dealers.
May you find that "once in a lifetime treasure."*

And to The Silver Fox and Diamond Lil

Acknowledgments

My husband said not to mention how much his support, belief, and encouragement have meant to me, because that's what love is. So I won't. My son and daughters, however, who have been superb cheerleaders, won't mind, so I'll thank Patrick for his astute eye, Kelly for wanting to bang me on the head when I was ready to quit—not to mention for keeping my grammar in check, Sharon for her positive attitude, my daughter-in-law, Karen, who told me to "go for it," and my granddaughter Typhany, who is stoked her Nana made it.

It's one thing for family to cheer you on. That's a given. But, to have an agent like Nina Collins, that is quite another matter. I would not be here, if not for Nina. From day one, Nina, whose inner beauty is indescribable, never wavered in her belief in the series and in me. Whatever success I may have, I share with her. I will never be able to thank her enough. And then, there is my editor, Jennifer Civiletto. Oh, I pity the writer upon whose shoulder she does not not reside. Jennifer's exquisite eye, romantic heart, and simpatico are gifts I will cherish.

Many thanks to Wayne Oberti, M.D., F.A.C.E.P., F.A.A.E.M., aka Dr. O—my erudite cousin and Olympic torchbearer, for his medical expertise and sense of humor; to Bobby Phillips, Salinas Police Department; Buck Melton, Carmel Police Department; and Gary Gray, former Deputy District Attorney, for all their contributions.

Last, but certainly not least, my gratitude to Chassie West and Sheldon Siegel, two acclaimed, award-winning authors who so generously gave aid and friendship, and sustained this fledgling writer when she was ready to pack it in. And to Craig Leslie, author and teacher extraordinaire, who gave me the confidence to see this through when he told me to hire a gardener. Thank you all, dear hearts.

DEALING IN MURDER

1

The blood-soaked sweatshirt was making Molly Doyle gag. Gingerly pulling it away from her body, she was thankful for the police windbreaker she'd been loaned. With her hair tucked up in a baseball cap, wearing jeans and sneakers, she was ignored by the invading television reporters. Slumped against the police car, fighting nausea, she looked like a rookie unable to handle her first dead body. She wanted to kick herself for not having her wits about her yesterday when she bought the desk from the dead woman. If only she hadn't been so greedy, so anxious to get to the other garage sales, she might have thought to check the damn desk. It hadn't occurred to her it might be locked.

And now, because of a stupid little key, she was a major player in a murder investigation. Eyeing the cluster of police huddled around the body in the driveway, she turned away from the patrol car and stole a glance at the growing crowd beyond the yellow tape. Mumbling ever so politely above the sounds of the surf behind them, the residents of Carmel's Scenic Road were soon joined by beach joggers and tourists drawn to the pulsing lights of the three patrol cars blocking the village's most traveled and expensive residential street. The magnificent view of Carmel Bay, and its famous white sand beach, took second place to the grisly scene before them.

Molly pulled the brim of her cap down, sucked in her breath, and pounded her fist against the car. She should have left after calling 911. The natural instinct to be a good citizen was going to kill her chance to start over. Ordered by the first cop on the scene not to leave, she knew it was the beginning of the end. The minute the cops checked her out, as she knew they would, she'd have to leave Carmel.

Reaching for the tiny crucifix she'd worn since her twelfth birthday, her lips moved rapidly, silently repeating one Hail Mary after another. Catholic Guilt told her she was praying for herself and not for the soul of the dead woman. The frequent litany quickly became hypnotic. A Zen state she once joked to Sister Agnes, her early mentor and harshest critic. Within moments her body finally began to relax. It was then it struck her. The revelation gripped her so firmly she had difficulty breathing.

"For want of a nail . . . the kingdom was lost" flashed across her mind. *For want, of a key, my new life here is over. What is a key, if not a little thing?*

Little things. Her life was a road map of "little things."

Her father's imprisonment was over a bracelet. A small chest inspired her career. The end of her marriage began with an offhand compliment. A woman died in her arms this morning because she'd forgotten to ask about a key. Insignificant things. *Little things.*

Her shaking hands were finally steady enough to rummage in her bag for her cigarettes. Finding anything in the large sling tote was always an adventure. It was the one place she could safely rebel against her need for organization. Her hands felt a small pack of Kleenex. Tearing it open, she stuffed it under the sweatshirt, making a barrier between her skin and the victim's congealing blood. Finding the cigarettes and her father's old Zippo, she inhaled deeply, wondering how much longer the police would keep her here. She toyed with the urge simply to slip away. In the obvious confusion going on in the driveway, they might not miss her.

Problem was, she had given a preliminary statement to the first officer after he had examined the body. They knew her name and where to find her. After escorting her to the patrol car, he ordered her not to leave. The chief would want to speak to her. That was almost an hour ago. The thought almost made her laugh. The chief? She remembered in time that no matter how famous Carmel was, it was still a tiny village, and wouldn't have a homicide inspector.

She needed to tear off her clothes and shower, to scald away the dead woman's blood, to purge the memory of the victim's contorted face, her huge disbelieving eyes darting in panic as she struggled to say something. Choking on her blood, her words were thick and garbled. Playing the sounds repeatedly in her mind, Molly tried desperately to make them mean something. Was the woman calling for someone? A husband? A child? God? With a horrible start, Molly wondered if it was her killer's name.

Brushing ashes off the cop's windbreaker, she tried not to look at the blood on her jeans and sneakers. Instead, she focused on the driveway and watched as a small cloth barrier was placed around the body. She shivered again as her eyes fixed on the police chief and watched his hand chop the air as he barked orders. A bear of a man, he'd come lumbering in nearly a half hour ago. He was well over six feet, with unruly gray-flecked sandy hair and a ruddy complexion probably from a temper. Glad not to be on the receiving end of his obvious anger, Molly almost felt sorry for the young cops clustered around him. The arriving officer must have told him he'd moved the body.

At this point, she didn't much care. She hated cops. All of them. Especially her uncles. She knew the chief would glance at her statement, then ignore it and ask her to repeat everything all over again.

Tucking loose hair back into her cap, she forced her mind into replay. She had to sort her thoughts. Get her facts straight. *He'll want to know why I was here. What time I arrived. Did I know the woman hurrying down the drive when I got here? Can I describe her? Would I recognize her again?* She knew the drill. How would he play her? Hard? Soft? Sensitive? She remembered the intricate variations on the themes—the hardball techniques, the soft sell, the sympathy plays, the good guy–bad guy roles. It was all her uncles bragged about at family gatherings. A tally of how many suspects they'd finessed into jail often replaced baseball scores and football trivia.

Stay calm, she whispered over and over. *Don't let him rattle you. Carmel may be a small tourist mecca with a low crime rate, but he is still a cop. Cooperate, be patient. Don't jabber. Keep your voice even. Don't smoke too much.*

If only she'd asked about the key yesterday.

She left the apartment early enough this morning to stop for the key, check out Sunday's garage sales, and be back in time to shower and open the shop by ten. It would be a mad rush, but she had little choice. Carmel was packed this weekend, and she needed sales. Taking on the small, neglected antique shop was proving to be more than she had bargained for.

The shop had been filled with dusty junk when she'd

arrived two weeks ago. She'd scrubbed, polished, and re-arranged until the pain forced her to stop. How Max, her dear friend, current benefactor, and one of the top antique dealers in San Francisco thought the inventory qualified as antiques was beyond her. It didn't take long to realize a plundering mission was needed to find goods that looked somewhat appealing. It killed her to think she was reduced to selling such dreck. It was humbling no longer to be one of New York's top antique dealers. She had to keep reminding herself it was temporary. She'd be back on top again. Wait and see.

"Ma'am? You okay?"

Molly opened her eyes. "Yes, thanks."

"Chief Randall asked me to run you over to the station. He'd like to go over your statement."

Molly looked down at her clothes. "I have to change. I can be there in about an hour."

"Now, if you don't mind," growled Chief Kenneth Randall as he came up behind the officer. "This is a homicide investigation, not a fender-bender."

Molly was never good at listening to her own advice. She often joked it was genetic. When it came to authority, Irish genes were different. "I'm well aware of the situation," she shot back, "but I don't think you can force me to stay in these bloody clothes any longer."

"Oh, we know our rights, do we? What if I told you to take off that sweatshirt here and now? What if I told you it was forensic evidence?"

Molly stepped away from the patrol car, "Don't bully me. It's unbecoming."

With his eyes still on her, he yanked open the patrol car's trunk, pulled out a large plastic evidence bag, and handed it to her. "Put it in here and you can go shower."

The shock on her face made him smile. Jerking his

head to the car, he said, "Get in. You can take it off there. The officer and I will stand by the window."

Swallowing the long string of names she wanted to hurl at him, she removed the police jacket, threw it in ahead of her, and climbed in. Damned if she would let him get under her skin. She kept her face blank, removed her cap, carefully pulled the sweatshirt up over her head, and stuffed it in the plastic bag. She buttoned up the police jacket, pulled the collar up around her neck, and took her time stuffing her hair back up into the cap. Shoving open the door so hard, she nearly banged into the young cop. Handing him the bag, she turned to Randall. "May I leave now?"

"An hour. No more, or I'll have to send—"

"I'll be there." Molly said firmly.

She could feel his eyes boring into her as she walked away. Livid, it was an effort to keep her shoulders back and measure her steps. She was determined not to let him see how angry she was. With any luck he'd turn away and go back to his cop work. She knew his intent was to intimidate her and establish his authority. It wasn't a sexist thing. He was probably a cop at the end of a generation that operated that way. They were devout proponents of scare the bejesus out of you so lying would never enter your mind. Shake, rattle, and roll over, her youngest uncle used to laugh.

Besides, she didn't want him to see the decrepit El Camino Max had left for her use. God-awful orange, with rusted hubcaps, it had so many dents she'd lost count. She wasn't trailer trash, and he wasn't going to treat her as if she were. Even though the small truck made her feel like a down-at-the-heels scavenger grubbing for junk to sell at flea markets, she had to admit it fit her garage sale outfit of sweats, sneakers, and baseball cap. She'd learned a valuable lesson her first weekend searching for treasures. Dressed in three-hundred-dollar wool slacks, a cashmere sweater, and Ferragamo loafers, she had no luck bargaining and had to pay full sack for everything. The original asking prices were reasonable; but every dollar saved was a dollar closer to New Orleans.

New Orleans was her immediate choice. Well suited for her goals and talent, the city was famous for its historic appetite and almost slavish devotion to gracious living and one-upmanship. But with only nine hundred dollars to her name, it was impossible. She needed at least fifty thousand to begin again.

She knew she shouldn't complain. She was lucky to have this job, the free apartment, the truck, and the okay to buy her own merch and sell it in the shop. Three hundred a week, and 10 percent on shop sales was near the poverty line, but with no rent to pay and only herself to feed, she'd eventually make it. She gave herself five years. Eight hundred and thirty-three bucks a month. If God didn't put her on a back burner, and she made some *really* smart buys, she could be in the Big Easy sooner.

Slipping under the police tape, she managed to get to the truck quickly. Thanks to the police jacket, the crowd and now impatient media ignored her. Climbing into the truck, she shoved a cigarette between her lips, wiped the tears blurring her eyes, and fumbled for the Zippo. How long, she wondered, would it take this cop to find out about her? He'll be too busy today. Tomorrow he would run a check, then he'd know.

The incredible vista of Carmel Bay was lost on her as she inched her way past the growing crowd in the street. The towering Monterey pines, the pristine white sand, and the aquamarine surf crashing against huge rock outcroppings could have been a painted billboard on the freeway. Her only thought was what would happen when that swaggering cop got a rundown on her past.

Screw it, she thought. After fighting weeks of bitterness with a new sense of freedom, she was determined not to let this tragic event set her back, especially this overbearing cop. Pushing her fears away, she spent the next few blocks saying a prayer for the soul of the dead woman.

Pulling into the alley behind the retail complex Max had recently inherited, she checked her watch and calculated she'd have enough time to shower, go to the police station, and be back in time to open at ten.

She hoped Pablo wouldn't call before she got back. Max's current lover and self-appointed keeper of the keys was not one of her fans. It was hate at first sight, but she hadn't a clue why. She'd been a half hour late opening yesterday, and he'd torn her to shreds. It had been too great a buying day to let him get under her skin. She'd found a truckload of goodies, including the desk with the missing key.

Let him scream and holler. She'd tell him what happened. It probably wouldn't even faze the prickly jerk. What Max saw in him was beyond her.

2

*R*andall almost didn't recognize her. Though she seemed to him to be around five-ten, she carried herself with confidence. A lot of tall women had a habit of slouching, inching down to fit in. He'd already decided she was a bona fide hard-ass. Women like her didn't slump or slink, or hunch over. They took advantage of towering over the crowd. Used it to intimidate. "Empowerment" was the word that came to mind. "Imperious" was another. She was all that. It didn't take a brain surgeon to see what kind of a broad she was.

Better-looking than an hour ago, he noted, as she turned in the borrowed police jacket to the desk sergeant. She was pushing forty, he guessed, and her makeup was subdued and natural-looking, nearly hiding what appeared to be a recent scar over her eye. Jewelry was minimal. Gold Rolex watch, jade ring on her pinkie, simple gold hoops instead of those skinny hanging earrings that proclaimed academia, female angst, and membership in what he called The Sisterhood. Her voice was firm, full-bodied. That was a plus. None of that New Age speak with a dangling question at the end of every sentence. He actually became livid when answers to questions were prefaced by the question first.

She had the finishing school look down pat. Dressed in

tweed wool slacks, a brown cashmere turtleneck, and alligator loafers, she affected that simple classic look that
put most people off. Quiet elegance was always intimidating. A great tool to hide the real persona.

An accomplished student of face reading, he fell into
the routine automatically. Assessing her features, he
made brisk judgments—almost oval face, shoulder-
length auburn hair in a simple blunt cut, off her forehead, indicated a thinking woman with some measure of
vanity. Large, deep chocolate eyes told him she was
generous, family-loving, and affectionate despite a serious nature. Strong high-set brows, not easily impressed.
The nose was good. Narrow bridge said she liked to be
alone and was a chronic perfectionist. Wide mouth, full
lips, could talk forever. The dimple in her chin spoke volumes; determined to succeed, a good infighter. Not to
mention the cockeyed slant of her upper lip when she
smiled. Sarcastic or insolent? The contradictions were interesting, but he decided he didn't like her face. She re-
sembled his ex-wife too much. The same classy look, and
probably the same agenda. Me first. He understood
women who wore bright colors and expensive jewelry.
They were up-front and too fun-loving to play mind
games.

Standing in the doorway to his office, he watched her
for another moment, deciding how he was going to play
her. He made his decision, then made his presence
known, "Ah, the mystery woman cometh. In my office, if
you please."

Molly turned to his voice. She looked at her watch,
"Forty-five minutes rates a thank-you I would think."

"Yeah, sure. Thanks." Stepping aside, he waved her in.
"Have a seat. Would you like coffee?"

"No. Thank you." Molly took a quick glance at his large office. With moving boxes piled everywhere and two chairs pulled close to his desk, there was hardly enough room for her knees. "Coming or going?"

"First day on the job."

Too bad, she thought. "We're both newcomers. This is my second week." Rummaging in her purse for a cigarette, she asked, "What's with the mystery woman remark?"

Settling behind his desk, Randall smiled. "If you're looking for a smoke, forget it."

Molly set the pack on his desk and fished the Zippo from the pocket in her slacks. "I know it's kosher to smoke when one is being interrogated." She took her time lighting the cigarette, then exhaled slowly. "You haven't answered my question." She could see the irritation in his eyes. Provoking him was stupid and dangerous. She was playing with fire.

"You signed your statement as Molly Doyle, but the driver's license you gave for an ID is made out to Elizabeth Porter. By the way, you're not being interrogated. This is an interview, and blow that smoke downwind."

He watched her stub out the cigarette in an ashtray that shouldn't be on his desk unless he, too, was a smoker. She must be thinking *hypocrite and cop all in one.* Nevertheless, it was a peace offering of sorts.

"Both names are mine," she said. "I'm recently separated from my husband. I've resumed my maiden name. My father called me Molly."

"That where you got the Zippo?" Nodding at her briefly, he added, "Women don't usually tote big clunkers like that."

Looking at it still in her hand, she nodded. "My only legacy."

"Could be worse. Okay. Let's take it from the top. Why were you at Mrs. Jacobs's this morning?"

"It's all in my statement. I assume you read it."

"Of course I read it. Now I want to hear it." Randall shoved away from his desk, and smiled. "Look, Ms. Doyle, we got off on the wrong foot earlier. I apologize. I wasn't . . . ah, sensitive to your situation. I realize what a shock it was to find Mrs. Jacobs. but a verbal recount is important. It's hard to be accurate when you've just—"

"It . . . it was . . . horrible. She just . . . just fell in my arms, and . . ." Molly shuddered.

"Sure. Why don't we start from the beginning? You went to her house because?"

"I bought a desk at her garage sale yesterday. I was in hurry to get to the other sales, and didn't realize the drawers were locked. So I went back this morning around seven. While I was locking the pickup, I saw a woman hurrying down the gravel driveway. I didn't see her after that. I mean, I don't know if she walked or drove away. Anyway, I headed for the patio where the sale had been. Halfway up the driveway, Mrs. Jacobs was staggering toward me and literally fell into my arms. She babbled something, then nearly knocked me over. I didn't know she was dead. I mean, dying."

She reached for her cigarettes, then changed her mind. "What I mean is I thought maybe she was having a heart attack or . . . or something. I laid her down and . . . and then I saw all the blood. I panicked for a moment, then called 911." Grabbing the cigarettes, she quickly lit another. "That's it."

Gut instinct told him she'd been this route before. Quick with her mouth at the scene, she seemed almost too savvy. Now her recounting was precise and well-ordered. Checking her out became a top priority. He glanced at her statement, "Antique shop, right? *Treasures on Ocean Avenue?*"

"Junk shop is more like it. That's not fair," she quickly added. "It's just that I'm used to selling upper-end merch, and—"

"*Merch?* Trade lingo?"

"Merch . . . *stuff.* I won't repeat some of the other terms that dealers use to keep from getting too full of ourselves when we pitch six-figure items."

"Okay, back to the desk. You needed a key. Didn't you check it out when you were eyeballing it? I thought all you dealers examined everything with a magnifying glass." Since he rated antique dealers a notch above con men, the gleam in his eye was purposely rude. "You know, crawl under tables, turn chairs over. I can't believe you didn't check out the drawers to see if the lock was inset, or placed at the edge."

Molly's eye began to twitch. She didn't need reminding. Especially from him. How did he know about inset locks? Probably watched the *Antiques Roadshow*. Everybody thought they were experts and were hoarding merch instead of sending it to auction. The show was drying up the market. "It's a banged-up Chippendale repro, probably twenty years old."

"A repro? For shame. I thought you were an antique dealer."

The pulsing over her eye was out of control. "It was for the shop, not for sale. The former owner used a counter. I had it ripped out. I prefer a desk."

Randall looked back at her statement. She listed her employer as Maxwell Roman in San Francisco. "Your boss gives you that kind of latitude?"

"Yes. He's an old friend. He recently inherited the shop and the courtyard complex. I'm here to do some repositioning and market strategy." Molly gently touched the twitch just above the scar over her eye. She prayed he hadn't noticed.

"So, you people get your *merch* at garage sales, huh? I wouldn't let that out if I were you. If"—he grinned—"you don't mind a little advice."

Ignoring the barb, she said, "Mr. Roman suggested it. He said Carmel was filled with world travelers downsizing, and I should make it a point to—" She stopped suddenly. "Look, I've got to open in about twenty minutes, and—"

"I've got a murder here, Ms. Doyle. Your *antique* shop can wait."

"Yes, of course. I only meant . . . well, how about starting with 'I didn't kill her . . . I didn't even know her'? Or, we can try 'I just bought a desk. It was locked, and I went back this morning to see if she had a key'?"

"Seven's a little early for these things."

"I had other places to check out. I wanted to get ahead of the early birds." When she saw his blank look, she said, "The people who show up before the sale is to begin? Surely, you're familiar with the term?"

"Obviously you didn't."

He saw the confusion on her face. "The killer, Ms. Doyle. I'd say he, or she, beat you to the punch. I don't imagine that's occurred to you." He saw her eyes widen as his words began to sink in. "Murdered, Ms. Doyle. The word is 'murdered.' Hold the aftershock for later. Can you describe this alleged other woman?"

"*Alleged?* Strange word to be using just now. You can't possibly think I was making the other woman up. I just told you I didn't know Lorna Jacobs. Why the hell would you think I'd be lying?"

"Cop words, Ms. Doyle. The other woman?"

"Yes," she quickly answered. "I'm . . . I'm thinking."

He watched her dig deep, fighting to regain the image, or make one up.

"The sunglasses! Of course, I almost forgot. She was close enough for me to see they were tinted blue. And she had on a straw hat and a denim jacket, too." She shook her head. "It was so quick. The glasses caught my eye. It was overcast, and I guess I thought it was weird."

Impressed with her recall, or swift creativity, he probed further, "Tall, short, fat, skinny? Young . . . old . . . what color hair . . . what?"

Molly paused, "Short. Maybe . . . maybe five-five? Not fat, but not runway slim. Couldn't see her hair. Age . . . age is difficult."

Randall rose from his desk and looked down at her. *Bullshit,* he thought. *That description could fit a thousand women.* "Okay, that should do it for now. We'll talk again."

Letting out a sigh, Molly got to her feet. She hadn't realized how tall he was. Even with her height, he was impressive. Probably close to fifty. His eyes surprised her. She always felt that the old adage about eyes being the mirror of a soul was on target. How then had she misread her husband? She couldn't think about Derek now. Randall's were a faded blue. Must be useful when he was playing good cop.

At her side, Randall offered his hand, "Look, you've had one hell of a morning. I didn't make it much easier either."

Taking his hand, Molly forced a half smile. "I've never seen a dead person let alone—"

"Sure, it's tough. I'll stop by your shop when I need to talk again. Police stations make people nervous."

Still wary, Molly forced another smile. "I'm there seven days a week, from ten until seven."

"I think that's against the law unless you're an owner."

"Tell my boss's boyfriend."

"Oh, like that, huh?"

"And then some," she mumbled as she headed for the door.

3

If the two men at the sale hadn't loaded the desk into the truck for her yesterday, she might not have bought it. When Lorna Jacobs saw her hesitate, she'd called them over and promised them a deal on the sports equipment they'd been eyeing if they helped out. Quickly writing a check for thirty dollars, Molly drove off without even opening a drawer. The look and size was right, and it had been too cheap to pass up. Dealer's greed will do you in every time. Lured by the dozens of sales advertised, she had run around town like a madwoman, and still hadn't opened on time. She had to bite her tongue when Pablo called at ten-thirty and tore into her. Two months ago she'd have made mincemeat of him. She knew her emotions were still too raw to let loose. Beholden to Max, she found herself willing to back off rather than have a confrontation. She owed it to him to keep her lip buttoned. How long that would last was anybody's guess.

Randall was her real problem. When he found out about New York, he would hound her like a dog. While the charges of fraud had quickly been dropped, she'd still been through the process. It didn't make her a murderer, but she'd been booked, photographed, and fingerprinted. All her dreams of starting over were suddenly crashing around her. It wouldn't take long for the other shop owners in Carmel to find out she'd been implicated in a massive antique fraud. Someone in the police station would let it leak. Either at home, to a lover, or to the family pet. Small towns were like that. Innocent or not, once that got out, the shop would be dead meat. Max would blame her, and God only knows how Pablo would react. Without a leak, she still knew that until she could save enough to get to New Orleans, he'd make her life hell. When Max was in love, he was as blind as a bat. *I should talk*, she quickly thought.

She caught the ringing telephone and braced herself for Pablo's tirade. He didn't disappoint her. Going to great lengths to control herself, she finally managed to explain what had held her up. As expected, he wasn't moved. As she was still unnerved by the morning's events, his callous attitude finally pushed her over. Desperate to find some joy in the day, she cut loose, "I've had enough for one day, dammit! Don't ever speak to me like that again." Her attempt at bravado fell on deaf ears. Staring at the telephone, she swore, "The bitch hung up on me!"

Until late afternoon, she thankfully didn't have time to think. A steady stream of tourists kept her hopping. Mostly browsers, six total sales amounted to just under two hundred dollars. Feeling a full adrenaline hangover, she hung the CLOSED sign on the door and locked up. Hungry, exhausted, and screaming inside for a Jack Daniel's she could no longer afford, she knew she'd have to settle for the cheap Spanish wine she'd found in the garage. Her stomach lurched just thinking about it. But it was free, and it helped put her to sleep.

For now, tea would have to do. Heading for the tiny storage room off the sales floor, she plugged in the electric teapot. With a lovely cobalt china mug she'd found at a sale last week, and some stale cookies, she plopped onto a stiff Eastlake side chair and kicked off her shoes. Sheltered by a palm she'd plunked into a gaudy orange-and-red reproduction Chinese fishbowl, her unprofessional slump was hidden from the large display window facing Ocean Avenue, Carmel's main shopping street.

So much for her first weeks in Carmel. The perfect hideout, Max had said, laughing. A great place to re-group, to think about the future. Because of a precious few wonderful childhood memories, she'd jumped at the chance. It had always been a major treat to drive down from San Francisco with her parents and sister for a weekend outing. Building sand castles on the beach flashed in her mind. The laughter over the picnic lunches her mother packed that always ended up soggy, and the memories of her father losing beer bottles loosely set in the cold surf, were fragmented but still dear. Easier to re-call was the sharp scent of the pine trees and the way their branches whispered at night. She and her sister Carrie would lie awake in the small rental cottage listening to the surf crashing against the rocks they were never al-lowed to climb.

Returning to the charming seaside village left her with mixed emotions. Canopied with thousands of Monterey pines, and filled with a mix of Hansel and Gretel cot-tages and Mediterranean-style architecture, the village was, for a child, the next best thing to climbing into a Disney cartoon.

A haven for artists and writers after the 1906 San Fran-cisco earthquake, Carmel was perched next door to Peb-ble Beach, the wealthy community founded and once owned by Samuel F. B. Morse of Morse code fame. It soon became a popular hideaway with Hollywood's elite when Bing Crosby brought his Rancho Santa Fe golf tournament to Pebble Beach in 1947. The "Clambake," as it became known, eventually grew into the present famous AT&T National Pro-Am. Luring the finest golfers in the world, and celebrity amateurs, the tournament continued to attract tourists from all over the world. California's sparkling gem soon became known for its charm, strict building codes, a draconian city council determined to preserve its beauty. And then there was its most famous mayor, Clint Eastwood.

Looking back made her heart hurt. Quickly dismissing those faded days, she forced her eyes to wander around the shop. With a large display window facing Ocean Avenue, and another wall of glass showing the arcade leading to the courtyard shops, there were only two brick walls to use for artwork and to position large furniture. American-made Oriental carpets from the thirties, faded and threadbare, were scattered over the stone floor and did little to enhance the furniture she'd spent hours polishing. Chipped gold-painted picture frames cradling paint-by-number seascapes were flanked by tarnished copper coach lamps that had never seen glory days and shop-made wood sconces with dusty candles burned down to just under an inch. Mirrors, never knowing a bevel, had spiderweb cracks and cloudy glass. Despite all that, the shop, like the apartment above, had fantastic bones. A lovely fireplace, surrounded by a chipped marble mantel, took center stage on one wall, and the brick walls, sandblasted at some point, would be great backdrops for first-class merch. The beamed stucco ceiling, painted, Molly guessed, in the early thirties, was an Art Deco gem. With clouds and rainbows, a starburst sun and flying nymphs, it was glorious. Suspended from this fantasy, were two huge, triple-row wrought-iron chandeliers that were exactly right for the period. While it was glaringly apparent she wouldn't be selling fine art or eighteenth-century furniture, she counted her blessings for the roof over her head and a means to live. The shop was infinitely less grand than what she'd been accustomed to, and her lessons in stretching a dollar during her early years as an acolyte at Sotheby's would come in handy.

Lost in the whimsy of the fairy-tale ceiling, she almost spilled her tea. The essence of the morning suddenly struck her. *I was moments away from a murder. What if I'd been there earlier?* She might very well be lying on the ground next to Mrs. Jacobs, instead of sitting here feeling sorry for herself. The thought was chilling.

That's crazy. Or was it? Was Lorna Jacobs the victim of a robbery gone wrong, or domestic violence?

That might have been me two months ago.

The sore ribs and small scar over her right eye made it easy to recall nearly every nuance of that heartbreaking night.

She and Derek had been at the shop late. They stopped at a small Chinese restaurant Molly loved, and between the dim sum and Mandarin beef, he'd destroyed her life, her dreams, and her future. He wasn't subtle, hadn't set up an elaborate preamble, nor had the grace to use a decent metaphor to lead her into the second darkest moment of her life.

She could recall each word of his opening salvo. They were etched permanently into her heart, buried with other wounds. She could have been seated front row center at a Rocky Horror show. Her eyes blurred as his lips moved in slow motion. "There's no easy way to say this" her husband of nine years casually began.

"What?" She'd remembered laughing. "You mean that Louis XV commode I spent an hour convincing Mrs. Bancroft to buy is a fake?"

How that moment would come back to haunt her. How many wonderful, glorious, and to-die-for pieces, items she passionately praised to long-standing clients, were later reproduced and switched before delivery? She prayed she would never know.

"No jokes, Molly. I'm serious." Her husband, Derek, lowered his head, and looked around the crowded restaurant. Certain that nearby diners were out of earshot, he grabbed her hand. "It's Greta."

She didn't want to discuss Greta. She could kick herself every time she thought about the day she admired her artistry and complimented her in front of Derek. "I'm tired, save it. Selling a twenty-grand chest of drawers takes the sap out of me."

She had been admiring a seventeenth-century Chinese lacquered desk at a wholesaler in London, and called Derek over to see it. It was breathtaking, and Molly immediately said so. Chinoiserie was one of the few things that could make Molly weak in the knees. The late-eighteenth-century European method of painting Oriental-style figures and scenes on furniture and accessories, in the style of the Chinese, ranked neck and neck with French Art Deco furniture. Greta Winters, the master restorer responsible for the piece, overheard her, and introduced herself to Derek as Molly walked away.

She purposely hadn't lingered. The asking price, wholesale or not, was way beyond their means, and she was afraid Derek might be carried away. Not an astute buyer, he was short on knowledge and impulsive. He had a problem falling in love with pieces, and it often took all of Molly's persuasive powers to convince him their profit margin was too slim, the piece was too damaged to bring back, or, heaven forbid, had been restored beyond what was acceptable. "Bottom line," "profit margin," and "overhead," were foreign words to him. Had he, along with a brother who was a financial brain, not inherited the shop from their father, Derek would have been broke and a professional houseguest in the Hamptons.

Knowing it took formidable skill to clean away decades of grime and still save the original work, Molly remembered saying, "No easy feat," then walked away. Three words that changed her life.

She was floored when she returned from lunch with a client two weeks later to find Greta sipping espresso with Derek in the workroom. Surprised to hear she'd moved to New York, she was stunned to discover Derek had hired her without consulting her or his brother, Harry. The fact that they needed an in-house restorer was beside the point. The man who had worked for Porter's Antiques for forty years had recently retired, and they had been hard-pressed to find a replacement to match his skills. Unable to take advantage of quality pieces needing minor repairs or careful cleaning, they were often forced to make purchases that were showroom perfect. The cost was killing them.

Greta turned out to be temperamental and secretive. Allowing no one in the workroom when she was restoring a piece, she claimed extraneous dust and pollutants contaminated the air. Newly waxed or French-polished surfaces needed isolation. She even demanded Derek place a red light over the door. When it was on, absolutely no one was allowed to enter. The fact was, Greta was doing superb work. Profits were up, so she called the shots.

Molly could live with that. What she could not tolerate was her intrusion into the showrooms and interrupting her when she was showing the fine points of a seventeenth- or eighteenth-century piece of furniture. It wasn't unusual for her to dominate the conversation, and it would take all Molly's diplomacy skills to ease her away. When Greta wrongly contradicted her in front of clients twice in one afternoon, Molly was furious. Storming into Derek's office after killing herself to make both sales, Molly had referred to Greta as the "diva" and demanded he keep her out of her way when I'm selling."

Yes, she could recall every word. And, stranger still, she could even remember how hungry she'd been that night at the restaurant, how delicious the taste of ginger was on her tongue when she'd said, "It's always Greta lately. What now?"

"I'm in love with her," Derek had calmly announced.

Looking back, she realized the signs were all there. Why hadn't she seen them? The quiet huddles she thought were discussions over a new piece; the sudden private buying tips Greta took Derek to check out; showing up together at auction previews and merely giving her a wave. And then there was the private collection sale at a new friend of Greta's on Long Island. But then, she had no cause to wonder. Molly and Derek had been married for nine years, for God's sake. They talked about finally starting a family. Long overdue, she had argued just last Christmas. After Derek's father's death, it had taken a few years to return Porter's Antiques to being one of the top dealers on the East Coast. Molly had worked nonstop to garner merch worthy of their renewed clientele. It was time, she told Derek, to begin the next generation. She was tired of cuddling other people's children.

What a blind fool she had been.

Her rush from the restaurant was still clear, but her mind, in its limited mercy, could not blur the violent aftermath at the apartment. Her bewilderment soon dissolved into anger. Only a few moments behind her, Derek found her in the kitchen uncorking the bottle of Opus they'd bought as a gift for a client. When he began to yell at her for opening the two-hundred-dollar bottle of wine, she calmly poured a large glass, took a sip, then coldly said, "I plan to finish this while you pack." Silent for a long moment, he'd said, "Look, Molly, I'm really sorry." His apology, so blithe and utterly calm was more than she could bear. "Sorry? *Sorry?* That's rich! Tell me, *darling* . . . how long has this been going on? I might as well know." When he'd said since they first met in London, she lost it. "You've been sleeping with us both? Oh, God!" It was then she threw the wine at him. His shock, and then cold fury finally erupted. His slap was so swift, she didn't see it coming. Knocked off-balance, she stumbled, then lost her footing on the spilled wine. Derek's savagery left her stunned and defenseless. Her head caught the edge of the granite work counter. When she came to, he was gone. Blood rushed from a large gash over her eye, her ribs ached so much she could hardly breathe. Managing to get to the telephone, she called Cleo. Cleo Jones, her oldest and dearest friend from her days at Sotheby's, was the only one Molly knew who would understand and help her. The taxi ride to the ER was hazy, but she clearly heard Cleo read the note Derek had left. She had two days to pack and get out. He reminded her the condo belonged to his family, and she was no longer welcome. An hour later, she was told that two of her ribs were broken.

Anger was a constant companion those days spent in hiding at Cleo's apartment. Bitterness would come later.

She set down the teacup and covered her face with her hands. Gently touching the scar over her eye, she gritted her teeth, then laughed bitterly. At least her eye had stopped twitching. Considering what she had been through today, that had to be some progress.

Leaving on a few small lamps for night-lights, Molly wearily climbed the staircase leading to the apartment and went to bed.

∼ 4 ∼

*O*n Monday morning, Randall sat at his desk, shuffled his notes, and sipped cold coffee. After twenty plus years, he'd never figured out which, besides dirty cops, pissed him off the most—stupidity or arrogance. Molly Doyle possessed both. She was bare-assed stupid to think he wouldn't consider her a suspect, and she was arrogant as hell. As far as he was concerned, antique dealers were consummate crooks who lived to screw the rubes. Somewhere along the line, they'd decided they were not part of the civilian population. Cops felt the same, but they had cause.

Objectivity was the foundation of any investigation, and he was close to throwing it out the window. Besides her occupation, she'd immediately rubbed him the wrong way. She reminded him too much of his ex-wife. Diana was five-eleven. Doyle was five-ten. Diana favored that casually tailored East Coast look: cashmere sweaters and silk scarves, wool slacks that cost more than his, and Italian flat shoes. Molly Doyle could have been her twin.

He knew his real anger was with himself. He had been out on the beach running when the call came in and hadn't had time to change. It didn't look good. First day on the job, first homicide in ten years, and the new chief shows up in running sweats. The real rub was that they had to come looking for him. He'd been out on his morning run and dropped his pager somewhere in the bone-chilling surf. The department had an emergency, and they couldn't find him. With no chief—his predecessor was on his way to Alaska to fish—the small police department had been on its own. By the time they found him on the beach, half the force was on the scene, and, he suspected, had trampled over possible evidence.

While he had examined the body and grounds, snapped out orders, and waited for the deputy coroner, Molly Doyle had been cooling her heels next to a patrol car. Time enough, he reasoned, for her to throw together an acceptable excuse for going back on Sunday. *Keys my ass,* he thought. *Sorry, lady, you gotta do better than that.* People always opened drawers when they were eye-balling a desk. It was a natural action.

In the station by 5 A.M., he'd made two calls to friends at NYPD, and bingo, she was on the charts. Transferred to Detective Al Malatesta, Randall got an earful. Porter's Antiques had fraud charges pending. Elizabeth Porter, aka Molly Doyle, had been arrested and booked along with her husband, Derek Porter, and a Greta Winters. High-priced lawyers got them out on bail, and Porter and Winters left the country. Without them, the state had no case. They had to let the wife go. Malatesta was keeping tabs on Doyle in case her husband contacted her, and asked Randall to cooperate. It was probably a waste of time, he'd added.

"How's that?" Randall asked.

"Porter had other problems. The marriage hit the skids before this all came out. Porter and the Winters babe were doing the deed. I don't know the particulars, but I understand he kicked the missus out of the fancy condo his family owned. Married a long time, too. Must have been a hell of a shock. I saw the bruises on her face and the cut over her eye when we booked her. Guess he didn't like her reaction. Not to mention the money's all tied up in his family trust."

Randall shrugged the news off. Where he came from, this was a daily diet. "Yeah, I saw the scar. So what do you think? She a major player in this?"

"Naw. I checked her out from day one. My gut tells me she's clean. Family story is interesting though. Father and two uncles were cops. She has a cousin with the FBI, and a sister's who's a lawyer up in Seattle."

"Yeah? Tell me a story. I'm all ears."

"Takes place in San Francisco. The story's old, maybe ten . . . twelve years. Uncles are dead. One took early retirement and died of a stroke, the other ate his gun. Both were narcs. Father died in the joint of a heart attack. He used to be in homicide. His knee caught a bullet, was forced into early retirement. Opened up a used furniture store. The Doyle brothers had a little side business going on. Fenced drug dealers' jewelry through her father. The department kept it quiet, but her father did time."

Randall felt his neck burning. His distaste for Molly Doyle increased and spread across his face. "Great Norman Rockwell family, huh? Nothing like dirty cops to—"

"Hold it, Randall," Malatesta quickly cut in, "these guys were decorated. The name's still respected on the force. They'd—"

"Don't shit a shitter. I don't give a fuck if—"

"Yeah, yeah, I know all about your stint in Internal Affairs. Life isn't black-and-white. You should know that by now. Besides, they only lifted from scum."

He wasn't surprised by the comment. It was that attitude, increasingly embraced by burned-out cops, veterans of the losing battle with drugs, that ultimately convinced him to leave Los Angeles. He'd witnessed too many acts of brutality bred from such frustrations. Understanding their feeling of impotence, he could no longer send cops to prison for simply losing it.

His shorts were not exactly pristine, but he'd been wise enough to limit his largesse to a comp dinner, or a few belts here and there for minor favors. Cops on the take and working both sides of the street, however, was not what police work was all about. He let one walk, a former partner, and swore he'd never do it again. Besides being wrong, it was dangerous and stupid. His arrest and conviction record for dirty cops was still unsurpassed at Internal Affairs.

Randall reached for a cigarette, then broke it in half. Wanting to change the subject, he asked, "How the hell did the cousin make the Bureau?"

"Had the right stuff, I guess."

"Okay, keep in touch. I'm not saying I'm tying her to this, but I'm keeping my options open."

"Come on, Randall. Case of being in the wrong place at the wrong time. She's not a killer. She isn't the type."

Randall let that go. "Get that fax smokin' okay? I'd appreciate the full jacket. And, thanks."

Randall hung up. " 'The type'? There *isn't* one, asshole." How had Malatesta made it to detective? He immediately thought about an eighty-year-old grandma in Compton who poisoned her family. He had her cold, forensics had her locked, and when they took her away, he still couldn't believe it. He'd almost blown that case, and the memory still rankled, even after a dozen years.

He didn't like the options fighting for space in his head. He had a better read on Ms. Doyle now. No wonder she kept her cool with him. She knew the drill firsthand. Maybe Malatesta was right. Maybe she was simply in the wrong place at the wrong time. On the other hand, maybe the Jacobs murder was connected to what she'd left behind. The victim owned a gift shop, and her husband had a combination frame shop and art gallery. Coincidence? Maybe. Maybe they and Doyle had done business in the past, and she had come to Carmel to shut them up, or start in a new venue. Maybe there never was another woman at the scene. Maybe Molly Doyle was the murderer.

Okay. What went wrong? Blackmail? Randall broke a cigarette in half and stared at it. Malatesta said Porter's Antiques dealt in museum-type goods, megabuck clients. Big-time. He pulled out another cigarette and lit it as he heard the fax coming in. He snatched each page like a kid looking for a free pass to a Lakers game. Spilling ashes on his jacket, he devoured each word of the lengthy report. Fucking antique dealers. Six charges of fraud amounting to over a million bucks. *So, she comes out here, hooks up with Roman, another high-end dealer in The City, who recently inherited half a block of prime Carmel real estate on the main drag, Ocean Avenue.*

Randall was impressed. Three or four million there at least. Former owner was another antique dealer. Figures. Had terminal cancer. Died of an overdose. Was Roman involved, too? Maybe Lorna Jacobs wanted out so Ms. Doyle bumped her off to warn the old man it was business as usual.

He gathered up the file and set it aside. He was rambling. Living in Los Angeles for twenty years made it easy to become plot-oriented. However, it was crazy not to examine any avenue, no matter how bizarre or farfetched. Nothing would ever be solved if investigators stopped at evidence and common sense. The elements in the Jacobs case were skewed. He knew it.

He had a hard-on for antique dealers and was itching to fry one. Careful to maintain the flint-edged cop façade, few knew he was an astute toy train collector, or had a fine complement of wonderful French furniture. Burned twice by dealers at collectible shows when he first began, he had decided then and there all dealers were fair game.

What little sleep Molly engineered Sunday night was fitful. The lumpy mattress, still reeking of disinfectant, made a good night's sleep problematic. *I should have finished the bottle of wine*, she thought, as gritty eyes tried to make out the time on the clock. She'd set the alarm for six, and it was nearly seven. The cheap windup clock hadn't worked again. Her nightgown was damp, and her forehead felt sticky. She tried to brush away the fragmented memories of her dreams—sepia colored and frightening. She could only recall quick flashes. Tiny gushers of blood spurting from Lorna's nose and ears, and frightened eyes outgrowing her face. Her muffled words growing louder and louder as she floated to Molly with her arms outstretched. A ghost had invaded Molly's dreams, and it totally unnerved her.

Flinging away a faded quilt, she sat on the edge of the bed and stared out the French doors. Were it not for the dreams and the restless sleep, she would need little encouragement to stay in bed. Forcing her eyes to focus on the brilliant red bougainvillea vine clinging to the iron railing, she tried to erase fear with beauty. *Say another Hail Mary, hum a tune, do what you must,* she reminded herself, *but get off this merry-go-round of anxiety.*

She'd noted the changes in herself during the past week. Once the shop and apartment had been cleaned and reorganized, she found that her attention span and drive were limited. She had become tentative and doubtful.

Mired in a stagnant pool of melancholy, she found herself staring at nothing, biting her lips and forgetting what she was doing. It reminded her of those dark days when her father had been arrested. She'd been younger then, the stamina to bounce back had been easier to grab and hold. And, there had been Derek a few years later. How miraculous love can be to soothe wounds.

Logic forced her to admit her sense of betrayal would eventually fade. The shame and notoriety would wane. All this would pass. It was better to focus on her new state of being. When on the rise at Sotheby's, Molly had already earned a fine reputation before meeting Derek Porter. Besides years of hands-on experience, she had, as the trade would say, "an eye." There was no question in her mind that she'd be on top again.

Elizabeth Porter is dead. Long live Molly Doyle.

With a million things to do before opening at ten, she forced herself out of bed and headed for the tiny kitchen, with its ancient gas stove, chipped tile, and mismatched cracked dishes. The fuchsia walls hurt her eyes, and she squinted as she made coffee. Sid Wells, the former owner, was obviously taken with bright colors. While Carmel was frequently overcast and foggy, it was not England, for God's sake. Remembering that Carmel's best months were August to October, she vowed to repaint the kitchen soon. She'd have to wear sunglasses if she didn't. The rest of the apartment boasted the same Day-Glo treatment. Somehow Sid had decided lime green was perfect for the living room. Large and sunny anyway, it had a working fireplace flanked by bookshelves that reached the twelve-foot ceiling. Not in the mood to remove scores of dog-eared Westerns, detective novels, and art and antique reference books, Molly had given them a quick swipe with a dust rag. The room was well proportioned, with French doors leading to a lovely L-shaped tile balcony overlooking the courtyard and shops below, but the furniture was pure retirement home rejects. A drab, lumpy sofa covered in olive plush made her shudder. At least the two club chairs were slipcovered in a passable brown-and-tan plaid. The coffee table—a cut-down dining table—was rickety and marred with glass rings. Burns covered much of the threadbare floral rug. The one bath, which thankfully had a full shower, was at least a pale yellow and didn't clash with the intricate blue-and-green Moorish tiles on the floor and walls. The two bedrooms were a disaster. The larger of the two, which Molly used, was lavender, with another set of French doors to the smaller balcony. The second bedroom, a depressing muddy red, with a double set of windows facing Ocean Avenue, was relegated to storage and repairs. Yet while her new home was a far cry from the sprawling condo in New York, it was hers, and she could make it over in her image, not Derek's, or his family's.

It had taken her a full week to remove years of grime from the apartment and the shop. The merchandise was deplorable. It was a wonder Sid stayed in business. Considering the rent he made from this prime complex, he probably didn't care. Besides the shop, there was Flora's Boutique—an upscale dress shop—Bea's Florist, and Tosca's, a private label coffee bar. How Max Roman, one of the most talented and accomplished antique dealers in the country, had carried on a relationship with Sid was beyond her. Hadn't any of Max's taste or panache rubbed off? No matter, Carmel was her turf now. She'd find out what the tourist wanted, and she'd damn well get it. Her living quarters would get a makeover, too. She didn't mind scrimping to save for New Orleans, but she refused to live like a rat.

She wanted to cry after she hugged Max good-bye the day he brought her to Carmel. She almost didn't agree to run the shop for him. Survival was the enticement. With nowhere else to turn, she had had little choice. Seattle and her sister Carrie were out. They hadn't spoken since their father went to prison. When he'd died, Molly broke the silence and called to tell her. Carrie was curt, and refused to attend the funeral. Moving to Virginia to stay with her cousin Jack was out of the question. He didn't need her baggage to ruin his career with the Bureau. Her cousin Angela and her husband Armand begged her to come to New Orleans, but that wouldn't have worked yet. She needed time to let Porter's scandal fade. Otherwise, she'd be more suspect because of Armand. While Angela's career as a fine watercolorist was not affected by her husband's reputation, Molly's would have been. Armand was one of the finest copyists in the business. Reproducing Monet, van Gogh, Picasso, Rembrandt, Gaugin, or any old master for corporate and private clients, while legitimate—providing the artist signed his name to the work—was still too close to what Molly had left behind. She needed time to let the memories dim. The antique world at her former level was a small community. Gossip was equal to finding lost treasure.

Besides, Carmel and all its natural beauty was not a shabby place to start over. The pace in the immaculate storybook village was sleepy compared to New York. She might miss that. But she had gladly traded blaring horns for the towering pine trees that whispered each night. And the quaint streets were safe enough to stroll at night, allowing her to window-shop the scores of top-notch art galleries, antique shops, and boutiques. She realized she should be counting her blessings for being able to relocate to a city boasting one of the most spectacular coastlines in the country, not to mention pristine white sand beaches.

Taking her coffee to the living room, she paused at the open door to the second bedroom. Staring at the desk, Molly felt sick to her stomach. She wished she'd sold it to one of the kitchen helpers from the coffee bar in the courtyard. He'd offered a hundred bucks when he and a friend carried it up for her. She had to grin in spite of her morbid thoughts. She'd only paid thirty for it. A seventy-buck profit these days was big-time.

Focus, she reminded herself as she settled on the ancient sofa. First thing is to find a key. She remembered the box in the garage filled with dozens of old keys, brass handles, and glass doorknobs. With a little luck, she might find something that worked. If not, there was always a screwdriver. She would have to redo the finish anyway. Scratched, chipped, and bleached by the sun, the desk was a blight. It would take several evenings, but she would make it sing.

Gulping down a quick bowl of cereal, Molly glanced at the wall clock in the kitchen. Shaped like a cat, with a wagging tail, the paws told her it was only nine-thirty. At least the clock gave her a laugh each morning. Not a bad way to start the day. She had enough time to check out the box in the garage. Quickly making her way down the stairway off the balcony, she hurried across the stone courtyard into the side alley. The garage was huge, and a rarity in Carmel. Filled with dozens of boxes of old books, magazines, and flea market junk Sid no doubt meant to refurbish and sell, it was the remaining area Molly vowed to clean. She had asked Max for the keys to the cabinets lining the back wall and thought the shelves would be ideal for backup inventory. As usual, Pablo barged in and told her they were off-limits. A friend was using them while he was out of the country. Eyeing the cabinets, Molly did a slow burn. They were another reminder of Pablo and his officious attitude. She searched through the maze of boxes, shoving many against the locked cabinets to make a path. Finally finding the jumble of keys, she stuffed them in her pocket and headed back to the shop. Slamming the garage door shut, she locked the padlock and kicked the door. *Screw you, Pablo,* she thought.

After a long day of tire kickers, be backs, and uninterested husbands anxious to play golf, she headed upstairs. Fallout from yesterday lingered, and she was exhausted. Taking a frozen dinner from the oven, she sat in front of the TV and was startled to see Randall offering few comments about the homicide. Not wanting further reminders, she was about to change channels when he mentioned an eyewitness. She almost choked on mashed potatoes. When he declined to identify the witness, Molly slumped against the cushion in relief. For some perverse reason, she quickly switched channels for the other local news. She almost hoped to find them lagging a few moments behind. She was right. The anchor was just beginning his lead-in. The camera was slowly panning up the tree-lined street, playing up the expensive residential area and Lorna Jacobs's home. Up the gravel drive, the reporter opened with a report of an unnamed witness finding the victim. When Dick Jacobs, the victim's husband, was interviewed, Molly bit her lip. Her heart nearly burst. She almost wanted to reach out and tell him how terrible she felt for him. She wanted him to know his wife didn't die alone, that she had been there, holding her as she took her last breath. She wondered if she should call Randall and ask if she could meet Dick Jacobs and tell him. Without thinking, she clicked off the television.

The less she had to do with Randall, the better. She'd been a nervous wreck all day. Every time the tiny bell over the shop door rang, she cringed. She fully expected him to come barreling in waving her rap sheet in her face. Maybe he hadn't run a check on her. After all, why should he? There was no reason for him to suspect her. She didn't know Lorna Jacobs.

Yet she knew the necessary ingredients to make an arrest. Motive. Opportunity. Means. She'd been there . . . and she could have ditched the murder weapon.

Two out of three—not good odds.

5

*B*y Wednesday Molly couldn't avoid the desk any longer. She needed it badly. With the old counter ripped, the pine harvest table, cluttered with the telephone, charge equipment, and a small lamp, left little room to write up a sale and wrap it. Besides, the table was too valuable not to sell. She knew she could mark it for twelve hundred and jump at an offer of one thousand. Unless, of course, she was lucky enough to get a buyer who didn't know haggling was generally acceptable. She would begin restoration tonight.

She was tempted to call Pablo and tell him she'd sold a horrid set of oak chairs, two prewar silver trays that probably came out of a Sears catalog, and an embroidered footstool she was convinced surfaced from someone's basement. Including an ugly Chinese vase she'd put on hold, she managed to ring up eight hundred dollars. A banner day so far. For junk. Imagine what a good day with decent merch might be. She knew it was useless to telephone. In fact, it would be counterproductive. She would never get better quality merch if she were able to sell crap.

While her dinner cooked, she headed for the desk. She found some cheap furniture stain and black enamel paint at the hardware store. Undecided whether to try to restore

the original mahogany finish or paint it a glossy black,
she thought it was a good thing Randall wasn't a furniture connoisseur. She'd said the desk was Chippendale
style, but it wasn't. A bastard of styles was more like it.
The factory that made it some thirty or so years ago
hadn't a clue or, more likely, didn't care that the feet were
Georgian style, and the case was a butchered mix of
Chippendale and Sheraton.

The keys she'd found hadn't worked. Careful prying
with a letter opener did the trick. Dragging over a large
carton, Molly pushed up the sleeves of her sweatshirt and
opened the first drawer. It took her a good ten minutes to
clear all five. Each drawer was crammed. No wonder the
desk had been so heavy. The two bottom file drawers
were filled with rolled-up watercolors and three narrow
photo albums.

Intrigued, she sat on the floor and began carefully to
unroll the artwork. It wasn't long before the art major in
her gleefully took over. She immediately recognized the
style as Early California, a school that began in 1890 and
died off around 1940. Though not her major area of expertise, she nonetheless remembered it because it had begun primarily in San Francisco, and flourished right here
in Carmel. After World War II, the style of landscapes
with flat, muted tones went out of fashion as the pioneers
died off, and the new Young Turks began following cu-
bism and abstract impressionism.

Her smile grew as she scanned them. The landscapes
were wonderful. They didn't look terribly old, and she
wondered if a resurgence was afoot. Paintings from this
school were now in demand, and highly valuable.
Searching for a signature, or initials, or even a logo, she
was disappointed to find nothing. No real surprise. Practice pieces were usually unsigned. When she flipped

through the photo albums, she was perplexed. Nothing matched the watercolors. Nor were there dates of the photos, notes on location, season, or time of day.

The last item was a small bookkeeping journal. Idly thumbing through it, Molly saw it appeared to be a record of sales. Under the title of each work—none of which matched the watercolors or photos—was the medium— watercolor or oil—the size and type of frame, and pertinent color formulas. Opposite each entry was a bracketed amount followed by another of greater value. Quickly adding up the amounts not bracketed, she was impressed. Molly shrugged. Wishful thinking, probably.

Was Lorna Jacobs the artist? Had she forgotten they were in the desk? Molly felt a sudden unease, as if she were snooping into a secret Walter Mitty life hidden away in a desk drawer. She should call Randall and tell him what she found. In any event, she didn't feel right keeping them. Throwing the powders, brushes, and as-sortment of pens—all ballpoints, unfortunately—in a plastic bag for the trash, she carefully placed the water-colors and the journals in a carton. She'd decide later what to do with them. Turning to the desk, she sighed at the job ahead of her.

It had been years since she'd rolled up her sleeves and worked a piece. While the desk wasn't a precious an-tique, it still deserved all the care she could manage. It had a function to serve, and it must fit in with the look she wanted to create in the shop. Midrange opulence. It could be done. Rich fabrics for pillows, shiny copper, sparkling silver, colorful china and porcelain. She'd made a deal with Bea Thompson, who owned the florist's in the court-yard. Bea would fill the vases, chamber pots, and copper washtubs with stunning floral arrangements. A discount card advertising Bea's shop would be on display. Flowers always caught the eye. Molly had done it at Porter's, and it worked.

She was thankful Max reminded her on the drive down from San Francisco that first day that on the West Coast, shine sells. Chipped and worn-down paint, distressed wood and frayed silk coverings might be fine for East Coast connoisseurs, but out here, it better be old and look new. She'd had to wash every porcelain, ceramic, and china piece in the shop. Next, she had attacked the brass, silver, and copper until her hands were nearly raw. The furniture was not worth expensive wax, so when she found an old, rusty can of spray polish, she didn't bother to see if it had a silicone base. Silicone, she remembered, was a hardener, and if it expanded and seeped into the pores of the wood, it could eventually fracture it along with the finish. It was to be avoided at all costs. Whoever bought this crap, she thought, would ruin it anyway.

Her mind went back to a Christmas vacation she'd spent with Pop at the shop. She was in her junior year at St. Cecilia's, and it was the first time they'd ever had their hands on a quality piece. The small chest of drawers was a major turning point in her life. In the Queen Anne style, and from the mid–1800s, it was in brutal shape. But once she had seen and touched it, she knew her future. The lovely curly maple was so dirty, Pop wasn't sure he had the touch to bring it back. He had always made it a point of pride that, while he sold used furniture, it was always clean, and had a shine. Over the years, he'd picked up smatterings of quick remedies and discovered, by trial and error, mysterious concoctions.

Working every night, it took them two weeks to return the dainty dressing room chest to its original beauty. Slowly and carefully, they removed the surface grime, taking pains not to penetrate the patina, or harm the intricate pattern of inlay. Never strip, he'd always reminded. The beauty of wood, and the patina that evolves, took years. Layers of polish, even dirt and grease from hands, created the deep glow you saw on old pieces. Sadly, the Jacobs desk was not worth saving. Besides its mixed pedigree, it had been treated terribly. Sun-scorched and gouged, it even had initials carved on one of the drawer fronts.

Molly shook her head. The prognosis was bad. Strip it, sand it, and paint it. It was the best medicine for this ailing specimen. Her last-minute purchase of black enamel had been on target. She would give it a high-fashion look. She might even cover the chair she'd been using with the leopard print fabric she'd bought at a sale last week. A cliché maybe, but it was never out of fashion. She would have to remember all the little tricks now. Porter's hadn't needed them. That was then. This was now.

Covering the floor with newspaper, she moved the carton of watercolors to a corner. Realizing she'd rolled some of them a little too tight, she pulled them out and let them uncurl. She couldn't help but admire them. Whoever the artist, he or she was really very talented. Being more careful this time, she decided to roll each separately. One in particular caught her attention. There was something about it that seemed familiar. So intent on searching for a clue to the artist, she must have missed the subject matter. Laying it on the floor, she stood back and studied it for several moments. The landscape portrayed a typical California meadow bordered by eucalyptus trees with a field of poppies at the end of their bloom. She rarely saw works from this period and couldn't think why it seemed so memorable. The poppies stuck in her mind. Glancing at her watch, she realized it was ten. She wanted to get up early and start walking on the beach. The cold bracing air would do wonders for her disposition. Not to mention some much-needed exercise. She would give the desk a once-over with sandpaper and call it a night.

Rolling up the last of the watercolors, she couldn't shake the landscape from her thoughts. She was convinced she'd seen it before. But where?

The beach Thursday morning was a mistake. The wind was ferocious and colder than she'd expected. The chilling walk to Carmel's famous white sand beach, at the end of Ocean Avenue, should have given her a clue. By the time she hit the roiling surf, the sky grew darker. Keeping a safe distance from the waters' edge, she stared blankly at the disappearing horizon.

"Not your idea of summer, is it?"

She whirled to see Randall hunched next to her. "Jesus! Do you always creep up on people?"

"Trick I learned in the field." He laughed. "Being on sand helps."

His laughter threw her off. Maybe he wasn't planning on hauling her in after all. Maybe he was just going to watch her. Maybe he'd come to his senses and realized he had to establish a motive. *Good luck,* she thought.

A small gust of wind buffeted them. Stamping her feet again, she tried to think of something to say. They were not destined to be friends, he was not going to be a customer, and except for telling him about the watercolors, she was surprised to find herself worrying about conversation.

Briefly touching her shoulder, he said, "Better keep walking. Sand's too wet to stay put. Easy way to get a chill. A system's coming in from the Islands. When we get the tail end of it, they call it the Pineapple Express. They can get ugly."

Turning away at his touch, she decided not to mention the watercolors or the journal. They had nothing to do with his investigation. She'd be wise to distance herself totally. Again, she ignored her advice. "How are things going?" she blurted. "I mean, have you found the other woman?"

"Nope. The garage sale regulars couldn't tie your description to anyone."

"You mean no one came forward?" Before he could reply, Molly said, "I can't believe people! What harm would it do to—"

"Probably didn't want her friends to know she went to garage sales."

Molly stopped and turned to him. "Oh, please! I know cops and sick jokes are synonymous, but that was awful."

He looked at her for what seemed an eternity. "Know a lot about cops, do you?"

Molly willed her eye to stop twitching. He knew. "Maybe she was a tourist and left that day. Maybe she doesn't know what happened."

"My job is filled with 'maybes,' Ms. Doyle." Nodding to the ocean, he added, "Keep your eyes open when you walk down here. Don't ever turn your back to the sea. Stay off the rocks, too. People get washed away here every year. Four or five last year I heard. Landlocked tourists come out here and want to fool around the tide pools. I'd stay out of the water altogether. It's icy, and the riptides are devils. Hawaii this is not."

Squinting against the cold wind whipping around them, his eyes were unreadable. "Thank you, Chief. I appreciate your concern."

"The name's Randall. Forget the 'Chief' stuff. Just wanted to pass off some California logic."

"Didn't know Californians used it. From what I see, you people live up to your reputation."

"Now what the hell does that mean? Are we going to go tooth and nail again? What say we give it a rest?"

He didn't bite, she thought. *He doesn't know I was born in San Francisco.* Even so, she couldn't ignore his half-assed apology. "I couldn't help myself." She smiled.

"Yeah, well, I'd be careful saying stuff like that. People are touchy. Especially down under. Angelinos hate Northern Californians."

She had little choice but to go along with him. "Okay, I'll bite."

"Matter of inferiority. Culture-wise, I mean. The City has roots . . . tradition, old family ties. L.A. was a poor relation until the movies made it famous. But it drew too much riffraff to make it a serious city. It never had the strong ethnic districts that gave The City its history." Pulling his collar up, he said, "L.A. was too big, too spread out to create a personality. It used to be a desert surrounded by orange groves. San Francisco has hills, fog, soft rain . . . a beautiful bay and bridges."

She was beginning to feel uneasy. There was a chance he did know about her and was playing head games to check her credibility. She decided it had gone far enough. "I have to confess. I mean, I've been pulling your leg. I was born in The City."

"Really? Well, hell, I'm from there, too. Whereabouts?"

Molly wanted to rush the surf and hope a riptide would grab hold. How lucky could she be? "The wrong side of Nob Hill."

"North Beach."

"Randall doesn't sound Italian."

"My mother. Her family had an apartment block and a few restaurants. Ever eat at Casa Mia?"

"Oh, sure. Went with my family a lot. One of our favorites."

"That was our place. Folks are both gone. My cousin runs it for me."

Prepared not to like him, she thought it strange the way the towering man was feeling less a threat. She cautioned herself to be careful. She didn't need or want friends. Especially cops. Glancing at her watch, she quickly said, "I've got to get going. I've got a million things to do to get ready for the weekend tourists."

"If you plan to do a lot of walking down here, I'd stick to the path up on the street. A lot safer."

Molly eyed the long, wide beach. There couldn't have been more than a dozen people here at this time of the morning. Was he being considerate, or merely probing? Was he an early-morning beach stroller, too, or *was* she being watched? If he wanted to keep an eye on her, all he had to do was check the shop every day. She didn't like the possibilities. "I've always loved this beach. I'd hate to think it was dangerous."

"Nothing like that. It's the dogs. Gotta watch them. People bring them down for exercise, and they bunch up and run wild. Knocked a woman down the other day. Broke her arm."

"I'll steer clear of dogs. Thanks."

"By the way, ever find a key for the desk?"

"No. I finally used a letter opener."

He laughed. "Well, that's one way to do it. Find anything interesting?"

Molly kept her face bland. He was a hard man to look in the eye and lie to. "Hardly."

"Anything I should know about?"

She saw his eyes narrow ever so slightly. She was beginning to wonder if she ought to tell him after all. But how could the watercolors mean anything? She decided to keep quiet for the moment. For some reason, she didn't want to give them up. "Some old pens, a few paintbrushes . . . watercolor powders . . . some oil tubes."

"Well if you find a hidden drawer with a few million bucks stashed, let me know."

Walking away, she grinned. "Right. You'll be my first call."

6

The case stank. Just thinking about the foul-ups gave him heartburn.

Lorna Jacobs had been stabbed. The murder weapon was missing. Only Molly Doyle and some phantom woman had been at the scene moments after the murder. A silent homicide. Neighbors heard nothing. No shouts, no scuffle. No other witnesses. No one was getting a paper, going to church, or setting out for a lazy Sunday. The husband, Dick Jacobs, the eternal prime suspect, had an airtight alibi. He'd been down the coast in Big Sur all weekend. Half a dozen witnesses to vouch for him during the right time frame. That was disappointing. However, Randall thought that the guy had been unusually composed. He'd answered every question with the utmost courtesy, and very little emotion. An iceberg? Still in shock? He'd watch Jacobs closely on the day of the funeral.

Every resident on the street had been interviewed. The two employees at her jewelry store had been guarded, but offered few kind words about their boss. The husband had a combination frame shop and art gallery. His single employee was new, and hardly knew Lorna Jacobs. Tenants at her two rental houses in Mission Fields, a small subdivision outside the city limits, gave him an earful. Flood damage after the last El Nino had still not been repaired even though she'd collected on the insurance. Nothing to kill over. No kids, no relatives to interview. The smattering of friends had nothing to offer. An activist for unpopular causes, Lorna Jacobs was not liked. She was actually detested. Abrasive was a frequent description.

Lorna Jacobs had also made a few enemies in the city council. A familiar presence at town hall meetings, she was not bashful. Her zoning protests against expanding the business areas were widely known. She'd even accused the city planner of taking bribes.

Randall buzzed for coffee, then closed the file in disgust. Okay, he thought, she was a rabble-rouser. She flouted authority. So what? He leaned back and closed his eyes. She was fifty-three, still wore Birkenstocks, long skirts, and kept her hair piled up in a loose bun. That put her smack in the middle of the protest generation. So, she never got over it. Not a reason for murder. Or was it? Whom was she pushing? Whose skin had she given a rash?

He could spin his wheels over petty differences. He had few, if any, ties in the community to call on for scuttlebutt. No bartenders, waiters, or cabbies. A village this small should be full of busybodies who knew where every bone was buried. He hadn't a clue who they might be. Neither did anyone on the small force. They didn't have enough crime to cultivate a snitch patrol.

Staring across his desk at the growing rows of material neatly arranged on the conference table, he said out loud, "It's all here. The little truth that will tie this up is here. I'll find it. I'll damn well find it."

Reaching for a scratch pad, he saw Molly Doyle's name scrawled on it. He remembered he was going to stop at the shop. He wanted to take another look at her.

Watch the body language, listen to the cadence of her voice. Try and rattle her cage.

Seeing her at the beach this morning had been unexpected. She didn't strike him as the outdoor type. She acted okay. Normal, even. Didn't hide the fact she'd been born and raised in The City. She'd said Carmel beach had been a favorite. She had been there before. When? How often? Why? She had been in New York for years. He'd have to think about that. Who might know her in Carmel? He'd put his one and only detective on it. After setting up the Murder Book, he revamped the charts and chain of evidence forms. He'd been somewhat pleased to realize cutting-edge techniques hadn't been needed. The Jacobs homicide was Carmel's first in over ten years. He'd have to work it the old way. Might be fun. He used to be one of the best. He was curious to see if he'd lost his touch.

He stepped over to the easels lined up against the wall. One for each of the trinity—motive, opportunity, and means. Into the fourth day of the investigation, he was seriously past the crucial forty-eight hours. Any mystery reader knew that if a crime hadn't been solved by then, each passing hour spelled doom. Motive had few lines. Opportunity? Only Molly Doyle and Madame X. Means had one word . . . stabbed. Frustrated, Randall held back a few favorite phrases and kicked a wastebasket instead.

Forensics came up with a few gum wrappers and some loose change found in the gravel. Lorna Jacobs's clothes and body had yielded nothing. No foreign fibers or matter except cat hair. The undersides of her fingernails were clear and unbroken.

He'd thought about sending the rookie to attend the postmortem. After moving the body, he deserved to see the pathologist cut up the cadaver, pull out the organs, weigh them, and bag them. Randall hoped he'd turn green and puke his guts out. But he changed his mind. He wanted to be there. He had questions. Questions a rookie would never think of. Randall knew the majority of homicides were primarily gang-related around Salinas, and pretty cut-and-dried. Drive-bys and a few stabbings were the methods of choice.

The pathologist was a surprise. A virtual expert on knife wounds, he was well versed on entry angles, thrust pressure, and type of knife. Randall wasn't surprised to learn there were no defense wounds on her hands. Lorna Jacobs had been a big woman, almost six feet. Randall had given the pathologist a shopping list: Give me the angle of the entry thrust and a guesstimate on the height of the perp. Was the weapon a kitchen knife, an ice pick, a hunting knife, a long blade, short, wide, narrow? A specialty item? Was he or she right- or left-handed? How close was the perp to the victim when the knife went in? Was it a lunge stabbing? Was it close and quick? How much force had been used? Not enough for a man? Too much for a woman?

He had most of his answers. The pathologist was a whiz. Lorna Jacobs knew her killer. He knew who he was looking for now. Only a name was missing. He wasn't ready to make it Molly Doyle. Not yet.

7

"*H*elp!"

Molly turned to see Bea from the florist shop trying to wedge her way through the door. She was barely five feet, and her arms were loaded with a huge display of sunflowers. "Hold on!" she said. Rushing to Bea's side, Molly took the arrangement from her and set it carefully on the pine harvest table. "This is gorgeous! It's just perfect. So . . . so Country French."

"That's what you ordered." Bea grinned with pride. "I just finished it. I've got to run, my new computer arrived, and the box is sitting in the middle of the shop. Stop by for coffee Saturday, after you close. Maybe you can help me put it together? I'm new to all this technology stuff. I hired a tutor, but she won't be free for another week."

"I'll be there." She watched Bea leave. So much energy for such a tiny thing. Aptly named, she almost buzzed. Her shop uniform of red leggings, red turtleneck, and a bright-flowered smock gave her tiny frame and short-cropped black hair the look of a pixie from a storybook.

Bea had been the first shopkeeper to welcome Molly to Courtyard Del Sueno, as the complex was known. Bennie Infama, the son of Tosca's owner, had been at her heels. The woman who ran the boutique opposite her had been tight-lipped and aloof. Molly shrugged her off. Slick blond buzz cut, always dressed in black, and a turned-down mouth. Probably five-foot-four with spike heels. She reminded Molly of a ghoul.

Molly usually didn't care for tiny women. They made her feel awkward and clumsy. Bea was an exception. She oozed joy and kindness. Molly preferred giants like herself. Cleo was five-nine. That qualified. Five-eight was okay. Anything below that, she avoided. Lorna Jacobs, she remembered, was even taller.

Forget her. Forget all of it. Clear it away.

She'd gone to the beach again. Climbing into bed last night, she realized she needed to establish a routine of sorts. Like it or not, she was going to be here for a while. The best way to cure some of her ills was to feel grounded. Routines did that. She didn't see Randall, but in case he was a ritual stroller, she didn't want him to think his presence had scared her away, or worse, that she was avoiding him.

After the noon hour, she collapsed with a cup of tea. She hated tea, but she'd read it was good for smokers. A large, orderly group of tourists from Germany, all speaking excellent English, had just left. For almost an hour, she'd been busy writing up sales and wrapping sixteen mismatched china teacups, eight brass candlesticks, a copper kettle, four ceramic match strikers, and two phony French demitasse sets. When the tour leader assembled them outside, Molly let out a long sigh. She'd never handled that many people all at once. After she added up her sales slips, a huge grin filled her face. Nine hundred bucks. She used to sell mediocre paperweights that cost twice that. She almost laughed. She wasn't working with three floors of museum quality goods anymore. This was her real world now. She'd better get used to it.

Gulping down the tea, she decided to make a little tour

of the floor. The Germans made a dent in her smalls. She would have to get some fresh merch in pretty quick. The tiny storage room was running bare. Max told her that what was referred to as decorative accessories at her previous level, was called "smalls" at this price range. Decent smalls, he'd gone on, even at this midrange price, were not easy to come by these days. With millions of people watching the *Antiques Roadshow* spin-offs, he'd huffed, merch was drying up. Much of what used to go to local auction was showing up on the Internet. Even garage sales were skimpy, and what was available was overpriced. The thought of another weekend of garage sales had little appeal for Molly. She knew she'd have to go, but she wouldn't be the first to arrive.

Staring at the holes in her decorating efforts, she shook her head and laughed. She hadn't expected to be faced with the typical dealer dilemma so soon. First you worried if the merch didn't sell. When it did, you were pissed because you didn't have backup. Empty spaces signaled a dealer too poor to keep stock, or not talented or connected enough to replace it. Antique dealing was vastly different from generic retailing. Gift shops only had to order from a catalog, a sales rep, or spend the day at the wholesale mart. Antique dealers had to scramble, cajole, and hustle. Hours spent at auctions, with competitor dealers breathing down their necks, was exhausting. Buying trips in the boondocks were no longer viable. Trips to Europe, unless you were high-end, were too expensive.

Eyeing an array of blue-and-white Chinese export platters, she thought about calling Max and telling him how inexpensive the Germans thought everything was. "Maybe I should up the prices," she mumbled.

"Don't be silly," said a voice behind her. Turning

quickly, Molly's face was flushed. "Oops. That really sounded awful. What I meant was—"

The petite slender woman, probably in her early seventies, laughed. The deep throaty sound, a contradiction to her patrician face and bearing, almost made Molly laugh. Her silver-white hair was rolled back into an elegant chignon. Dressed in a simple linen sheath—a wonderful shade of yellow—she leaned upon an intricately carved ebony cane. Offering her hand, she announced, "I'm Bitsy Morgan. I used to own this whole dump. I sold it to Sid about five years ago."

Taking her hand, Molly smiled. She loved caustic older women. They carried brusqueness with such élan. "I'm Molly Doyle."

Bitsy Morgan gave her a long look, "Yes. I know who you are. You're the one who found Lorna."

Molly cringed. Ignoring her, she asked, "Care to join me for a cup of tea? I could use another. I just had a big group in and—"

Bitsy waved her off. "Okay, don't discuss Lorna. Tea would be fine." Glancing around while Molly got the tea, she settled on a Victorian revival sofa upholstered in red velvet. Smiling her thanks, she took a quick sip, then said, "Have to say Sid spruced up the courtyard pretty well. Too bad he let the shop go. Looks better. You do all this?"

"I moved and shoved until I was ready to scream. Not much to work with, but I think what we have shows well."

"Hard to sell crap, isn't it? Don't faint, honey. I did it for years. Paid the bills and kept me in Scotch. Then I found myself a rich husband. A customer, wouldn't you know." She laughed at her joke, then winked. "Kept at it for years, between our trips to Asia and Europe. Couldn't give it up. Loved the con too much."

"Shame on you! There's no con here. And, I really wouldn't call this crap. It isn't grand, but it's at least decent. I'm not lying on the tags. I called them as I saw them."

Bitsy took a small sliver flask from her bag and spiced her tea. "It's close to crap. Pure and simple. But it's what people want these days."

"Well, I wouldn't call the hallmarked Russian samovar in the window 'crap.'" Lifting her cup, Molly said, "Limoges china is pretty good, don't you think? The German tourists were happy."

"Sure they were," Bitsy said. "Considering European prices and the dollar difference, you're cheap. Honey, if you're under the competition, stay that way. Some of the dealers in town are too high for what they sell. Some of it's simple greed, but a few don't know their ass from their elbow."

Settling back, enjoying the first stimulating conversation she'd had in weeks, Molly said, "I took a tour the first week. Seems English is out, and French is back in."

Bitsy roared. "We haven't had good English stuff for years around here. This peninsula has been bombarded with British boardinghouse rejects. Hell, they've been pushing those prewar wardrobes for months. They even have the gall to call them *armoires*!"

Molly laughed. "I know. I saw a few. Tell me about the dealers. What am I up against?"

"Depends on where you came from, and how long you plan to stick around."

Molly avoided eye contact and poured more tea. "I'm from—"

Bitsy pulled out an ivory cigarette holder, and cut in, "Save it. I know all about you." Pulling a large silver cigarette case from her bag, she said, "Find an ashtray, will you?"

Molly's heart lurched. Her tongue suddenly felt thick. "You can't smoke in here." Forcing a tiny laugh, she added, "You know that."

Lighting her cigarette with a flourish, Bitsy's voice turned raspy. "Who the hell's gonna stop me? The new cop in town? If a customer comes in, I'll put it out." Leaning toward Molly, her gaze was soft, her voice gentler. "Sweetie, Max and I go way back. I'm here to help."

"Oh? It would have been nice if Max told me to expect you." Eyeing her carefully, Molly found an ashtray. Sitting across from her, she asked, "How did you know I found Lorna Jacobs? I wasn't mentioned in the papers."

"Max told me. Don't dwell on it, dear. Put it all away. New York included."

Bitsy saw the quick flash of anger on Molly's face. She placed a finger on her lip and smiled. "Not now. Later. We need a steak dinner and a few belts. First order of business is to get the show on the road. You need sales. You need dough to get to New Orleans and start that shop of yours. Before that can happen, you need decent merch. Now, what I had in mind was—"

"You seem to know an awful lot about my business," Molly finally snapped.

Stubbing out her cigarette, Bitsy gathered her things. Smiling to ease the tension, she rose, then said, "Max said you had a temper."

Rising also, feeling a need to tower over the older woman, Molly did little to hide the sarcasm in her voice, "Really? Max used to keep confidences well. What else has dear Max—"

Understanding her move, Bitsy turned away and headed for the door. "It will keep."

"No, it won't! Who the hell do you think you are, coming in here and—"

"It's a long story."

This was bordering on madness. Eyeing the empty shop, Molly spat, "I've got time. Why should you care what I do?"

Bitsy's smile was pure melancholy. "That's a longer story."

Slowly making her way to the door, Bitsy paused to examine a display of Haviland china. "I've sold this pattern so many times, I've lost track. Here it is again." Turning back to Molly, she looked at her for a long moment, "Funny how the past keeps cropping up." Giving a quick wink now, she said, "Get a good night's rest. You'll need it. I'll be back."

~~ 8 ~~

*T*he day had been unusually warm for July. Normally overcast in the morning, real summer didn't start until late August. Hovering near the eighties, the sound of pinecones popping all over town made tourists edgy. Too hot to shop, they were irritable, thirsty, and spent most of the day at the beach. Molly had had only three customers all day. By the time she closed, the streets were in gridlock and many of the restaurants on Ocean Avenue had lines of restless customers on the sidewalks waiting for tables. With so many excellent Italian restaurants in town, the aroma of garlic, onions, and herbs filled the air. Next to Chinese, Italian food could make her melt. It was a pity she couldn't afford to eat out. She knew she could splurge once a week, but determined to be disciplined, food was a weakness she must control. Besides the expense, she had only a tiny portion of her wardrobe with her, and maintaining her weight was a major priority.

Ignoring the hunger attack, she made her way to Bea's shop. She wasn't in the mood to set up a computer, but she'd promised. The visit from that strange woman, Bitsy Morgan, bothered her. She hadn't been able to get her off her mind all day. She had half a mind to call Max. How dare he discuss her with a stranger? She owed him a lot, but kindness had its limits.

She found Bea locking up. "Oh, Molly. Can we do this another time? I've just found out there's a memorial service for my landlady at the beach." Throwing her keys in her bag, she said, "She was a real bitch, but I don't want her husband throwing me out because I didn't show proper respect. I've moved four times in ten years." She looked at Molly and shook her head. "Finding a house I can afford for me and Buddy in Carmel is almost impossible. I've had him since he was a pup. I could never give him up. All those Silicon Valley people are buying up houses here, and the rents are obscene!" Checking her watch, she said, "I've got to get moving. Listen, I really appreciate your offering to help me with the computer. I just hope that customized program for the shop will be easy."

"I'm sure it is. Call me when you're ready. Good luck finding parking space at the beach."

"Well, if I don't, it won't be because of mourners. I doubt if very many people will show up. Nobody liked her. I mean nobody. I guess if you add the cops, there might be ten people or so."

"The cops? Was her husband a cop?"

"No, he's actually a nice guy. I was only kidding. I guess you didn't know my landlady was the woman that was murdered Sunday. Lorna Jacobs? You must have seen it on the news."

Molly carefully kept her face still. "Yes . . . yes, I did."

"The police have a *real* job on their hands for once." Rolling her eyes, she lowered her voice. "I can think of five or six people who might have done her in."

Not sure if she was serious, Molly's eyes narrowed. "Oh, come on."

"Here comes Bennie. Ask him if you think I'm nuts."

Bennie Infama was one of those rare people who could

bring a smile to any face. Hard muscles, baseball cap worn backward, oozing energy, dancing dark eyes and blue-black curly hair, he was charm incarnate. He and Bea had gone out of their way to make Molly feel welcome. "Ladies! I come with a request."

"Make it quick," Bea said. "I'm on my way to Lorna's service."

"You going after the way she treated you?" He shook his head, then flicked the underside of his chin with his fingers, "No disrespect to the dead, but that bitch is on her way to hell. She was a murder waiting to happen."

Recognizing the universal Italian symbol of ill will, Molly was intrigued, "Was she that bad?"

"Hey, don't get me started." Squinting at Molly, Bea asked, "Didn't you go to her garage sale?" Before Molly could answer, she said, "I've been meaning to tell you . . . a good customer was in later that day bitching about missing out on the desk. She saw you through the window at the shop and swore up and down it was you. Was it?"

Molly hesitated. She didn't want any connection with Lorna Jacobs known, but it was pointless to lie. "Well . . . yes."

"Ugh, wash it with Lysol. The woman was a pig. "Turning to Bennie, she said, "What do you need? I've got to go!"

"We've got a trash problem. All the cans were knocked over, and Molly's garbage was all over the alley. Good thing you bag the kitchen stuff."

"Bet it was those raccoons again. I'll put some bunges on my handles," Bea said. Waving a finger in the air, she added, "We can thank Lorna for that, too." Easing away, she said over her shoulder, "Fill Molly in on Raccoon-gate."

"We got an overpopulation of raccoons. A little kid over in Pacific Grove is in bad shape after eating some feces out in the garden. Horrible tragedy. Traps were set, and a lot of them died. Lorna staged a protest and had a TV news crew over to her place watching her lay out food and water. Half the county wanted her head."

"Defiant, or an animal lover?" Molly asked.

"Definitely defiant. She was like that. Contrary as hell. The kind of person who searched for causes, you know? She tried to close us down at Tosca's because we wanted to add a few things to our menu. Claimed there were enough places to get sandwiches." Bennie looked away for a moment, then crossed himself, "Hey, I don't mean to speak ill of the dead, but I'm not shedding any tears. The bitch lived for turmoil. You were lucky you didn't know her."

Having a difficult time keeping her face blank, Molly couldn't help the need to defend Lorna Jacobs. "She must have had some redeeming qualities. No one is all bad."

"I'll give you a ten spot for every one you can find that liked her. No . . . take that back, make it a hundred," Bennie said.

"Too busy to take a census. Next time there's a trash problem, holler. I'll give you a hand."

"Naw, forget it. I'm going to call Max and have him put in a small Dumpster. We need one anyway." About to turn away, Bennie shook his head. "Funny thing is, your trash can seems to be the most popular. It was dumped over the other morning, too. Maybe you've got a nosy competitor, or something."

That seemed bizarre. Frowning, she said, "I'll watch what I throw away."

"Good idea. Those colored powders and tubes of paint were a real mess. Whoever was digging around stomped

them all over the bricks. I had to hose the alley down."
Backing away, he gave her a wave. "Stop in for coffee
more often. I got a new blend I'd like you to try."

Stuck on what he'd just said, her smile was automatic.
"Great. I'll do that."

Feeling an unease she couldn't identify, and not
thrilled that someone was searching her trash, she decided to walk off the edgy sensation. Heading out of the
courtyard, she turned without thinking toward the beach.
She hadn't planned to go that far, but once there, she
wondered where the memorial service was being held.
Curving around Scenic Drive, Carmel Beach ran a good
two to three miles. Not anxious to walk that street so
soon, she realized the mourners could be gathering anywhere. Chanel low-heeled pumps were fine for the shop,
but not for hiking along a packed-dirt footpath. Her feet
were already feeling the impact of the long trek down to
the beach. With two hours of light left, she figured she
could make it as far as the first curve in the road. It was
the least she could do for the woman who had gasped her
last breath in her arms.

By the time she reached the curve, she could hear music. Looking down from the footpath onto the beach, she
saw a small group near a large outcropping of boulders
half-submerged in the pounding surf. Gathered around a
table covered by a white cloth and filled with trays of
food and a makeshift bar were, she quickly estimated, at
least twenty people. Maybe she should have taken Bennie
up on his challenge. Three guitarists stood to the side
playing classical music.

Finding a spot under a gnarled Monterey pine, Molly
watched people shift from group to group. She spotted Bea
with a rather loud bunch apparently sharing something
funny. Her arm was linked with Dick Jacobs's, and another

woman's. Their laughter struck her as out of place, but then, she quickly realized, not everyone mourned the same. Irish wakes were notorious for ribaldry.

Squinting against the slowly setting sun, Molly watched Dick Jacobs. She couldn't explain the kinship she felt for the disliked woman. It bordered on being macabre, yet it was real. She shouldn't have come. The fewer who knew she'd been the one to find his wife, the better. Feeling like a nosy neighbor spying on a party next door, Molly drew closer to the tree.

She continued to watch for a few more moments, then said three Hail Marys for Lorna's soul. Turning to leave, she almost tripped over her sore feet. Not twenty yards up the curving, tree-bordered path, she saw Randall. Hands shoved in pockets, he seemed to be looking right at her. A white-hot flame raced through her. The bastard was following her after all. She should have remembered cops frequently go to the funeral of an unsolved homicide victim. God only knew what he was reading into her being there, half-hidden by the trees. She had half a mind to trot down and join the group. Better yet, she ought to walk right up to him and say hello. *Bet that would blow his mind.*

For once, good judgment overtook her temper. Turning away slowly, as if she'd been watching the surf, she headed in the opposite direction. She'd have to take a side street back. It was steeper, longer, and over bumpy asphalt. With no sidewalks in the residential part of town, her feet would be screaming all the way home. She'd suffer the pain rather than walk past him.

Lighting a cigarette, she aimlessly strolled past the homes, stopping every now and then as if she were sightseeing. If he were still watching, he'd be bored out of his skull by now.

Her feet were in genuine pain by the time she hit the first sidewalk. Pausing in front of a gift shop, she saw the reflection of his patrol car in the window. He was looking straight ahead, but she knew he had spotted her. Taking her time, she stopped every now and then to lift one foot from a shoe and wiggle her toes. Keeping her gaze casual, she continued to search for him. After two blocks, she stopped in front of an art gallery and spotted him again. Pretending to be interested in the group of small oil paintings in the window, she turned slightly and saw him park up the street. Moving at a snail's pace, she headed for another gallery a few doors away. With almost a hundred galleries in town, it was an easy stop-and-go tour.

When she reached the next gallery, she suddenly forgot all about Randall. The connectors from her eyes to her brain did a somersault. Perched alone, on a baroque easel, was a large watercolor that could have been a twin to any one of the ones she had found in the desk. The stylized Early California milieu and colors were identical. Even the landscape bore a similarity to the region portrayed in the series of watercolors. A fidgety surge of excitement filled her. She leaned in closer to the window, searching for a signature. So mesmerized by the coincidence, she hadn't noticed the sign to the right of the work that bore the artist's name. Finally spotting it, she rubbed the scar over her eye as she searched her brain. Lawrence Toby did not ring even one tiny bell. Definitely not one of that era's big-name artists, he would be easy enough to check out.

Her eyes glued to the artist's work, she fumbled in her tote for the small notebook she always carried. Blowing out her breath in frustration, she had half a mind to dump it on the sidewalk. *Get a grip*, she silently swore, *or buy a smaller bag*. Patiently setting the tote down, she hunched down and shoved aside keys, wallet, sunglasses, and cigarettes until her fingers found the small leather book. Pulling out the micro pen from its holder, she quickly rose to her feet and jotted down the artist's name, date of birth, and death.

Curiosity was pumping her blood so fast, she could almost feel heat on her cheeks. She itched to get into the shop and investigate. But how? She was a daily prisoner from ten until seven. Noting the shop times on the door, she sighed. Ten to six. Pablo be damned, she decided to open at eleven tomorrow. If she got caught, she would have to think of something.

Lighting another cigarette, Molly exhaled slowly. Her mind was going full tilt trying to sort out a number of thoughts. Turning back to the watercolor, she shook her head. The similarity was too close to shrug off. Nodding, she finally concluded that the watercolors she had found in the desk must be simple practice works. Artists frequently emulated the styles of well-known painters. It was good training. "No," she mumbled, "That doesn't compute. Lawrence Toby couldn't have been famous enough to bother with. The few names that came readily to mind, Armin Hansen, Percy Gray, and Theodore Wores, were artists whose works transcended the genre and frequently showed up at auction. But Lawrence Toby?"

No longer interested if Randall was still following her, she ended her charade of browsing and headed home. Reaching the shop, Molly went up the street stairs to the apartment. Wincing at each step, she rummaged for the keys. Instant success brought a smile to her still puzzled face. Shouldering open the heavy, iron-studded door, she stepped inside, gingerly removed her shoes, and made the kitchen her first stop. She was famished, and in dire need of a cup of coffee. Plopping yet another frozen dinner in the microwave, she headed for the bookcases in the living room.

Filled with old antique price guides, detective novels, and Westerns, the shelves also contained a rather large selection of art books. When she'd cleaned the apartment, she had been too tired to tackle the books. There were, she estimated, a good two hundred filled with dust and mold. Max hadn't wanted them, and Pablo merely shrugged and told her to trash them. Loving old books, even if torn and tattered, she hadn't the heart to destroy them. Now she was glad. They were sufficiently out-of-date possibly to prove useful.

Pulling off dozens of books, even those remotely related to art, she stacked them on the floor next to the sofa. She was sick of Lean Cuisine, but the thought of cooking for one was unappealing. Gulping down dinner, she took two swallows of coffee, then reached for the first book.

If she couldn't find Lawrence Toby, she knew the library was her next stop. With Carmel being a celebrated art haven for several decades, she was certain its library would be well stocked with reference material.

In any event, she was determined to discover how on earth fresh watercolors by an artist who died more than forty years ago were in that cursed desk.

9

*W*hy the hell had Molly Doyle been down at the beach last night spying on the memorial gathering? Morbid curiosity? Old-fashioned respect for the dead? He didn't think so. How about guilt? Randall wondered for the tenth time this morning. As far as he could tell, she'd stayed up on the path. She was already there when he arrived. He thought he was well hidden by the trees, but he'd bet she made him. Waving a car past him, he jaywalked across Ocean Avenue, and headed for his meeting with the district attorney. Randall had a plainclothes man video the mourners. He wanted a clear picture of who attended and bet the killer was there. They often were. Where did these "memorials" come from anyway? Couldn't they wait for the coroner's office to release the body and have a proper funeral? Seemed like a poor excuse for a beach party. Bunch of juveniles who wouldn't admit to being middle-aged. The whole world was tragedy nuts these days. Candlelit vigils, flowers, and crosses erected at accident and homicide scenes, ribbons on trees, bunnies, balloons, even Beanie Babies. When he went out, he wanted his ashes scattered in the sea. No service, no wake, no nothing. No tears to shed, no life to celebrate. *When I'm gone, I'm gone. End of story.*

Pausing a half block from Molly's shop, he thought

about stopping in, then changed his mind. It was too soon after last night. If she hadn't spotted him at the beach, she might have seen him following her in town.

The case was getting under his skin. It was like a silent movie. You had to be a lip reader to know what the actors were really saying. Maybe he'd been away from civilian homicide too long. Putting away cops was easier. The variables were fewer. Yeah, he'd wait until tomorrow. He'd have to play it a little smarter with her, pretending that she was a dirty cop who knew the tricks of the trade. This wasn't what he had in mind when he left Los Angeles. Carmel promised to be an easy stroll into retirement. A no-stress, no-brain-drain job.

Passing the shop, he kept his eyes straight ahead. If she happened to see him, it would appear he was just walking past. Nodding to strangers, he waved at phantoms, and smiled to nonexistent acquaintances. He was on his way to an early lunch meeting at Daria's with Dan Lucero, the DA. If the meeting were a bust, at least he'd have a great lunch. The premier gathering place for bigwigs on the Monterey Peninsula, he had had dinner at Daria's twice when he'd been up from Los Angeles to look over the police facilities. A cross between the old Chasen's in Beverly Hills, and the Russian Tea Room in Manhattan, its excellent food had been a major factor in his decision to take the job. Knowing Daria DeMarco some years back had been another bonus. It had been a good twenty years since he'd seen her. She'd played a major role in helping him break up a drug ring operating out of L.A. Her estranged second husband had been a key player in moving drugs up and down the coast. They'd killed a full bottle of Gentleman Jack catching up during Randall's first trip to Carmel.

Next to his train collection and antique furniture, cooking was his only passion. After his divorce nearly ten years earlier, he'd taken an early vacation and spent two months in the kitchen of his restaurant, glued to the chef. Finally, Angelo, whom he'd stolen from a hot trattoria in Los Angeles, threatened to cut his hands off if he didn't leave.

With only a block to go, he slowed his pace and began to discard the various roles he would portray to the preening, cocksure jerk who probably wanted his head. He'd missed meeting Lucero on his first trip. The DA had been on a goodwill tour in Sacramento kissing political ass. Randall remembered him from a criminal justice seminar last fall in San Diego. Tall, trim, wavy brown hair; the ideal Adonis to capture the female vote. Lucero dressed in tailored Italian suits, crisp white shirts, perfect ties, and big, gold cuff links, of the kind no one wore anymore. You couldn't miss him. The buzz was in his favor, however. He was well liked, admired for his legal acumen, and had an enormous agriculture constituency with megadeep pockets. Lucero, it was said, had his eye on Sacramento.

Nodding hello to Daria, Randall couldn't help but grin when she jerked her thumb behind her and tilted her head. He gave her a salute, and found Lucero in the most prominent banquette. Dan Lucero and two bulging briefcases filled the leather booth, forcing Randall to take a chair from a nearby table. The DA was sunk into the supple folds of the leather as if it were his private domain. Randall had to bite back a laugh. *Lucero couldn't resist telling me this is his world and he considers me a temporary visitor.* He quickly took in the other men's features. Most prominent were his thick brows. Randall immediately knew what he was up against. Dominant and abrupt nature. Combine that with a nose that hooked slightly downward, a sure sign of ambition, Lucero was all a DA should be. His only weakness, Randall mused, were his large brown eyes. Like Molly Doyle, his affection was tempered by a serious nature, but his loyalty to his family was intense. Randall could understand that; it was a strong Italian trait. The goddamned chin was going to be trouble. Bullheaded, persistent, and determined. Like Molly, Lucero had a natural dimple. In fact, Randall had one, too. Carmel was going to be very interesting.

Lucero's maneuvering reminded him of lunches with writers and directors when he'd been, for a brief time, one of the many police consultants to the movie industry. Stature at an expensive restaurant, one designated as the watering hole for your profession, was a historic part of the power process. The need to mark your territory—booth, table, or corner—was vital to your status. It always amused him to realize the need seemed greatest for politicians and lawyers.

Quickly going through the ritual—handshake, taking the measure, polite banalities—Lucero lost no time. "We should have met last Sunday when this homicide went down. Why didn't you have the courtesy to call my office?"

Randall kept his temper with the waiter hovering. He looked up, smiled, ordered a J&B soda, then quickly settled on a Cobb salad. He'd put on a few pounds and decided to go the rabbit route today. Lucero waved the waiter away. "You know what I like. Oh, Chris, tell Bruno to go easy on the pesto. I've got a sour stomach today."

Randall watched this little display; another exhibit of his familiarity, then replied calmly, "Until I make an arrest, there's no need to call you."

Lucero hunched over the table. "This is a small community. We work together up here, Chief. Arrest or not, you should have called."

Randall nodded thanks to the waiter as he served their drinks. Taking a long swallow, he carefully set the drink down, moved in to meet Lucero's still-hunched posture, and said, "The name is Randall. I was a little busy Sunday. My priorities were too stacked up to be making courtesy calls. Besides, I figured you had enough unsolved bullets flying around in Salinas to keep you busy."

Moving back to the deep folds of the booth, Lucero's eyes took on a hard glint. "Good answer." Taking a sip of his martini, he added, "I want a full report on my desk ASAP. I want to walk every step with you on this. I want—"

"I want a few things myself. Number one is support that works. I've got a good force, but facilities and equipment need updating. If you can make that happen, you can walk to the can with me for all I care."

King of his turf for so long, Lucero was not accustomed to being interrupted or spoken to with so little respect. Flashing a well-honed grin, the most important tool for a politician, he decided to let Randall's breach of etiquette pass for the moment. He was new. He'd learn. "You'll have what you need. We want to wrap this puppy up quick. There's a lot at stake here. For both of us. Homicide, other than gang bangers, is big-time here. It rarely happens. Media coverage on the Central Coast will be relentless. Hell, they'll be running this all over the state. It's not good for tourism."

"Yeah, well, I'm on the bubble. Not you."

"Your performance reflects on me."

Randall leaned back and laughed. "Hey, hold it. Don't give me that political crap. I've been there, okay? My wins or losses are mine. They don't rub off on you." Digging into his Cobb salad, he waved his fork in the air, "You're two years away from reelection. When I nail this bastard"—he looked Lucero in the eye now—"and you can bet your ass I will, then we'll applaud your efforts on the campaign trail, okay?"

Lucero studied Randall for a long moment. Giving his full attention to the steaming *pasta con figole e pesto*, he savored two lengthy samples, then carefully dabbed his lips, set down his napkin, and said, "Let me give you an overview of the terrain, *Randall*. You're an ex-big-time L.A. cop working in a tiny little burg that couldn't find its ass in a windstorm. Tech support is limited because nothing, well, rarely, happens. General homicide is as rare as a two-bit whore. When one breaks, it comes down on every criminal justice system on the peninsula. My office takes the heat if nothing happens. This particular homicide is important, because—"

Randall was almost in Lucero's face. Only the fact they both had façades to maintain kept him civil. "*All homicides are important.* I've never known one that was *particular.*"

Lucero laughed. "You must have been the terror of Internal Affairs. I'll bet everyone quaked when you sneezed."

Randall hated games. He'd thought he'd left them in L.A. But, what the hell. "They shit their pants."

"Okay. Let's eat. Lunch is getting cold." Eyeing Randall's salad, he said, "Mine is, anyway." Between bites, Lucero ordered another round, then said, "Okay, here's where I am. I'm going for one more term as DA, which, I'll probably win. Then it's attorney general. I'm going to Sacramento again to discuss strategy. That says it all."

Randall noticed Lucero ate like a true *paisano*. He didn't use a spoon to twirl the pasta onto his fork. It was great show when in Rome, but working-class immigrants ate with gusto. It was funny, he thought, how a little thing like that could fuck up first impressions. There might be more to the guy. Maybe. "In spades." He finally answered. "I got the big picture. It's the little one that needs focus. I need two investigators."

Lucero set down his fork, sipped his drink, and winked, "In return for?"

Randall decided to stick with first impressions. "Excuse me? This isn't a board game. I'm without a seasoned detective. I can't promote within, because right now, I don't have time, nor do I have the manpower to spare. May I remind you that you are obligated to cooperate?"

"Maybe. It all depends."

The urge to dump Lucero's lunch in his lap was overwhelming. Maybe a good old-fashioned pistol-whipping in the alley might work. Setting his napkin on the table, Randall eased his chair back. Pulling out his wallet, he threw two twenties on the heavily starched linen. "I don't cut deals with politicians. I don't like plea-bargaining. And, I particularly don't like ambitious lawyers. You either give me the investigators, or I go over your head."

He waved to Daria on the way out. "Best Cobb I've had since the Derby closed."

"That's a first-class compliment, and I take it humbly. Most people don't know the Brown Derby invented it."

"Yeah . . . well, life goes on. See you later."

Outside the restaurant, he fished a cigar from his pocket, plunked it in his mouth, and rolled it around his lips like a true *Cubano*. Pausing at one of the dozens of jewelry shops in town, he stared in the window, glancing at custom-made rings and trinkets and concluded Lucero was a piece of shit. *Dumb fuck just had to see if I was a puss. If he checked me out, which he should have, he'd know not to deal me off like that.* Lucero reminded him of college jocks who never grew up. The kind who typically relegated women to locker room jokes, knowing jabs, and sleazy chuckles. A sub rosa club that never lacked members.

While his ex-wife might not agree, Randall felt he'd at least made the leap to a mature male. All things considered, he thought of himself as solid, dependable, and more or less enlightened. He respected women who knew their place, he gave to charity, he liked dogs, went to Mass on Easter and Christmas, and didn't pad his expense account. His opinion of the human race, however, was not flattering. He had special compartments for the species—fair, bad, and worse. People, he learned early in his career, were born thieves, crooks, and killers. Only circumstances, peer pressure, and the lack of a clear-cut opportunity to get away with something kept humanity more or less in check.

Continuing to stroll, he set up a work schedule in his mind for the investigators Lucero would send over. There were still interviews pending. Lorna Jacobs's inventory was primarily custom work from local jewelers. He'd already heard rumbling that she was a slow pay. Bank records and personal history needed to be examined. He'd gone through every inch of her house with the criminalist—personal and business files, computer disks, her hard drive, clothes, laundry, garbage—the usual gamut.

Staring at the end of his unlit cigar, he had to admit he was almost embarrassed to have Lucero's people around now that he thought of it. He'd have to tell Lucero the crime scene had been contaminated. While the responding officer was waiting for him, and Molly Doyle was cooling her heels, the automatic sprinkler came on. In a panic, the officer moved the body away from the spray. An inch could spell disaster. Any foreign objects were history. A seasoned officer would have covered her with a tarp. Standard issue, stowed in the trunk. Randall knew what happened. The rookie panicked, and when he realized what he'd done, he figured the pathologist would assume the ground condition was due to the early-morning drizzle. He as much as admitted it that morning. Poor fuck was ready to wet his pants. He let him off with a warning.

Ms. Doyle, however, had failed to bring that little point to his attention. Why? Why not? With her family background, she probably knew it would cover her tracks. But what tracks? Did she have any? Fiber match wasn't pertinent. The woman died in her arms.

All the photos of the crime scene were wrong. Once the position of the victim is in question, or improperly handled, the scene is compromised and contaminated; speculation and deduction become the only tools available.

Stabbing his cigar in the air, he punctuated each thought. Impression prints on the lawn and the gravel were destroyed. The only given was the time of death. Even Molly Doyle and the mystery woman were sketchy. Everything else was a crapshoot. This wasn't the first case he'd had to salvage from error. Shoving the cigar back in his mouth, he mumbled, "Won't be the last either."

10

*S*tanding in front of the desk, admiring the soft black gloss she'd been able to achieve, Molly was waiting for Max to answer the telephone when she saw Randall walk past. Wanting to keep an eye on both the street and the floor, she'd angled the desk next to the wall near the front window. Now she could watch for potential customers and any reaction to her displays. *How nonchalant he pretends to be,* she thought. *He hasn't the guts to come in and face me.*

Max's voice interrupted her silent venting. Breathless as usual, he told her Pablo was on his way down with a full truck of merch. "My shipment from France arrived early, and I've got to make room. It's a mixed bag of stuff. See what you can do with it. Pablo has all the paperwork . . . you'll probably have to lower some prices. What I can get here won't fly down there. You decide. Call me tomorrow. I must run, darling, Mario's in town and I'm meeting him for lunch."

"Our Mario?" Molly asked wistfully. Mario Bono was one of the top decorators in the world, and an old customer.

"Who else?" Max said. "I'll give him your best."

"Don't," she quickly said. 'I . . . I don't think I want him to know where I am. I mean, he might blabber." It killed her to even say it, but she knew it was better to keep a low profile. The fewer people who knew where she was, the better. At least for now.

"Oh, yes. Of course. Well, be good."

"What the hell else can I be?"

"Now, now, this will all blow over. You'll be back mixing with the crowd in no time," Max gently teased.

"Ever the optimist." She laughed back.

"I'd never have made it this far in life if not." He let that linger, then added, "Molly, darling, I know Pablo has been a trial, but for my sake, give . . . give him some time, will you? His life hasn't been easy either."

Molly sighed. "For you, anything. But I won't take any more of his shit. Fair warning, okay?"

"It's a deal."

"By the way, why didn't you tell me about Bitsy Morgan? I mean, who is she, really?"

"Oops, I didn't think she'd stop by so soon."

"That isn't the point, Max! The point is—"

"Sweetheart, don't get your Irish up now. We only want to help."

"You know I love you dearly, but telling some stranger about my problems is—"

"She's not a stranger. I mean, well, let her tell you, okay? Don't shut her out. She's a hell of a dame, and I mean that as a compliment."

"I'm thrilled you adore her, but that doesn't mean I have to."

"Look, love, I've really got to go. *Ciao!*"

Molly hung up, checked her watch, and calculated Pablo should arrive in about two hours. This was the worst possible day to have to contend with him. She'd had little sleep again. Tossing and turning most of the night, she finally got up at three. She sat in the darkened living room trying to sort out the crazy dream that brought her awake. Wearing an artist's beret, Lorna Jacobs was knee deep in boiling yellow surf, her arms flapped like a huge, ungainly bird, and she kept shouting at Molly. Just as that fateful morning, Molly had no clue what she was saying.

Shaking away the thought, she remembered that the Bitsy woman was coming back. That was all she needed. Pablo and Bitsy in one day. She had enough time, she estimated, to get rid of her and make room for the new merch. Between trying to figure out her dream, her plans to check out Lawrence Toby, and the news that Pablo was on his way with God only knew what, her thought processes were fritzed to hell.

If she were lucky, Pablo would be gone by midafternoon. She could close for an hour and get over to that gallery. Molly hardly had time to finish her thoughts when Bitsy swept in. "I don't keep regular hours, you might not see me for days, but when I'm here, honey, I can sell with the best of them."

Dressed in a stunning mocha raw silk suit, the woman was a veritable knockout. With her personality, including the bawdy air she liked to affect, and flashing eyes, Molly realized she could probably sell camels in Hawaii. But she didn't need her. She had a hard enough time keeping busy. Besides, Max hadn't mentioned her working here. Trying hard for his sake, Molly smiled. "I'm sold, but honestly, we really can't afford anyone now, Ms. Morgan."

Making herself comfortable on a love seat, Bitsy threw up her hands, "Who mentioned money? I'm just bored. Besides, you need me."

Jesus! Molly thought. *How the hell am I going to get through to her?* She had to play this gently. She didn't want to alienate anyone who seemed to know more about her than she would like. Pulling up a paisley-covered footstool, Molly said. "Mrs. Morgan, there's hardly enough to keep me busy as it is."

Pulling out her cigarette case again, Bitsy said, "You can't continue to work seven days a week, sweetie. You have to have time to get to the house sales, the auctions, you need—"

Molly quickly interrupted, "Please, don't smoke again. A shipment from Max is on the way, and I don't want—"

Bitsy let out a roar. "You don't want Pablo to smell it, right?" Seeing Molly's lips harden, she added, "Yes, I know the unpleasant little bitch."

"You seem to know everyone," Molly said.

"Pablo was Sid's friend. Max hired him after Sid died. Let's just say we've had our moments." Seeing the look of surprise on Molly's face, she returned the cigarette case to her bag. "Look, I'll get out of your hair for today. I'll clear this with Max. He'll see the logic." Rising from the love seat, she stepped over to a small walnut side table and picked up red glass bowl. "Tell me, is this ruby or cranberry?"

Molly's eye began to twitch. "What does the tag say?"

"It doesn't. Which tells me you don't know. The customer will know that, too. Can't have that and pretend to be an antique dealer."

Molly touched the pulsing spot over her eye and rose from the footstool. Bitsy threw up a hand to stop her. "This is why you need me. When you sold high-priced smalls in your fancy shop, didn't you detail your tags with dates and artisans? Didn't you differentiate between Meissen, Nymphenburg, and Hochst?"

Molly took a deep breath. "Of course, but—"

"But what? You think *junk* doesn't need a description?

Let me tell you honey, collectors of ruby and cranberry glass are serious. Besides, junk is relative. This merch may not be period Louis XV, Queen Anne, or Jacobean, but it's not that shabby." Moving to a sideboard, she pointed to a charming milk jug. "Is that a Ralph Wood, or a recent reproduction?" Picking the small jug up, she examined it carefully. "You're asking thirty bucks for this . . ." Glancing at Molly, her face still bland, she said, "It's real, and it's worth three hundred." Moving quickly, she grabbed another jug and looked at the tag. "This is what? Creamware or Staffordshire salt glaze?" Turning her back on Molly, she said over her shoulder, "Don't answer. It's Creamware. Change the price to two-fifty. You're losing your ass here, darling." Heading to the door, she turned dramatically. "Those flow blue platters you have in the window are repros. Made in Hong Kong every day. Let them go cheap. Fifty bucks each would be fair. A lot of people only want the look, anyway." Stopping at the pine harvest table, she added, "This is real. Check out the pegs. Up the ticket to twenty-two hundred." Giving Molly a broad wink, she said, "See you tomorrow."

Watching her leave, Molly fumed. She knew the harvest table was real. Too worried about sales, she'd grudgingly lowballed the price. The moment Bitsy was out the door, she threw her hands on her hips, and rattled, "Bet *you* don't know the difference between English Queen Anne or American, *sweetie*! Bet *you* couldn't date a secretary's pediment! Tell, me darling . . ." She began to rant as she moved about the shop. ". . . when did a bonnet top come into vogue? How's 1735 to 1770? Or, a baroque arch? Why, Miz Bitsy, honey, the English used it between 1690 and 1720. Of course, you wouldn't know us Yankees didn't catch on until 1730. Now, that swan neck over there"—pointing to an imaginary example—"had a short run: 1760 to 1780." Smiling nastily, she said, "Better change that tag to twenty grand."

Plopping down on the Victorian love seat she absolutely loathed, she mumbled, "That's all I need. Miz Know It All and Pablo in one day." Just the mention of Pablo's name brought her to her feet. Between her bruised ego and a floor that needed to be cleared, she swore, "Shit!" Checking her watch, she figured he was halfway to Carmel. In the middle of moving small furniture aside, and vowing to be pleasant when he arrived, she stopped in her tracks. *So, Miz Bitsy knows Miz Pablo. Well, well. And Pablo had been at the shop with Sid. Interesting. Why hadn't Max told her any of this?*

Then, she wondered, why was Max the heir, and not Pablo? The only possible answer was that Max and Sid stayed close. But did Max have to inherit Pablo, too? It was none of her business, but she was itching to know. It might explain some of Pablo's hostility. She expected that his initial animosity toward her was simply jealously. She and Max had a history he didn't share. She expected it to cool down after the first week in The City. After all, she wasn't entirely unlovable. In the end, she decided it was old-fashioned envy. She'd been where most dealers only dreamed of being. High-end in New York.

On the other hand, she guessed, it could be simple disdain. She was sure he knew about Derek and Greta. Max promised he hadn't told a soul, but knowing gossip in her business ranked second only to profits, she had her doubts.

Medium height, slim as a pencil, and a bottle blond. Pablo was a walking ad for *GQ*, in his button-down shirt, crisp khakis, and tasseled loafers. His only positive quality, Molly often thought when she wanted to choke him, was his uncanny gift of looking fresh all day. His face always had that just-out-of-the-shower glow, and his clothes were invariably wrinkle-free. She sometimes thought she hated him just for that. Her hair was usually wispy by midmorning, and her lipstick never seemed to last more than an hour. Cleo said it was constant anxiety. Pushing hair back and licking lips were sure signs.

Accompanied by two helpers, both in starched, one-piece, dark green coveralls, with TREASURES embroidered over the breast pocket, Pablo lost no time in barking orders. "We can't be double-parked for more than a half hour. Get that shit in here on the double. Furniture first, boxes second, then rugs."

In like a whirl, he carelessly dropped a large manila envelope on the desk. "Here's the inventory. Speaking of which, the one you sent from here did not follow the format I outlined."

Ready to be sweet, she smiled. "It was the best I could do without a computer. Cross-referencing would have taken me days longer."

"I've brought a computer. You can do it over." Glancing at her sideways, he asked, "You *are* computer literate I hope?"

"Of course," she replied evenly.

"Thank God for little favors. I loaded the custom program we use in The City. Follow that exactly. I'll want a full report every Monday. We got you a fax, too. Use that for the reports and any communications."

Good, she thought. *Now I won't have to speak to you.* "Where exactly do you expect me to put all this equipment? The desk won't hold it, and the storage room is half a closet."

"I give a fuck. You figure it out."

Molly held her breath. "When do you expect your friend to return?"

His eyes roaming the floor, he turned sideways. "What friend?"

"The one using the cabinets in the garage. If I could use those for stock, I'd be able to put the computer in the storage room."

"I told you they were off-limits. Forget it." Standing in front of the desk, he said, "God Almighty! Where in the hell did you find this piece of crap? It's beyond gross."

Molly thought a few Hail Marys might work. She tried, but her tongue got twisted. "At a garage sale."

"Get rid of it."

"Replace it then." She shot back. "Oh, and by the way, where are my last two checks? You're supposed to send one each Friday. I'm missing two weeks."

He gave her an insolent stare, then said, "Get your report right, then I'll see about it." Turning away, he looked over the showroom and blew out his breath. "Why isn't this cleared? The truck is loaded. We'll never get everything in here. God, you're useless! Why Max ever—"

"That's it!" Molly exploded. Weeks of enduring his rudeness and caustic remarks finally detonated the bomb ticking in her. Determined to be as crude as possible, she screamed at him. "Who the fuck do you think you are to talk to me like that? You're nothing but a hired hand, you little prick!" Nearly in his face now, she had to hold back from shoving him against the wall. "I don't work for you. I work for Max, got it? You no longer give me orders, understand? You get those checks down here by FedEx. I'm working seven days a week, nine hours a day without even a lunch break. In case you didn't know it, that's against the law, fucker."

She had to give him credit. Not one perfectly arched eyebrow moved. The baby-smooth skin on his face was still. His grin, however, was grotesque.

"Don't threaten me, you stupid cow." Striding past her, he purposely bumped her shoulder with his. Marching out to the sidewalk, he waved one of the helpers aside. She couldn't hear what he was saying, but the sharp gestures of his hands told her he was taking his venom out on the innocent helper.

As she clasped her arms tightly, her anger was still at a rolling boil. Elated by her bravado, she gritted her teeth and forced herself to stay put. Watching from the window, she saw him stalk off down the street. The helper, who had taken the brunt of his anger, came in. "Uh, Miss? Pablo said we were to clear out the center of the room and unload real quick. If you can get more of the fragile stuff out of the way, we'll . . ."

Nodding quickly, Molly replied, "Of course. I'll get them on the staircase." It was difficult to keep her voice even, but she managed a tiny smile. "I'm sorry he yelled at you. It was my fault. He's mad at me."

"We're used to it," He said. "He's an *artiste*. You know what they're like."

"Really, is that what assholes are called these days?"

"Guess you've never seen his work. He's really good. Don't know why he's fooling around with antiques. Don't worry about the yelling. You must have given him hell. No one does. He's really pissed. He took off."

"That's the best news I've had all week," Molly said over her shoulder. Finding a large silver serving tray, she began loading china cups, vases, figurines, and anything that might break. By the time she had half the staircase full, a mélange of thoughts crowded her mind. *Pablo's an artist . . . was friends with Sid. Bitsy knows him . . . Bitsy knows Max. Bitsy knows about me. How just too cozy for words. What kind of a snake pit have I fallen into?*

With her arms full of silver pieces, Molly realized she'd better put the CLOSED sign on the door. The truck seemed to be attracting a curious crowd. Pasting a smile on her face, she announced a new shipment to three women about to come in, and that they were closing for the day. Overwhelmed by the amount of merch Max had sent, she knew she wouldn't be ready to open the next day. Redecorating and tagging would take her into the early-morning hours as it was.

With the smalls out of the way, Molly edged her way around several of the new pieces of furniture. The quality was immediately apparent. Disaster could be imminent, Wall Street could be crumbling, there could be riots in the street, but lead a dealer to a gem or two, and caution was thrown to the winds. All thoughts of Pablo, Lorna Jacobs, or Lawrence Toby vanished as a smile lit her face. The mix of excellent Country French, genuine Old English Pine, and two American walnut gate leg tables, that might possibly be period, was delicious. She might make an antique shop out of this place after all!

She had no idea what the boxes of smalls held, but she was eager to tear them open. When one of the helpers brought in several paintings, she rushed to his side. "Oh, let me take those. I'll stack them behind the desk."

"I've got half a dozen more. Want them here, too?"

Her attention caught by the first one he set down, she nodded. "Oh, yeah . . . sure, that's fine." Bending down to get a closer look, she sucked in her breath. That rare shiver of excitement that came with discovery hit her hard. The surge of blood that rushes to the brain, and makes the knees weak and the hands shake, was indescribable. Was it possible? Was this a Hassam? It couldn't be. Max wouldn't let something like that out of his hands. About to pick it up to read the signature, the helper was at her side with the other paintings.

"Oops, I think that's a mistake. That's one of Pablo's."

"Not on your life," Molly quickly said. "I know this artist."

"I'm positive. I've seen it in the shop. He copies work all the time. Keeps his hands supple, he says. He's got a little studio in back of the shop. Max uses them for background sometimes." Lowering his voice, he said, "Pablo even gets the signature down pat." Realizing he was giving away state secrets, he quickly added, "But they're not for sale. I mean, Max won't allow it. You ought to see the Rembrandts! Max puts them with his heavy-duty stuff. He must have grabbed that by accident."

Unable to believe Pablo was a copyist, Molly was not about to let it out of her sight. "Well, I'll hang on to it and call Max in the morning." Giving it one more glance, she thought, *Armand could pull this off, but Pablo?*

"I don't know. He'll have a royal fit if he finds out."

Brushing her hands together, Molly said, "Let me worry about that. You're in the clear."

When they left, Molly locked the door. The smile she'd kept pasted on turned to a somber slash. That Max was using fake art for background was, in her mind, deceitful. As a group—herself included—antique dealers were, at one time or another, slightly shady. Prone to embellish value, praise quality, overprice goods, and hedge on provenance, it always paid to heed that old Roman saying—*caveat emptor*, buyer beware. She'd been as guilty as anyone. It was easy to add a few years to a piece, forget to mention that drawers had been replaced, or tack on a phony countess as being a previous owner. But it was hard to believe Max would step over the edge so far. She hadn't gone to Max's shop when she arrived from New York. She'd had enough of antiques and art. All she'd wanted was a familiar shoulder to cry on and a trusted face to believe in her innocence.

Heading to the storage room to make tea, she was in dire need of some Jack Daniel's to give it a kick. She ought to break down and buy a bottle to stash back here for days like this. Carrying the tea back to her desk, she plopped down and surveyed the damage. Max's men had been great about positioning the larger pieces. They'd been saints to shove and move for her. She couldn't believe it was already four. Gulping down the tea, she realized how hungry she was. She had to see Bea and tell her she wouldn't be able to help set her computer up tonight. She could grab a coffee cake from Tosca's to tide her over.

The sun-filled courtyard was in full bloom. Bougainvillea cascaded over the iron balconies, trumpet vine climbed the walls, and the center fountain bordered with masses of mixed impatiens was gorgeous. It suddenly struck Molly how little notice she'd given to her surroundings. So filled with self-pity these past few weeks, she hadn't taken the time to fully appreciate her good fortune. Since the area was filled with late-afternoon shoppers sipping espressos and pastries, she had to wend her way through the crowded iron tables and bistro chairs. The sounds of laughter and happy conversation suddenly lifted her mood. The relaxed atmosphere of Carmel was beginning to get to her. So used to the fast pace of New York, it was still hard to slow down when she went from point A to point B. Her days were beginning to seem like those in someone else's life. Maybe it was the salt air. Maybe it was the soft sounds of the crashing surf she'd begun to listen for before closing her eyes at night. Maybe it was that crazy cat clock in the kitchen that gave her a laugh every morning. Maybe she could be happy here.

Bea's shop was swamped. Giving her a quick wave, Molly said, "Rain check on the computer setup? I've got a huge delivery to sort out."

"Good idea," Bea said. "I'm dead on my feet. It's been a day. I'm not in the mood to pay attention. I'll call you when I have some free time."

"Great."

Back in the shop with two huge slices of Tosca's special apple cake Bennie insisted she try on the house, Molly devoured one and set the other aside for a later treat. Filled with energy, she wondered if it was the sugar, or the exhilaration of finally telling Pablo off. She'd spent so many years polishing mannerisms to match her clientele—the muted cultured voice, the slow gliding walk, the poised stance, she'd forgotten how good it felt to let loose.

Looking over the large walnut wardrobe, an ungainly 1930s monstrosity that Max's men had placed against the wall behind the desk, she opened the accordion doors and discovered someone had fitted it with moveable shelves. It was perfect for the computer and fax.

When the phone rang, Molly blew out her breath. *Now what?*

She let it ring four times. It was after seven. She knew it was either Pablo or Max. Grabbing the phone on the fifth ring, she wasn't surprised to hear Max's voice. "Darling!" He laughed. "I've just heard the most outlandish tale from Pablo. I hope it's all true. I'm so thrilled to see my old Molly back."

Surprised Pablo was such a sniveling tattletale, but relieved Max wasn't angry, Molly said, "I tried, Max. Honestly, I did. But he crossed the line this time."

"I know, darling. I just wanted you to know I understand. Oh, but you should have heard the poor dear! The connection on the cell phone was fuzzy, so I'm not sure I got it all, but what I did hear was marvelous! I'll get a replay when he gets home. It won't be easy keeping a straight face."

"He should have been there hours ago."

"He's staying over to visit friends. I don't expect him for another day or two."

"Swell, just keep him out of my hair. By the way, the merch is absolutely great. And, thanks for all the computer stuff. As soon as I price out, I'll fax you the info."

"Take your time, darling. Say, Bitsy Morgan called. Take her on. She'd be a great help."

Molly dropped her head in defeat. "Max! There isn't enough for two people."

"I insist. How awful of me not to realize you were captive. Besides, how on earth can you find new goodies trapped in the shop all day?"

She hated the idea of losing commissions. She needed every dime she could make. And she wasn't sure how they would get along. Bitsy Morgan may be an old hand, but she didn't need any more lectures. "I really don't see—"

"Molly, look on it as a favor to me. Bitsy and I were in the game together eons ago. She saved my little tush more than once. The woman is a veritable walking antique encyclopedia."

"I've had my first lesson."

"Have her in on the weekends. That way you can hit the auctions."

Molly blew out her breath. "That's the only time I make decent sales."

"She doesn't need the dough, darling. The woman is richer than Croesus."

"Then why?"

"Bored out of her skull, sweetheart. Look, I've got to run. Mario's still in town, and we're having dinner with Anne G."

Staring at the mess before her, she laughed. It wasn't so long ago that she'd be dining with the likes of Mario Bono and Anne Gorman. Now she was a shopgirl again, stocking inventory and marking price tags. "Have a wonderful time, Max. And . . . thanks again for everything."

The wistful tone in her voice slipped past her resolve to be upbeat. Max caught it immediately. He was a prince not to comment. "No, darling girl, thank *you*."

Bracing her midriff with one hand, she was using her hip to inch a sideboard across the room when she heard a rapping on the front window. Thinking it was someone trying to get in on the new goodies before tomorrow, she ignored it. When the rapping became louder, and more insistent, she finally turned around. The scowl on Randall's face was enough to make her feel faint.

11

*I*nvading the room like he was on a mission, Randall scooted past her. "What the hell are you trying to do? Put your back out? You modern women think you're Amazons, for Christ's sake. Where do you want this ugly thing?"

This is it, Molly thought. *He finally checked me out. Just what I needed. What a great way to end the day.* "It's not ugly! It's . . . well, plain." She saw the look on his face. "How's unattractive?"

"Ugly, and watch your manicure," he said, laughing as he took hold of the other end. "Don't lift. I'll do the donkeywork. You just sort of guide it."

Between them, they had it quickly in place. "You sure this is where you want it?"

"Perfect. Thanks."

"Cover it up with something, will you? That's an eyesore."

Molly wondered if this was some new preamble cops learned at sensitivity training. Start out with humor, then come in low and dirty? She had little choice but to play along. "Come on, it's not that bad. These carved Victorian things are popular now."

Picking up the sales tag dangling from a drawer pull, his eyes popped open. "You want fifteen hundred bucks for this thing? You people are crooks. I wouldn't use it for firewood."

"I wouldn't either, but hey, taste is subjective. So, Chief, are you in the market for antiques? It's after hours, but I'd make an exception for you."

Surveying the jumble of boxes, rolled rugs, and general chaos, he said, "Knock off the 'Chief' thing. But, yeah, come to think of it. If you run across any Stickley pieces let me know."

She couldn't help it. She couldn't let this pass. "You're kidding, right? I wouldn't have figured you for that ugly Mission stuff."

He gave her his blank, slit-eyed stare he used to put people off. "What's wrong with it?"

"Oh, let me count the ways. Besides being really boring, it's unimaginative, sterile, and it has peaked. Way overpriced, but a marketing dream while it lasted. In fact, Stickley is making those lines again. I figured you for Directoire . . . or maybe Louis Phillipe."

Moving a box off an Eastlake chair, he sat down and stared up at her. "Come again?"

"Late-eighteenth-century French. Neoclassical. Masculine, yet classic. Very sophisticated."

"You are a charmer, Ms. Doyle."

"I've been called worse. Care for a cup of tea? I'm out of coffee."

"Sure, I like tea." Eyeing the disorder, he laughed. "You'll be up all night with this." Moving aside a few boxes, he cleared a narrow aisle and leaned over to look at a chest. "An old herbalist in Chinatown got me drinking it last year. He said green was the best for smokers. I have a few cups every day. Nice chest." Patting his pocket, he said. "Got any fancy crystal ashtrays lying around?"

Molly had to laugh. "Okay, I smoked in your office, you can smoke in mine. Just don't turn me in." Shoving aside wrapping paper on her desk, she found an ashtray, handed it to him, then said, "I'll plug in the teapot. I drink green, too, Chief. You're in luck."

Inhaling deeply, he said, "Nix, the 'Chief' bit, okay? It's Randall."

"Fine," she answered over her shoulder, "You can drop the Ms. crap, too." Returning quickly, she pulled up a chair, placed a cardboard box between them, and crossed her arms. *No sense in prolonging it,* she thought. *Might as well get it over with.* "Nice of you to drop in."

Randall sat back and smiled. "I saw you working your tail off and thought I'd say hello."

"And?"

"Okay, so this isn't social. I need your help. I'd like you to get together with a police artist and see if we can come up with a drawing of the missing woman."

She hoped he took her sigh for surprise and not relief. "She still hasn't come forward?"

"Nope. I want to get this out to the media. If she's from out of town, she might catch it on the news and give me a call."

"Of course. I'd be happy to help. I have got a woman who's going to start working with me soon. In fact, she might be in tomorrow. I can call you and let you know when I'll be free."

Hearing the kettle whistle, Molly excused herself. The sooner he was gone, the better. His penetrating eyes made her feel he could read her mind. Besides, she was still feeling guilty about the watercolors. It wasn't as if she'd stolen them, but her continued silence made her feel like a sneak thief. Returning with the tray, she said, "Listen, I can come anytime. Good God, finding that woman is more important than this shop being closed for an hour or two. In fact, tomorrow would be perfect. I'll be closed for a day or two anyway."

"Good, I'll set something up for tomorrow morning." Grabbing his mug, he took a sip and said, "Excellent. A lady of many talents." Before she could answer, he got up and began roaming again. Sliding past three chests plunked in the middle of the room, he said, "Who's coming to help you move this stuff?"

When she didn't answer right away, he turned and looked at her. "Figures. Your boss didn't plan very well. Guess he's into that independent women stuff. Hell, if you ladies can be firemen and carpenters, I guess you don't need muscle anymore."

Her silence only made him feel worse. "Personally, I don't think women should be cops, either. But what the hell, what do I know? Gotta get with the times, I guess."

She was determined not to let him get under her skin. For some reason, he delighted in trying to rattle her. "As a matter of public relations I'd keep those opinions to yourself. Carmel has always been very enlightened. Ahead of the crowd, one might say."

His eyes were twinkling now. "Yeah, like Berserkley-ville." Swinging his empty mug in the air, he said, "I'm only kidding. I admire women who can make it on their own." Setting the mug back on the carton, he smiled. "Thanks, Molly. I appreciate your cooperation. Let's see if we can flush this mystery woman out."

At the door, he turned. "By the way, I collect trains, too. Run across any of them, let me know." Pausing for a moment, he added, "What? No smart remark?"

Molly grinned. "Nope. It's a heavy-duty market. Good investment."

"At least we've found some common ground. By the

way, you give up walking the beach already? Haven't seen you lately."

Not sure if he was being friendly, or probing, Molly said, "I've been working late. That extra hour of sleep in the morning helps me make it."

"I was afraid I'd scared you away."

Opening the door, she smiled. "I don't scare that easy."

He paused at the sidewalk. "No. I don't think you do."

12

Up at six, after only a few hours' sleep, Molly headed for Tosca's at seven. Arranging for two of Bennie's busboys to help move furniture, she barely made it back to the apartment to catch the phone. Randall would pick her up at ten. Salinas was only fifteen minutes away, and he'd assured her she'd be back before noon. She no sooner hung up, than Bitsy called. She'd spoken to Max and knew about the new shipment. Did Molly want her to come in and help? Molly assured her she'd be fine, two of Tosca's kitchen helpers were coming in early to move rugs and furniture. Until they were in place, she didn't want to unpack smalls.

Totally ignoring her, Bitsy said, "Well, I'll stop in later anyway." She was off the line before Molly could protest.

Slamming down the phone, Molly headed to the bedroom to change. Eyeing her wardrobe, she wondered how on earth she was going to maintain an image with only six pairs of slacks, a dozen sweaters, five silk blouses, and six pair of shoes. The rest of her clothes were at Cleo's in New York, and God only knew when she'd return from London. When Molly left to visit Max, she had no idea she'd end up in Carmel. Determined to save every penny for New Orleans, she battled the urge to drop in at Saks down the street. Instead, she made a quick trip to

Target in Sand City, where she found jeans, tee shirts, and sneakers in record time. Opting for jeans, she threw on a black cashmere turtleneck and sneakers.

Molly could see Randall listening carefully as she gave the police artist the description of the other woman. She watched him check his notes, and knew he found no deviation from her initial description. Did he think it only proved she had her routine down pat or that she was telling the truth? She thought he still wasn't certain which to believe.

Heading back to Carmel, Randall thanked her again. "Too bad we couldn't put a face to that figure." Shoving a cigarette in his mouth, he punched in the lighter and shook his head. "Gonna be tough for anyone to recognize a straw hat and blue glasses."

"I know. I'm sorry I didn't notice more. Every time I see someone wearing blue glasses, my heart stops. A woman passed the shop the other day wearing a pair. I almost dropped a *millefiori* paperweight. Thank God it wasn't a good one."

"Okay, I'll bite. What the hell is that?"

"Oh, come on, Randall. You've seen them."

When he shook his head, she explained, "Glassblowers fuse strands of colored glass into a cane and slice them into thin sections. They end up looking like flowers. Millefiori . . . a thousand flowers."

"Oh, yeah. Is that how they do that? You gotta know a lot of stuff to be in your business." Noticing she wasn't smoking, he said, "Come on, break the law with me. Have a smoke in a patrol car."

"I'm trying to cut down."

"Won't work. Either go cold turkey or take your

chances. I keep breaking them in half, but it's too expensive."

Finding her own, she said, "You convinced me. Truth is, I felt funny smoking in a police car. You didn't smoke on the way over, and I was dying."

"Yeah, well, what the hell. If some good citizen wants to make a complaint, I'll be sure it gets lost." Watching her face break out in a smile, he continued to prod. "How'd you get in the antique game? I mean, what was the attraction? Old furniture seems kind of boring to me."

Staring at the passing traffic, her eyes seemed fixed on a past so distant, she had to pause. "A small chest. My father . . . my father had a used furniture store on O'Farrell. I helped out after school and on the weekends. One afternoon he showed me some new arrivals. One of the pieces was a small, delicate chest of drawers. It was . . . it was perfect."

Turning to him, she couldn't help but smile. Disaster might be looming, but get a dealer talking, and the moon could fall. "The proportions were exquisite. A wealthy woman in those days would use it in a dressing room, or a large walk-in closet. It had three drawers . . . the pulls were only simple brass knobs, but the marquetry was gorgeous. It was walnut, and the inlays were Greek keys in ebony. I'd never seen anything like it before. It . . . it captured me." Realizing she was rattling, she said, "It sounds crazy, but I fell in love. For the first time, I looked at furniture with different eyes. I mean, you can't get too excited about ratty couches, painted iron hospital beds, or barnyard chairs. But this chest was like a fantasy. I could picture it in a penthouse on Nob Hill. How we got it, I'll never know."

Randall was startled by the brightness in her eyes and

the way her face seemed to glow. "No kidding? That's all it took to get you hooked? A little thing like that?"

Molly almost winced. "Yes," she said softly, "a little thing like that."

"So, how'd you learn the trade? Did you go to school, or something?"

Still thinking about the chest, Molly almost didn't hear him. "Oh, no, well, I mean I've got a fine arts degree, but it's a hands-on education. I went to work for Max when I was in my senior year, then through college. He had a shop on Union Street then. I had six years of learning from a master. He bought a building in Jackson Square just after I graduated. I stayed for another year, then he made some calls and got me on at Sotheby's in New York."

Lost in thought, she hadn't noticed that she'd spilled ashes all over her sweater. Quickly brushing them off, she asked, "What about you? Why a cop?"

His eyes focused on the road, his laugh was almost terse. "Do I have a 'save the world complex,' or am I trying to subordinate my true criminal instincts?"

"Both sound good to me. You pick."

"I just don't like to see bad people do bad things and get away with it."

"Oh no, you don't get off that easy. You're deeper than that, Chief."

"Think so, huh?"

"I know so. How did you end up here, in Carmel?"

"Got tired of L.A. Simple as that. Took early retirement. I don't fish, I don't hunt, and I don't play golf. I wanted to keep my hand in the job, but on my terms, so here I am."

"What about family?"

"What about them," he snapped.

"Jesus, Randall! Do you have a wife? Children? Brothers . . . sisters? Pets? You started this, you know."

Giving her a side glance, he said, "Okay, calm down. I'm divorced, okay? Have been for ten years. Got a daughter up at Stanford. That's it. I'm an only child, my folks are gone, and I don't have a pet. Interrogation over?"

" 'Interview' is the word here, I think."

Throwing back his head, he laughed. "Touché."

Pulling into Carmel, Randall double-parked in front of the shop and had her door open before Molly unhooked her seat belt. "So, what happened to that small chest? You never did say."

"My father sold it the day after it we finished restoring it."

"You must have been crushed," he said kindly.

Molly looked up into his eyes, and without blinking, said, "You know, I didn't realize until now that I still am."

Turning on small lamps in the shop, fluffing pillows, Molly idly wandered around the boxes that needed unpacking. Memories of that small chest filled her thoughts. In all the years since, she'd never run across another like it. *Someday,* she mused. *Yes, maybe someday I'll spot another.*

Bitsy arrived only moments later. Eyeing all the boxes, she was almost giddy. "What fun! I can't wait to see what Max sent down."

On her knees, unwrapping gold-veined Venetian wineglasses, Molly was startled by her voice. Realizing she'd forgotten to lock the door, she carefully set the glasses on a table and headed for the door. "I should have locked this damn thing." Her voice was a little short on purpose. It was time to set the pecking order with this woman.

While she respected Bitsy's age, she wasn't about to let her come in and take over. She might not know much about cranberry glass, or blue flow stoneware, but she sure as hell knew what Max had sent, and this was her milieu.

Setting a picnic basket on Molly's cluttered desk, Bitsy gaily announced, "I stopped at Bruno's and got some goodies. Cold chicken and avocado sandwiches, pasta salad, and a wonderful Merlot. Hope you have some decent glasses." Before Molly could respond, Bitsy headed for the Venetian glasses she'd just unpacked. "Rinse these out, honey. I'll set this up." Looking around the shop, she rolled her shoulders comically. ". . . somewhere. Oh, and see if you can find a couple of ashtrays. I smoke like a chimney when I'm working."

Edging her way back to her desk, Molly recited three Hail Marys so quickly barely finished one before starting the next. "I think we need to have a little chat first." Stepping over an open carton, Molly lifted a chair and placed it in front of the desk. "Have a seat, Bitsy." Setting the picnic basket on the floor, she picked up a wad of wrapping paper, flung it to the floor, and nearly slammed the ashtray on the desk.

Very quietly, Bitsy sat, crossed her legs, adjusted the pearl-encrusted collar of her pale blue jumpsuit, and said, "A bit testy, are we? Been up all night with this stuff I guess."

Molly fell into the chair, raised her hands to stop Bitsy, and said calmly, "Yes, I am testy. I'm also not in the mood for—"

"I'm overwhelming you, is that it? It's my way, darling. I can't help it. I can't change at this age."

Molly didn't like the amused glint in her eyes. She recognized the time-honored challenge right away. Bitsy was as much as telling her she'd been around more blocks than Molly would see in a lifetime, and she'd led the way at every turn. "I'm sure there are those who find you charming. Max included. However, I don't need a mother, Ms. Morgan. I don't need you to take me in hand."

"Your mother was a lovely woman. It's heartbreaking to think you barely knew her before she died."

Molly felt as if she'd been punched in the chest. Her mouth fell open, and she had to grip the edge of the desk for support. "My mother?" Blinking quickly, she could feel hot tears forming at the corner of her eyes. "What do you know about my mother?" she demanded.

"May I smoke?" Bitsy asked softly.

Molly could only nod. Her throat was too dry to speak. Shock waves pounded her head.

Taking her time, Bitsy reached into her bag. Setting the silver cigarette case on the desk between them, she slowly inserted a cigarette into an ivory holder. The only sound in the room was the expensive snap of her gold Dunhill lighter. "Your mother and I grew up together, Molly, my dear."

Speaking without her usual snap and rasp, Bitsy continued, "Your mother and I, poor and skinny, were true Wild Irish Roses. Maeve Connovan and Fiona Fitzpatrick. That was us. I married late in life. Almost a spinster by those days' standards. Today, thirty is common. He was a Merchant Marine, but he had a way about him that . . . well, I moved to San Pedro to stay with his family while he was out to sea. I miscarried twice. After I lost the second baby, Teddy died of malaria in Singapore. Your mother, bless her soul, packed a tuna fish sandwich, hopped aboard a Southern Pacific, and slept sitting up all the way from The City to San Pedro to keep me from slashing my wrists. She stayed with me for two months. Your father was a prince then. He wired enough money for the both of us to come home. My folks wouldn't have me back, you see."

Pausing to remove the cigarette from the holder, Bitsy stabbed it to death. Ashes flew all over the mess on the desk. Her voice rose slightly. "I was already pregnant when we got married. I had a brother in the seminary, and I'd brought shame to the family. Teddy's folks were nice enough, but I couldn't stand the constant reminder. I moved in with your parents. When your dad got hurt on his beat and opened the store, I helped out for room and board. That injury was such a blow to him." Shaking her head, she said, "He could have gone a long way on the force. Bastards wouldn't even give him a desk job. In those days, cripples were sent packing with hardly enough disability to buy beer. Anyway, when you were born . . . you were a latecomer too, it perked him up."

Molly's eyes were brimming with tears. Bitsy made a play at wiping her own. "We may have come a long way, baby, but we can still cry at the drop of a hat." Reaching for another cigarette, Bitsy laughed. "Hell, I promised I'd tell you this over a steak dinner."

Molly's throat was so tight, she could barely speak. "Chicken and avocado is fine." Reaching across the desk, she took a cigarette, lit it, and smiled uneasily. "Please, don't stop."

"Well, I stayed with you and your folks for another year. When your mother got on her feet, I found a little apartment nearby and went to work for Max. When your sister was born, I slept on a cot in your room until your mother could manage."

Seeing the surprise on Molly's face, she laughed. "Yes, Max and I go back that far, honey. Anyway, I married again a few years later, and moved to Reno. My husband was a rancher. Hell, he owned half of Nevada. He's the one who started calling me 'Bitsy.' We traveled all over the world. I kept in touch with your folks, sent your mother perfume from London, a gold-tooled Bible from Rome, a coconut from Honolulu . . . she got a kick out of that!" Pausing to blot her mascara, Bitsy looked away, almost unable to continue. She cleared her throat. "Rollo and I were in Paris when your mother died. You must have been about—"

"Ten." Molly said quickly. "I was ten. Carrie was eight."

"Yes . . . yes, that seems right." Rising, Bitsy glanced at the glasses Molly had been unpacking. "What say we open some wine. I'm a little parched."

"Good idea." Going for the glasses, Molly said, "I'll wash these and be right back." It was a perfect excuse to get hold of her emotions. She needed to get away for a moment to catch her breath. Halfway to the storage room, she stopped. "I don't have an opener."

Bitsy's raspy laugh was back. "Hell, honey, do you think I'd come unprepared? Got one in the picnic basket."

Within moments, they were on their second glass. "I heard about your father's . . . troubles." Avoiding Molly's eyes, she searched for a napkin to set under her glass. "We were in The City just before it happened. I didn't stop in to say hello." Clearing her throat, she quickly went on. "Your father and I had some issues by then. I'm afraid he didn't like my sending your mother gifts from all over the world. A reminder, I guess, about the life she didn't have. Anyway, I'm not surprised you didn't recognize my name." Looking away for a moment, she finally said, "At any rate, we were headed for the Islands again. Always loved those cruises."

Stealing a quick glance at Molly, she then said, "Rollo died of a heart attack a few years later in Athens. I sold some property and opened a shop in Beverly Hills." Swirling her glass, she laughed. "I made a killing, let me tell you. Those movie people were so hungry for class, they kept me scouring Europe for years. After a time, I got tired of the gig. I came up here, bought a spread in Pebble Beach, and opened this little place. I did okay, but it was boring, you know? I sold out to Sid. I had plenty of dough, and my feet were itching, so I did the world tour again."

"I'm speechless," Molly finally said.

"I told you I'm overwhelming." Bitsy laughed.

Taking a deep sigh, Molly felt a need to apologize. "I'm so sorry for earlier. These past weeks have been—"

"Not another word. You've had a lapful, honey. Look, I know about New York." Pouring another glass of wine, she hovered over Molly's glass. "Come on, let's kill this."

When Molly nodded, Bitsy filled her glass. "I've sort of kept an eye on you. Max told me about your marriage years ago. You never saw me, but I'd pop into Porter's every now and then. I just wanted to get a look." Her smile was almost shy. "I used to change your diaper. I had to see how you turned out." Giving her a wink, she laughed. "Not bad I'd say. Your mother would have been very proud of you. Anyway, when the shit hit the fan, Max did call me. I lied that first day, by the way. Max was literally in tears. He told me he was going to have you come out, so I suggested—"

Molly almost spilled her wine. "I have *you* to thank for this?"

Bitsy shrank back. "Well, honey, it seemed a good idea at the time. Staying with Max much longer would have done you in. I knew Pablo would drive you nuts. Between Max and me, you had a chance in Carmel to start over. Of course, I didn't think you'd end up being the only witness to a murder, but . . ." Looking at Molly with an almost guileless gaze, she added, "It hasn't been all that bad, has it?"

Molly shook her head. "I don't believe this. How the hell did I end up with two fairy godmothers? No pun intended. And I don't want to talk about finding Lorna Jacobs. I still don't know how to deal with that."

"Hell of a shock, I'm sure. Lucky it was you."

Molly finally realized there was no getting around Bitsy. Giving her a look that left little room to plead her innocence, Molly said, "Okay, I'll bite. Why?"

"If it was someone who knew her, I doubt they'd have called 911."

"That's disgusting. I can't even imagine it."

"You didn't know her. I can't think of anyone who did who isn't relieved she's out of here. I almost feel sorry for our new police honcho. He's going to have a suspect list a mile long."

"Do you include yourself in that list?" Molly almost laughed.

"I'm sure he'll eventually get around to talking to me. I consigned a collection of Art Deco jewelry with Lorna. I bought it in London years ago when it was cheap and out of fashion. I ran into Lorna and Dick one night at the La Playa. I was having drinks with some of the dealers in town." Bitsy thought for a moment. "Did you meet him?"

Molly frowned, "No. Of course not. He wasn't there . . . I mean, when—"

"I meant at the memorial. I saw you up on the street."

"Oh, well, I was out . . . walking. I didn't think it appropriate for me to go."

"Well, he's a sweetheart, by the way." Bitsy went on. "Anyway, we got to talking, and she was telling us about a client that was looking for Art Deco baubles. If any of us ran across some, to let her know. I told her I had some, and I'd stop by." Digging out the sandwiches, Bitsy offered one to Molly. As she began to unwrap hers, she continued, "To make a long story short, I left her with around four or five grand worth . . . my cut, by the way, and wouldn't you know she had a robbery a few weeks later."

Having just taken a bite of her sandwich, Molly could only reply with a frown.

"A reply is not required. If you haven't guessed the next part, I'll tell you. Her insurance had somehow lapsed." Bitsy eyes opened wide for effect. "She said she couldn't remember getting a renewal notice. Ergo, we were all out of luck. Me, and a half dozen other consignors. Naturally, the jewelry was never recovered."

Carefully wiping her lips, Molly shook her head. "But—"

"No buts allowed." Bitsy shot back. "She as much as told us all to get lost. Them's the breaks, she said. She had her losses, too. And she wasn't responsible to make anything good. A few tried to sue her, but nothing ever came of it. The lawyer fees would have been more than their loss. I could take the loss, but the others, well, they were pretty hot."

"I think you should tell the police. It might help the investigation."

"Not me, honey. I don't want to get involved. I'm not going to blow the whistle on my friends. Let that cop do the dirty work."

While all this was fascinating, Molly was still trying to

digest this woman's connection with her family and Max. She was also annoyed with the way she'd been manipulated into coming to Carmel. Glancing at her watch, she realized the day was rapidly drifting away from her. She had planned to take a break, scoot over to that art gallery, and get to the library before it closed. "Well," Molly began, "now that it seems we're . . . old friends of sorts, I'd love to go on, but—"

Bitsy interrupted again. "I know. You're up to your ears, you have your own ideas how you want this place to look, and you don't need me, so get lost."

Molly laughed. "That wasn't the way I'd put it, but since you brought it up."

"Okay. I'm quick for an old bag." Giving her a wide smile, she added, "I know you've got a lot to mull over, so I'll leave you in peace."

Helping her with the picnic basket, Molly felt ashamed. She didn't want her to think she was being dismissed callously, and she had been, after all, close to her parents. "I can handle this unpacking, but, how about taking you up on that steak dinner? I'd love to hear more about—"

"Wonderful," Bitsy quickly answered. "Let's meet at the La Playa tomorrow around seven. That give you enough time around here?"

"Seven it is."

She had no recollection of ever hearing her father mention a woman named Bitsy. It wasn't a name easily forgotten. Mystified by her apparent connection with her family, she decided to table her confusion. She wasn't ready to go back in time again. The mere mention of her mother filled her with pain. The few memories she had were fading each year. Tucking away her thoughts, she put her brain on hold and forced herself to focus on unpacking the dozens of boxes.

Molly was so surprised by the beautiful pieces that the time passed quickly, and she was shocked to realize it was after six. Making a considerable dent in the stacks of boxes, she began to wonder how she was going to display it all without the shop looking like a zoo. An accomplished student of layering, Molly could mix, match, and create tableaux with the best of them. However, it was an art. Just one wrong move, and the effect was destroyed. She had so many wonderful pieces now; it was going to be difficult to choose. She decided to sleep on it. Give it a fresh look over tomorrow. Right now, the most pressing thing on her mind was Lawrence Toby and the watercolors she'd stashed upstairs behind three rolled Oriental carpets in the closet. Whether or not to put that exquisite cobalt-and-gold Derby potpourri bowl on the mid-nineteenth-century Louis XV style side cabinet or the Regency rosewood chiffonier, could wait. Until she got inside that art gallery, she couldn't care less whether the gold accents on the Derby clashed with the brass inlay on the chiffonier. In any event, the brass needed cleaning, and the marble top was splattered with wax drippings from candles.

Realizing it was too late to get to the gallery or the library, Molly sidestepped the littered staircase and gingerly made her way up to the apartment. All she needed was to break a leg. Nearly two hours with Randall and the police artist, Bitsy's admissions, and unpacking boxes had worn her out.

A sudden longing for a cup of cocoa filled her. Shadowy memories of her mother again flitted through her mind. They were so few now. The effort to catch them left an ache. Discovering she was out of milk, the cocoa lost its appeal. Settling instead for Café Français, she put the kettle on, then opened the window over the sink.

Resting against the chipped tile counter, she closed her eyes and listened to the pounding surf rolling in at Carmel Beach.

Sinking into the sofa, she warmed her aching hands on the hot mug and tried to absorb all that Bitsy had told her. Maybe it was the Irish in her, but she was surprised to realize she was angry. She didn't like the feeling of being emotionally captive. Whether she grew to like Bitsy or not, she was now obligated to endure her powerful personality. "Overwhelming" had been Betsy's own description. Molly could hardly argue the choice. Good intentions or not, she'd been deftly manipulated by two experts. No signs of senility with Bitsy or Max, she finally had to laugh. Given the years they'd had to perfect their skills, Molly pitied anyone who got in their way.

She had two more stacks of art books to scan before bed. Holding back a yawn, she wondered if she was wasting her time. How sinister could some watercolors be? More, who the hell cared who painted them? All this sleuthing was probably a classic case of Much Ado About Nothing.

In spite of her fatigue, Molly continued the search for Lawrence Toby. Down to three books, she had to quit. Her eyes were burning and rolling around in her head. Passing the spare bedroom on her way to bed, she paused briefly. She glanced in the corner where the watercolors were stacked behind the rolled Oriental rugs. Shaking her head, she wondered again why she was going to so much trouble. She'd be better off if she just trotted them over to Dick Jacobs and be done with them. Taking in the rest of the room, she wondered if she'd ever have time actually to get merch of her own. The space in the garage was the perfect place to clean and repair out of Pablo's prying eyes. She thought about calling Max and forcing Pablo to give it up. She could play hardball with the best of them. *Damn right*, she thought. *Molly Doyle's in town, and she means business.*

Randall moved out from under an awning across the street as Molly's apartment lights went out. After a leisurely dinner at Daria's, he was too full of *vitelo tonatto* to sleep. Walking around town, he found himself across the street from her shop. It was close to eleven, but when he saw her lights on, he'd thought about dropping by. By the time he'd made up his mind, it was too late. He was still bothered by the sketch the police artist had produced. Molly hadn't deviated one bit from her original description, but it still smelled. The final product was too ambiguous. He had no defining elements to rely on. Not even a hairstyle, a face shape, mole, pimple, or scar. Short woman, not fat, but not runway slim, she'd said. A denim jacket. Standard fare around here. Jeans, and a medium-sized straw hat with a normal brim, not even a colored band, beads, or feathers. Blue-tinted sunglasses. Must be millions of them out there. A thousand people could fit the description. He didn't like it.

He was finding a lot of things not to like besides a going-nowhere homicide. An understaffed force, a district attorney who thought he was the Second Coming, and now his daughter might be coming down from Stanford for a little bonding. The timing was bad for a visit. He hadn't the time to spend with her, but then, he reluctantly admitted, that very point had been the beginning of the enmity between them. He'd been a weekend father when he was with Homicide Robbery. It got worse when he moved to Internal Affairs, but it didn't change the hours that never seemed to end. The move, however, made little difference to his wife's social life. Though she was married to someone viewed as a piranha within the closed police community, his new job hadn't tarnished Claire's standing in her social circle. Coming from old Pasadena money, her charity pals in L.A. could have cared less. He'd been at least thankful for that. Being an absent husband bothered him less than being an absent father. Wives come and go, he'd once hear some dumped guy say, but kids are forever. He felt bad about Annie. Maybe they could make up for lost time now that he was only an hour or so away. He and Claire had parted ways years ago. Growth problems, the shrinks would say. He'd never been into her social whirl. Wintering in Palm Springs, lounging by the pool, and playing golf was not his idea of fun. Divorce was never a question of why, only when. The *when* turned out to be his ex-partner at Homicide. Claire had a penchant for guys who packed heat. Maybe it was an aura women fell for. He'd given up trying to figure it out. Randall hadn't carried a gun since he moved over to IA. As head of investigations, he sat at a desk.

Cupping his hand around the lighter, he inhaled deeply while he stared at Molly's darkened windows. He couldn't seem to get her out of his mind. She had been busy as bee sorting that place out. Going about her business as if life were normal. Acting as if she were innocent.

He covered the three blocks to home in a matter of minutes. His new condo, conveniently across from the low-key, plain-looking building that was in reality, the police station, was still filled with unpacked boxes, and, he had to grin, wall to wall Directoire and Louis Phillipe furniture he'd collected since his divorce. How the hell had she pegged him so well? Smart cookie. Maybe too smart.

He'd made some headway at least. Lucero finally sent

over two investigators. So far, they'd learned a lot about Lorna Jacobs. A shit stirrer par excellence. She'd threatened a city councilwoman over a zoning decision in front of a packed town meeting, threw dead fish at the mayor of Monterey during a town hall meeting over expansion on Cannery Row, was being investigated by the State Labor Commission for labor infractions, had two civil suits pending over repairs not made to rental houses after the last El Nino flooding, and six small claims suits for non-payment of jewelry consignments at her store. Her newest trick was the raccoon problem. The woman had suspects waiting in line.

His normally prime suspect, the hubby, had an airtight alibi. Left the rabble-rousing to his wife, kept his nose clean, and ran a profitable frame and art shop. Quiet, unassuming, polite and a busy community volunteer. Worked the Bach Festival for the past fifteen years. Solid. Salt of the earth. Pillar of the community. Sensitive. A nineties kind of guy. Yeah, sure.

$\mathcal{T}$he day promised to be nasty. Sultry and close, a lightning storm was parked over the bay. According to early-morning news flashes, the light show was so lengthy and rare, even old-time locals were astounded. The multiple strikes of lighting had already created power outages along the coast, and apparently had started several forest fires in Big Sur. Molly grabbed her raincoat and baseball cap from the storage room. A little thunder and lightning was not going to prevent her from her mission. Throwing her hair in a ponytail, she locked up and hurried to the gallery.

In fact, she decided, the storm couldn't have come at a better time. With power flicking on and off, and everyone talking about the nonstop clapping of thunder and the sky lighting up, her leaving the shop wouldn't seem strange. Even her disguise appeared normal.

Casually sauntering into the gallery, she paused to give the impression she might not stay. A young woman came out from behind a freestanding panel, and said, "Hello, can I help?"

Molly gave a start. "Oh, yes, thank you. I ran for your awning to get out of the rain, and I noticed the watercolor in the window." Turning to a large oil near her, she said, "Oh, and that's very nice, too."

"I'm glad you chose our awning." She laughed. "This storm is driving all our visitors back to their rooms. Let me give you a little tour." Standing near the oil Molly mentioned, she began her sales pitch. "This particular piece is one of my favorites. The artist is John Karman. This work represents Carmel as it looked during the first quarter of the century when we were a tiny village. Don't you think he's marvelous?"

Good, Molly thought. *She actually thinks I came in to get out of the rain.* Eyeing the oil, she pursed her lips. "Actually, I prefer landscapes. The one in the window caught my eye."

"Ah, the Toby. He *is* exceptional, isn't he?" Giving Molly an energetic smile, she added proudly, "He was the owner's father. Very sought after, you know. It's a shame Mrs. Martyn is out today. She's an amazing authority on Early California painters."

"Really?" Molly questioned. "I'm from Boston. I'm not familiar with West Coast artists. Shame I missed her."

"We have more. Let me show you. If any interest you, I can arrange for Mrs. Martyn to meet you tomorrow."

Following her, Molly's eyes scanned the gallery, taking in the white grass cloth walls, overhead lighting, and pale sisal carpet. Very simple and perfect backgrounds for the large inventory of art. Potted orchids in Chinese bronze cachepots were tastefully scattered about the showroom on excellent quality chests and tables. A few abstract sculptures in marble stood on bronze and marble plinths in strategic corners. Heavy gilt frames made much of the art, mostly frothy seascapes geared for the tourist trade, look spectacular. Astute dealer, she thought. Gold frames meant important works. It was an old trick to rid dealers of artists whose work didn't move. A Queen Anne oyster-veneered chest caught Molly's eye. It was all she could do to restrain herself. She quickly noticed it had had some restoration, but Molly figured it to be early eighteenth century. Running her hand over the top of the chest, Molly finally said, "This is lovely. Do you sell antiques, too?"

Stopping midstride, the young woman said, "Oh, that old thing? No, it's just to set off the art and to hold the orchids. Mrs. Martyn loves orchids. She has a florist change them every week."

Fighting the urge to correct her, Molly made a mental note to check back with the owner and offer to buy the chest.

"Here we are." She smiled over her shoulder at Molly. "Aren't these wonderful?"

Clenching her hands in her pockets, Molly held her temper and smiled. "Hmm, yes, very nice." There were three Tobys. Two on the wall, and one on an easel. It took only a few moments to recognize that the one on the easel was a reverse rendition of one in the desk. Colors, scale, and size were almost identical. *Now what,* she thought? *What the hell does this all mean?* The watercolors were too fresh to have been Tobys. They *were* practice pieces. Was Lorna using this artist as an example of the Early California style? Why Toby? Why not use a better known artist? Moving closer, Molly let out a sigh.

The young woman mistook it for awe. "Yes, he *was* wondrous. It's such a pleasure to sell his work."

Nodding politely, Molly said, "Very nice." A sudden thought struck her. "Umm, what price do you have on this?"

"Mrs. Martyn is asking fifteen thousand for this particular piece. It's titled *Laguna Night*. These four were acquired just last week from the estate of a private collector. Mrs. Martyn was thrilled when they were offered. She almost didn't put them in the shop. *Laguna Night* happens to be one of her favorites. The one in the window, *San Pedro Moon*, is twenty-two." Pointing to the wall, she said, "The one on the left, *Sheppard Grove* is eighteen, and the other, actually my very own favorite, *Long Beach Memory*, is twenty-three. What makes these in the shop particularly exceptional is that they are all *plein air*. You see, as a child, Ms. Martyn frequently accompanied her father when he painted." Standing back, she uttered almost reverently, "These were his last, so you can see . . ."

Saved by another series of thunder, Molly was glad the idiot didn't hear her snort. She had to get a grip. She was itching to tell her these works were lucky to get twenty-two hundred. "Yes, of course. It's the colors I'm not sure about. They might not fit in with the area I had in mind." Molly quickly interrupted before the bonehead started another breathless sales pitch. She had to say something, anything, before she lost it and told the woman she was an imbecile and totally off her ass. *Plein Air*? Who tells salespeople this crap? Excuse me, but that French term means, literally, *open air*; working directly in the ambiance of light and atmosphere, otherwise known as the great outdoors. Impressionist artists, whose theme was to offer a quick impression—images that were a moment's slice of life—used the method.

These pictures, she wanted to shout, were filled with minute detail in the style of English romantic landscapes à la John Constable and JMW Turner. While the Tobys were light-years away from the skill or execution of either of those brilliant artists, it was, nevertheless, a favorite and recognizable style. Detail, detail, detail! This Lawrence Toby shouldn't even be considered an Early California artist! Swallowing her indignation, she pretended to be interested. "Well, I'd like my husband to see them. We're looking for his study."

Her eyes lighting up with the prospect of a sale on her own, the young woman quickly handed Molly her card. "Why don't you let me know where you're staying? I'd be happy to arrange a private showing for your husband. I'm sure Mrs. Martyn would love to meet you both."

"No." Molly waved her hand. "I mean, we're with friends. I don't have their number with me. Maybe we can drop by tomorrow." A sudden inspiration struck her. Showing interest in only one artist might not be wise. She wasn't sure why, but the instinct was strong enough not to ignore. "I saw some other work when I came in." Sauntering to the opposite wall, she mused, "These are interesting." Pointing to an oil of a grove of eucalyptus trees, she asked, "What can you tell me about this artist?"

"Lovely choice. Ina Hubble is the artist. She was one of the original Early California artists. Claiming the light was extraordinary, she lured many of her contemporaries to Santa Barbara. Unfortunately, she was not very prolific, and has only recently come on the market. We have four of hers. Women artists of that period are very popular now. I think Mrs. Martyn's pricing is reasonable and very competitive. This one is eight thousand."

"Hmm. Yes, it's very . . . peaceful. Have you any other women artists?"

"You're in luck, or rather, we are." She giggled. "We just got two in by Rowena Webster." Tilting her head slightly, she lifted her chin and winked. "Ms. Webster was rumored to be an early paramour of Randolph Hearst. Of course, most of her work was done near San Luis Obispo." When she didn't get a reaction from Molly, she added, "You know . . . near San Simeon? Hearst Castle? *Citizen Kane*?"

"But I thought Mr. Hearst built that for—"

"Oh, Mrs. Martyn tells me she was before Marion Davies. Mrs. Martyn does her research, let me tell you."

Following her toward the back of the gallery, Molly checked her watch. She had to get moving. The power, already flicking on and off in the gallery, made her anxious to get to the library before the town went dark. Besides, she still had a few dozen boxes to unpack. "I really have to get going."

"Oh, I hate for you not to see them. We just got them back from the framers. The original frames were just too horrible."

Following her to the back of the gallery, Molly stood back and appraised the two paintings. They were quite unremarkable. "Hmm, I don't think this is what we're looking for."

"These," the salesgirl hurriedly said, "will be in the range of four to five thousand. However, I think they have a good chance of appreciating very fast. Women artists of that period are just coming into their own. Value could double in a year."

"Really? How wonderful. Actually, I know next to zilch about art. I just buy what I like." She moved to the door. "I really have to go. I'll tell my husband. Maybe we can stop in tomorrow. Thank you so much for your help."

Just before she reached the door, the power went off. She didn't see the woman outside reaching for the door, and almost knocked her over. "Oh, I'm so sorry," Molly said. "That was close."

Soaking wet, her hair flattened to her head, the woman ignored Molly's apology, and hurried past her.

Stepping outside, Molly returned to the window display to get another quick look at the Toby. She was startled to see the drenched woman staring at her. Pretending not to notice, Molly turned away, and muttered, "What the hell is her problem? A little rain never hurt anyone. Probably jealous of my baseball cap." It *was* rather fetching, with its three gold stars on the black brim.

Running to every awning she could find on her way to the library, Molly zigzagged her way to Ocean Avenue, then took her chances in the downpour and crossed to the landscaped meridian dividing the street. The dozens of towering pines and redwoods that shaded seasonal annuals were swaying like hula dancers and throwing off rainwater like open spigots. Carefully scooting between the slow-moving cars, Molly made it to the library. She was in luck. The power was back.

The scholar in her was bursting with questions. She hardly noticed the blazing fire in the massive fireplace, the floor-to-ceiling multipaned windows, or the comfortable lounge chairs filled with retired gentlemen in sport coats and ascots no doubt lost in sagas of ancient sea battles. The reference section was larger than she'd expected, and she was delighted to discover that the art section was extensive.

A fine arts degree did not make one an expert. It was virtually impossible to be proficient in every art or antique style or period. However, besides a general overview and the fundamentals to find a job, it had taught her how and where to look for the accepted expertise of each of the hundreds of categories and subcategories. The fields were enormous, not to mention the vagaries of each classification.

The first book she cracked was Mantle Fielding's *Dictionary of American Painters, Sculptors and Engravers*.

Considering Carmel was an acclaimed artists' colony,

she was right in assuming the library would be a gold mine of information. With the many volumes at her disposal, an hour passed before she realized the time. Between the sharp cracks of thunder, and a few flickering lights, she managed to find more than she'd expected. Unprepared for such a volume of information, she'd neglected to grab a notebook and had to make cramped notes on the back of old shopping lists and a wrinkled envelope she'd found at the bottom of her bag.

It didn't take long to realize Lawrence Toby was a middleweight amongst the long list of his contemporaries. Surprisingly, Rowena Webster and Ina Hubble were not mentioned. A little strange if they were so involved with the early movement. As for Toby, she'd found only two listings of sales in *Leonard's Index*, the bible for art sold at auction. Webster and Hubble were not listed at all. But if they'd been in private collections, that would make sense. Without the many price indexes published annually, collectors had no way of staying on top of the going rates for the thousands of artists sold on the auction block all over the world. Gallery sales and private purchases are just that, private.

While Toby was listed in Eden Hughes's *Artists of California, 1786–1940,* he rated only two small paragraphs. His output seemed to be meager; maybe twenty or thirty works, at most. Again, Webster and Hubble were not listed. Noting the time, she quickly returned the reference materials and thanked the librarian for her help. She had to get cracking. Besides the waiting boxes, she still had to see if Bea wanted help with the computer and then she had to meet Bitsy at seven.

On her way back to the shop, she decided to call the Archives of American Art at the Smithsonian first thing in the morning. Maybe they had something on Toby. The nitty-gritty would come from the old-timers who knew the art world inside out from day one. They could scrape away the varnish and get to the heart of any artist. They could tell her habits, vices, routines, work schedules, friends, family, pets—every nuance of an artist's life from cradle to coffin. One call could provide reams of statistics and insights on any artist worth a damn from da Vinci to Calder. Once upon a time, and not so long ago, she had access to these people.

Returning to the shop, she took off the damp raincoat and cap, took down her hair, and stared at the mess before her. She could call Cleo. Heading for the stack of boxes, she angrily opened the first one handy. No, she couldn't call Cleo. She hadn't the nerve to ask for her help. Not after the way she'd been shunted off to London because of Porter's fiasco. Not that London was a bad transfer. In fact, Sotheby's promoted her. They knew Cleo had been duped, along with everyone else. Derek and Greta had pulled the same con with art as they had with furniture. Offer the real thing, then substitute the phony later. With Porter's sterling reputation for integrity, they had never been questioned. They'd parted as friends, but Molly's shame was still too deep to ask for her help. Max, unfortunately, didn't have access to the people she needed.

She was beginning to wonder if all this detective work was really necessary. Her first impression was probably right. The watercolors were studies by an amateur. So what if Lorna Jacobs was a closet painter. What did it matter now? The woman was dead. If only she would stay out of Molly's dreams.

⚊⚊ 14 ⚊⚊

*B*y late afternoon, Molly had the boxes of smalls finally unpacked. It was a good thing she was closed. With power on and off all day, it would have been a zero sales day. Turning on the portable radio in the storage room, the hot topic was the freak storm. Several trees were down in Pebble Beach and Carmel Valley, the surf was incredibly high, and winds were playing havoc all over the peninsula. The fires in Big Sur were out of control, and firefighters were rushing in from all over the state.

China dinner sets, porcelain figures, crystal glasses and compotes, and silver hollowware littered the floor and every available surface. Molly's eyes were glazed, and she was close to being giddy. Sets of leather books stacked on the floor were ready to totter at any moment. The staircase, still loaded with the old smalls, added to the look of a pirate's cavern of hidden spoils.

Molly had to laugh. It was a typical antique dealer dilemma—feast or famine. You bitched if you didn't have merch, and then you bitched when you had too much. And it didn't end there. When you began to sell off, you bitched about not being able to find comparable quality goods to replace what you'd just sold. At least her sense of humor was returning, and for that, she was grateful.

Carrying a tray of cloudy crystal decanters, she made a

mental note to buy a box of Efferdent. The denture cleaner was a trade magic potion used to remove mineral stains. Maneuvering the stairs like a tightrope artist, she managed to get the door to the apartment open without dropping the tray. Entering the spare bedroom, she set it on an old table she'd found in the garage. If Max's stuff looked this dingy, it was a wonder he sold anything. Maybe he ought to spend less time power lunching and more time keeping tabs on the way Pablo was running things. There were at least six pair of lamps with dusty silk shades, several Oriental vases and large bowls that were dusty and dull, and umpteen pieces of silver badly needing polishing. The few small Oriental runners he'd sent down needed spotting. Molly rolled them loosely, leaned them in the corner along with the others, and nearly squashed the box of watercolors. She was about to pull the box out when she realized it was almost five. The rugs would do little damage between now and when she returned.

Running in to freshen up, she was out of the apartment and at Bea's shop in less than ten minutes. If the power held, she'd have Bea up and running by six-thirty. She found Bea ready to close. "Still want to get that computer set up?"

"Absolutely! I can't wait to get started. I've already unpacked everything and set the equipment where I'll use it. I thought that might make it easier for you." Bea smiled. "I was going to call you today, but I got so busy, the time just flew. This storm is driving me nuts. I'm ready to plug my ears with cotton. I can't remember thunder cracking like this hour after hour. One of my customers, Jim Vanderzwaan, is a weather guy on TV, and he said this system is really rare. It might keep up all night." Giving her a mock shudder, Bea said, "Reminds me of one of those dark and stormy night things on TV. I'll call in our pizza order and we can get started."

"Oh, listen, I'll have to pass. I promised a . . . a friend I'd have dinner with her. I should have called you."

"That's okay, I'll get a small one then. I'm going to stay late. I've got a dozen cachepots of orchids to set up for an opening, and three anniversaries."

Molly walked behind the counter and took a moment to look over the equipment. "I'll get it hooked up, set up the printer, then I'll load that custom software. Do you have an extra phone for your modem?"

"Hey, a complete fool, I'm not. Even I knew I had to call Pac Bell!" At her side, Bea pointed to the outlet. "Got it in a week ago."

Molly laughed, "You'll be surfing the net before you know it! Weather like this isn't ideal for set-up, but I think we'll be okay. I'm going to have to move the printer closer. Do you mind if I take some of your stuff off the lower counter?"

"Decorate to your heart's content. Give me whatever is in the way, and I'll stash it somewhere."

Moving aside boxes of ribbons and gift wrap, Molly picked up some loose papers and nearly shrieked. "For God's sakes, Bea!" Picking up a handgun by the barrel, her face was ashen. "What on earth are you doing with this . . . this thing?"

Rushing to her side, Bea took the gun from her. "Shit! I forgot to put it back in the drawer. I'm sorry. I didn't mean to scare you. I've had some crank calls lately. Loud breathing, then a lot of just plain hang-ups. I don't have that caller ID thing. I hate all this techno crap. Getting this computer is a major concession for me." Biting her lips, she let out a sigh. "I should really bring Buddy with me. He's gentle as a mouse, but looks ferocious."

Perching on a tall counter stool, Molly shook her head. "You should call the police. Seriously, let them handle it. At least ask Bennie to walk you to your car at night."

Placing the gun in her cash drawer, Bea shrugged. "If I get another call, I will. I didn't think of asking Bennie. I hate to bother him. He's so busy. Besides running Tosca's, he's like a godfather around here. Got a problem? Ask Bennie. Maybe I'll run over later and ask him. Anyway, let's get on with this darn monster." Pretending to shiver, she laughed. "I'm scared to death of computers. I just know I'll botch something up and lose all my records."

"Everyone feels that way at first."

It didn't take long to get up and running. While Molly loaded Bea's custom software and ran through the system, Bea continued work on a massive display of lavender roses. Pausing for a moment, Molly complimented her. "Gorgeous! Absolutely to die for. Who's the lucky customer?"

"An anniversary at Spanish Bay. Some hotshot mogul from San Francisco wants to surprise his wife. I just love guys like him!"

Finally ready for Bea, Molly called her over and ran her through the basics. Waiting at each step as Bea took notes, she kept an eye on the time as she explained each procedure. Finally, she said, "I've got to run. I'm supposed to meet my friend in fifteen minutes. I'll stop by tomorrow night and we can run through it again."

The relief on Bea's face was almost comical. "Oh, could we? I'm really lost. I hate to admit it, but I can't even type."

Molly couldn't help but laugh. Bea was the least affected person she'd met in a long time. "Stop worrying, it's a breeze. You'll be asking me to install games before you know it."

Giving Molly a quick hug, Bea said, "You're a gem. I'm so glad you took over the shop. It's fun having you here."

Touched, Molly could only smile. "Well, I haven't really been much fun lately, but I promise to make up for it. By the way, can you tell me how to get to the La Playa Hotel?"

It had, at least, stopped raining. Willing to take a chance it would stay dry, Molly decided not to take the pickup. She hated to be seen in it. Besides, the six-block trek would make up for the beach walks she'd abandoned. Heading down Ocean Avenue, she made it to Camino Real, where she was to turn left. Still having trouble getting used to the smoking ban in bars and restaurants, Molly decided to take advantage of the next two blocks and get her nicotine craving under control.

Taking a deep drag, she paused at the corner and let her eyes roam over the manicured garden of a lovely home across the street. The simple tranquillity of tree ferns, azaleas, and hydrangeas was like soothing eye candy after the past few days. She was about to cross the street when out of the corner of her eye she saw a car stop suddenly at the corner just to her right. Pausing in case the driver was going to turn her way, she stepped back and saw it was Randall. He didn't look her way, but continued across the street heading south toward the beach. She couldn't believe it. He was actually following her! She knew she hadn't been imagining it the night of the memorial.

Taking an angry drag on the cigarette, she fought the sudden urge to turn around and go home. If not for Bitsy, she would have. Easily finding the hotel, she admired its lovely Spanish-Moorish design, quietly elegant, yet wonderfully inviting. It was too bad she wasn't in a better mood to appreciate it. Bea said the gardens were to die for.

Adjusting her eyes to the darkened lounge, she found Bitsy comfortably ensconced at the bar, chatting with the bartender. Rushing to greet her, Bitsy nodded to the waiter, who led them to their table. "The gang is kind of quiet tonight. Dick Jacobs is here. The man with him is his lawyer." Bitsy pointed them out as they were seated. "The usual bantering and witticisms are being replaced with medleys of sympathy and mild pats on the shoulder. I'd like you to meet the regulars. After we order, we can scoot over and say hello."

"Another time, if you don't mind. I'm bushed, and I'd really like a quiet night." She wasn't in the right mood to socialize. Bitsy was a handful as it was. She knew it was prudent to meet the other dealers, but she wanted to be ready for the dozens of questions they'd throw at her. Where was she from? How long had she been a dealer? What was her specialty? When she saw the disappointment on Bitsy's face, she amended, "Maybe after dinner? I haven't eaten all day, and I'm starving." Visions of a fat filet and baked potato swimming in butter replaced the urge to throttle Randall. A few shots of Jack Daniel's would help purge his face from her thoughts.

"Sure, we'll do that. You'll get a kick out of them. Besides, it's good business to know your competitors. Not that we're adversaries. An armed truce, you might say. Ah, hell, you know the drill. No different than that bunch you ran with in New York. Huggy, huggy, kissy, kissy, stab in the back for Missy." Laughing at her joke, Bitsy didn't see Molly's eyes shoot up. The woman joining Dick Jacobs was the same one Molly had nearly collided with at the gallery earlier in the day. Wet hair or not, the woman was stunning, and hard to miss.

"Who's the woman with Dick Jacobs?" It was out of her mouth before she could stop herself.

Lowering her menu, Bitsy half growled, "Rhonda Martyn."

Surprised that she was the owner of the gallery, Molly tried to sound nonchalant. "Oh, really? Are they old friends?"

Bitsy waved her off. "They've been having an affair for years. It's common knowledge."

Molly mulled that over as they gave the waiter their orders. Questions were running over themselves in her mind. Tiny shivers bedeviled her spine. It was all she could do to keep her toes from wiggling. She needed a cigarette. She had to think. Taking a large sip of her drink, she tried to sort out the alarms going off in her brain. Renderings of Rhonda Martyn's father's work were in Lorna Jacobs's desk. Dick Jacobs had a gallery and frame shop. Rhonda Martyn had a gallery. Connections that could be coincidence. But were they? What did it mean? Did it mean anything at all?

Molly nearly drained her glass. When their second drink arrived, Bitsy excused herself. "I'm just going to run over and tell the gang we'll join them for dessert."

Gone before Molly could stop her, she watched her head for a large booth two tables away. She quickly counted eight people. A woman with a henna rinse leaned into the table and whispered something to two pudgy bleached blondes, making them laugh. Two other women were captivated by a story told by an extremely well dressed older man, a startling contrast to the loud patterns and colors on the women. Dealers, particularly women, had a penchant for costuming. Either stark blah, or over the top. For some reason, many seemed to think selling antiques or art required an exotic appearance. Molly quickly amended that. Rhonda Martyn was an exception.

Rising to greet Bitsy, one of the women was wearing a flowing Queen of Sheba shawl over her ample shoulders, and one of the blondes who joined her had a French beret pinned to the side of her upswept hair. When another got up, Molly almost spilled her drink. The woman was actually wearing a cape made from a paisley shawl over a skintight black jumpsuit and black stiletto-heeled boots.

What the hell happened to the urbane Carmel she remembered? Unique among artist colonies, and still bohemian to the core, it somehow managed an enviable reputation for style and conservative elegance. With the thousands of tourists coming in every week, the shopkeepers now must think they needed to costume themselves in order to be remembered.

Molly was halfway through her steak by the time Bitsy returned. "Oh, honey, I'm sorry to leave you like that. When the girls get to talking, nothing can stop them." Eyeing her cold dinner, Bitsy pushed it away and waved for the waiter. She ordered another drink, then laughed. "I had a late lunch. I'm not all that hungry."

Molly couldn't get the Dick and Rhonda connection out of her mind. She had to know more about the woman. "Tell me about Rhonda Martyn. I get the feeling you don't like her."

"Got the smell of a hoity-toity wanna-be. She moved here a few years ago and opened up her gallery." Giving Molly a smirk, she laughed. "Like we need another? Nearing a hundred in a town two miles square is, to my way of thinking, overkill. Anyway, she's done well, especially with her late father's work. He apparently was one of the finer Early California artists. Art's not my thing, but I'm sure you know they're all hot now. Dick does a lot of her framing. Guess that's how it all started. Anyway, Dick and Lorna were kind of the odd couple. Different backgrounds mostly. Her family had money, his did not. She was better educated, Vassar, the grand tour, different set of friends. He came off a ranch in Utah and got as far as art school. Artsy friends of hers in Boston introduced them. Lust at first sight, probably. Well, hell, it was still the free love time. Anyway, they ended up going in different directions after they moved here. She got all caught up in causes; he just wanted to paint and sell art. His work didn't do much. Had too many styles, clients got confused."

"Is he talented?" Molly asked casually. "I mean, could he have made it if he'd stuck it out?"

"Who knows? Most don't. I doubt it, though. He's too passive. You know you have to promote yourself these days. Look at Neiman and this Kincade guy. You have to push your work, get out and be somebody . . . convince people you're the hottest ticket in town. No different from selling antiques. Get word of mouth going that a particular style is hot . . ." Bitsy threw her arms in the air and laughed. "*Voilà!* It is!"

They were on their coffee when Dick Jacobs and Rhonda Martyn stopped at their table. Looking haggard, Jacobs reached for Bitsy's hand and squeezed it. "Thank you so much for the beautiful flowers at the memorial service. I've been meaning to call."

"I'm so glad you liked them." Bitsy said. "Rhonda, dear, you look ravishing as always. Darlings, I'd like you to meet an old friend." Turning to Molly, she introduced her. Dick smiled hello, and Rhonda nodded, and then looked away, making it obvious that she was not interested in conversation. As Bitsy and Dick chatted, Molly stole a quick glance at Rhonda.

She hadn't had a chance to get a good look at her when she nearly knocked her over at the gallery, nor did she make eye contact when she'd seen her staring at her through the windows. Rhonda Martyn's age was hard to determine. Her skin was nearly flawless, or skillfully made up. She could be anywhere between forty and fifty. Medium height, and very slim, she carried herself with nonchalant grace. Her short, soft blond hair was expertly cut, and she wore a tasteful charcoal suit dress with élan.

Focusing on Molly, Dick said, "I was planning on dropping by your shop. I just learned today you're the person who bought my desk. I'd like to buy it back. I've had it for years. Lorna thought I didn't want it, but it was a mistake."

Molly was dumfounded. She hardly knew what to say. How on earth did he know about her? "Oh? Well, I . . . I sold it. I'm so sorry."

"What?" he blurted. "You couldn't have. It was locked. What I mean is, I have the keys. You couldn't have possibly—"

"Oh, that! Well, I managed to get it open. It wasn't that difficult." Reaching for her coffee, Molly said, "I hardly had it in the shop an hour, and it was sold."

"I . . . had some personal items in the drawers."

"Oh? I didn't find a thing. Well, I mean there were some paper clips, a few pens . . . a few brushes." Pretending to think, she finally added, "Some watercolor powders . . ." Before she could finish, he abruptly turned to Rhonda. "It's been a long day. Do you need a lift?"

Reaching for his arm, she patted it gently. "No, thanks, Dick. I've got my car." Nodding to Bitsy, she said, "Stop in sometime. I've got a new artist you'd love." Turning to Molly, she hesitated briefly. "Nice meeting you."

Molly nodded, then turned to Dick Jacobs, but he was already on his way out.

Bitsy was silent for a long moment. Pretending to read the dessert menu, she finally said, "So, you bought Dick's desk."

Molly fiddled with her napkin, then pushed her coffee away. "I bought a desk at her sale. I didn't know it was his."

"How'd you end up going back on Sunday?"

Beginning to feel uncomfortable with all this questioning, Molly said, "To see if she had the keys." Checking her watch, she saw it was already after nine. Covering a yawn, Molly smiled. "Can I take a rain check on meeting your friends? I'm bushed." She wasn't tired at all, but it seemed an easy way out.

"Of course, darling. You run on, I'll see you tomorrow."

When she reached for her wallet, Bitsy stopped her. "Put that away. I told you it was my treat."

"Thank you. We didn't get a chance to do much reminiscing, did we?"

Bitsy squeezed her hand. "Oh, we have plenty of time for that." Hesitating for a moment, she said, "If you're walking home, be careful. Carmel isn't a sleepy little village anymore, but I guess you found that out already."

Pulling on her coat, Molly said, "Yes, and I won't forget it . . . ever."

↞ *15* ↠

Outside the hotel, Molly was relived the rain hadn't started again. Still under the canopy, she frantically fished a cigarette out of her bag and quickly lit it. Heavy clouds had cast an inky cloak over the village. Without moonlight, or streetlights, it was pitch-black.

Remembering Bitsy's warning, the prospect of walking eight blocks in the dark was not thrilling. She was almost thankful she'd have to walk in the street. Maybe Randall might swing by and give her a lift.

Once she got to Ocean Avenue, she'd feel better. The shop lights and busy restaurants were less spooky. The Dick and Rhonda show continued to baffle her. Small town or not, the art connection between them made her feel uneasy. Wanting his desk back didn't make her feel too comfy either. And that intense stare Rhonda had given her at her gallery made her even more determined to find out what was going on.

In the middle of the street, Molly carefully avoided the parked cars and the trees soaked by rain. Lighting one cigarette after another, she rationalized it would make a good weapon if someone jumped out behind a car.

Something was not right in the heavens. She knew it. She could feel it. In spite of her anger with Randall, she was almost ready to call him and hand over those cursed watercolors. He'd probably think she was crazy. Maybe she was. But if she itemized the points, she might not be. Lorna Jacobs is murdered. The desk is loaded with watercolors in a style similar to those in Rhonda Martyn's shop. The artist is Lawrence Toby. The owner of the shop is his daughter. His work does not warrant her prices. He was, at best, a fair Sunday painter. She has one watercolor in particular that is nearly the mirror image of one in Rhonda's shop. There is another, from the desk, she knows she's seen before. Okay so far.

Rhonda Martin gives her a hard look at the shop. That's reaching, she thought, but leave it in. Then, Dick wants the desk back. When she lied about selling it, his charm quickly disappeared. Reaching the first sidewalk and shop lights, she slowed her pace and stopped before a jewelry boutique. Partial to gold, she stared at a display of exquisite abstract designs, and absently fingered her midsize wide gold-hoop earrings. She'd seen one of the Rothschild women in Paris wearing an almost identical pair. If they were good enough for a Rothschild, she'd reasoned, they were good enough for her. Derek hated them, but she didn't care. Focusing on a gold necklace of overlapping triangles, her brain snapped into replay, and she caught her breath. The trash cans! Bennie said her cans had been popular. The bag of paints and powders had been smashed all over the alley. Smashed in anger? Rage? What?

Whirling away from the window, she flattened her back against the cold glass. The tip of her cigarette was waving around like a beacon. *What the hell have I stepped into?* She was on the verge of being terrified, and her eyes darted wildly up and down the deserted street. Noting a familiar shop across the street, she realized she was only steps away from Rhonda's gallery. The last place she wanted to be. She'd have to walk a block out of her way, but it was worth it. The mere thought of that woman started her eye twitching.

By the time she made it to the shop, she nearly skidded to a stop. The front windows were dark. She could have sworn she left the night-lights on, then remembered she hadn't. She didn't want the disorder visible. She eyed the dark outside stairway to the apartment as she groped in her tote for her keys. She'd forgotten to replace the burned-out light over the door and wasn't in the mood to climb the steep stairway in total darkness.

The moment she entered, a series of lightning flashes lit up the street. The violent cracking booms that followed nearly stopped her heart. The sudden longing for her Day-Glo rooms brought a brief smile to her tight lips. Making her way to her desk, she snapped on the small lamp and headed for the littered stairs.

Unlocking the door to the apartment, she switched on a lamp in the living room. Turning to go back down and douse the desk lamp, she changed her mind. Sidestepping the mess on the stairs wasn't worth the effort. The chance of someone out in this weather poking their head in her window was too remote to consider. Dropping her tote on a chair by the sofa, she shrugged off her raincoat and was headed for the kitchen when she saw the draperies on the French doors fluttering. "Shit!" she swore. Running to the doors, she nearly slipped on the puddle of water spreading across the hardwood floors she spent hours hand waxing. Fighting the downpour that erupted, she pulled the door tight and locked it.

Sidestepping the puddle, she headed to the kitchen for paper towels. Turning the kettle on, she grabbed a wad of towels and returned to the living room. On her knees, sopping up the mess, she found a trail of smaller puddles leading to the worn Oriental carpet almost a foot away. "How the hell did it blow in this far?" she mumbled. Shaking her head, she returned to the kitchen with the sopping towels and fixed tea. Back in the living room, she turned on the rest of the lamps, picked up a dirty ashtray, then froze. A series of wet spots ran across the carpet toward her bedroom. Panic slowly started in her stomach and quickly rose to her throat. Very carefully setting down the cup and ashtray, she snatched up the portable phone on the coffee table and ran to the door leading down to the shop. Thank God she'd shoved her keys into her pocket. Easing the door open, she squeezed through to the steps, locked it quickly, ran down, and turned on more lights. Wasting little time, she punched in 911.

Forgetting the police department was only blocks away, she was amazed at how fast Randall showed up. The two officers with him were quickly dispatched to cover the courtyard staircase from her balcony and the street entrance to the apartment. Taking her keys, Randall gruffly ordered, "Stay the hell down here and do not come up unless I call you. Got that?"

Molly could only nod.

When she saw him pull a gun from inside his sport coat, she quickly made the sign of the cross.

"For crissake! Knock that off." He saw the shock on her face and grinned. "Cop humor. You should know that."

The comment didn't register as she watched him stealthy climb the stairs. All she could think of was someone was in her apartment.

What seemed an eternity was only ten minutes. When Randall stood at the top of the stairs and called her, she nearly fainted with relief. "Okay, come on up."

Following him into the living room, she stood hesitantly near the door while he slipped on a pair of thin latex gloves and carefully unlocked the French door. "All clear, Parker. Go around the front and get Wilkins. Head back to the station and get the kit print."

Turning back to Molly, he holstered his gun, checked his watch, then said, "Got any coffee?"

When she didn't answer, he waved his hands in front of her face. "Hello?"

"Oh, sorry. I, ah . . ."

Waving her off, he laughed. "Sure, sure . . . I know. Scared the hell out of you. That's normal. Best thing now is to do something with your hands. Make a pot of coffee. We'll be here for a while." Following her into the tiny kitchen, he eyed the bright colors, and said, "Hope to hell you didn't do the decorating around here. This looks like shit."

Thankful for his presence, but still angry with him for following her, she said, "While I'm grateful for your help, I have to say your bedside manner has a lot to be desired."

"Only kidding. Classy broad like you wouldn't do this. Guess ole Sid was color blind."

Setting out cups on a tray, Molly snapped, "I didn't know Sid, and don't refer to me as a broad."

"Hey! I meant it as a compliment, okay?"

"Find another," she shot back.

Easing out of her way, Randall shook his head, then followed her to the living room. "I'll do that. Now, can we get some details down for the record? Start at the beginning . . . when you first realized someone had broken in."

Settling on the lumpy sofa, Randall looked around. Taking in the gouged coffee table, the worn rug, the faded flowered draperies, and the two tattered side chairs, he shook his head. "How the hell can you stand this? I'd be out all night if I had to come home to this."

Surprised by his continued lack of tact, she said, "I'm not in a position to complain. The rent is free. I'll do some painting when I have time. Right now I've got a load of new stuff to set up."

Ignoring the sharpness in her voice, he glanced at the fireplace. "Does it work?"

"I was told it did. I haven't used it yet."

"Those books yours?"

Molly's eye started again. He had some nerve playing nicey-nicey when he had been following her all over town. Gently tapping the twitch over her eyes, she said, "No, they belonged to Sid. Max didn't want them, so I'm the lucky winner."

"Read a lot?"

Grabbing the cigarettes from the table, she stuck one in her mouth and let it dangle as she reached for a book of matches. "Can we get on with this? I'm dead tired." She struck the match so hard, it fizzled and died. Taking in a deep breath, Molly tried again. She knew he was watching her, and that made her angrier. Exhaling slowly, she stared at him.

Randall pulled a small notebook from his inside pocket, and fumbled around for a pen. "After you."

Molly began with locking up at six and going over to Bea's, then to dinner with Bitsy. It wasn't until she noticed the French doors open and was cleaning up the rainwater that she realized someone had broken in. She gave him the time she left the La Playa, and told him she'd walked around town a bit. "I don't get much opportunity to see what all the shops are offering."

"Not a great night to stroll around town."

Really? Then why the hell were you out? "It wasn't all that bad. A little rain never hurt anyone." As angry as she was with him, she had half a mind to tell him about the jumble of elements and nebulous threads she'd been developing. It was almost impossible not to jump up and see if the watercolors were still behind the rolled-up rugs. While she'd been waiting for the police, her earlier suspicions grew stronger and suddenly made sense. The why of it still eluded her. Instead, she told him what time she got home, then added, "When I saw the trail of water leading to my bedroom I realized someone had broken in."

"You're sure everything was locked when you left?"

"Both outside doors were locked. The door from here to the shop was locked." Shaking her head, she sighed. "I'm sure I checked the French doors before I left. I know the one in my bedroom was locked. I do that every morning before I go downstairs." Looking past him to the balcony, she nodded. "Yes, I did lock them before I left tonight. I remember because I set some food out for the courtyard cat."

"Anything missing?"

"I . . . I don't know. I mean, I got the hell out of here and called 911. I haven't had a chance to look. I've got a set of ivory miniatures and some jewelry—"

"Check it out. I'll get the coffee."

Hurrying to her bedroom, Molly pulled open the bottom drawer of her dresser. Her rosewood jewel box was in place. Holding her breath, she opened it and sighed with relief. Everything was as she'd left it. Checking the closet, she saw that nothing was missing. She had so few clothes with her; it would be easy to see if anything was gone. Returning to the living room, she said over her shoulder, "I should check the spare bedroom. I'm using it for storage and a workroom." Turning on the light, she went directly to the rolled-up rugs she'd stacked in the closet. The watercolors were still there. They hadn't been touched. Quickly glancing around the room, she saw that everything was as she'd left it.

"Nothing's gone," she finally said.

"What about downstairs?"

Molly shook her head. "The door was locked."

On their second cup of coffee, Officer Wilkins showed up with the equipment to dust the doors. "Is that really necessary?" Molly asked. She wanted them out of there. She had to think, to put her suspicions down on paper, see if she could connect the dots and come up with a picture. "It was probably some kid looking for money or credit cards."

"Or maybe a rapist who bugged out when he found the place empty. Yeah, I think it's necessary." The hard look on his face left little room for argument.

It was midnight when they were ready to leave. "I'd get dead bolts on the doors," Randall said. "An alarm system would be better. Especially with the shop downstairs. If your boss whines about the cost, have him call me. I'll make sure he comes through."

Seeing him to the door, Molly pretended to yawn. "That won't be necessary. Max will be beside himself when I call him."

"Glad to hear it. Look, lock up, leave the lights on. He won't be back. Not tonight, at least."

"Thanks," Molly groaned. "Some good news at last."

"I was only kidding. Unless he's a real sicko, repeat visits are rare. Once the cops show up, the venue's too hot. Get some sleep. You look dead on your feet."

Molly was too revved up to sleep. She carried the tray to the kitchen, left it on the counter, then turned on every lamp and overhead light in the place, including the bathroom. Retracing her steps when she left earlier in the evening, she distinctly remembered locking the living room French door. The locks were old; maybe they were easy to pick. A pro would know how to work them. Okay, she thought, let's play pretend. What would a pro want with her? He'd go for the shop, not the apartment. Unless, of course, he knew about the door going down into the shop. That would make sense. Then again, why would he want to climb back up to the apartment, then down to the courtyard? That would be risky, going back and forth. Antique shop robberies were more frequent than people knew. Vans were a common sight in front of an antique shop. For all anyone would know, it was just another late-night delivery, or someone loading up to head for a show. Fill up a van, set up a table at a flea market a hundred miles away, then pocket the cash and drive away whistling. It happened every day, all over the world.

The thunder and lightning was beginning to play out its last hurrahs, and the pelting rain had slowed to a soothing patter. By the time she'd carefully placed the watercolors between bath towels and rolled them up in one of Max's Oriental runners, the rain had finally stopped. Stepping out onto the balcony, she let her eyes adjust to the dark, then quickly headed down the stairs with the rug and hurried to the garage. Once inside, she reached for the light switch, then changed her mind. *That's silly,* she quickly thought. *So what if I'm down here? Who cares?* According to Randall, her uninvited visitor was probably long gone. Just in case, she flipped on the light, then ran the bolt across the door. Relieved, she turned back to the dusty cavern and froze. All the boxes she'd stacked up against the cabinets were shoved into the middle of the floor up against the El Camino. That didn't make sense.

She had the only key. "Of course . . ." she said out loud. "Her Highness was here. Maybe he let his friend in to get something." Setting down the rolled-up rug, she walked over to the cabinets and stared for a long moment. There were six cabinets and six padlocks. Far too many to be wasted on one of Pablo's chums. A devilish grin spread across her face. It stayed there all the while it took her to remember where she stashed that big ring of keys she'd found down here.

Considering the pack rat that Sid was, she hefted the heavy ring of keys and smiled. Surely, a padlock key would be part of this ancient collection. Finding three, she smiled again. Pablo's friend would have to make do with only five now. She'd do a little rearranging and stash the rug and a few boxes in one. Tomorrow she would buy a new padlock. Combination, of course.

The thought of screwing over Pablo gave her such a lift, she almost forgot what drove her here. When all the cabinets were unlocked, Molly laughed as she flung each door open. Standing back to eye the contents, she was stunned. Expecting to find a battered suitcase, a carton or two filled with an old toaster or coffeepot, or odds and ends of kitchenware, she found instead shelf after shelf of unframed canvases carefully set into vertical dividers. Her hands shook as she reached for the closest one. Carefully pulling it out, she leaned it against the doorframe and bent down for a close look. Rising slowly, her eyes roamed the dozens of dividers in each cabinet. Moving to the next set, she pulled out another canvas. Her eyes immediately went for the signature. Subject matter was irrelevant at this point. By the time she'd pulled six more, her hands were shaking. "Oh, my God." was all she was able to manage. Her brain was so muddled at that point, she barely heard the latest series of thunder. Ina Hubble,

Rowena Webster, and Lawrence Toby! An inventory here that could quickly add up to thousands upon thousands. Quickly returning the artwork, she closed the cabinets, and replaced the padlocks.

In a daze, she opened the door to the El Camino, pulled back the driver's seat and managed to fit the rolled-up runner with the watercolors into the small storage space. Doubly cautious, she turned off the light and inched her way out of the garage. Raining again, she risked getting soaked as she let her eyes adjust once more. Searching the alley, she saw a few stray cats huddled between the wall and the small Dumpster Bennie ordered. Both were bright orange tabbies, and she felt sorry for the poor things. After art galleries, stray cats were the second largest population in Carmel. Bennie had warned her not to leave food out, but she couldn't bring herself to ignore them.

Drenched by the time she made it to the balcony, she kicked off her shoes once inside, locked the French door, and headed for the bathroom to shed her soggy clothes. In her robe, she collapsed on the sofa and closed her eyes. Confusion and intrigue were making her brain ache. The twitch over her eye, now at full throttle, was driving her nuts. She knew right off those cabinets were not just a handy place to store inventory. No dealer in their right mind would relegate high-priced stock to a dank, dirty garage. Filled with questions, suspicions, not to mention a real touch of fear, she had never felt so confused. She could call Max, but what would that really accomplish? What if he was a part of this? How deeply involved with Pablo was he? Where would *his* loyalties lie? Love was blind, lust was blinder.

It didn't take a rocket scientist to know talking to Randall about this was out of the question now. After what she had left in New York, he'd be all over her. She'd never be able to convince him she wasn't involved. He was already skeptical about her.

Filled with an adrenaline rush she couldn't shake, she headed for the kitchen and pulled out a bottle of Sid's Spanish Terror. If this was the only way to nod off, so be it. Settling back on the sofa, she drained the first glass. By the time she finished her third, she lit one more cigarette and settled back. Keeping an eye on the long ash she was prone to ignore, she finally felt her body begin to relax. Stubbing out the cigarette, she headed for bed.

16

*M*olly had a lot to think about. The dots were coming together. The shape of the picture was still hazy, but a faint outline was beginning to emerge. Living alone was still new to her and the silence in the apartment this morning was suddenly annoying. She needed to think, to plan her scene with Randall. Even the sound of the news would make her feel less antsy. Turning on the TV, she clicked the remote until she found CNN. Just hearing the anchor's voice made her feel better. Visions of that movie with Janet Leigh in the shower forced her to double-check the doors before she'd headed for the bathroom. She almost considered leaving the shower curtain open, then decided the mess on the floor wouldn't be worth it.

She had to call Max about the break in. It was going to take all of her resolve to sound normal. While she was at it, she decided to tell him about her checks Pablo hadn't sent.

Drinking coffee by six, she was longing for a warm, buttery croissant. She needed comfort. She had half a mind to run down to Tosca's and splurge. Damn the calories, or the budget. She was taking this penny-pinching regime too far. A few croissants weren't going to kill her budget.

She knew Bennie arrived early and would let her in.

Heading down to the shop, she turned off the extra lamps, slipped a Kenny G cassette in the stereo, and decided to send Max a fax about her overdue checks. She wanted it official, in hard copy, not verbal. It was too early to call him anyway.

Visions of croissants and a steaming espresso with lemon and a touch of whipped cream put a tiny smile on Molly's face as she locked up and briskly walked through the arcade to the courtyard.

Concentrating on sidestepping large puddles of water on the uneven bricks, Molly didn't see the cops until she reached Tosca's. The door to Bea's shop was open, and two police officers stood outside with a clearly agitated Bennie. Last night's intruder must have made the rounds and tried to break into Bea's. She was about to join them when two paramedics came through the alley with a gurney. When she saw them approach the police, she held her breath. She felt like a stick figure in a freeze frame. Talking nonstop to the officer, Bennie was waving his hands and gesturing. In the middle of his gyrations, he turned and saw her. Sprinting toward her, he shouted, "Stay there, Molly. Don't . . . don't come over here. It's . . . it's Bea."

Molly's hand flew to her mouth. "Oh, God! What happened?"

Bennie grasped her shoulders. "You gotta stay calm, okay? Don't fade on me, okay? Promise?" He saw her mouth open, ready to speak. "I can't make this easy . . . so . . . so give me some space here."

"For God's sake! What happened?"

Taking a deep breath, he said, "It's Bea. She's . . . she's dead."

"What? No . . . that can't be! I . . . I was with her last night . . . she . . . she was . . ."

As Molly's shoulders slumped, Bennie held on tighter. They didn't see Randall approach. Standing behind Bennie, he said, "She was *what*?" Towering over both of them, the dark scowl on his face was pure horror. "Answer me, goddammit!" He pulled Bennie away from Molly and was almost nose to nose with her. "You have a fuckin' bad habit of being the last to see people who turn up dead."

Pressed up against the building, trying to put as much space between them, Molly shook her head back and forth. "That's . . . that's unfair . . . and cruel."

Moving to within inches of Molly, Randall stared down into her eyes. The hard, chilling look suddenly had the opposite effect on her. Shoving him in the chest, she yelled, "Get the fuck away from me." Her voice was shaking with anger. "How dare you treat me like some street punk!" Emboldened by the shock on his face, she hurried on, "I . . . I left Bea at a quarter to seven. How do you know I was the last to see her?"

That only stopped Randall for a moment. Pulling out a pack of cigarettes, he offered her one. "Calm down, for God's sake. And lower your voice."

Shoving the pack away, she yelled, "Calm down? You're nothing but a loudmouthed bully."

Bennie was knocked out by Molly's bravado with the chief of police. His hands were nervously going in and out of his pockets. Moving a step closer to Randall, he said, "Uh, I'll have one . . . I mean, hell, I'm kinda nervous myself. I found her."

With his eyes locked on Molly's, Randall side-handed the pack to Bennie. Pulling it quickly away, barely giving Bennie time to grab one, Randall took one out and gave it to Molly. "Peace pipe time. Have a smoke with me."

The pleading twinkle in his eyes won her over only

slightly. Cupping her hands around the light, she exhaled quickly. She waited until he lit his, then asked, "When . . . when did she . . . ?"

"The deputy coroner is just finishing up. He figures she's been dead around six hours. Won't know for sure until the postmortem."

She didn't even try to hold back the tears. "Oh, God! Poor Bea! I . . . I just can't believe it. What happened? I mean, was it a heart attack, or . . ." Her voice trailed off, then she whispered, "Poor little thing." Then her eyes widened. "Six hours?" Pausing to calculate, she said, "Then—"

"Yeah, she blew her brains out and we were only a shouting distance away and never heard a thing. Thunder was pretty strong around then."

Molly's legs almost crumpled. "*She what?*"

"Suicide. The place is a bloody mess."

Molly turned away and braced herself against the wall. Her voice was just above a whisper. "Impossible . . . she wouldn't . . ." She looked at Randall. "I don't believe it. We had plans to work on the computer again tonight. I mean, she was fine . . . she was . . ." Shaking her head, she mumbled, "She was . . . just across the courtyard. Why didn't we hear something? You were here . . . you left at twelve." Molly's voice drifted.

Bennie's eyes were darting between them so fast, he hardly smoked. "Hey, what's the secret code here? What's going on?"

Before Randall could answer, one of the officers shouted, "Hey, Chief. The Deputy Coroner's done. Can I let forensics in?"

Randall's face turned a bright pink. "Put a lid on it, will you? Being the Village Voice isn't in your job description." Turning back to Molly and Bennie, he ordered, "Stay put. I need to talk to both of you."

"I'll take Molly over and give her some coffee." Shaking his head like a wet dog, Bennie added, "I need a triple espresso myself."

"Yeah, fine." Randall said over his shoulder as he lumbered back to Bea's shop.

Wrapping his arm around the shaken Molly, Bennie said, "Come on, we'll have some coffee and—"

"Poor Bea. God, I can't believe this."

"I know. I can't figure it either." Unlocking the café's towering folding French doors, he whispered in awe, "Man, you got pretty dangerous with him. Made me wanna cry and run to my room."

Molly wiped the tears streaming down her face. "He's a goddamned bully. A little couth would go a long way."

Leading her into the café, he sat her down and ran behind the counter to snap the coffee machines on. "Yeah, but, hey, he's a cop. They've got the power."

"To protect and serve!" she shot back. "Where is it written they can push and shove and get in your face? This isn't L.A. for God's sake."

"This is true." Taking a deep breath, he said, "Okay, we have to pull ourselves together here. Want something sweet? Kinda take the acid out of your throat?"

"I was on my way here for croissants. I don't know if I'll ever be able to eat one again."

"You can't go though life thinking that way. You want plain, almond, or chocolate?"

Molly shook her head. "Anything is fine."

"Almond it is. Let me warm 'em up, and I'll join you."

In no time, he was at the table with a tray loaded with espresso, sliced lemons, cream, and a basket of croissants wrapped in a linen cloth. "Just like Rome hey? The Via Veneto or something?" Shrugging in an old world manner, he pretended to pinch her cheek. "Come on, Molly. I was crazy about Bea, too. I'll go to pieces later." He gave her a quick wink. "It's a guy thing. Private."

Reaching for his hand, she squeezed it. "I know you were. I didn't know her very long, but she was a darling. Always so cheerful. I . . . I just can't believe she'd do this."

Serving her a croissant, he asked, "How did she seem last night? I mean, was she down, or moody or pissed about something?"

"She was her usual perky self. I set up her computer, we laughed about technophobia—"

"Excuse me?"

"Being afraid of computers. Screwing up."

"I'd appreciate it if you two would refrain from discussing this case until I've taken your statements," Randall said as he entered.

Bennie jumped up. "Oh, hey, sure. Listen, how about coffee or . . . ?"

Eyeing the table, Randall said, "I'll have the same. Big cup espresso, okay?" Flipping the linen napkin open, he added, "A couple of chocolate croissants for me."

Taking a seat next to Molly, he set a small recorder on the table. "When Bennie gets back, we'll be civilized, have our repast, then I'll take your statements. Fair enough?"

Avoiding his stare, Molly said, "Fine. Whatever."

Since small talk was almost sacrilegious, they ate in silence. When their cups were empty, Bennie jumped up. "Refills all around?" Randall merely nodded. He was staring at Molly playing with crumbs on her dish.

"Put the closed sign on your door. The courtyard is shut down for the next few hours," Randall ordered.

"Oh, okay, sure." Scurrying behind the long glass display case filled with pastries, Bennie nervously did as he was told. Back at the espresso machines, he asked, "Can I make a few calls? I gotta let the help know to come in later."

"Make it quick. I've got a full day ahead." Turning to Molly, he said, "Look, I'm . . . ah . . . sorry about out there. I was pissed. That little Bea was a sweetheart. I bought some plants for my office from her. Kind of got to know her. I guess I lost my objectivity for a minute."

Turning her face away, she said, "You need a few lessons in comportment."

"I've been told that."

He had a smile that totally infuriated her. It was arrogant and comical at the same time. She never knew when he was putting her on. The more he used it, the sharper her tongue became. "Most of your life, I'd bet. It just doesn't seem to sink in."

"I'm working on it."

"Yea, I'm thrilled."

Randall shook his head and gave her that grin again. "You just have to have the last word, don't you!"

Molly turned and faced him. "Not always."

"What the hell does that mean?"

Staring out the window, she said, "Figure it out. You're the cop."

Bennie's return with fresh cups was perfect timing. Randall glared at Molly, then turned on the recorder. In a calmer voice, he identified himself, gave the date, time, and location and noted the reason for the interview. He then identified Benny and Molly for the record. "Mr.

Infama, the manager of Tosca's, discovered the suicide victim, Ms. Bea Thompson, and has given the first officer on the scene a written statement. I will therefore begin this interview with Ms. Doyle. Ms. Doyle was the last person to see Ms. Thompson—"

"You don't know that," he quickly interrupted.

Randall inhaled deeply, then said, "Yes, excuse me, Ms. Doyle. You are correct. I apologize for my assumption. Now, would you please describe your evening with Ms. Thompson."

"Thank you, Chief Randall. I met Bea a little after five last night to set up her new computer, give her an overview of Windows, and walk her through logging on and off. I was there until a quarter to seven. I was having dinner with a friend, and I had to be at the La Playa at seven."

"Tell me, Ms. Doyle, did you notice anything unusual about Ms. Thompson? Did she seem nervous, distracted . . . pensive?"

"She was her usual happy self . . . nervous about the computer, but we laughed about that." Thinking for a moment, she quickly turned to Bennie. "Did Bea see you about walking her to her car at night?"

Bennie squinched his eyes. "Say what?" Looking at Randall, he said, "She never said a thing. What the hell's going on around here?"

Randall turned off the recorder. "Look, you two. I ask the questions, okay? You don't chitchat back and forth. I'll do the follow-up." Clicking the recorder back on, Randall explained the cut, and noted the time again. Staring at Molly, he said, "Please explain your last remark regarding Ms. Thompson contacting Mr. Infama."

"Bea told me she'd been getting some crank calls.

Hang-ups. I told her to report it to the police, or at least ask Bennie to walk her to her car if she was leaving late."

Bennie slapped the table. "Oh, man! Why didn't she tell me?"

Hitting the switch again, Randall turned to Bennie. "I'm not going to tell you again to keep your fuckin' trap shut. You open it again, and I'll haul your ass out of here."

The recorder was back on, and again Randall explained the cut. "How did this conversation regarding crank calls come up?"

Giving Bennie the high sign to be still, Molly continued. "Well, while I was making room on the lower work counter for the equipment, I saw a handgun. It was under a pile of papers and ribbon. It freaked me out. I asked her to put it away. She laughed, then put it in the cash drawer, and that's when she told me about the calls. We were supposed to meet again tonight after closing to run through the routine again."

"That's it?"

Molly nodded. "That's it."

"No other conversations? No female heart-to-hearts?"

"No. Look, I didn't know Bea all that well."

"So, you're not aware of any personal or business problems?" Randall asked.

"Except for hating her landlady and all the grief she'd given her, she didn't appear to have any . . ." Molly could have kicked herself. She hoped Randall wouldn't ask her who that was. Any connection to Lorna Jacobs would only muddy up the waters.

"Really? Did you know that was Lorna Jacobs?"

Shit. Avoiding his glare, she reached for her espresso. "She mentioned it the night of the beach memorial."

"What kind of problems?"

"Oh, uh . . . repairs not made after the flooding a couple of years ago."

"That was it?"

"Yes."

"I'm going to ask you something now, and I want you to be as objective as you can. Don't get huffy on me, and don't think I'm out of my gourd, okay?"

The look on her face told him she was already of that opinion. Throwing up his hands in a peace gesture, he said, "Bear with me. This is vital. I want you to close your eyes and recall the woman you saw leaving Lorna Jacobs's house the morning of the murder."

Still staring at him, she said, "Do we have to go over that again?"

"Please. As a favor."

Giving him an impatient smirk, she said, "Then what?"

"Please cooperate, Ms. Doyle. Keep your eyes closed until I tell you to open them."

Folding her arms around herself, she closed her eyes, then nodded.

"Please respond, Ms. Doyle. This is your statement. Nods won't do it."

"Yes . . . all right."

"Take that image . . ." Randall began slowly, ". . . and see if it fits Bea."

Randall saw her arms stiffen and her lips tighten. He gently gripped her arm. "Come on, Molly. Don't fight me here. Could it have been Bea?"

"Aw, man! That's not fair!" Bennie blurted. "Bea couldn't even kill a snail if it was in her plants!"

Keeping his eyes on Molly, Randall's voice was a guttural snarl. "Shut the fuck up Bennie!" Watching Molly's lips fold in as she bit them, he understood the struggle.

He knew all about denial, about not wanting someone you knew to be guilty of a crime. His voice was gentle again. "Think about the height, the frame . . . the walk. *Could it have been Bea?*"

When she didn't answer, he said, "Okay, open your eyes." He snapped off the recorder, then nodded to Bennie. "I need another refill."

Glued to his chair, Bennie couldn't take his eyes off Molly. "It wasn't her, was it!" he pleaded. "Don't let him—"

"*Bennie!*" Randall shouted. "Am I gonna have to run you in for obstruction?"

Reluctantly, Bennie rose and cleared the cups. Molly remained silent. Randall checked his watch, clicked the recorder back on, then let out a slow breath. "Give it a minute to absorb. Forget you liked her. Forget you even knew her." When she still didn't answer, he added, "Look, I have a good reason for asking. Peel away the denim jacket, throw off the straw hat, dump the sunglasses."

Bennie stood behind Randall. His face was like melted wax. His eyes seemed to fold into themselves as they fixed on Molly. She could almost hear his silent plea to deny it all.

"It could have been," Molly almost whispered. It killed her to admit it, but she realized it was possible. Bea could have fit the description. Her height was close, and her tiny frame would easily be disguised. "The jacket was big. A size two or five could have been under it. She . . . she had a straw hat under the counter. But . . . but the sound Lorna made . . . it . . . it didn't sound like Bea's name."

Bennie's face was ashen when he set the cups down. "I don't fuckin' believe this. Bea wouldn't—"

"Hurt a fly. Yeah, yeah, tell me about people. Whatever

Lorna Jacobs tried to say wasn't necessarily her killer's name, Molly," Randall said. The fatigue in his voice was pitiful.

Signing off on the recorder, he reached for his cup and sipped thoughtfully. The smirk was gone; the eyes were tired and surprisingly softer. Looking at Molly, he said, "Bea left a suicide note confessing to killing Lorna Jacobs." Forestalling any outbreaks, he quickly threw up his hands. "Don't open your mouths! This is not for publication. The only reason I'm telling you two before I make it public is because you are here and part of the immediate scene. She claimed it was an accident. They got into a hassle over the flood damage and Lorna lost it and came at her with a knife she was using to cut down some cardboard boxes. She said they struggled and Lorna got stabbed."

"All this time . . . all this time, and it was Bea. Little Bea . . . right next door . . ." Molly shuddered.

"Bullshit." Bennie whispered. "It's bullshit. Bea was like a little bird. She couldn't . . ."

Reaching over to calm him, Molly said, "Bennie . . . she was as strong as an ox for her size. She used to carry huge displays over to me . . . she unpacked the computer stuff and hefted it up on the counter. I know how you're feeling, but . . . but—"

Bennie was furious. "You believe this shit? You really think she did it?"

Molly closed her eyes. "Oh, God, Bennie! She confessed! What more do we need to know?"

Randall stood up, pulled some money from his wallet and set it on the table. "I'll need you both over to the station later. We have to go over your taped interview, get it on paper, and . . ." He let his voice trail down as Molly bent her head and began to cry. Looking at Bennie, he said, "Bring her with you, okay? Come together."

Bennie nodded, "Sure." Handing Randall back his money, he added, "Don't insult me, huh? This isn't business. You should know the difference."

Randall's smile was terse. He knew Bennie was hurting, but he wasn't in the mood for a smart-ass punk to remind him about manners. "Cops have to be careful these days."

17

*D*eclining Bennie's offer of coffee after leaving the police station, Molly promised she'd stop by later. Noticing the police tape was down, she still couldn't bring herself to walk through the courtyard just then. It would never be the same, for any of them. Bea's vibrant personality and the wonderful scent of spring from her shop was horribly stilled. Molly wondered if she'd ever be able to scoot over to Tosca's without thinking of her. Alone in the shop, with the closed sign still on the door, she sat huddled in a large Deco leather club chair Max somehow mixed in with all the Continental goods. The buttery leather was soft, worn smooth by countless owners whose history would forever be a mystery.

She wasn't sure which astounded her the most, that Bea was Lorna's killer, or her suicide. Either was almost too bizarre to believe.

Quick flashes of their laughs last night over the computer plagued Molly. She tried to search for some clue, some tip-off that Bea had it in her mind to kill herself. It didn't make sense. Who orders pizza when contemplating the end? Who worries about booting up? Who would continue to care about crank calls? In her mind, suicide meant depression or guilt. Okay, Bea was feeling guilty about Lorna's death. But, if it was an accident, why not come clean? Why not admit to Randall she'd been the mystery woman and explain it was self-defense? Considering Lorna Jacobs's hostile reputation, a jury would probably have let her off. Any tiny comment or look or gesture that might have given away her feelings of guilt was invisible to her. She hadn't known her well enough to note the shadings of her nature. In fact, the only time she remembered seeing a frown on Bea's face was the night of the beach memorial. Perpetually up, constantly humming or smiling, Bea certainly didn't act like someone who had recently killed her landlady.

Dragging herself over to the desk, Molly was about to open the top drawer for a cigarette when she snatched her hand away. The damn desk! She was beginning to hate the very sight of it. Slumping onto the chair, she pulled open the drawer and fished around blindly for the pack she swore was there. Finally finding it under the multipage inventory Pablo left, she shoved one between her lips, and searched her pockets for the Zippo. Holding back a scream, she pushed papers around the top of the desk, hunting for the book of matches she'd taken from the La Playa. Just as she was ready to throw everything to the floor, she heard the bell over the door ring.

Looking up, the cigarette dangling from her lips, she was about to tell the woman entering that she was closed, when the stranger asked, "Need a light?"

Molly took the cigarette from her lips and shook her head. "No. I'm quitting." Rising from the desk, she said, "Today. Right now, in fact."

As tall as Molly, the woman smiled. "Sure. That's what we all say when we're pissed." Pulling a lighter from her bag, she said, "I quit every day. Mind if I join you?"

She was the kind of woman other women hated on sight. The kind of woman other wives kept away from their husbands. Tall, blond, slinky, and sexy did not adequately describe Daria DeMarco. Tall, jet-black hair with lustrous Cleopatra bangs, well-rounded and sensuous, painted a more vivid picture. The wide, open smile on a face with cheekbones Cher could only imagine made Molly want to throw a sack over her face.

Molly threw up her hands. "Oh, hell, why not? I'll quit tomorrow." Picking up the cigarette, she leaned in for the light, then sat back down at the desk. "I'm closed for inventory, but have a seat anyway." Finding the ashtray, she moved it between them and smiled. "I'm Molly Doyle." Leaning across the desk, she offered her hand.

Taking it quickly, Daria DeMarco smiled and introduced herself. "I own Daria's down the street. I wanted to stop in earlier and welcome you to town, but it's been crazy. I figured you could take a break." Glancing around the mess, she said. "Looks like you had a good raid somewhere."

Molly welcomed the laugh that flew out. "Sounds like you've been in the business."

"No, not me. I have my own kind of madness. Temperamental chefs, no-show busboys, dishwashers with phony green cards, and waiters with Ph.D.s. Schlepping around for antiques is not for the fainthearted." Seeing the look on Molly's face, she added, "I knew Sid for years. I've heard the horror stories. He used to have a decent shop. The last few years he let things go."

"That makes me feel better," Molly said. "I was beginning to wonder how he made the place work. The stuff was pretty awful when I got here."

"I guess it didn't matter when he found out he was dying."

"I didn't think about it that way," Molly looked away for a moment, then sighed more to herself than to Daria.

So wrapped up in her own problems when she arrived, she hadn't considered how unimportant this shop must have been for Sid.

Sensing she'd embarrassed her, Daria said, "Hey, who would? Anyway, I just wanted to drop in and invite you over for a Welcome to Carmel dinner." Checking her watch, she snuffed out her cigarette and rose. "I've got to get back. Look, come by anytime."

Walking her to the door, Molly said, "Thanks very much for the invitation. That's really nice of you."

"Not really." She grinned. "As much as I'd like you to think I'm a grand person, I have to be honest with you. I had a deal with Sid, and thought I'd pass it on to you. He gave me first crack on any new silver and copper serving pieces, odds and ends of china and flatware. When you drop in, you'll see why. In return, he came to dinner once a week on the house."

"Really?" Looking around the shop, Molly waved her arm. "My boss sent a truckload. In two more days, you'll be dazzled. You might regret it . . . it won't be cheap."

Turning at the door, Daria said, "Nothing good is." Pausing for a moment, she added, "I heard about Bea. I guess you got to know her well. I mean, being so close and all."

Surprised the news had traveled so fast, Molly hurriedly said, "Not that well, but I'll miss her." Nodding at the spray of silver and red roses in a wine cooler on a mahogany center table, she said, "Bea did that just the other day. I hate the thought of throwing them out when they begin to wilt."

Daria moved to the table and gently touched one of the petals. "I understand. She did my flowers at the restaurant. I don't know where I will find anyone to replace her." Smiling faintly, she said, "I mean . . . her, not just a florist."

"She was a joy. One of the few bright spots of this place."

Patting Molly's shoulder, Daria said, "It's tough being the new kid on the block. Especially in Carmel these days. We're constantly being bombarded with smart-ass newcomers who think they're gonna show us how to run a business. You wouldn't believe their failure rate! I'll give you a tip . . . be nice to the old-timers, don't try to set the world on fire. Big-city tactics don't work here." Opening the door, she turned. "Oh, and stay the hell away from town council meetings."

Molly gave her a mock salute and laughed. "Got it! Come back tomorrow afternoon. I'll be ready for you."

Watching her leave, Molly wondered what it must be like to look like that. She doubted if she had many women friends. Some women are born with an aura so strong, it sent danger signals for miles around. She'd met a few in New York, but none could match this one.

Not in the mood to face the unpacking left to do, she slumped back into the comfort of the leather chair. Confronting Randall was shoved aside. She'd had enough of him for one day. Besides, all her dots were beginning to fade. With Bea confessing, what had her suspicions to do with anything anyway? So what if she suspected a con was in the works? More to the point, she could be dead wrong. At any rate, it had nothing to do with Lorna Jacobs. Bea's confession confirmed that.

Shaking her head at the wonder of it all, she knew the best thing now was to get back to work. By the time she gathered all the empty cartons and bubble wrap, she found herself in a better mood. Cradling a wonderful pair of black-and-white Staffordshire spaniels in her arms, she nearly dropped them when the door flew open with a crash.

"Was that Daria I saw leaving here?" Like an imperious matriarch, Bitsy had both hands on her ebony cane. Her face was almost rigid with scorn.

Carefully setting the expensive spaniels on an English butler's desk, Molly held her temper. This was just too much for one day. If Bitsy kept this up, she'd long for a retirement home. Very sweetly, Molly replied, "Yes, and isn't she something?"

"That's a mouthful, honey. Stay away from her. She's trouble. The woman leaves dead men in her wake. When you bury two husbands before you're thirty, something isn't right."

Kicking aside a small empty carton, Molly threw her hands on her hips. "Excuse me? Look, Bitsy, I appreciate your local acumen, but, dammit, I'm nearly forty years old and I think I can decide who I might like to know."

Sauntering over to the leather chair, Bitsy sank in and said, "Mark my words. Keep your distance. Her first husband committed suicide. Ran his car into a tree in Pebble Beach. His mother Francis and I are dear friends. Poor dear still isn't over her loss. Her second husband was a—"

"Enough!" Molly screeched. "Enough, okay? I've had enough of death, murder and. . . . and—"

"Yes, I heard about Bea. I was having my hair done, and . . ."

Molly threw another small carton across the room. Bouncing off a walnut dresser, it landed on a stack of books and knocked them to the floor. "This goddamned place is like a—"

"A village, darling. Need I say more?"

"Please don't! And please, don't presume you have the right to tell me who to know, or who to associate with."

"I just don't want to see you get tangled up with the wrong kind of people," Bitsy said.

"You're unbelievable." Molly sputtered. "The woman kindly invited me to a Welcome to Carmel dinner at her restaurant. I don't think that constitutes immediate friendship. And, if I chose to be friends, that's my business, not yours."

"Well, she does buy a lot of silver and china. Used to buy tons from me. Sid found her some nice pieces." Bitsy gave her a smile.

"Hypocrite." Molly laughed.

"I'm really sorry to hear about Bea. Talk around town is you and Bennie found her this morning."

"That's not true," Molly said cautiously. "Bennie found her. I was on my way to Tosca's when I saw the police there."

Fingering the fringe of a Chinese silk piano shawl draped over a bookcase next to her, Bitsy said, "I've never understood suicide. Guess I'm too stubborn to let desperation get me down."

Picking up the books she'd knocked over, Molly avoided looking at her. "Not everyone's that lucky."

"You make your luck, honey. Some people just don't have the knack."

━∾ *18* ∾━

By six that evening, the shop was almost respectable. All the furniture was in place and glowed from a light coating of wax. Tomorrow would be smalls day. The prospect of polishing all that silver and washing china and porcelain after a quick dinner was not riveting, but she had to get open. One more day of redecorating was all she could spare. Remembering her promise to Bennie to stop by, she searched for her shoes, quickly slipped them on, and locked up.

Avoiding Bea's shop, she headed straight for Tosca's. Bennie saw her right away and pointed toward a table in back. When he joined her, she was immediately struck by the dark shadows under his eyes. Setting down espresso, and a slice of the apple coffee cake she loved, he sank onto the chair. "Man, I'm beat. How about you?"

"I can't say it will be a day I'll soon forget," Molly replied between quick sips of the steaming brew. "I tried to keep busy so I wouldn't think."

"Yeah, I cleaned equipment and did inventory." Moving his cup in circles on the table, he finally said, "I'm sorry about this morning. I mean about losing it when you said Bea could have been the other woman. You had to do what was right."

Closing her eyes, she took a deep breath. "God, Bennie. I never made the connection until Randall asked. I've tried all day not to think about her."

"I called Max and told him about Bea."

Molly's eyes flew open. "I meant to call him. What did he say?"

"Don't worry about it. I'm supposed to keep him up to date on stuff anyway. Randall beat me to it. Max was sick about it. He said he'd call you later on. He was crazy about Bea. The whole gang around here was . . . Sid, Pablo, Max." Bennie paused for a moment, smiled a little sadly, then said, "Anyway, Randall told him the shop was off limits until he releases it. He told Max he'd get Bea's brother to contact him about clearing the shop out later. I knew she had a lot of orders to drop off, so I called Randall a little while ago to see if a couple of my guys and me could deliver 'em. He said no. Nothing goes until he says so." Draining his cup, he shook his head. "Man, Rhonda's gonna be really pissed! She's got some fancy opening going on the next day or so. Bea had to special order some rare orchids for her from Seattle. Don't know what's going to be done about them."

Molly's droopy eyes shot open. "Rhonda?" Biting her tongue, she had to warn herself to be careful and play dumb. "Who's she? Why is she going to be mad? The poor woman's dead, for God's sake!"

"Rhonda Martyn. She owns one of the hottest art galleries in town. *Mucho dinero* kind of stuff. She gets . . . I mean, got all her flowers from Bea. They were old friends. Well, sort of. Overheard them a few times going hot and heavy. Guess it was over the orchids. Anyway, Bea used to work for her at the gallery. Quit last year and opened up her shop a few months after Sid died."

The dots were taking shape again. It was hard not to

bolt out of the chair and run back to the shop to think about this new information. Searching for an excuse to leave, she made a serious dent in the coffee cake. Maybe the sugar might give her brain a kick-start and she'd come up with something plausible without hurting Bennie's feelings.

Before she could come up with something, he said, "So, Daria stopped by, huh?"

Molly blew out her breath. "Jesus! The eyes and ears of the world seem to be following me lately." Throwing her hands up, she said, "Yeah, yeah, I know . . . it's a small village. If I hear that one more time, I'll scream. I really will."

Bennie laughed. "Don't get paranoid. Daria called and told me. She's my cousin."

"Your cousin? Oh, sure . . . silly me. It's a small village!"

"You said it, not me," he said. "Yeah, anyway, Daria and I are first cousins. Dan Lucero, the DA, is our third cousin. He says we're fourth, because he's been after Daria for years, but she won't give him the time of day. Bella Trattoria up the street? That's Vince Palucci, my first cousin, and then Tony Braggato, who owns Nona Rosa's down on the wharf in Monterey, is another cousin. Half the restaurants on the peninsula are owned by family." Grinning now, he added, "Italians around here are connected."

"You're doing a great job of making me feel better, Bennie, but *basta*, okay?"

"Listen, all I mean is . . . well, you're a good person, and I told Daria she should come over and say hello. I know you don't know anyone, and with Bea gone . . . I mean, I thought maybe she could cheer you up."

Reaching for his hand, Molly leaned over and kissed his cheek. "That was very sweet of you. Thank you. I really mean that."

"I just don't want to see you get in the dumps. Go have dinner and a few laughs. It will do you good. I've got family here, it's easier. When you're alone, it's tough."

This sweet young man was prompting more tears than she wanted to shed in public. Draining her cup, and taking the last bite of the coffee cake, she said, "Speaking of food, I've got a dinner warming in the oven."

"Sure. Oh, hey, my sources tell me Randall's going to make an announcement on the news tonight about Bea and Lorna. Case closed, I guess."

"Your sources? Bennie! You sound like an undercover cop."

Bennie grinned. "I overheard Randall call Dan Green over at Channel Eight when I delivered the espresso machine he ordered from me."

"Thanks for telling me. I'll watch Bravo with dinner instead of the news."

Her mind at full throttle, she had to slow it down. She was jumping around too fast. Nothing was making sense. The dots were going haywire. Thinking made her hungry. Staring at a freezer full of frozen dinners, Molly thought about taking Daria up on her offer, but the fact that Daria hadn't bought anything yet stopped her. She couldn't very well eat first and sell later. Hunger for good food was no excuse for bad manners. Lying to Bennie about dinner in the oven was a good excuse to leave. Or, she wondered, was it really his mentioning his large family, and her not having friends that made her pretend not to be a lonely stick figure living on frozen dinners.

The frozen pot roast was horrible. Throwing it in the

garbage, she boiled water for pasta, found a cube of butter, a bottle of dried Italian herbs, and a half-full carton of grated cheese. If she was going to figure out what was going on in sleepy little Carmel-by-the-Sea, she might as well have something good to eat. Setting the Pyrex bowl brimming with pasta on her lap, she turned on the TV to an old Fred and Ginger movie, grabbed a notepad, and, between bites, listed all the names involved and tried to connect the dots.

Setting down the bowl, she shook her head. It was a waste of time, she finally realized. It still didn't make sense. So what if Bea used to work for Rhonda, and Rhonda was screwing Dick, whose wife died in her arms and was murdered by Bea? How did her buying Dick's desk, which he wants back, fit in? So it was filled with artwork duplicating Rhonda's father's. Another so what? Dick and Rhonda were lovers. It means nothing. And then there were the cabinets in the garage. How did lending them to a friend of Pablo figure in all of this? Maybe he owned the collection of the two women artists. Rhonda's featuring them could merely be a coincidence. Watching Fred and Ginger whirl around a glittering Hollywood set, she poured a glass of Sid's wine and nearly choked on the first swallow. Sid! Bennie included Sid and Pablo in "the gang." If Bea hadn't opened her shop until after Sid died, how did they all know each other? Carmel might be a cozy little place, but everyone there couldn't be that connected. And, Sid was dead, too. An accidental morphine overdose, Max had told her. Really?

Killing the last of the wine, she stared at the TV screen, then tore the paper off the notepad and balled it up. Close to being bombed, she pretended she wasn't staggering and carefully made her way to the kitchen. By the time she was finished, her head was pounding, and her stomach was acting up. Stopping in the doorway to the extra bedroom, she stared at the jumble of silver she'd planned to polish that night. With extraordinary grace, she did an about-face and barely made it to bed.

*F*or the first time in days, Molly slept like a lamb. Awaking refreshed, her head clear and her stomach normal, she said a prayer of thanks for Sid's Spanish wine. Taking a long shower, she threw on jeans and a tee shirt, found her sneakers under the bed, and headed for the kitchen. She put her brain on hold, downed two mugs of coffee, then hauled several pieces of silver into the kitchen. In under an hour, she had two trays filled and ready for the shop. By ten-thirty, all the china and porcelain was washed, the silk lampshades dusted and sponged, and the remaining silver and copper were ready to place.

By four, the shop was ready for business. All inventory stickers were in place and the new price tags made. All that was left was to enter the new information into the computer. As much as she hated to admit it, Pablo's custom software was a dream. The cross-referencing was concise and buyer-tracking info was priceless. She still had to price the artwork Max had sent. She'd made a list of the artists and figured she'd hit the library to see if any were listed in the auction price guides. With a little luck, she might have some decent art to sell. It suddenly dawned on her she'd forgotten to call the Smithsonian about Lawrence Toby. While she was at it, she'd check out Hubble and Webster. Her connect the dot game might have been far-fetched, but she was still determined to find out what was going on with these artists. Using a thick marker, she made a note to remind herself and placed it on the desk.

Finding Daria's number in the phone book, she jotted it down and was about to call when she saw Randall staring at her through the window. Giving him a cautious smile, she watched him head to the door. Setting down the phone, she unlocked the door.

"Got a minute or two?" he asked.

"Sure. Come in." Closing the door behind him, she remembered to lock it again.

Standing in the middle of the room, he said, "Looks good. Better than I expected." Giving her a sideways glance, he said, "I mean, it was a hell of a mess the other day. I'm surprised you managed to finish it so quick." Turning to face her, he added, "Considering what you've been up against lately."

Heading to the desk, she said, "Work does wonders for the soul. Helps keep your mind busy." Dumping the ashtray into a wastebasket, she placed it in view, then quickly lit a cigarette. She saw him place a manila folder on the center table displaying Bea's last arrangement. He picked up a fallen petal, rubbed it between his fingers, then brought it to his nose. "I love roses. My mother used to have them all over the garden. The house was always filled with them." Turning to her, he smiled. "She wouldn't put them in the restaurant. Said it made the place look too fancy."

Molly smiled, but said nothing.

Picking up the folder, he flapped it against his hand as he stopped before a stuffed owl in a glass case. It was a rare find these days, and highly collectible. "Don't let Fish and Game see that. They'll drag you out in cuffs and not wait for an explanation. Then again, I guess that owl is too old to fall under the Endangered Species Act."

She ignored that and watched him wander, eyeing an Edwardian burled walnut bureau, running a hand over the soft damask of a wing chair, picking up a nineteenth-century brass sundial. He looked at price tags, opened drawers, read the titles of leather book sets, until she thought she was going to scream. As if he read her mind, he sauntered over to her and pulled up a chair. Placing the folder on her desk, he made himself comfortable, lit a cigarette, and opened the folder. "Mind telling me about it?"

Molly moved to her chair, pulled the folder toward her and saw what she'd been dreading for days. Her rap sheet. Photo and fingerprints. Statement, the works. She flipped the folder closed and slowly pushed it back. "What's to tell? It's all there."

"I'd like to hear your side of it."

"What's the point? I had nothing to do with it. My ex and his . . . his girlfriend were behind it. I was cleared of all charges and released."

"The point, I think, is pretty clear. In view of what's been going down here, we need to talk."

"I don't see the connection."

Crossing his leg, he leaned back and gave her his terse smile. "Well, you know, I wouldn't have either a few days ago. But, gosh, the modern miracle of technology kind of made me change my mind. I got some interesting information this morning from forensics. A couple of years ago, it would have taken a few days to come up with what they gave me like zap. Now"—he snapped his fingers—"it's only hours." Stubbing out his cigarette, he leaned back. "Your prints were on Bea's gun."

Molly stared at him as if he were insane. "I told you I

touched the gun. I told you how I found it. I handed it to her!"

"You didn't tell me you touched it. You said you saw a handgun and told her to put it away."

"I must have. I'm sure I told you." Looking down at the desk, she tried to recall the scene in her mind. Her hands began to move over the desk. "I was at the counter . . . sitting like this. I moved some papers and ribbon." Her hand hovered over the desk as she tried again to remember. "I saw the gun"—reaching for the ashtray, she picked it up—"I . . . yes, I picked it up by the barrel." Her eyes narrowed then, and she repeated, "The barrel. Got it? I never touched the grip!"

"Like a good cop's daughter would."

Her head snapped up. "Leave my father out of this!"

"Ease up. Got any coffee?"

Jumping to her feet, she clenched her fists. "Get out of here!"

"Sit down. I'll get it. You take cream, right?"

Molly watched him head for the storeroom. Grabbing another cigarette, she barely got it lit. It wasn't improbable that he might arrest her. Innocent or not, he could make a case if he wanted to. But he'd be hard-pressed to make it stick. A few Hail Marys now seemed to be in order.

He shoved the mug under her nose. "Take a few swigs. I doctored it up a little." Patting his breast pocket, he said, "I came prepared."

Eyeing him warily, she was losing patience with his attitude swings; steely eyed frowns, grins, laughter . . . all part of his repertoire no doubt. Sipping the coffee, she winced. He must have poured half a flask in her mug. Her eyes never left his as she took another swallow. "Are you through with the mind games? Your routine is a little too erratic. Seems to me you're out of practice."

"I guess you know quite a few."

"I grew up hearing most of them. Probably a few that might surprise you."

"I'm always open. Right now, I've got to make a few decisions. Maybe you can steer me in the right direction. Here's the story. I've got a possible suspect in a homicide that doesn't ring true. I mean, the suspect has some connections that, while remote, could be plausible. I'm thinking maybe I've got a business deal that went wrong . . . the vic's husband and the possible suspect push a similar product, okay? Well, the vic's hubby, the statistical prime suspect, has an airtight alibi, so I gotta cut him loose. I'm thinking maybe the wife, the vic that is, is targeted to scare off the hubby. Got that so far?"

"We're on the same page," Molly said.

"Fantastic."

"Not much of a stretch."

"Okay. Now, what makes me wonder about the possible suspect is, I get two names on a scene of the crime statement, and I find out the possible suspect made a buy on something that doesn't work. A big goof, I'd say. Then I check this person out and find—"

"Can we cut to the chase?" Molly snapped. "Better yet, let me finish the story. First, let's dispense with the 'possible suspect' crap. Plain English instead of cop shoptalk, okay? Out of the starting gate, you lose your objectivity with me because I'm an antique dealer. My take is you've been had a time or two. Okay, I understand, it goes with the territory." She saw his eyebrows rise, and stopped him. "Like they say, been there . . . done that. We're not saints, but we're not all crooks, either.

"Now, here's the way *I* see it. Because you have no suspect, and probably no murder weapon . . ." Seeing his eyes narrow, she knew she'd been on target. Quickly going on before he interrupted, she added, "I am assuming this, of course, because whatever killed Lorna wasn't still in her and it wasn't near where she fell into my arms. Add to that, the arriving officer moved her when the sprinklers came on. Now your crime scene is zapped. What do you do? You follow me all over town." The surprise on his face was too funny for words. It at least gave her some satisfaction. "First at the beach memorial, then all the way home. You've walked past the shop at least a dozen times, and you followed me the other night when I went to the La Playa."

"Shit, was I that obvious?"

"I told you . . . you're out of practice. Then, to add insult to injury, you cleverly had me finger a dead woman yesterday as the mystery woman at Lorna's." Sitting back, she crossed her arms. "I have to be honest, that just dawned on me. And, no, I did not fake the intruder thing." She was on a roll now, and everything suddenly fell into place. She knew why he was unsure of nailing her. "There was no way I could have killed Bea. You'd been following me, so you knew when I got home. That's how you got here so quickly after I called 911. How could I have come home, killed her, come back . . . cleaned myself up . . . changed clothes and called you within . . . say, ten minutes? And you were here until *after* midnight. You said yourself Bea must have done it around midnight."

Clapping his hands, he shook his head and laughed. "*Bravo! Bellissima!* Except, you forgot something."

Molly felt faint. What had she forgotten?

His eyes almost glimmered. "The suicide note."

"What about it?"

"That's what I want to know. Tell me about it."

Slapping her hand on the desk, she nearly knocked over the ashtray. "Enough with the Columbo shit, okay! How can I tell you about something I haven't seen?"

"Oh, that's right. I didn't show it to you."

Beyond exasperation, she reached for another cigarette. "You're beginning to bore me."

"It was on her computer screen." He saw her eyes widen, and then he knew.

"That's impossible," Molly whispered.

"Why is that?"

"Bea didn't know how to boot up. I mean, she made notes, but she was confused. I was supposed to go back tonight to show her again how to get up and get through Norton. Besides, I didn't even get her into the word processing program. I never opened it up. She had no idea how to access. In fact, I hadn't even set up her printer driver." Molly's hand flew to her mouth. It was a full moment before she said, "Bea didn't kill herself. She was murdered."

It took the wind out of her, but she saw where he'd planned to go all along. "Time of death is never precise. It can go minutes either way . . . you . . . you think I killed Bea after you left. You think I wrote the suicide note on the computer." Almost breathless now, she hated the words her mind forced her to say, but she had to get them out. "You think *I* killed Lorna, and that Bea saw *me* leave. You think I found out Lorna was Bea's landlady, that she was angry with her, and that gave her a motive."

"Bingo." Lifting his mug, he toasted her. "Couldn't have put it together better. I could take this to the DA and see what he thinks."

Randall watched her face collapse. He was waiting for the lip to curl, or the twitching over her eye to begin. Instead, he saw a frozen mask. Only her eyes hinted at the terror taking hold. He was disappointed. But not with her, with himself. This was nothing more than payback for her not taking his guff. He knew it was wrong, because he liked her sass. Best of all, he admired her brain, and found sparring with her fun. He wished they could have met under different circumstances. Molly Doyle, he was beginning to discover, was one of a kind. And he knew more about her than she realized. What was more important, he knew she wasn't the killer.

He toyed with letting her suffer for a few more minutes, then changed his mind. "But, I won't, because you didn't kill Lorna or Bea."

Nearly crumbling from relief, she pressed her palm over the twitch that was ready to explode. "You are a bona fide prick. You knew all along I was innocent, and you—"

"I had to be sure." Reaching for his flask, he asked, "Refill?"

Molly let out a long sigh and pushed her mug to him. "You bet your ass I do."

Feeling a surge of satisfaction, Randall grinned. "Call it gut instinct, call it—"

"How's lack of evidence?"

"Yeah, that's good, too."

Cradling the mug with both hands, she nearly drained it. "So, now what?"

Taking a deep swallow himself, relieved she hadn't tried to kill him, Randall said, "I went on TV last night and announced Bea's suicide and confession. Her brother is a wreck, but the DA is happy. As far as the killer's concerned, the case is closed. So, now—"

"You're up a creek without a paddle."

"One might say that."

Her sadness for Bea was unfathomable. Murdered for what? A killer was still loose. *Who's next?* she wondered. Not all the seemingly bizarre threads she'd been trying to weave between Lorna and the others might not be so far-fetched after all. Would Randall think she was nuts if she told him her idea? She looked at the roses and knew right away she didn't care if he laughed in her face. It was the least she could do for Bea. "Maybe not," she finally said.

Randall looked at her hard and long. "I'm waiting."

Molly took a deep breath and put her hands up. "Okay, but don't interrupt me."

Barely blinking, he said, "You've got the floor."

She tried to read his face, but it was blank. Taking a moment to organize her thoughts, she began with finding the watercolors in Dick Jacobs's desk. All the while she ticked off each person, each event, each suspicion, and how they might be connected, he remained silent. Finally, she added, "I don't know what this all has to do with Lorna's or Bea's death, but I'm determined to find out. And, I'd bet my life Max is not a part of this. I know this man, he's . . . well, not quite a saint, but he'd never touch anything like this. He doesn't have to."

Leaning over, he poured them both more coffee. He took out the flask, and set it on the desk. "Help yourself."

Molly added only a few drops of the brandy. She was already beginning to feel a light buzz. "You think I'm crazy, or what?"

Finishing off the flask, he said, "Yeah, like a fox. So, that's why you slipped out in the pouring rain the other night. Wilkins thought you were nuts."

"Wilkins?"

"One of my officers. He was at your apartment, remember? He went after the print kit."

"You had one of your people watching me? All night?"

"Just to be sure your uninvited guest didn't stop back." He saw the conflict in her eyes. He knew she wanted to thank him, yet perversely wanted to yell at him again. He wasn't sure which he preferred. "Part of the job. Okay?"

She gave him a tentative smile. "Yeah, okay. I'm not sure, but I think I'm supposed to be appreciative . . . so thanks."

"Now, what have we got here? An art scam that began to unravel? A jealous lover who wants the ole lady out of the way? Was Bea somehow a witness, or did she figure it out and was blackmailing Rhonda or Dick?"

"Are you going to let me help you with this?"

"No. Absolutely not." When he saw the stubborn set of her chin, he stared at the dimple in it and remembered his initial face read. Stubborn to a fault. Determined to win. This was going to be fun. "Are you nuts, or what? How the hell can you help me?"

"I just gave you some possible motives." She smirked.

" 'Possible' is the key word here." Pulling out a cigar, he saw her eyebrows rise. "I'm not gonna smoke it. I'll just roll it around, helps me think."

Molly laughed. "I really don't mind. I love the smell of cigars. Good ones that is."

"Oh, this is good, believe me. One of Fidel's finest." Taking her cue, he took his time lighting it.

"Lovely. Now, will you let me help?"

"Why should I?"

She wished she could cross her toes. She was going to lie big-time now, and it somehow seemed the right thing to do. "I can get art world information unavailable to you. The people who can give me what I need—"

"We need. *We* is the key word here."

"Okay, okay. Anyway, you wouldn't have the first clue who to talk to, or where to dig."

"And you do? Last I heard you were on the outs with that group."

So much for lying, Molly thought. "I have a friend who's still connected. She'll do it for me."

Randall studied his cigar with utmost interest. "Let's sleep on it."

"Sleep? Please!" she shouted. "I haven't had much since I got here."

Randall laughed. "Yeah, well, you've been a little busy getting mixed up in murder."

"You haven't been much help, either," she snapped.

"True. Okay, here's what I'll do. You get me the info you seem to think will put some of this together, and I'll take it from there. Will you do that for me?"

"No, not for you. For Bea."

"A damn fine reason."

≈ *20* ≈

*T*he spectrum of emotions these past months that had left her sleepless and fitful, not to mention the constant eye twitching, seemed now to belong to another person. The sudden feeling of relief might have made her almost giddy were it not for Bea. When she saw how seriously Randall took her suspicions, she began to wonder if she'd turned those watercolors over sooner, Bea might still be alive. It was a premise she didn't want to accept. She wasn't sure she could live with such guilt. Randall had to let her help him.

At least she could look him in the face now and not measure every word, or wonder when he was going to drop the other shoe. It was clear he would become a presence in this life she must have in Carmel.

Plugging in the teakettle, she remembered she was about to call Daria when Randall arrived. At her desk, she found the number and dialed. Surprised to hear from her so soon, Daria said she'd be right over. Molly eyed the silver pieces she thought Daria might like, then nervously fussed with the display. Anxious to make a substantial sale, she had to laugh. She'd sold priceless antiques to mega tycoons, and here she was feeling like a novice waiting for her very first customer. Pouring the tea, she noticed how chapped her hands had become from polishing all the silver. The clear nail polish she used was chipped, and a faint residue of furniture stain clung to her cuticles. All signs of a poor dealer up all night cleaning merch and praying for a decent sale the next day.

Dressed in a chef's white jacket and black-checkered pants, Daria was there in minutes. "I'm helping with dinner prep"— she laughed—"we're shorthanded again." Eyeing the shop, she said, "This is fabulous!" Making her way to six deeply chased silver trays Molly had mounted on sturdy wood plate holders, she sighed. "God! I don't know which I like best." Moving to an Art Deco cocktail shaker, she picked it up and smiled. "I'm glad these babies are back in vogue. They've been hell to find. My bartender loves to show off with them." Running her hands through her incredibly thick hair, she turned to Molly. "Let me wander, okay? You've got so much here I have to think."

"I know the feeling. I thought Max was nuts to send all this silver. Guess he knew you'd be interested."

"Bitsy Morgan probably told him. I've never met the man. Bitsy and I go back a little. You should probably know I'm not one of her favorite people. Anyway, you'll hear the rumors soon enough."

Leaning against the desk, Molly folded her arms. "I'm not a gossip, and I don't like those who are. If that includes Bitsy, so be it. Since Max has decided she's to work with me on the weekends, I've got to get along with her. I've already set some ground rules. I decide who my friends are, not Bitsy Morgan. Besides, I've got baggage of my own."

Examining a Regency repousse compote, Daria said, "Welcome to the club. It's not very exclusive. It only means you've lived." Noting the hallmark on the compote, she nodded. "Good marks. This would be great for flowers."

"I guess I've lived a bit then. I've never thought of it in those terms."

Daria's smile was kind. "Works for me." Moving to an English gate leg table, she eyed the dozens of unmatched silver plate forks, knives, and spoons. Taking her time, she turned several over, and held some as if to judge their weight. With no further comments, she inched her way to the silver plate vegetable dishes and meat platters. Molly couldn't tell if she'd looked at the price tags and began to wonder if she was really a tire kicker, or simply looking for a new friend. She didn't care. She liked Daria, and that, in itself, was a great sale.

After a few more moments of wandering, Daria pulled up a chair at the desk. Taking out her checkbook, she said, "I come up with four grand for all the trays, the flatware, and the serving pieces. How's thirty-six hundred sound? I've got a resale license, so you can consider me a dealer."

The woman had a calculator for a brain. She was good, Molly had to give her that. She'd examined almost two dozen pieces and noted the prices without being obvious. And, she knew the 10 percent knockdown was the minimum discount usually given to dealers. Thrilled with the sale, Molly still had to make it sound iffy. "You're clearing me out of silver!"

Daria grinned. "Deal . . . or not?"

"Are you kidding?" Molly laughed back.

Pleased, Daria wrote out the check. "I'll send one of my guys over to pick this up later."

"Anytime. I'll bubble wrap it up and—"

"Don't bother. You've got enough to do. Just box them

and throw the receipt inside. I've go to get back to chopping onions and garlic. Come by for dinner tonight. We'll celebrate."

"I'd like that," Molly said. "I could use a little fun."

It took nearly an hour to write up the sales tags, enter the info in the computer, and pack up Daria's booty. She might have gaps in her decorating efforts, but the 10 percent commission she'd just made was certainly worth it. She knew Max would be pleased, especially since she'd only lowered his tags by 5 percent.

Daria had been a welcome diversion, but now that she was gone, Molly's mind was cluttered with a number of scenarios she wanted to offer Randall. A little soft music might help untangle some of her wilder notions. She headed for the storeroom and sorted through the dozens of CDs she'd found in the apartment. Sid Wells might have been a lousy decorator, but his taste in music was so close to hers it was almost eerie. Between Kenny G, Gershwin tunes, the Eagles, Brubek, and Keiko Matsui, she was in music nirvana. Deciding on Matsui and a few others she hadn't played, she set up the five-disk player and turned up the sound. Stepping back into the showroom, she was startled to see the back of a man leaning over her desk and riffling through the paperwork. He was dressed in tattered jeans, his leather jacket was scratched and mottled with stains. The hair straggling from his limp and dirty Indiana Jones hat, was long and oily. One of these times, she swore, she was going to remember to lock that door when she was closed. "Excuse me? Those papers are private. Put them down and get the hell out of here."

Turning at her voice, he said, "Hey, chill . . . no big deal."

Furious with his attitude, she said, "Really? Well, it's a big deal to me." Moving quickly to the desk, she gathered up the papers and turned them over. "Out."

Glancing around the shop, he smirked. "I saw Daria leave. What'd she buy? More silver? She's a sucker for the stuff. I've got half a dozen pieces in my van she'd like." Pulling a card from his jacket, he threw it on the desk. "Name's Milo Kraft. I specialize in smalls. I sell to all the dealers around town. I can get you anything. Just name it. Tiffany, Sèvres, Imari, Derby, Meissen . . . old, new, fakes. Give me a shopping list, I'll have it in a week."

Not wanting to even touch the card, Molly said, "I'm not authorized to buy from pickers." It was a lie, but she wanted him out. Without pickers, dealers would starve. They were a mainstay of fresh merch. This one was a bottom feeder of the trade, pushing flea market junk, garage sale castoffs, and most likely turning a blind eye to stolen goods. His type were not above Dumpster diving. Every time a new shop opened, or management changed, they crawled out of the woodwork. "You'll have to contact the owner."

"I'll call Pablo. We're tight. He used to buy from me all the time."

"Pablo doesn't own this shop, and I don't take orders from him."

He laughed as he saw her hand inch toward the telephone. "You don't have to call the cops. I'm legit." Shoving his hands in his pockets, he made a point of sauntering to the door. Stopping at the center table, he picked up the petals Randall had earlier touched so gently. "Now that Bea's history, I can put you with a friend of mine for your flowers."

His crass insensitivity was more than she could stand. "Get the hell out of here."

"Hey . . . chill, okay? My friend is cheap. She deals in day-old stuff."

It must have been the fury on her face that finally pushed him to the door. Opening it wide, he sucked in the damp air, then glanced over his shoulder. "See you around."

Molly quickly locked the door behind him and watched through the window as he sprinted between two cars and stomped across the planted meridian in the middle of Ocean Avenue.

"Pig," she mumbled. She wanted to pour Lysol over everything he'd touched. Creeps like him made her squirm. She'd seen enough of them come in and out of her father's small used furniture shop to spot them a mile away.

Molly picked up the petals on the table and bit her lip. "Oh, Bea, if what I think is going on is right, maybe . . . maybe you'd still be here. I don't know how you fit into all this, but I'm going to find out."

She opened the shallow middle drawer of the desk and emptied a small paper clip box. Gently, she dropped the petals into the box and stared at them. She didn't need a reminder of the guilt she felt. It was deep enough to be a constant companion, but she wanted them where she would see them every day.

Forcing a smile on her face, she checked her watch. It was almost six. Daria said to come early so she could spend some time with her before the hordes showed up. Rushing upstairs to freshen up, she made sure all the doors were locked and left most of the lights on. She still hadn't replaced the burned-out light on the outside stairs and made a mental note to do so. She had so many things to remember now, she decided to get a notebook and keep a list on the desk. It dawned on her that with the computer, she could check out Toby and the other artists there. She made a note to call Cleo. A small gleam lit up here eyes. Wait until Pablo saw the telephone bill! She and Cleo could talk for hours.

Remembering the radio forecast of possible rain, she grabbed her raincoat. Outside the shop, she shoved her hands into her pockets and filled her lungs with the salty damp air. Like a tonic, it seemed to rejuvenate her. She turned back to the shop window and smiled. Her displays looked great, she was going to meet a new friend, have a wonderful dinner, and help solve two murders. What the hell else could one want?

She remembered Daria's was on Dolores, but when she reached the corner of Ocean and Dolores, she couldn't recall which end, north or south? Opting for the north end, she knew she had time to double back if she was wrong. As small as Carmel was, it nevertheless was a little confusing. It was easy to meld all the dozens of unique buildings into one great mind photo. By the time she reached the middle of the first block, she recognized a few of the shops and knew she'd made a mistake. Crossing the street to avoid a line of people she'd already waded through, she stopped to catch her breath. The soft drizzle that had started shortly after she left was now rain. Spotting an awning over a restaurant two doors down, she pulled up the collar of her raincoat and made a quick run for cover. Leaning back, close to the window, she smiled at a few tourists. "Mind if I barge in?" Laughing, they waved her in. When two more people joined them, Molly inched herself to the edge of the awning to make room.

Glancing over her shoulder, she looked into the window. Her heart stopped. Seated at one of the two window tables was Bitsy and Pablo. On the white tablecloth was a pair of blue-tinted sunglasses.

She never thought she'd be so happy to see Randall. Standing at the hostess podium with Daria, the smile on his face froze. "You look like you've seen a ghost."

Molly's hands were shaking as she unbuttoned her raincoat. "Worse."

Taking hold of Molly's elbow, he nodded to Daria. "We're going to the bar. Can you get us a table off the beaten path?"

"I'll go you one better, follow me. You can have my private hideaway."

Following Daria down a plush burgundy-carpeted hallway, Molly couldn't help but notice the several heavy gilt framed oil paintings filling the walls. Her eyes bounced back and forth until she had to stop. "Who *is* this artist?"

Randall's eyebrows hit his hairline. "Whoa . . . I thought we had a crisis here. Who the hell cares who the artist is? Are we on the same page here, or what?" When he saw Molly hadn't heard a word, he muttered, "Can't you turn it off?"

Daria smiled. "Can a swabby ignore a whorehouse?" Turning away from him, she stood next to Molly and folded her arms. "Mackie O'Brien. She's local and a close friend. I'll have to get you two together. Great, huh?

I'm a sucker for her stuff. There's more in the dining room."

"Truly gifted." Molly said.

Passing behind them, Randall said. "I'll be at the bar. When you two can find some time, drop by."

Reaching out to stop him, Molly had to grin. "I'm sorry. Occupational hazard. I love antiques, but art is my real passion."

Shoving his hands in his pockets, he eyed the picture before him. "Okay, so this artist has perfectly captured a soft, foggy morning. You can almost smell the wood fire burning in the storybook house and imagine a small boy in knickers yawning over his morning porridge. Yeah, okay, sweet." Jerking his head toward the end of the hall, he asked, "Shall we start again? The private room?"

Ushering them into her sanctuary, Daria said, "I'll get Manuel in here to take your drink order."

Randall nodded, and, as soon as she left, he looked around, then said, "Okay, let's get this over with. I don't want any more distractions. It's a great room, right? Daria knows her stuff. Giving the table a rap with his knuckles, he muttered, "Good Brittany piece. I figure the pine dresser to be English . . . mid 1800s. The majolica on the shelves are probably a mix of Italian and French, some period, some new, and the side chairs . . ." Pulling one out and giving it the once over, he shook his head. "I'd lay odds they're beech wood. Maybe George IV. The cane panels have been replaced." Stepping back, he looked down at the carpet, and hesitated for a moment. "Possibly Serapi . . . early twentieth century." Giving Molly a glance, he pulled out a cigarette, lit it then said, "That about do it? Can we get down to what ever the hell had you so spooked now?"

Sinking into one of the chairs, Molly's eyes narrowed.

"The carpet is Bakhtiari, Persian . . . late 1890s. And, yeah, that about covers it."

Joining her at the table, he placed a heavy crystal ashtray between them. "Baccarat, right?"

"Okay! I got the point."

Satisfied, Randall sat back and said, "Good. Now, care to fill me in?"

By the time Molly told him about seeing Bitsy and Pablo at the restaurant, and the blue sunglasses lying between them, the waiter knocked and entered. They gave him their bar order, then Randall asked for two menus. "I think we'll be dining in here."

"The thing is," Molly began, "Bitsy has made it a point of letting me know Pablo wasn't one of her favorite people. She hinted at having a run-in or two with him. So this little tête-à-tête seems a bit strange. And when I saw those glasses . . ."

Pulling a pair of sunglasses from his pocket, Randall handed them to Molly. "Show me how they were positioned."

Molly took them then briefly closed her eyes. She placed the sunglasses between her and Randall, lens facing left. "In the middle of the table, facing the window. Bitsy on my right, Pablo on my left." She paused for a moment, then added, "Bitsy is right-handed. I think." Rolling her eyes, she swore. "So is Pablo."

"Okay, it can go either way. Just depends on how they were held in the hand before setting them down." Giving her a wink, he smiled. "Good work, Molly. First-rate deduction."

Folding her arms, she slumped in the chair. "Only it doesn't tell us a thing. Except one of them owns blue sunglasses. I wouldn't call Pablo exactly short, but Bitsy would qualify."

"And they both have ties to Lorna Jacobs, and knew Bea. If we can connect them to Bea, we've got a starting place to jump from. What do you know about this Bitsy Morgan?"

Before she could answer, Daria arrived with their drinks, and menus. "Both Jack Daniel's fans I see. Makes life easy. I'll be back with a bottle and some soda. I think you two might need quick refills."

"Grab a glass and join us." Randall said. "You might be able to help out here. I need someone who knows the lay of the land. I haven't had time to develop—"

"Snitches?" Daria asked.

"Connections," Randall corrected. "Local historians."

Sensing Daria's discomfort, Molly quickly said, "This room is wonderful. You've got a really great eye. I can see why you call it a hideaway. I could happily spend hours—"

"Save it," Randall snapped. "Daria knows what I mean."

Daria saw the anger fire up Molly's eyes, and she had to laugh. "I do. But, thanks, Molly. This is the only place I can get away from bores and wanna-bes."

"Does that mean I can come in?" Dan Lucero stood in the open doorway and gave Randall a mock salute. "Manuel said you were back here." Sauntering in, he eyed the drink tray, then smiled at Molly. Offering his hand, he introduced himself. "So, you're the lady who found Lorna Jacobs." Seeing the look of surprise on her face, his laugh was almost sarcastic. "Being the DA around here, I sometimes get to read homicide reports." Dismissing Molly quickly, he draped an arm around Daria. "Is this a private party, or can anyone join?"

"Did I forget to mention jerks, pests, and over-the-hill studs?" Daria said.

Placing a loud kiss on her cheek, Lucero laughed. "So, Chief . . . ah, excuse me, *Randall* . . . having a little celebration here? First big case in the bag thing?"

"The suicide of a sweet woman is not something to celebrate, Mr. Lucero," Molly said as she rose and reached for her tote. Nodding to Daria and Randall, she said, "Another time? I'm not very hungry."

Lucero held out a hand to stop Molly. "Sweet woman or not, she was a murderer. So I won't apologize."

Molly looked at Randall for guidance. It didn't take much to recognize the tension between the two men. And, it appeared he hadn't told the esteemed district attorney the truth.

"I'd hate to see you miss tonight's special," Randall said. Looking at Daria, he asked, "Veal Shanks à la Pomodoro, right?"

Trying to decipher the hidden messages going on, Daria could only nod. "Right. Please stay Molly."

Randall saw the confusion on Molly's face. It was time to lay all the cards on the table. "Pull up a chair, Lucero. It's still the same ball game. We're just going into extra innings."

Lucero's eyes went from Molly to Randall, then to Daria. "We all got box seats here?"

Randall nodded. "Molly is our new coach, and I just recruited Daria as a scout."

Between soup and salad, three baskets of garlic bread, and a prime year, according to Lucero, of a bottle of Clos du Bois Merlot, Randall and Molly enlightened Lucero and Daria.

"What makes you so sure about this?" Lucero asked Molly.

"There are few artists with little or no major reputation that can command the prices Lorna's asking. Lawrence

Toby is not one of them. She's riding the trend for California artists and creating a false market. An old trick, by the way. It's done every day with antiques." Looking at Randall, she said, "I'd say Mission furniture is a recent one. It's ugly, unimaginative, ungraceful, and reeks of being poor. Anyway, the pictures I saw in her gallery were not painted some sixty-odd years ago. I could bore you with the details, but I won't. It would take hours to explain pigments, varnishes, oven aging, and technical details, but let's just leave it at the pictures are raw. And, they're too carefully executed to be *plein air*, which was the style of most Early California artists." Seeing Lucero wasn't up on art lingo, she added, "Painted in real time. On the scene in the open air."

"You people are crooks," Lucero said.

Staring straight at Randall now, she said, "Not all of us."

"I wish you would have had the courtesy to come to me with this before now. I told you I wanted to walk this with you," Lucero said to Randall.

"I wasn't sure until yesterday," Randall lied. From day one, he had been determined to keep Lucero out of the loop. He read Lucero as the type to jump too soon, and he didn't want him going off half-cocked with unrealistic demands or press conferences. "When Molly came in tonight and told me about this Pablo and Bitsy duo, things began to click in a different direction."

"I don't like bringing the public into this," Lucero said as he poured wine all around. "This isn't a cozy movie of the week on TNT. This is dangerous work. It takes trained specialists to—"

"Aw, cut the crap, Lucero," Daria finally said. "Randall is right in asking me to help out with local background. He has no clue about village intrigues or gossip. He needs to know who's screwing whom, where the bad blood is, where deals went bad, and why. I can get him that, and you know it."

"Okay, but what about little Miss Molly here? What's an antique dealer—"

"You're not much of a nineties kind of guy, are you?" Molly said. "A few lessons in couth might go a long way."

Randall drained his glass and laughed. "Way to go, Molly. Watch her, Lucero, she's got a mouth on her. I'm just glad she's found a new target. Listen up, Dan." Randall smiled. "You don't mind if I call you Dan, do you?" Not waiting, he went on, "Molly can get info I wouldn't know where to look. Her contacts in the art world will be invaluable. We know a scam is going down. Why it led to a double homicide is *what* we need to know. Besides the standard motives of greed or blackmail, I think someone wanted out."

"As art scams go," Molly interrupted, "this is small-time. Not six or seven figures or icon artists auctioned at the big houses."

"But it's enough, to keep it going," Randall said. "Daria is going to gather the scuttlebutt on this group. Molly will get into the artist's background. I'll be running a check on everyone."

"Where do I fit in?" Lucero finally asked.

"In the driver's seat when the time is right."

Expertly twirling pasta on his fork, Lucero smiled. "I like that." Looking up, he said, "Hey, come on, you guys, *mangia.* Eat up!"

Randall sat back and winked at Molly and Daria. "Profound advice, Counselor."

Standing in front of the shop, Randall said, "Your window looks good. I might even be tempted to drop in. My

daughter's coming down from Stanford this weekend.
Got to get a birthday present."

"She is? That's great." Turning back to the window,
she said, "With everything that's been going on, it's a
wonder I ever got this place ready for customers. Would
you like to come in for coffee? Maybe look around for
your daughter? I'll give you a good price if you find
something." Molly hoped he'd play cop and check the
apartment out. Still a little queasy about Bitsy and Pablo,
she didn't want to take any chances she might have had
another uninvited guest. She'd rather he thought she was
being polite.

"Still spooked, huh?"

"Caught me red-handed."

"I don't blame you. I noticed the light over your outside stairs is still out."

"I keep forgetting to replace it."

"Get the locks changed yet, or the alarm system in?"

Unlocking the door to the shop, she said, "Nope."

"Okay, coffee sounds good. You fix it, and I'll take a
tour."

By the time Randall checked the shop, the apartment,
and the garage, Molly had coffee and a sliver tray of
cookies on the scarred coffee table. Helping himself,
Randall said, "I'd block off these doors tonight before
you go to bed. First thing tomorrow, get a locksmith over
here and change everything. Then call your boss and get
an alarm in here."

"I will. I promise. Then I'll call Cleo." When she saw
the blank look on his face, she said, "Don't worry, she's
my best friend and one of Sotheby's art experts in London." Taking a moment to give him a quick recap, she
added, "Cleo can get all the info we need. And she's very
discreet." Filling their cups, she shook her head. "I just

can't figure why Bitsy acted like Pablo wasn't one of her favorite people, then has dinner with him."

"Could be she's blowing up a smoke screen. Are you sure they didn't see you?"

"Positive. I had my back to them and my collar up around my face. I was only there for a moment or two."

"Lucero came in when you were about to enlighten me. Tell me about Ms. Bitsy."

"It's a 'small world' story. I'm not so sure I believe it all, but Max vouches for her. Anyway, she claims she and my mother were close friends. They grew up together in The City." Molly paused, reached for a cigarette, then repeated all that Bitsy had told her. "I don't recall my father mentioning her, or even Max in stories about the early days in the business. Apparently, it was her idea for Max to have me take over this shop. She thought Carmel would be a good place for me to regroup. By the way, Bitsy had a consignment deal go bad with Lorna. I don't know if you know that. She said there was a robbery, and Lorna wasn't insured. She and a few others got left holding the bag."

Randall sipped his coffee and reached for a cookie. He seemed engrossed in the chocolate swirls and didn't say a word. Finally, he said, "I know about the robbery." What he didn't tell her was that he knew Bitsy was one of the consignors, and that his investigators on loan from Lucero blew questioning her. By the time they realized they'd dropped the ball, Bea was dead. "Interesting little group. Pablo is a talented artist, Bitsy claims he's not one of her favorite people, they meet for a cozy little dinner, and they're both tied to your Max character. Does anything bother you here?"

Molly thought for a moment, then said, "Antique people are a tight crowd. It's not unusual for spiderweb connections."

"That's not what I mean. Think about it. Bitsy maneuvered you here, right? Isn't that what she told you?"

"So? I don't follow." The minute she said that, she realized where he was going. "Oh, come on! You think I was set up and it didn't work? That's reaching. Who the hell knew I'd be at Lorna's in time for her to fall into my arms?"

Randall waved her off. "No, that's not what I meant! This group isn't *that* sharp. *What* I think, is"—he grabbed another cookie and paused—"if Bitsy claims to be tight with your family, maybe she knows about the hubby of this cousin in New Orleans and figured to wrap you all up together in their little game. Considering what went down in New York, they might figure you were in on the scam there and . . ."

Molly was almost breathless. "How the hell do you know about Angela and Armand?"

Popping another cookie in his mouth, he said, "It's my job."

"Any other little bits of family history you might like to share with me?"

"Sure. Your sister made partner in her law firm a few years ago, she's been having an affair with the senior partner for three years, she drives a Beamer, owns a fancy condo, and—"

"I don't want to hear about her," Molly said.

"Hey, you asked." He saw the pain in her eyes, and he suddenly felt like a shit telling her about her sister. He could have ended with the cousins in New Orleans. "Back to the subject at hand, keep an eye on Miz Bitsy. Try to draw her out."

Still smarting from the news of her sister, and how much Randall knew about her family, she couldn't help but grin. "Draw her out? She never shuts up! She's already let me know I'm a novice when it comes to midrange merch. I didn't get in this business to sell cranberry glass or Haviland china. I could care less about brass candlesticks, milk jugs, moth eaten books, or half the junk in the shop. It's a means to get out of here, that's all."

"You sound like a snob, Molly. Don't let your customers hear you."

"I give a shit, okay? I *am* a snob. I, at least, admit it."

"Hey, we got two murders to solve. How about making more coffee?"

She gave him a stare, then picked up the tray and headed for the kitchen.

"A few more cookies, if you've got 'em."

Returning with a full dish of cookies about to spill off the edge, she set them down and said, "I forgot to tell you a few other things. Bitsy said Dick Jacobs used to be a pretty good artist. He didn't make it because he couldn't find his style. Oh, and she warned me to stay away from Daria. She said she was bad luck, or something."

He ignored the comment about Daria. He knew her story. It wasn't his business to enlighten Molly. "Dick, too? This place has more artists than squirrels. Anything else you've neglected to tell me?"

"No. I just forgot, that's all. I mean, it didn't have anything to do with Lorna or Bea."

"Look, Molly. You gotta let me know stuff like that. It adds up."

"I thought you knew. You seem to know everything else. Besides, Bitsy wasn't a part of any of this. I just didn't think—"

"I know," he said kindly, "But it's little things that . . ." He saw her shudder and was immediately concerned. "What?"

"Little things! Not again!"

Pulling out a cigar, he rolled it between his fingers. "Care to share that?"

Molly eyed the cigar, and reached for her cigarettes. Offering him her Zippo, she said. "I had a revelation the day I found Lorna. It suddenly struck me how *little things* had played a major role in my life." She told him it was a bracelet that sent her father to prison, and her offhand compliment of Greta. "And I've told you about the chest already."

"I know." His smile seemed almost sad, "You wonder sometimes if you'd only turned left instead of right, a whole different path might have been avoided. Life, my mother used to say, was simply a series of zigs and zags. Some good, some not so good." Catching himself, he lit his cigar, stared at the Zippo, then said, "So, tell me about the bracelet."

It wasn't a subject she wanted to recall, but she thought he probably knew the story anyway. "I don't really know much. Or don't want to remember. At any rate, a woman at a cocktail party in San Francisco saw her stolen bracelet on a guest. It was easy to spot, she'd designed it. Intertwining gold serpents with emerald eyes. The police were called. It was all very discreet of course; this party was on Nob Hill. They questioned the woman with the bracelet in the butler's pantry. She told them it had been a gift from an old friend. Needless to say, it was traced to my father. The bracelet had ended up as part of loot taken from a drug bust. The officers who made the bust were my uncles. They helped themselves to jewelry now and then, passed it on to my father, and he fenced the pieces and split the proceeds."

"Who was the woman?"

Molly looked away, then shook her head. "I don't know. I never found out. Now that I think about it, the details were pretty sketchy. The department was anxious to keep it hush-hush. All I remember is my father admitted to everything, and before I knew it, he was in prison. The shock and the pain was more than I could bear. I adored my father. It took years for me to . . . well, if it hadn't been for Max, I'd have been on the street."

"I understand. You don't have to—"

"No . . . it's okay. I guess you're used to this kind of thing."

Filling their cups, Randall said, "I was a big shot at Internal Affairs in L.A., and I never got used to cops turning. It happens more than people think. In your father's case, I guess his bitterness turned to payback. I don't know about your uncles."

"Guess you've had a pretty good picture of my life."

Avoiding her eyes, he nodded. "I had to. You knew I would." Checking his watch, he said, "Look, tomorrow's another day. I've got a lot to think about now. What say we secure these doors and wrap this up." Rising, he hitched up his slacks and helped her move the sofa against the French doors in the living room. Chairs were placed under the door handle in the bedroom and front doors. "That should do it. Got anything downstairs that might work for a spoiled brat at Stanford who brags to her old man she used to play tennis with Chelsea?"

"Let's take a look."

Finally settling on a small oil painting, Randall smiled at the price tag. "A bargain, I'd say. This looks like turn-of-the-century Lake Tahoe."

"Turn it over," Molly suggested. "Once again, you seem to know your stuff."

Randall grinned. "I already did."

Giving him the superspecial gift wrap, she handed him the package. "Since you already seem to be on top of an-

tique lingo, I won't insult you then by telling you this is
not called an oil painting. To those who know, as I am
certain you do, it's called a picture. However, just in case
that aspect of the biz was not one of your specialties, I
thought I'd mention it."

"I'll pass that on to my daughter." Heading out the
door, he said. "Just in case she doesn't know." Turning
back for a moment, he added, "First thing tomorrow?"

"New locks, alarm system, and call Cleo. Then call
you to meet for strategy."

Giving her his squinty-eyed look, he nodded. "You'll
do."

*T*rue to her word, Molly called a locksmith, and then Max to order the alarm system. She got his answering machine and left a message.

Next call was to Cleo. They had departed friends, vowing to keep in touch as they'd laughed over past adventures and an uncertain future. "Darling!" Cleo's hoarse voice rang out. "I'm so glad you called. I was going to give you two more weeks, then I was going to call you. We've been close for too long to let Derek keep us apart."

Molly laughed. "You are irreplaceable! Oh, how I miss you. You sound horrible."

"Blame it on London weather. But, oh, what a charming evening I had. The cold was worth it."

Molly could almost envision Cleo in her flat lounging on plump, lace-edged pillows, a cashmere robe casually draped at the foot of the bed, and velvet embroidered slippers tucked neatly by her night table. A stack of the latest art books would be teetering next to her favorite tortoiseshell-and-silver clock. Five-eleven and reed thin, Cleo's tawny Jamaican elegance could have made her one of the world's top models. Her love of art, and her almost encyclopedic knowledge, led her instead to Sotheby's, where she became one of their resident experts. Under her tutelage, Molly learned how to dress, how to look and act Park Avenue, how to charm the Asian and European high-rolling collectors, and more, how to do it with élan.

On the telephone for nearly an hour, Molly related her weeks in Carmel, then laughed as Cleo told her about the crew at Sotheby's. "They are a unique group, let me tell you. But then, you know the Brits. Anything exotic and irreverent is a breath of air to these poor sods."

"Oh, to be a fly on the wall." Molly laughed. Finally, she said, "I need your help."

"Is it Derek again? I hear he and his paramour are in Lisbon."

"Lisbon? That could only mean one thing," Molly said.

"Exactly. They'll be at it again before long. They just better keep out of England. I'll fry Derek's prick until his balls sizzle."

Molly couldn't keep back the laughter. For all her silky smoothness, Cleo could swear with the best. She used to keep the men in the back room at Sotheby's in stitches. "No, it's not Derek or Greta. But God help them if they run into you. Here's the problem . . ."

The lengthy shopping list Molly gave her made Cleo laugh. "Oh, but darling, this is child's play. I'll have it all together in a few days. Will a fax do?"

"Perfect," Molly said. "Then you agree, Toby is a lightweight?"

"Absolutely. Ina Hubble and Rowena Webster do not ring a bell. Not even a tiny chime. But not to worry. You'll have it all . . . down to what they ate for breakfast, who they fucked, who they turned down, and what they drank."

After spending the morning at the station, Randall walked across the street to his condo for lunch. He had a lot on his mind, and cooking cleared out the cobwebs. He'd called his old narc buddies in San Francisco and got the full jacket this time on Molly's father. It pissed him off to think a man that dedicated had been dumped like a can of garbage. Desk jobs were always around for good cops hurt in the line of duty. He must have made a few too many enemies in City Hall. Ignoring the unpacked boxes, in the living room, he headed for the compact, but well-appointed galley kitchen wide enough to house an island chop block. He'd had little time to set up house, but he made sure the kitchen was stocked. Examining the hanging iron pot rack over the small Wolf stove for his favorite omelet pan, he realized he was out of eggs. The condo had been half a million, not expensive for Carmel, but he meant to stay here until the end, and in that sense, it had been a bargain. His expenses were minimal. He'd collected all the furniture he wanted, and his only other vices were toy trains and Cuban cigars. Between his retirement pay, the Carmel salary and the profitable restaurant in San Francisco, it was easily affordable. He knew he could never live in The City again. It wasn't the same. All the characters were gone. Of course, he'd found out they were gone in Carmel, too—died off or run out by IPO punks driving property values higher than ever. Carmel was never cheap, but it was reaching madness.

The job was supposed to be a breeze. With nearly 60 percent of Carmel residents being weekend owners now, crime was a joke. The jewelry stores had been taking a hit the past few years. He was almost glad he had something to sink his teeth into. Except for Bea. If he'd had a network, and more investigators, her death might have been avoided.

Leaning against the granite counter, he stared at the black-and-white mosaic-tiled backsplash. He decided to move his murder book to the condo. For all intents and purposes, the case was closed. He didn't need to have curious eyes at the station wonder why it was still out, or see the coroner's report on Bea. The killer must have thought no one would notice the bruise on her neck. Stopping the blood flow to the carotid arteries was all it took to knock her out before killing her. The way he and the pathologist figured it, the killer then stood behind Bea, put the gun in her hand, and pulled the trigger. The killer would've needed to be well protected from the blood splatter, but that was easy. A towel would do the trick. Forensics had very little for him. Too many shoppers made it almost impossible to focus on anything. Nailing the killer, however, was a given. He hadn't lost his homicide touch. Chasing dirty cops only used half his brain; now he could put the whole thing to work again.

He also needed to get his boxes unpacked and make room for the new setup. Checking his watch, he heard his stomach grumble. He was to meet Molly at the shop in a little more than an hour. Bad idea. Being seen together was out. They were in real time now. Punching in the number to her shop, he set up a meeting at Daria's for seven. "We'll use her back room again. When you leave, go down your back stairs, through the courtyard, and out onto Dolores. Go right, up to Ocean, and head up to Sixth. Make another right and you'll see an alley between two shops. That will take you to Daria's delivery door. Walk right in through the kitchen and ask for Manuel. He'll call Daria. Don't worry about him, he's been with her for years." Once that was settled, he called Daria and told her to expect Molly.

Fixing a quick sandwich, he mulled over the recent discoveries in Bea's files. Her lease with Max Roman was only a year old, signed just a few months before Sid

Wells died. She'd paid no key money, a miracle in itself considering Carmel commercial spaces were at a premium, and it wasn't unheard of for landlords to rake in five figures just for the privilege of signing an exorbitant lease. He wondered how the hell most of the shopkeepers were making it. Bea's rent, however, was only two thousand per month. That bought a kiosk here, if you could find one. The fact that she made a five-grand deposit in her checking account two days after she signed the lease, and previously worked for Dick Jacobs, gave his brain some real lessons in gymnastics.

Randall's latest instructions set Molly's eye twitching. She tapped it gently and forced herself to calm down. He was right. It would look strange if he kept coming in the shop. Especially with Bitsy around Fridays and weekends, and dropping in throughout the week. They really shouldn't be seen together if she was going to help. Further thoughts were interrupted by the FedEx man. When he handed her the letter pack Max had said was on the way, she wanted to hug and kiss the poor guy. Tearing it open, she found not only her overdue checks, but this week's, and another check for five hundred dollars. The short note from Max was sweet and dear. The extra money was hazard pay. Having to deal with Pablo, he'd hastily jotted, was more than she needed just now. He would be out of town for a few days, he'd added, and wanted her to meet him at Sanford's on Sunday. It was going to be, he'd put in quotes, an auction right up her alley. Sanford's was the premier auction house on the West Coast, and Molly could already feel the tingle of excitement. He'd meet her there at nine sharp, and reminded her to bring the shop's checkbook.

Waving the bonus check in the air, Molly grinned. She

only hoped the El Camino would make it to The City and back. She hadn't been to Sanford's in years, and was suddenly looking forward to getting out of Carmel, if only for the day. When she saw a young couple enter, she stashed the checks in the desk, and smiled. "If I can be of help, let me know. Otherwise, I'll leave you to browse." Pretending to ignore them, she watched them out of the corner of her eye as they split up and wandered slowly through the shop. Well dressed, or not, they could be thieves. She'd had to fill the gaps left from her sale to Daria with an assortment of smalls that could easily be shoved into a bag or pocket.

Moving over to the center table that held the last arrangement Bea had made, Molly picked up a few more rose petals and sighed. Gently smoothing the petals in her hand, she felt her eyes water. If she had any qualms about the plan she was going to propose to Randall, these petals gave her the courage. She knew she was in for a battle, but in the end, he'd have to agree. Moving back to the desk, she emptied the paper clip box and placed all the petals in an envelope in the top drawer.

By the time the couple walked the room, they were ready to buy. With great glee, and no super sales pitch, they bought two small tea tables, the Eastlake chair by the potted palm, and a pair of English barley-twist candlesticks. She loved customers like this. They knew what they wanted, and she hadn't had to interfere. Gracefully helping them set out their new treasures on the sidewalk, Molly chatted with the wife while her husband went for their van. The crap furniture was finally moving. Looking around, she nodded. It never failed. Bring in good merch, and you can sell off the junk in no time.

It was turning out to be a great day. A supersale, a bonus, and new locks with everything on a master key that only she had. When she caught Max before he left for his trip, he said to order an alarm system and have the bill sent to him. He was near tears over Bea. She hadn't realized he'd known her that well. His anger with Pablo over her checks was another eye opener. After asking her to give him some slack, she was surprised at his temper tantrum. He said he was going to wring Pablo's neck. That should be a Kodak moment.

━ *23* ━

"*A*re you out of your mind?" Randall's face was almost blotchy. "I've heard some pretty stupid ideas in my time, but this one is—"

"Hey! That's what you thought was going on when I was a suspect."

Uncorking a bottle of wine, Randall said, "You never were a suspect."

"Bullshit!"

Looking up, he said, "Watch your mouth. I knew you were clean with this. I just—"

"You just what?" She laughed in his face. "Wanted to rattle my cage?"

He laughed with her. "I just wanted someone to spar with, okay?" Filling their glasses, he winked at Daria. "You wouldn't happen to have—"

"It's on the way." Smiling at Molly, she said, "Deep-fried zucchini."

"You *are* joining us?" Molly asked.

"I'll be in and out. I've got a big party coming in. High-rolling golf nuts from Canada. They've been playing Pebble all day, so I can imagine the wine will be flowing along with the bragging. Groups like that need personal attention. I do have some news for you, though." At the door, she winked. "See you in a few."

Molly knew she had an uphill battle with Randall. She decided to play it a little slower. "By the way, I'd like to give you those watercolors and the journal. I don't feel comfortable having them around."

Still angry at her idea, he pretended to look over the menu. Nodding, he said, "Yeah, sure, good idea."

"I've got to go to The City on Sunday. Max wants me to meet him at Sanford's."

Still looking over the menu, he mumbled, "Great. Have fun."

Opening her menu with a flourish, Molly realized this game could go on for hours. "Okay, be stubborn. You know it would work."

"I'm thinking about veal Parmigana, what about you?"

With the large menu covering her face, she said, "Pasta Putanesca sounds good."

"It's a close second to mine, but you'll love it." He watched her set the menu down, then reach in her tote and pull out her cigarettes and ever-ready Zippo. "Nice of Daria to let us smoke in here, don't you think?"

"Wonderful." She smiled politely.

"It's out of the question. I won't have you on my prayer list."

"You have one? I've got one, too. I haven't added you, though. Should I? I mean, if you don't break this case—"

"Dammit, Molly! If you think I'm going to let you waltz into Rhonda Martyn's gallery, you're not playing with a full deck."

As she leaned into the table, her eyes were sparking. "I can do it! Who better than me to offer an artist new to her collection?"

"No."

"Hear me out. First off, somebody, either Lorna or Dick, and if my hunch is right, Pablo, too, is faking dead

artists. Now, maybe . . . just maybe, Lorna was one of the
artists and she wanted more money, or she wanted out.
She's knocked off, and that leaves Pablo and Dick. I
haven't figured out where Bea comes into all this, but
maybe she knew about the scam and wanted in, or out. At
any rate, they might be minus an artist, or in the market
for another."

"You're reaching here." He knew she was close, but he
didn't want her puffing up with success. "Suppose it went
down that way. Where the hell are you going to come up
with an artist?"

"Armand! He's the best! He can match any style, any
artist from the sixteenth century to Grandma Moses!"

Almost head-to-head across the table, Randall said
softly, "No."

Molly wanted to smack him. Controlling her voice, she
said, "You'll never get her then."

"You're sure she's the one, and not Dick Jacobs. Why?"

Settling back in her chair, she felt she'd won some
ground at last. "Gut feeling. When I met her that night
with Bitsy at the La Playa, I could smell ambition on her.
Bitsy said she was a wanna-be, but she didn't have to.
The energy coming from Martyn was incredible. Dick Jacobs is a wuss. Easily led. All you have to do is shake
hands with the guy. Wet rag."

Randall played with the bread basket, turning it every
which way. Finally selecting the perfect piece, he
slathered on soft butter, mounding it carefully and filling
each corner. "I can't authorize some crazy Cajun to paint
fakes, Molly. I could get my ass burned from here to
Sunday."

"This is no different from those stings you cops are always pulling off. How about narcs posing as dealers?"

"That's different."

"Baloney."

Before he could answer, his cell phone rang. Molly watched his face turn from annoyance to surprise, then a cold anger. The tightening of his jaw made her quickly reach for another cigarette. When he slowly put the phone back in his jacket and pushed away from the table, she didn't dare speak. She watched him play with the half-eaten bread, then rise. "Dick Jacobs just took a header off a cliff down by Big Sur. Sheriff's Patrol found the car parked at one of those vista spots. Both doors were open, so he checked it out. Found the note on the driver's seat addressed to me." Looking away for a moment, he added, "Something about being despondent over his wife's death."

"Oh, my God!" Taking a deep breath, she said, "I don't buy it. Not for one minute."

Randall nodded. "Neither do I. Get hold of your Armand. Tell him the truth, tell him what you need, then have him call me."

Daria returned with the deep-fried zucchini just as he was about to leave. Seeing Randall almost at the door, she said, "What? The bread's not fresh enough? No, it's the butter, not soft enough. I thought so. I told Manuel . . ."

Randall gave her a brief smile. "I gotta run."

"You want a take out bag for the road?"

Checking his watch, he said, "Don't wait up." Looking at Molly, he thought for a moment, then said, "On second thought, it's the sheriff's jurisdiction. I won't be long. Can you stick around? We're on the bubble now."

"You couldn't pry me out of here. I'll call Angela and Armand while you're gone."

"The sooner, the better. Bring Daria up to speed while I'm gone."

By the time Molly filled Daria in, finished her pasta, and drained two glasses of wine, she was ready to burst. "And now Dick Jacobs." She shook her head, then quickly crossed herself, "We've got to stop Rhonda."

"Hey, let's not have a *mea culpa* here," Daria said. "This isn't your fault. How could you possibly know?"

"I had a feeling, and I didn't act quick enough. I mean, I didn't really *know*. I just felt something was wrong. It was like hearing a song on the radio for the first time, only you know you've heard it before. Not déjà vu stuff, but—"

"I understand, Molly. Believe me, I do. Nevertheless, there's no way you could have prevented any of this. Even if you'd given Randall those watercolors right away, he wouldn't have known what it all meant. Besides which, they wouldn't have proved a thing. It would be like doing a crossword with half the page missing."

"I know . . . but—"

"No buts! Look, try your cousin again while I get coffee and dessert."

"Just coffee. I can't eat another thing. I've been living on frozen food so long, my stomach is rebelling."

Molly watched Daria leave and wondered why Bitsy was so down on her. It had to be jealousy. She thought her first impression of Daria was sound. Besides, if Randall trusted her enough to let her know what was going on, that was good enough for her. Waiting for Angela to answer, Molly tried not to think about Dick Jacobs. What had Daria said? *Mea culpa? Yes,* she thought, *by my fault.* But, she reminded herself, she was right in saying that even if she had given Randall everything earlier, it wouldn't have made much sense then.

When Armand finally answered, Molly wasted little time in pleasantries and catch-up. Careful not to mention the homicides, she only told him she was cooperating with the local police on an art scam. "Yes, Armand, they know about New York, and that I wasn't a part of it. That's why they want me to help. It's my art background they need. Yes, I told them you were absolutely legitimate, and that you were the finest copyist in the country." Pulling the phone from her ear as he spent a long moment reminding her whom he could copy, she finally broke in. "I'm not sure who I want you to do, I just need to know you'll help."

Armand's silky Cajun soft drawl was almost gooey by then. "But of course, *chère*, I will do this thing for you. What fun it is to be needed by the *gendarme*! I will not be cheap, however. You tell this Randall that, *oui*?"

"Of course. But, Armand go easy, okay? This is important for me." She gave him Randall's telephone number and reminded him twice to call. With promises of rock-bottom prices and work even the finest experts in the world would have trouble with, Molly exchanged telephone kisses and promised to call Angela soon.

It was ten before Daria had another chance to sit with Molly. "Manuel will take over now. I've had it." She smiled as she sank into a chair. "My feet are killing me today. Twelve-hour days are par for the course, but I think age is creeping up and shouting in my ear." Seeing the look on Molly's face, Daria laughed. "Hey, I'll be forty-eight this year. I've been doing this for twenty-two years. It catches up."

Molly was astounded. "You haven't a wrinkle on your face!"

"Good genes. It's an Italian thing."

"Olive oil and garlic," Randall said. "Best medicine around."

Pulling up a chair, he joined them. Daria was already

standing. "I'll get your dinner." Pausing, she added, "A bottle of Jack might be handy. I'll see if I can find one."

Lighting a cigarette, he said, "Is she one in a million, or what?"

"At last we can agree on something. I got hold of Armand. He's agreed to help. He'll call you tomorrow. What about Dick Jacobs? Did you tell the Sheriff's Department your suspicions?"

"Nope. Not time yet. Let them do their thing. I don't want any leaks on this. I'll get my ass kicked later, but so what." Giving her his special squinty-eyed look, he suddenly said, "Hey, you're beginning to sound like a partner. I'm the cop, here, not you."

As Molly was about to comment, Daria arrived with Randall's dinner. Molly decided to let the man eat in peace. For the moment anyway.

Finally pushing his plate away, Randall said, "Excellent. I couldn't have done a better job."

Rolling her eyes, Daria said, "Gosh, thanks."

"Here's where we are. Dick Jacobs is, for all intents and purposes, a bona fide suicide. Despondent over his wife's death, he couldn't find a way to carry on, blah, blah, blah. Forensics is going to have one hell of a time finding anything, if they even bother to look. That's assuming, of course, they take his note as gospel. I sort of leaned in that direction, so maybe they may just go through the motions. By the time they got his body off the rocks, the poor man was so cut up and bruised . . ." Seeing Molly's face turn white, he said, "Well, anyway, they'll do the autopsy, then file it. Okay, Daria, you've got the floor. What have you got for me?"

Kicking off her shoes, she rubbed an ankle, then said, "Dick Jacobs and Rhonda Martyn have been an item for some time. Maybe two years. Manuel's cousin does housework for a Mrs. Langley, who happens to live next door to Lorna and Dick. She overheard Mrs. Langley tell her husband about the shouting match Dick and Lorna had the night before she was killed." When she saw the look on Randall's face, she asked, "They didn't come forward with that?"

"Nada."

"Well, I'm not surprised. Anyway, she told her husband she kept hearing Lorna say she wanted out."

Slapping the table with her hand, Molly said, "See? What did I tell you?"

Ignoring her, Randall motioned Daria to go on. "That was all she could make out. Next item," Daria continued. "Pablo and Rhonda had a little tussle in Dick's shop the other day. One of my steady lunch ladies was in and couldn't wait to tell me about it. A born gossip, I guess I was the handiest to blab to. She'd been in to see about some framing, and she could hear loud voices in the back workroom. She was close enough to hear Pablo giving Rhonda hell. She knew Pablo from when he worked for Sid, and being an art patron of sorts, she knew who Rhonda was."

Almost preening with I-told-you-so's, Molly nevertheless kept quiet. She watched Randall digest this latest news, then finally asked, "Do you know how long Pablo worked for Sid?"

Daria thought for a moment. "I'd say he was around for at least two, maybe three years. In fact, he worked as a waiter for me for a few months when he first got to town. Came from L.A., I think. No, Reno. I remember now, he gave Harrah's as a job reference."

Drumming his fingers on the table, Randall remained silent for so long, Molly and Daria began to exchange questioning looks. Finally, he said to Molly, "Bitsy's due in to work tomorrow, right?" When Molly nodded, he said, "She'll probably know about Dick. It will hit the eleven o'clock news tonight. Act surprised, okay? But, that's all. Let her talk all she wants. Stick around the shop for about an hour, then split. I don't want you to have to make small talk with her. Stay away on Saturday as much as you can. Come in late. By then, she'll be bursting to talk about it. Might even have some interesting tidbits to drop. You're going to The City on Sunday, right?" Before she could reply, he quickly said, "You'll have to give her your key on Saturday. Don't sweat it . . . you can rekey on Monday if you're queasy about it."

"I won't be back until late. How will I get in?"

"Have her drop it here," Daria said, then snickered. "That should be a laugh. We're not what one would consider close." Eyeing Randall, she turned to Molly. "Bitsy and my former mother-in-law were tight. Enough said?"

⚊ 24 ⚊

On her way to San Francisco Sunday morning, with Randall's minimap to guide her through the maze of changes made since she'd left nine years earlier, Molly replayed Saturday with Bitsy. True to Randall's word, Bitsy arrived in a flurry of drama. "Oh, that poor, poor darling of a man! I can't believe he'd do such a thing! It wasn't the perfect marriage . . . we all knew that, but to . . . to end it like that is just dreadful."

"There is no perfect marriage," Molly remembered saying. She also remembered quickly adding, "Well, I'm no judge. But he must have loved her."

Watching Bitsy wander the shop, moving a vase an inch here, a figurine on a stack of books there, she wondered how long she could stand still and not scream at her to leave things alone. "Well, it's really a sad ending." Bitsy finally managed. Grabbing her tote, Molly headed for the door. "I won't be long, just a few errands. Have fun!"

Have fun? In the short hour she'd been gone, the prima donna sold over four thousand bucks' worth of furniture. Fighting elation and the urge to wring Bitsy's neck, Molly was in a mood by the time she closed up.

Checking Randall's clear printing on the map kept confusion to a minimum. She was nearly in shock when she saw how huge San Jose had become. You had to be living in the Gobi Desert not to know it was the hub of Silicon Valley, but Molly remembered San Jose as a dusty, sleepy town in the middle of olive groves, and plum orchards. It was hard to take her eyes off the sprawl it had become. The spurts of intimidating drivers, even on a Sunday morning, were more than she'd bargained for. Speed limits in California, she decided, were totally ignored. She cringed when she saw the speedometer frequently hit eighty. Relying on cabs for so long, she knew her driving skills were a little rusty, but these people here were really nuts.

As she drew closer to The City, she shuddered thinking about yesterday. Having no clear idea when Cleo's faxes would come in, she'd quickly finished her errands, then spent most of the morning running up and down the stairs from the apartment checking the machine. When Bitsy offered to keep an eye peeled for them, Molly quickly told her not to bother. "Anything I should know about?" she'd asked. Molly told her it was research on ivory miniature pictures for an out-of-town client she'd had earlier in the week. It was almost noon before they started to arrive. When the first one started to pop out, Molly was halfway up the stairs. Thankfully, Bitsy was busy with a customer. Rushing to the machine, Molly sat at the desk pretending to update the weekly report to Pablo she'd send next week. No longer feeling obligated to cringe under his whip, she decided to play with his head and send them a day or two late from then on. She was, however, not anxious for the confrontation she expected when Pablo realized he couldn't get into the garage without her key.

By the time the fax was finished spitting out papers all

over the floor, Molly had almost twenty pages. *Bless Cleo*, she thought. *As usual, I owe her.* She spent most of the afternoon poring over the information Cleo had gathered. She couldn't wait to show it to Randall. His daughter was due in that day, and they'd planned to meet the next night at Daria's.

When she arrived at Sanford's, she had ten minutes to spare before meeting Max. The Upper Market Street location where Sanford's had reigned for years was seedier than she remembered. Parking, even on Sunday morning, was at a premium. Her luck held out when she spotted a car in front pulling out. After Christie's and Sotheby's, Sanford's was the third largest auction house in the country. Sanford's Annex, where she was to meet Max, had been generally used for run-of-the-mill and low-range items. Max told her the Annex had been retired, but was open today because of a specialized preview at it's more prestigious location around the corner, the Main Gallery. The Main Gallery, Molly remembered, was a little more civilized. The Annex was a cavernous warehouse with cement floors and soaring ceilings. Freezing in the winter and stifling on a warm day.

Max had been careful to warn her not to remember the old days when steals were the soup of the day, and the majority of the crowd was dealers. Scoring deals now was blind ass luck. Most of the buyers were caught up in auction mania, and prices were frequently past markup range. Every now and then, Max said, he could steal a few things, but not like before. However, he'd added, one never knew and the thrill of the chase was still alive. Auctions were, after all, a crapshoot. Molly could feel the excitement of the chase as she locked the El Camino. The tingle racing up and down her spine was a sure sign. With

half the country into auctions, flea markets, and antique
shows these days, and judging by the number of cars, she
wouldn't be surprised if she went home empty handed.

Standing outside the entrance, and stylishly dressed as
always, Max was holding court with a small group of
men. He was tall, and slightly pudgy, and his snow-white
hair, tousled just enough to look rakish, was nearly glis-
tening. It was hard to believe he was creeping past seventy. In his professional uniform—navy cashmere blazer,
checkered shirt, bow tie, tan wool slacks, and custom-
made London loafers—he took care to tell the world he
was successful, and a man of taste. Max was an anachro-
nism; many dealers dressed down at auctions hoping to
be inconspicuous to the public, and, as strange as it might
seem, to other dealers. The rationale, however, was
twofold. If the public knew you were a dealer, they often
tried to eavesdrop, sneak a look at the notes on your catalog, and attempt to judge the value of items you planned
to bid on. For dealers, the message was, business is slow,
or I'm not a threat. The big giveaway was spending too
much time examining a piece. Too much interest meant
the estimates in the catalog were off, and maybe the item
was a sleeper. Or, interest was so great the cost be
damned. Previewing at auctions was an art, and Max had
taught Molly well.

The men with Max—mostly in their mid thirties—
were also well groomed, and were probably dealer or
decorator cronies. Despite the petty jealousies, the ram-
pant and often outrageous gossip mill they kept alive with
every breath they took, antique dealers and decorators,
were cousins in crime, and a close-knit club that rarely
admitted outsiders. Relishing a day amongst her own,
Molly felt her eyes take on a shine. Oh, but it was a great
business! And, no matter what, she wouldn't trade it for

the moon. Giving the small group a quick look, Molly knew they were hardly hangers on. One or two, she quickly judged, might be neophytes, cultivating Max as a possible angel for future buys. It was hard to tell. Max, she knew, financed buys for more than one handsome and talented young dealer. She could think of at least a half dozen well-known dealers he helped claw his way to the top. The rest, she knew, were the real McCoy. Probably the best and brightest The City had to offer. High-end dealers knew their tribe. It was a look, a stance, a manner, but most of all, it was style. Besides, Max didn't associate with losers or wanna-bes. Pablo, she realized, must be an aberration. Max's circle consisted of the cream of the crop. They spoke the same language, knew the same people, and could tell tales to rival Liz Smith.

Certain she didn't know this small group, she sighed with relief. It would be easier being Molly Doyle from Carmel, than a shamefaced Elizabeth Porter from Manhattan. While they probably wouldn't recognize her, they would certainly know of the scandal. That thought halted her in the middle of the street. What if one of them did recognize her? What then? Cower, lower her eyes, or look at him straight on and stare him down? She was beginning to think this trip was a bad idea. Max hadn't seen her yet. Maybe she should turn around and go home. She could call him on the cell and tell him she had the flu.

In a nanosecond, good ole Irish genes kicked in. Squaring her shoulders, she nodded to herself. *Screw them.* She had nothing to be ashamed of. Pasting a big smile on her face, she headed straight for Max. Her fears were unfounded. There wasn't the slightest sign of recognition. After a round of introductions, Max took Molly by the arm, and waved. "Time to split up, boys. We'll meet here after the auction." Leading her on, he paused, then called over his shoulder, "Don't forget lot 94! That's mine, you devils!"

"Are we pooling today?" Molly asked. "Or are you just calling your lots?"

"Molly, hush! You know pooling is illegal," Max said with utmost sincerity.

"Sure. Since when has anyone paid attention?"

"Honey, we're *known* here. You know that! Sanford's would spot that in a minute. I just want lot 94, that's all."

Molly didn't believe him for one minute. Pooling was an ancient tradition, and still widely used by dealers. An old trick, and Max was a master. All over the world, dealers would get together, select a group bidder, and establish top prices for lots by mutual consent. Then, they would sit back and hope to hell the group leader scored. The object was, to avoid bidding against each other and driving prices up, and to send a signal to the civilian audience that certain items held little interest. The fewer people bidding on a lot, the less the feeding frenzy. Get twenty hands raised on a lot, and *voilà!* Prices went over the top. Actually, Molly always thought it was brilliant crowd control and consumer psychology. When the auction was over, they'd meet, usually at a safe bar, conduct their own private auction, and hopefully walk away still friends.

Holding her elbow, he leaned in close. "Here's an extra catalog. I've marked a few items you should have for the shop. Since Clint and his cronies bought most of Pebble Beach, I'm anticipating some very big names flitting through town soon. I want the shop upgraded as soon as possible. You've only an hour before show time, so, darling, try not to let the boys see you eyeball." Seeing the look of surprise on her face, he laughed. "Oh, yes, I know how good you are. Just don't underestimate them, that's all. A few of them are new to my crowd, and I'm keeping an eye on them." Gesturing toward the area around them, he said, "The layout is not the same as when you came with me in the old days. To our right, is the better quality stuff. Facing this exalted section, are several glass cases holding comparable decorative accessories: china, silver, ivory, bronzes, and porcelain figures. The side and back walls are covered with an amazing range of art."

Molly was already taking it all in. Nodding in time with his tour guide drone, she scanned the area for herself. Anxious to be on her own, she was impatient to see everything. The tingling was driving her nuts. "Behind the better crap," he drawled, "is the real junk. Odds and ends from the sixties and on. Pure dreck." Tapping his nose, he said, "However, one never knows what I might have missed."

"I doubt it," Molly responded. "But I'll take a look."

"Oh, do! I've salvaged some marvelous funk from there and made a mint. Oh, I could tell you tales! Now, if you go straight down this aisle, the smalls room is on your left. Not much this time, but you be the judge."

"What's our plan of attack?"

"Take a gander at what I circled, make your own marks, then meet me at the espresso bar. We'll ponder together and decide who will bid on what. When the auction starts, I'll sit in front, you take the back. I don't want the boys to think we're close. Just boss and manager, okay? They get so jealous at times, I want to scream."

"What if we want the same pieces? Who gets first dibs?"

Checking his watch, Max muttered, "We haven't much time, darling."

Molly held her grin. *So, that's how we're playing,* she thought. *A few months ago, he'd have to fight me to the wall for a piece.* "I might find something suitable for the apartment. A few rugs and maybe some decent furniture." She said over her shoulder, "Those cold floors are a bitch, and the springs have sprung on the sofa."

Giving her an air kiss, he said, "Of course, my love. How thoughtless of me. We'll steal a few things, I'm sure."

Pulling him back, she asked, "What about the Main Gallery? Anything over there?"

"Molly! Please, scoot along! It's full of trains! Can you believe it? Toy trains!"

Molly's eyes lit up. "Really? I've . . . I've got a customer asking about them."

Looking around to see if anyone he knew was nearby, he scolded, "Darling, don't let anyone hear you. I mean, trains?"

"I'll check it out later."

"Not with me," Max said rolling his eyes.

Molly wandered off smiling. Dear Max. Image was all. Deciding to take a look for Randall after the auction, she finally began her stroll. Eyeing the icy and foggy gray concrete floors, she saw they were haphazardly covered with scores of Oriental, Persian, and Chinese rugs in every color and condition. Some were terrific, but many were worn, soiled, and frayed. She marked two lots for the apartment. Glancing up, she could see dozens of light fixtures, hanging from rafters just below the soaring metal roof, a few absolutely grand, but most grotesque. Leaving the glass cases for last, she headed for the furniture. The art, she quickly saw, was weak. Old world scenes in chipped and broken gold frames kept company with some of the most god-awful abstract junk she'd ever seen.

She soon marked a half dozen items that might be

worth taking on. Stopping before a petite lady's secretary, she pulled out a drawer, checked the dovetails and was surprised to find them irregular and obviously hand-cut. There was just about the right amount of wear on the side panels to make her interested. She quickly dated the piece to the early nineteenth century, just before the onset of machine-made furniture in midcentury. Stepping back, she carefully examined the case. One side was blistered. Sunburn . . . must have stood next to a window for years. The finish needed work, but it was intact and original. The bookcase top fit the lower desk case perfectly. This, she was happy to see, wasn't a marriage. The practice of fitting two similar pieces together to pass off as a whole, was not uncommon. The legs were in fair shape, and she'd bet they were hand-turned. Opening the glass doors on the bookcase, she held one at an angle to see if the glass was replaced, or wavy as the original should be. The leather writing pad was hashed. It would have to be replaced. West Coast wanted perfect. It would be honored back East for its age and sense of history. Also, the key was missing. *Great*, she thought. *Another one.*

Quickly managing the examination in only a few minutes, she shrugged as if disinterested, then walked away. At an overcarved Victorian sideboard, Molly used the top to circle the lot number, then drew a box and wrote the number 5. Next to that, she drew a larger box, and wrote 15—2. Her private code to remind her she'd go five hundred for the desk. After getting it in shape, she would tag it for fifteen hundred to two thousand. In less than a half hour, she'd listed ten lots. The secretary, two Louis-XVI-style chairs with lovely carved arms and caned backs, but missing cushions, a graceful Queen-Anne-style tea table with a cigar burn smack in the middle, an old Chinese tin tea canister that would make a great lamp, two English soup tureens in luscious deep blue and white, an Edwardian glass-topped display table she could use for small items and jewelry, and a pair of water-damaged window seat benches that would be smashing next to the fireplace in the shop. Though many of the pieces were "of the style," they would end up, after hours of work and effort, handsome and respectable merch. Adding up her boxes, she came up with three thousand, not including the buyer's premium of fifteen percent. Too many people forgot to add the auction house sales commission when they walked up to the window to pay. Her larger squares totaled, on the low end, eleven thousand, and the high was a delirious nineteen thousand. Ten percent of that helped the New Orleans fund very nicely.

On her way back to Max, she took a few more minutes to eyeball the crowd. What kind of species was this? She knew her crowd in New York. Besides the usual dealers and decorators, it had been mostly tire kickers, wealthy bored women looking for an odd piece or two, the rabid collector, the upwardly mobile executives searching for a statement piece, and the newly rich computer and Internet moguls wanting instant class. This crowd was alien to her.

Learning a long time ago not to judge a buyer by his or her looks or clothes, she had to mix common sense with past experiences. Dismissing the young couples there with children, pegging them to be on a budget, and perhaps looking for an odd table, or dresser for the nursery, she did not consider them serious bidders. Next, she watched the over-forty crowd: what they examined, how long they paused before an item, whether they handled it, turned it over, or discussed it. How often they made notes in their catalog, and how many were together. This group was usually trouble. She hated them with a passion. They fell into two categories; those with spendable income intent on upgrading, or dealers. Next, she focused on the Asians. A good percentage of the crowd, they seemed more interested in the French-style furniture and the large assortment of ivory and bronzes in the glass cases. The next group, and possibly the most dangerous, besides dyed-in-the-wool collectors, was the gay contingent, which seemed to be the largest present. Seldom alone, and usually paired, she found them mostly interested in anything English or French. Stylish, adventuresome, and daring, they unerringly managed to spot the best pieces. Able to pull together any number of styles and make a room sing, Molly knew she'd have trouble with the secretary and maybe the two benches.

Then there were the collectors. She'd spotted five or six right away. The nemesis of every dealer at auction. In a shop, they were treated like monarchs. At auction, they were loathed, and watched like potential shoplifters. Such beings were rabid. They would drive bids beyond the pale, hanging on like mad dogs with a bone. They had been known to ruin their marriage, mortgage themselves silly, steal, cheat, and rob kids' college funds, all because of the fanatical need to possess the object of their personal mania. "Greater love hath no man," she once heard an angry wife say, "than his collection." It was better than sex, she'd told her sympathetic listener.

But, oh, how Molly loved collectors. They were such easy prey.

Bent over their catalogs, Max began rattling off lot numbers that held his interest. When he gave her the lot number for the secretary, she shook her head. "Boring. It doesn't fall into the three *N*s. Not good, not better, not best. Needs too much work. I'd pass."

"Really? I rather thought it was sweet. It does need
TLC, but my man can easily remedy that. Oh, I'm disappointed."

"Go for it anyway," a voice said from behind. "She
only wants it for herself."

Molly looked up to see Pablo sneering at her. Every
four-letter word and combination she had in her New
York repertoire was ready to roll off her tongue. With exceptional control, she said. "Gosh, what a surprise. I
thought you were on vacation."

Ignoring her, he pulled up a chair. Looking at Max, he
said, "Charles is watching the shop. We had two fantastic
sales this morning. The Coromandel screen and the
George II tallboy are history." Giving Molly a sideways
glance, he continued grandly, "Twenty-two grand for half
an hour is—"

"You must be exhausted," Molly broke in. "With your
limited experience, I'd say that was high-anxiety time."

He would love to have slapped her. It was written all
over his face. With only a tiny huff, he said to Max, "I
don't feel like sitting around here all day, if you don't
mind." Getting up abruptly, he leaned down, whispered
something in Max's ear, then left.

"That was vile, Molly." Max giggled.

"Please! He asked for it."

"But you do want that sweet little secretary, don't
you!" Before she could lie, he laughed. "I always said
you had an exquisite eye. Of course, I helped you perfect
it, but nonetheless, it's true. I remember telling everyone
at our table the night of Ivana's wedding about you."

An inveterate name-dropper, Max sometimes got his
people a little confused. "I think it was Donna Karan at
last year's Armory show."

"Oh? Well, whatever. If you want the piece, go ahead."

"If I can grab it for five hundred, I will."

"Anything in this crazy business is possible. Okay, I think we're in accord on the rest of your marks. The limits you set are doable. You have my blessings." Glancing at his Rolex, which he kept in perpetual view, he handed her a bidder's card. "We'll meet back here when we've finished, pay for the loot, get someone to load you up, and hit the road. Let's go, darling, it's time to party."

As they headed for the rapidly filling seats, Max said, "Oh, I almost forgot. Stop by for drinks after. You and Pablo can have your own corner of the room."

Not wanting to seem ungracious, but unwilling to spend one minute around Pablo, she said, "Let's see how long this takes. I've got a long drive home, and I don't relish fighting these drivers in the dark."

While she searched for a decent seat in the back of the long rows of folding chairs, she wondered again if maybe Pablo or Bitsy had seen her the night they had dinner together. She'd told Randall they couldn't have, but she really wasn't that sure. Bitsy hadn't acted like they had, so maybe she was just overly nervous. Settling into her chair, she wondered how long she could stand the cold metal seat. As soon as the auctioneer reached his podium, all thoughts of discomfort and the Pablo and Bitsy show were gone. To Molly, an auction was the best and only show in town. Not a place for the faint of heart, the auction house is an energizing experience tailor made for pirates, robbers, gamblers, and cutthroats.

She particularly enjoyed getting a bead on auctioneers. They were a special breed. To be successful, one must be a born predator, adept at mesmerizing the crowd and keeping it in one's power. The best were those who could grab an audience with small bursts of humor and keep the crowd eager to buy. Many houses have two to three auctioneers working a sale. Each maintained a separate style and pace, purposely creating an imbalance that often threw the novice. The slower auctioneer, reminding Molly of turtles, draws out his words, pauses to check his list, stumbling occasionally on a word, lulls you, annoys you, makes you bored and drowsy, and ready to bid just to stay awake. The faster auctioneer, who rattles on with the speed of lightning, barely taking a breath, was Molly's favorite. Dubbing them rabbits, she loved the way they kept everyone alert and insecure, snapping off bids with such speed, you jump right in afraid you'll miss out, and frequently pay more than you'd planned. Oh, but it was a great show, and she could feel her juices flow just waiting for it to begin.

She wasn't disappointed. Opening the auction was a rabbit, and, she quickly noted, one of the best she'd seen in a long time. In his mid-to-late thirties, he was impeccably dressed in a dark suit, good tie. His slightly wavy black hair was short, and his eyes danced and bounced around the room like greased lightning. The first hour flew, and they'd gone through one hundred lots. Sixty per hour was the average. This guy was great! Marking the hammer price for each item, she'd study the catalog later to determine this market. It was imperative she learn the West Coast crowd; what they wanted, what they were willing to pay. This was war, and she had to know the enemy's strengths and weaknesses. At least one-third of the lots reached or passed retail. Thankfully, none of her choices had been a part of that group. She also kept an eye on Max. Shifting her bottom on the cheap seat, it was easy to follow the elegant flutter of his bidder card. The little devil had been busy bidding on items he failed to mention.

At the end of the second hour, she was dying for something to drink. Afraid she'd lose her seat in the standing-room-only crowd, she suffered in silence. Besides, some of the lots she'd marked were about to come up. It was past time for a turtle, and lo and behold, the auctioneers switched places. Mr. Turtle was older, probably in his sixties. A pro, no doubt, and conservatively dressed. After managing to take the French chairs, the tea tin, and the display case, she backed off on the Queen Anne table. Doubling what she'd marked, it was hard to keep a straight face. First lesson at auction, keep a poker face. Don't react, no matter what. Never let anyone know what you're thinking. The tureens, both in the same lot, were up next. Molly was ready with her bidder card. When they opened at five hundred, she rested the card on her lap and watched them quickly hit twelve hundred. When the hammer fell at two thousand, Molly knew a collector was on the loose. Two of her marked lots to go. The secretary and the window seat benches. She managed to pick up two good carpets for the apartment, at least.

Starving by then, and wishing she'd taken the time for breakfast, she thought about the sandwiches for sale at the espresso cart. Losing her seat, even at this stage, wasn't worth it. Molly estimated the crowd was over three hundred, with at least two dozen people on their feet. Biding her time, she soon found her patience had paid off. She stole the window seat benches for one hundred. Thrilled no one had seen their potential; she had a hard time not gloating.

Finally, it was time for the secretary. Keeping an eye on Max, she was surprised to see Pablo sneak down the middle and, bending down next to his seat on the aisle, whisper in his ear. Before she could think what this sudden appearance meant, the secretary was opening at three hundred. Molly almost laughed. That was a sucker open if she ever saw one. Similar to low and high estimates in catalogs that were too low, opening a quality item for chump change was another ruse to pull you in and get the action going. She was surprised to see Max's card shoot up. What was wrong with him? He knew better. You hold off, waiting for the amateurs to either jump in, or wait a beat, then slowly lift your card. Realizing she had no way of outbidding him, she decided to run him. Maybe it was time for the student to teach the teacher. Pablo, she had no doubt, was behind this. Raising her card, she countered at three-fifty. Other bidders came in, lured by the low price. The bidding quickly escalated. Max kept his card high, never once lowering it. At six hundred, Molly joined the fray, jiggling it at seven. A man next to her got in on the frenzy and knocked the bidding up to eight hundred. Still a bargain, she gave him a tiny smile, and said, "It is a lovely piece, don't you think?" Ignoring her, he took the bait and didn't lower his arm. Two more bidders, two and three rows up, joined in, and within seconds, they were at twelve hundred. Molly knew Max wouldn't back out now. Dropping her card, she sat back and watched the fun. When the hammer fell at two thousand to Max, he turned around, wagged his finger at Molly, then blew her a kiss.

At the cashier's window, he threw his arms around her and laughed. "Oh, you wench. Thought you were going trot out with that little gem, did you? For shame. Where did you learn to be so sneaky?"

"From you, dear heart. In my other life."

"Well," he said, hugging her to him, "you cost me. You're going to have to pay. Take it to Carmel and make me some bucks." Pulling back, he gave her a challenging smile. "If you can." Thinking for a moment, he said, "I just realized, you can't possibly get all this into that baby truck. I'll have one of my boys pick everything up and schlep it down later next week."

Caught up in the excitement of the chase, she forgot to consider how she'd get everything back to Carmel. "Brilliant idea. In that case, I'll run over to the Main Gallery and check out the trains for . . . for my client, then head home."

"Oh? You're not stopping by?"

"No, I really should get on the road. I hate to admit it, but I'm bushed. I haven't had this much fun in weeks."

Time enough for a quick smoke. She was having a nicotine fit and longing for coffee and something to eat. The streets, she noticed, were as filthy as they'd been when she used to come to auctions with Max. Once inside the Main Gallery, she quickly remembered the old place. The room dividers were still upholstered in gray carpet. The floors were at least covered with better-quality Oriental rugs. The dozens of glass cases, holding hundreds of toy trains, tracks, and station houses, stopped her. Unprepared for such volume, she made her way to a counter to find a house catalog. She was astounded to discover there were fourteen hundred lots being offered. All a single collection of one man. A quick blurb announced this offering was only one of two more slated for the following year.

Randall would go nuts if he saw this. Then her heart fell when she saw that the price of the catalog was twenty-five dollars. A few months ago, that wouldn't have mattered. With fifteen dollars in her wallet, and just enough gas to get home, there was no way she could buy a catalog. She hadn't had time to deposit her checks, and frankly hadn't thought she'd need much money to make the two-hour trip. Eyeing the string holding the catalog to the back of the counter, she glanced around quickly, then snapped it off. Quickly shoving it into her tote, she stood at the counter and stared down into the glass case. Pretending to examine a bright red engine, she drummed her fingers on the glass as if in thought. She didn't want to rush away in case anyone had seen her look over the catalog and put two and two together. When her eye began to twitch, she realized it was time to go. Leaving the showroom, she prayed no one saw her.

The hilarity of what she had just done overtook her. Sprinting to the El Camino, she quickly unlocked it and was laughing so hard, she nearly fell in. Pulling out of the parking space, she turned to watch for traffic, then saw Pablo across the street looking in her direction. Certain he hadn't been inside looking at trains, Molly could only think of one reason why he was there. He was watching her.

There was a slight tremble in her hands as she gripped the steering wheel. She took deep breaths all the way down Potrero to the freeway. When she was sure she was in the right lane for the San Jose turnoff, she was finally able to calm down. Why was Pablo watching her? She had some dots she'd neglected to link. Since Bea knew she'd found Lorna, Pablo probably knew, too. Despite Bitsy's remarks about him, she could have told him, since they were apparently tight enough to have dinner. What really spooked her were the sunglasses. She had had a hard time turning her back to Bitsy on Friday and Saturday. She laughed now remembering how she'd jumped when Bitsy came up behind her in the storage room. Because Max backed her story about being an old family friend, it didn't mean she was off the hook. And, Molly reminded herself; her age didn't preclude her from using a knife on Lorna, or even killing Bea. The more she thought about Bitsy as a suspect, the more she was determined to watch her step around her. She had to admit, though, that woman could really sell.

Her mind zigzagged between the growing list of players and possibilities all the way to San Mateo. When her thoughts settled on Bea, she sighed. Randall said he was going to release the shop to her brother next week. Apparently, the brother was taking Bea home to Oregon for burial. Molly wondered if anyone was going to arrange some sort of memorial. She'd have to ask Bennie. Maybe, she thought, she might just go to Carmel Mission and say her own prayers. It was the least she could do. Besides, she hadn't been to Mass since she'd left New York.

She'd been meaning to visit the famous Carmel Mission. Whenever the family made the trek to Carmel, mass at Mission San Carlos Borromeo de Carmelo was always a must. Being too busy, she knew, was a lame excuse. Saying a quick prayer for all the Masses she'd recently missed, she was busy thinking as she approached Palo Alto. Noting the exit sign for Stanford, she wondered how Randall's weekend with his daughter had turned out, and if she'd liked his gift. By the time she hit San Jose, she was trying to formulate a concise presentation for Randall from Cleo's faxes. There was so much to tell him, she hardly knew where to begin.

25

*B*y the time she drove into Carmel, it was nearly eight. Ocean Avenue was still packed with parked cars. Most of the day tourists from the inland valley and the Bay Area to the north seemed to be taking a leisurely day. Exhilarated from the auction, and keyed up for her meeting, she was tempted to ignore Randall's instructions to do the circular walk to Daria's. For two cents, she'd drive right over and park in front. Pulling into the garage, she parked the orange monster and patted it on the hood. "You did a bang up job, sweetie. Not one hiccup or tiny stall. You may not be a beauty, but you're one hell of a ride."

Only two blocks to go, and it started to rain. Molly had totally forgotten the newscast last night calling for light showers. The tail end of another storm coming in from Hawaii was due to hit late Sunday. If she didn't hurry, she'd be a drowned rat. As much as she liked Daria, she wasn't ready to show up with her hair plastered to her head, or her mascara running. It was hard enough to be in the same room with her without feeling like Olive Oyl.

Just as she reached the back alley to the restaurant, it started to pour. Covering her head, she quickly scooted into the kitchen, fluffed out her slightly damp hair, then smiled to the dishwasher as she hurried through the maze of kitchen help moving like whirling dervishes. Holding a large tray filled with what appeared to be appetizers, Daria caught Molly's eye. "Just in time. I'm taking this in to Randall and Lucero. They've gone through two bread baskets already, and are ready for a second bottle of wine."

"Are they antsy?" Molly asked. "I told Randall I'd get back by eight. It's only quarter to."

"No," Daria responded, "just growing boys still sparring and taking each other's measure."

Eyeing the tray, Molly knew it wasn't one she'd sold her. Without thinking, she ran her fingers over the heavy gadroon edge. "Ahhh, Sheffield . . ." She sighed.

Daria smiled. "It's a beaut, isn't it? I got it for a song at a flea market."

Molly's eyebrows rose. "Lucky you! These babies go for a mint."

"Well, hey, we've got to be lucky sometimes in life. Nothing like the thrill of the chase, right?"

Molly squeezed her arm. "Sometimes the chase is more fun than scoring a treasure. I've got to take you to an auction. You'll have a ball."

"Been there, done that. I don't go anymore. I can't control myself."

"Come on! I promise not to let you get crazy."

"Ha! You won't be the first to try. We'll see. Maybe."

Following Daria to her private room, Molly said, "I didn't know the DA was going to be here again. I have to admit, I'm not very comfortable with him."

Carrying the huge tray with ease, Daria stopped just outside the door. "You couldn't keep Lucero away if you tried. He's not a bad guy, Molly. I've known him most of my life. Behind all that politico bullshit, he's really a good person. Dedicated as hell. As soon as he stops trying to outmacho Randall, our new chief will come to the same conclusion."

Reaching for the doorknob, Molly said, "Okay, if you say so."

When Molly entered, the sight before her almost took her breath away. The table was gorgeous. A mixed array of fine china, heavy silver flatware, crystal wine and water goblets, surrounded a stunning bouquet of yellow gladioli with small trails of ivy just barely touching the starched damask cloth. If all the tables in the restaurant proper were set like this, Molly could see why Daria was so successful. The food, she had to admit, was also first-rate.

When Randall and Lucero rose, she felt like the belle of the ball. "What a way to catch a murderer!" she blurted. "Count me in on the next homicide."

Lucero laughed. "Hey, Molly! I like your spirit." Giving Randall a wink, he added, "I just hope to hell you know what you're doing, 'cause I don't like your plan."

"Well," she said as she took a seat, "wait until you hear the rest of it. But not until after dinner. I don't want to spoil this elegant setting."

Setting the large tray on a stand next to her, Daria sat opposite Molly and grinned. "Come on, don't keep us in suspense. We've been waiting all day for this little pow-wow." Passing Molly a dish filled with appetizers, she said to Randall, "Molly needs some wine. Let's loosen her tongue."

While Randall poured Molly's wine, Daria heaped the remaining dishes with deep-fried artichokes and zucchini, lamb-and-mint-stuffed mushrooms, and calamari with pesto. Glad now she hadn't eaten all day, Molly could hardly contain herself as she remembered her manners and waited until everyone was served.

After a few moments, Randall said, "Okay, Molly. Enough of this. Let's hear about the faxes. Lucero and I are heading for a third bottle of wine. If you drag this out until after dinner, Lucero will be on his ass before long."

"Speak for yourself," Lucero shot back. "Italians are brought up on wine. I'll drink your Irish ass into the ground."

Daria winked at Molly. "Uh, I guess he doesn't know Randall is—"

"I'm *mezzo-mezzo*." Randall smiled at Lucero's surprised look.

"Well, hell, why didn't you say so?" Reaching over to fill Randall's glass, he said, "That makes all the difference in the world."

"Seeing I'm outnumbered here," Molly said, "I guess I won't wait until after dinner. Cleo's faxes verified what I'd already guessed. Lawrence Toby is an insignificant lightweight. He never made the grade, never would, never could. Rhonda jumped on the Early California artist trend and created a false market for her father. Without a *catalog raisonne* of his work no one would have a clue."

"Say what?" Lucero and Randall said at almost the same time.

"It's a compilation of work. The entire body. It's used to chronicle an artist's output."

"So what if there isn't one? What does that prove?" Randall asked.

"For one thing," Molly began, "it helps stop forgers from creating work that never existed. There are any number of reasons to—"

"Save it," Randall said. Looking at Lucero, he added, "Don't get her started, okay? We'll be here all night." Turning back to Molly, he said, "What else have you got?"

It was amazing, Molly thought. Only two weeks ago she would have been hammering back at him after a remark like that. Now, she knew his barbs were actually affectionate. Pretending to ignore him, she said, "Four years ago, Sotheby's turned down six Lawrence Tobys. The next year, Christie's did the same. Late last year, Skinner's followed suit."

"Hell, this is more fun than cooking," Daria said. "Why is that important?"

"Most auction houses, the big ones anyway, have a policy of guaranteeing works painted after 1870 to be authentic."

"And?" Lucero's fork was midway to his mouth. "Don't stop now, for crissakes!"

"They wouldn't touch them because all the works were submitted by Rhonda. According to Cleo, the auction houses were leery. Toby wasn't well-known, his work was blah, and she demanded low estimates of ten grand. With no catalog, that alone says volumes."

"Got it," Randall butted in.

Molly ignored him. "So, next step? Create a market. Get the prices up, establish a history, then make more and hit the auction circuit again."

"Sounds like a lot of work," Lucero said.

"Not really," Molly answered. "It's done all the time. Just do the math. Ten, maybe twenty pictures going for ten grand? You're the heir, you have limitless inventory? Without the catalog, who's to say how much the artist put out?"

"What about the other two?" Randall asked. "The two women stacked up in your garage?"

"Ah." Molly's eyes lit up. "They don't exist."

"What? This sounds like an old black-and-white movie," Daria said.

"Webster and Hubble are pure fabrications. Cleo's resources, experts of the era, I might add, vow those women are phony. Gerald Lytton, one of Cleo's friends, and close to ninety, was one of the original patrons of the Early California group. He knew them all. Fed and housed quite a few of them when they were broke. He insists the women never existed."

While Daria cleared the table, she said, "It sounds like little Ms. Rhonda has herself a stable of competent artists. Something Carmel has always been overpopulated with . . . to keep her shop rolling in dough."

"Then," Lucero took over, "she has a palace revolt. Someone wants out, wants more *dinero,* or maybe ups the blackmail ante. We're rehashing old ground. We did this scenario last time we met. Only thing that bothers me is why you're so sure the pictures by Rhonda's father are fakes. I mean, at this point, all we've got is your say-so. So how do you *really* know?"

"Okay, fair question," Molly said. "To begin with, I have a master's in art. Now, that alone does not make me an expert. And"—she raised her hand for emphasis—"I'm not claiming to be one. I am known, in my former life, as having a good eye, and not just for antiques. I learned the old way, at Sotheby's. I worked under a woman who *is* considered an expert, and she taught me how to see. In Lawrence Toby's case, I think the work is bogus. There is a lack of spontaneity for the style they pretend to be offering. We won't go into that now."

"Thank God," Randall muttered.

Giving him a sharp look, she added, "The dumb asses used acrylics!" Seeing the blank looks on their faces, Molly said, "Acrylics weren't available in those days. But, for the sake of argument, suppose they used oils. I'd still have seen through them. I could bore you with detail, but I won't. I'd have to get into pigments, varnishes, even oven aging." Seeing their rapt attention, she felt the thrill of success. She had them, she knew it. "Oils take years to dry, gradually acquiring a certain look as they pass through the stages. They have a depth and luster, while acrylics still look a little plastic. Over a period of time, oils will often crack, yellow, and darken. Even if they'd been cleaned and revarnished, they'd have a different appearance from what Lorna's showing. Acrylics don't age like oils. They just don't. If they'd even used oils, they'd have a different look. They'd be raw."

"Raw," Lucero repeated.

"It means they weren't painted sixty-odd years ago," Randall explained.

"So," Daria broke in, "they've got a great little factory going on until someone puts a kink in the machinery. Lorna's the first, then Bea maybe holds Rhonda up for more hush money. When she's history, Dick gets the shakes. Rhonda has her hands full then. She has no choice. He's got to follow."

"And," Molly jumped in, "she's now out of artists!" Looking Lucero full in the face, she said, "That's where I come in."

"No. I told you before . . . you're only an advisor," Randall snapped.

"You can't pull this off without me! Besides, you owe me."

"Excuse me?" Randall looked at Daria, then Lucero. "Did I miss something here?"

"If you hadn't put me through such a wringer with all that cat and mouse baloney, I'd have told you about the watercolors and journal earlier."

"So?" Lucero asked.

"Bea might still be alive." Looking around the table,

she decided to push the good ole Catholic guilt button. "This is my chance at redemption. You owe me the opportunity to right a wrong."

Randall threw his napkin on the table. "I don't owe you shit." Leaning into the table, his face only inches from her, he said, "I've already got a standing order for flowers at a cemetery. I don't need another."

Lucero studied Randall for a moment, then nodded. He'd been there before. Pulling out his cigar case, he offered Randall one. "Fresh off the boat. Take one."

Still staring Molly down, Randall reached for the cigar. Hardly blinking, he said, "Your input has been invaluable. In fact, without you, I doubt we'd have come up with the motives. But it ends there. Okay? By the way, your Armand called me, we're set up for some pictures, and Lucero and I will be interviewing undercovers for the sting."

Smarting from the look in his eyes, Molly looked away. *They can't pull this off without me,* she thought. *The art and antique world has its own language, its own way of doing business.* "Then let me sit in on the interviews."

"Why?" Randall said in a calmer voice.

"Because you don't know how to set your person up."

"A sting is a sting," Lucero said.

"That's where you're wrong, and that's where you'll fail. Humor me for a moment." Taking a deep breath, she felt Daria's hand on her shoulder for support. "I just left an episode in New York that puts me in an eminently credible position." She saw Randall's eyebrows rise, and hurriedly added, "I wasn't part of it, but Rhonda doesn't know that. I can speak her language, don't you see? I can let her think I masterminded it. That I have the resources to back me up. I can tell her I'm broke, and I have an artist who can copy anyone."

"You're forgetting something," Randall said quietly.

"What?"

"Pablo."

So intent on convincing them, she'd totally forgotten about him. "Screw him," Molly said.

Daria grinned at Lucero, whose eyes shot open. Randall gave her his basic squinty-eyed look, then said, "He's not my type. However, he can't be ignored."

In the silence that fell upon them, Daria said she'd see to their dinner. Molly concentrated on clearing the bread crumbs from around her plate. Ignoring them both, she sipped her wine, lit a cigarette, and generally avoided eye contact. Finally, Lucero said, "Look, Molly. Randall doesn't need my okay to pull this off, or to enlist private aid. It's not always kosher, but it's done. Like *Law and Order* on TV, he does his thing, I do mine. But here on the peninsula, we've got a lot of small communities, and when something like homicide goes down, I try to work closely with law enforcement. We've got three murders now and it's seriously dangerous. This woman is ruthless, to put it mildly. Randall and I just can't condone your waltzing into her gallery and placing yourself at risk."

Frustrated she hadn't been able to make them see the holes in their plan, never mind the reality of Pablo hovering near, she snuffed out her cigarette, and broke in, "I understand. Really, I do. It's just that . . . well, to use cop talk . . . your people can't walk the walk, or talk the talk. You don't realize what a small, specialized world the art and antique racket is. The minute Rhonda starts asking questions, you have to be able to drop the right names. You have to know the artists of that time. What they produced, who would be best to replicate, and why. Or, as she's done with Webster and Hubble, whose style would be best to emulate and how much product can be passed off."

Breaking his silence, Randall said, "Okay, then you coach our people. Will you do that?" Shaking his head, he added, "Give us a break here, for God's sake!"

"She's still got Pablo. Maybe it won't work. I've seen his work. He's very good."

"We've got to take the chance. I want to nail her so bad, it's keeping me up at night," Randall muttered.

Before Molly could say more, Daria returned with Manuel to serve dinner. The only sounds in the room were Lucero's hands rubbing together as three different platters of pasta were set before them. "Get through this and we'll see about some osso buco, or maybe roast duck."

Praising Daria for the wonderful dinner, she said, "If we keep meeting like this, I won't be able to fit into my clothes. I don't have much with me as it is."

"It makes me happy to see people enjoy our food," Daria said.

"That's all well and good," Molly answered, "but you won't give us a bill, and you've cleaned me out of silver. I've got to keep my part of the bargain at least."

"What bargain?" Lucero asked.

"None of your business," Daria shot back. Looking at Molly, she said, "It's my contribution to the cause." Spearing her gnocchi with gusto, she added, "I've got more news if anyone is interested."

"Let's hear it," Randall said.

"Pablo used to be a male nurse."

"Okay. And?" Lucero queried.

Lost in her own thoughts, trying to formulate a stronger argument to convince Randall to let her approach Rhonda, Molly suddenly remembered the artwork she'd kept from Max's truckload of new merch. The only thing she had to figure out was how to use it. Catching up on the tail end of Daria's news, her mind flashed on Sid Wells. *"That's how he got into the picture!* He took care of Sid."

"Yep. To the end. And, they were not lovers, by the way. Sid was not gay. Just a little effete. He played it up though. He claimed it was good for business. We had a lot of laughs over that."

Molly's head swung from one face to the next. "Is it possible? I mean, maybe we've been looking in the wrong place."

"I'm sorry, but you people have lost me," Lucero said as he pushed away from the table. "Who the hell is Sid Wells, and what has he got to do with any of this?"

Randall seemed to be fixated on one of the many French bistro posters in the room. When he didn't respond, Molly had to nudge him. "Think about it! Pablo— the blue sunglasses!"

His eyes still on the poster, he said, "Might be Bitsy's, too."

"Hey!" Lucero shouted. "Can we all get on the same page here?"

Molly told him about Sid Wells and his connection to Max. "He had terminal cancer and died of an overdose. Max told me it was suicide."

"Okay, I see where you're going, but if Pablo's the one we want to look at, why off ole Sid? The guy's days were numbered anyway."

"Maybe Sid knew what was going on and wanted a clear conscience before he headed upstairs? Maybe he threatened to blow the whistle? Maybe Pablo, or Rhonda, or any of the above, decided to . . ." Molly paused, then said, "Maybe that's why he left the shop to Max instead of Pablo!"

"So does that let Rhonda off the hook?" Daria asked.

"No," Molly answered quickly. "She's the only one who stands to gain from the phony art. I mean, *really* gain. Of course, she has some legit artists in the gallery. But she has to fork over 40 percent to them."

"Then what was Dick getting out of it?" Daria asked.

Molly smiled. "What price love?"

Daria's answering smile was brief. "Silly me."

"Forty percent? Is that all an artist gets?" Lucero's mouth was hanging open. "What a bunch of fuckin' crooks."

"Standard practice. Some galleries get more. They have the overhead, the artist doesn't. I'm not saying it's fair, it just is," Molly said.

"It's still a crock," Lucero said.

"You people are giving me a headache," Randall finally broke in. "Too many *maybes* here."

Tapping Randall's arm, as if to slow him down, Lucero was intrigued. "Hey, this is good. You gotta throw some shit on the wall to see what sticks. Go on, Molly."

"Uh, well, that's all I can think of now." *Except for one other little thing.* Willing to risk a few raised eyebrows, and maybe a smirk or two, she finally said, "Well, Daria said she thought Pablo was from Reno." Taking a deep breath, she added, "So is Bitsy."

"You got any aspirin?" Randall asked Daria.

"Stop it," she told him. "I can see your brain going into overload. Molly's got some great points, and you know it."

"This is getting too muddy," Randall said. "Maybe you ought to change locks again tomorrow."

"Oh, that's right. Bitsy dropped off your key earlier." Digging in her pocket, Daria said, "I almost forgot." Handing an envelope over, she added, "She gave it to

Manuel. I was thankfully in the kitchen when she got here."

"Maybe you should stay at the Pine Inn tonight," Lucero said. "We can charge it to the county."

"Don't be silly," Molly said with little conviction. "I . . . I'll be fine."

"You can stay with me," Daria offered. "I've got plenty of room."

"No, really, but thanks. If I did that, they might know we're on to them. I'll leave all the lights on."

"I'll send a patrol around every hour if you'd feel better," Randall said. "In fact, I'll make sure you're watched when you leave here."

"Stop it, okay! I'll be fine." Sneaking a quick glance at Daria, she said, "But I will change the locks again tomorrow. I'll tell Max I lost the key . . . or something."

"Charge it to my office," Lucero said. "I'll write it up as witness protection." Seeing the startled look on Randall's face, he said, "Hey, we got to take care of our own, right?"

Molly smiled to herself. For the first time since all this began, she felt the thrill of a small victory. They knew they needed her now. More, they knew she knew.

26

*H*er brief thrill of victory was short-lived. When she reached the shop, the stairway to the apartment was pitch-black. She'd forgotten to change the lightbulb again. Besides being tired, and a bit pissed off with Randall and Lucero, she was beginning to realize the danger she might be in. All in all, the dark stairs did not make her feel warm and cozy. She couldn't go through the shop. She'd bolted the upstairs door from the inside in case Ms. Bitsy decided to nose around while she was gone. As far as she was concerned, the woman was definitely not to be trusted. Those blue glasses might have been Pablo's, but Molly wasn't taking any chances. Passing through the arcade leading into the courtyard, she headed for the back staircase. At least the soft glow of the shop lights and the illuminated fountain gave off enough light so she wouldn't trip over her feet.

Bursting at the seams from the sumptuous dinner, Molly wished she'd stopped at the pasta. The chocolate mousse was the real killer. What she needed was a cup of tea to settle everything. Slumping down on the sofa, she sipped slowly and ran the evening's conversations through her mind. The Bitsy/Pablo/Reno connection was bothering her. Bitsy must have known Pablo in Reno. But when? Before she sold out to Sid, or after? It was just too cozy to be a coincidence. She knew Randall felt that way, too. He'd had little to say tonight, except telling her she was not going to play a major role. And, to suggest she might change the locks again.

Great, she thought, *what do I do now, stay up all night?* She began to think she should have gone to New Orleans after all. Fighting gossip and suspicious looks would have been a hell of a lot easier than trying to help catch a killer. And, she thought, as she looked around the room, she'd be living in better surroundings. The guest-house Angela and Armand had offered was paradise compared to this. Maybe a little too much, with all its flowing mosquito netting and the heavy antebellum Victorian Gothic furniture, but her creature comforts had been taken for granted for so long, the contrast she faced now was getting to her. It was, she knew, Daria's lovely table setting that raised this ugly mood. Too many memories of a past life. Ashamed for being so shallow, she slammed the chipped mug on the coffee table so hard, it actually swayed. Disgusted with herself, she threw her feet on the table and surveyed her kingdom. The only good-looking thing in the room were the books flanking the fireplace. Lighting a cigarette, she decided she'd better get the place lit up.

Unbolting the door to the shop, she hurried down the stairs to turn on every lamp. Moving in such a flurry, she hadn't noticed the missing pieces. Stepping back, she scanned the room and swore, "God damn her!" It was suddenly apparent Bitsy had been at it again. Making a quick mental inventory, she counted six chairs gone, a tiger maple drop leaf table, a small mahogany cabinet, a painted pine chest of drawers, at least three lamps, and most of the blue-and-white willowware. The only joy was that the ugly red Victorian sofa was gone. Turning in a complete circle, she noted other smalls missing. "In one day!" she nearly screamed. "I bust my ass to sell an ash-tray, and that old bat cleans the floor in one day!"

Her competitive nature was threatening to overpower her. Gritting her teeth, she headed to her desk and saw Bitsy's note, with several sales tags attached. Shoving it aside, she fell into the chair and stared out the window onto Ocean Avenue. It wasn't until she swiveled away from the window that she saw faxes sitting in the machine's out tray. Sucking in her breath, she prayed they were not from Cleo. If Bitsy was there when they came in, she and Randall were dead meat. Checking the trans-mission time at the top of the first page, her body almost collapsed in relief. They were only an hour old.

Bitsy's sales marathon quickly forgotten, Molly de-voured the pages so fast, she had to remember to breathe. Oh, God! When Randall sees what Cleo dug up on Rhonda Martyn, he'll . . . he'll what? Tell me what a great job I've done, thanks a bunch, see you around? Maybe that would be best after all, she finally concluded. He was probably right. He needed a pro to handle this woman. Especially now. Turning back to the window, she let her mind drift as she watched a few stray cars slowly drive by, and a couple peer into a gift shop across the street. *I don't belong here*, she thought.

Folding the new faxes in half, she took them with her as she checked the front door, and headed up the stairs. Bolting the door behind her, she looked down at the faxes, then threw them on the coffee table. Her head was beginning to ache. Battling her desire to help, and now, her real fear after reading the faxes, she wandered around the living room like a flimsy ghost. Stopping at the book-case, she had half a notion to take a book to bed. There hadn't been time to read lately, and she missed it. Scan-

ning the shelves, she had to laugh. She wasn't into Westerns, but what the heck. Discarding the first two she'd
pulled, she spotted *Call of the Wild* by Jack London, an
early favorite as a child. She flipped it open and found an
envelope slipped between the last two pages. It was
sealed and had no writing on it, so she took it over to the
floor lamp and tore it open. As she sunk back onto the
sofa, her momentary shock turned into a nervous giggle.
Nine one-thousand-dollar bills fluttered in her hand. She
turned them over at least three times to make sure they
were real. Satisfied they were indeed, she had to hold herself back from throwing every book off the shelves.

By one in the morning, she'd found twenty-three thousand dollars. By two, when she pulled the last book from
the two built-in cases, she nearly fainted. Once again,
tucked in the back, she found another envelope. It contained much more than money.

On the floor, surrounded by books, she had a hard time
clambering to the sofa. As she read the three-page hand-
written document, she literally held her breath. Finding
almost half of the money she needed to get to New Orleans was suddenly unimportant. Running to the bedroom for her tote, she dumped its contents on the bed and
scrambled for Randall's business card. He'd scrawled his
home number and cell phone number on the back, and
she could barely read his writing. Hoping she'd deci-
phered the numbers correctly, she punched them in so
fast, she had to hang up and start again. When a sleepy
woman's voice answered, she almost hung up. Taking a
deep breath, she asked for Randall. Surprised to find a
smile on her face when she was told she had the wrong
number, she quickly shrugged it off. In fact, she wouldn't
be surprised if he had met someone. After all, he was a

handsome man. There was an aura of power about him that undoubtedly some women found alluring. And he did exhibit, on occasion, a sense of humor. Just because he had a hard head didn't mean he was totally unlikable. Exchanging a zero for a six, she tried again. When he picked up on the third ring, she nearly shouted, "Get over here right now. I've got the proof you need to nail Rhonda."

In sweats and sneakers, Randall was there before Molly could finish her second cigarette. Watching from the spare bedroom window facing Ocean Avenue, she saw him jog under the arcade and head for the courtyard. She had the French door open as soon as he hit the balcony. The moment he entered and saw the mess on the floor, he said, "Redecorating? You woke me up for this?"

"Very funny." Thrusting the papers she'd found in his face, she said, "Grab a seat and read this!"

Randall eyed her warily, took the papers and headed for the sofa. Reading through quickly, he set them on the table. Looking at the mess on the floor, he said, "Don't tell me, you found this in one of those books. How'd you know to look there?"

"I couldn't sleep so . . . so I was rearranging." She didn't want to tell him about the money. The legality of ownership might be dicey. And, she didn't need a morality lesson on top of everything else just now.

He looked at her strangely, then said, "Just a lucky pick, uh? A one-in-a-million kind of thing."

She didn't like the look in his eyes. She slipped into the easy chair across from him. "Out of the blue. Maybe it's fate."

"Don't start with the *maybes* again. I've had enough for one night."

"Well?" Pointing at the papers, it was all she could do to contain herself. "It's all there . . . the whole shooting match from the beginning!"

Rubbing his eyes, he let out a big yawn. "It doesn't mean a thing. A confession from a man who has been dead for six months or so does not mean diddly. We don't even know if Sid wrote it."

"But he lays out the whole scheme. He admits to organizing it. He names Rhonda, he lists Dick as the artist for Toby, and Webster and Hubble. Jesus, Randall! It's a confession from a dying man wanting to clear his slate."

"So what's it doing hiding in an old Western? Who put it there? Why?"

"How the hell do I know?"

On his feet, he yanked up his sweats and shook his head. "It won't hold up. Besides, we already know about the scam."

"But—"

"In the act, my dear. I've got to get them in the act. After that, I can tie in the motives. Until then, we're up shit creek without a paddle."

Bitterly disappointed that her great find had fallen so flat, she slumped down in the chair and crossed her arms. "Sorry I woke you."

At the French door, he said, "Glad to see all the lights on. Don't forget to call the locksmith tomorrow."

Ignoring him, she turned her head away.

"Molly . . . hey, you did good, okay? It's just not enough." Halfway through the door, he stopped. "Oh, Lucero and I would like you to take a look at an undercover we decided to use. She's from his office. Can you be at the Doubletree in Monterey tonight at eight? Room 403."

Still not looking at him, she said, "Sure, fine. I'll be there."

"You going to lock me out?"

Heading toward him, she realized she was acting like a sullen brat. "I forgot to ask how your daughter liked the painting."

"She didn't show."

Molly reached out and touched his arm. "I'm so sorry. She probably got her dates mixed up, or something."

The look on his face made it clear he didn't want to talk about it. "Yeah, sure. Something like that."

"Uh, listen, how about some coffee?"

She saw him hesitate, but his eyes told her he really didn't want to be alone. "I've got some great lemon cookies. How about it?"

"I could manage a few."

When she returned with the cookies, he laughed. "These midnight meetings have got to stop. People are going to start talking."

"We could become notorious."

When she leaned over to set the tray on the table, he touched her cheek.

Startled, Molly froze for a second. "Coffee should be ready, I'll be right back."

She found her hands shaking as she poured coffee into two mugs. She hoped he hadn't seen the flush that was burning her face.

Randall was at the French doors when she came back with the coffee. "How about a rain check. I've got an early meeting tomorrow in Salinas." Giving her a nod, he was out the door before she could comment.

After she heard him reach the courtyard, Molly slammed the tray on the table, then shoved the sofa

against the French doors. Biting back a few choice
words, she ignored the coffee and cookies and pulled the
wad of money from under the cushion of one of the club
chairs and headed for bed. The joy of finding the confession, even though it didn't seem to be the case breaker
she hoped, and the incredible luck of all this loot, suddenly seemed irrelevant.

Angry with herself for flirting with Randall, for that
was exactly what she knew she'd done, she stared at the
stack of bills in her hand. With half the means of setting
up her own shop, she thought about lowering her expec-
tations a notch. Maybe she ought to leave now. Let Randall solve the case on his own. She could start a little less
grandly. She could also sell the miniatures and make her
nut. She quickly dismissed that idea. The miniatures were
her long-term security blanket. She'd already discovered
how fragile her future was. She wasn't about to tempt fate
and gamble her one ace in the hole.

Shoving the money under the mattress for the time being, and still bristling from Randall's quick exit, she
mumbled, "Well, he didn't have to touch my cheek either." Throwing her clothes over a chair, she pulled a soft
cotton nightgown on, and said, "New Orleans, here I
come. Randall's on his own." First thing in the morning,
she'd call Max and tell him to find a new manager.
Maybe Ms. Bitsy should take over. The old bag was out-
selling her ten to one anyway. Pulling the quilt up around
her ears, she closed her eyes, and mumbled, "Fuck it.
Fuck all of it."

During her morning coffee, Molly thought about calling
Angela to see if the guesthouse was free. Armand had a
habit of harboring old cronies on the run from ex-wives,
and, on more than one occasion, forgers running from the

law. First call, even before Max or Angela, was Cleo. Without her help, Randall would be at a dead end. Oh, shit! She'd forgotten to give Randall Cleo's faxes. Rushing to the phone, she began to punch in his number, then stopped. She'd promised to meet him tonight in Monterey. She wasn't sure if she could face him now. "Screw him! I'll give them to him tonight, and that will be the end of it. He'll probably just tell me it doesn't prove a thing anyway."

Down in the shop by nine, she shoved aside Bitsy's note and called Cleo. Not finding her in, she left a message on her answering machine and called Max. Before she could say more than hello, he was rambling on about the additional merch he was sending with her auction buys. "I've got a *wooonderfull* sofa for the apartment, dear heart. Forest green damask, with two needlepoint wing chairs. And"—he was almost breathless— "three rather nice Kelims for the living room, and—"

"Max?" She had to stop him before she lost her nerve. "That's just great, but I need to talk to you about the shop."

"Darling, I only have a few minutes. We'll talk later, you're doing a fantastic job, and I can't thank you enough. Now, listen, I've thrown in a few coffee tables. You might want to schlep one upstairs. Do what you will with the rest. They're not really fun pieces, but you can use them for display. Pablo will be down with another truck."

"But, Max—"

"I really must run, my love. I'm on a committee with Anne G, and I don't want to be late for our board meeting. Kiss, kiss."

Molly stared at the dead phone and wanted to scream. Just yesterday, she'd been complaining about living like a poor mouse, and now, she could care less. "Go run to your little meeting," she snapped. "Fine! Wonderful! I'll get this shop back together, then I'm out of here." She walked the floor and began mentally redecorating. Two tables and three chests had to be repositioned to fill in Bitsy's sales gaps. Decorative accessories had to be re-done, along with placing lamps and smalls. And, she still had to fax last week's reports and call the locksmith back. She crossed her arms and roamed the shop, eyeing spaces for some of the merch upstairs. Checking her watch, she returned to the desk and called Angela. When Angela's machine came on, Molly contemplated an early cocktail hour. Instead, she pulled a few dollars from her tote and headed for Tosca's.

She tried to avoid looking at Bea's shop. It was virtu-ally impossible. She wanted to cry when she saw the butcher paper covering the widows. Turning away, she al-most collided with Bennie.

"Hey, Molly. I've been meaning to stop over."

"I know, me, too. Got any apple cake? I need a pick-me-up. It's too early for Jack Daniel's."

Benny laughed. "That's the spirit."

Molly spent a good hour chatting with Bennie, stuffing herself with apple cake and ignoring the calories that would pile up. She was in a dangerous mood, and at this point in her life, food was a wonderful panacea. Check-ing her watch, she saw it was almost eleven. She was an hour late opening. Bennie finally noticed the time, and said, "Hey, you closed today, or something?"

Wiping crumbs from her silk tee, she shook her head. "Nope."

When that was all she said, Bennie took a seat. "What's up? Something I can help with?"

"Nope."

"Okay, so we aren't having a memorial for Bea. I tried, honest, but she didn't know enough people to fill six parking spaces. I mean, her customers are scattered, and—"

Stopping him with her hand, she said, "It's not that, honest. It's . . . it's other things."

"Oh, sure. Sorry, I didn't mean to pry. By the way, I talked to Daria this morning. She told me a big shebang was already in the works for Dick Jacobs. I'm not going. I didn't know him. Should have a packed house, the man was well liked. 'Course that doesn't mean a thing in Carmel. Memorials are big around here. All the leftover flower child generation bums flock to them. We have an overflow of New Age hippies, candle burners, and the Save the Ant people still hangin' around." Taking a sip of espresso, he crooked his little finger, and grinned. "Most of them don't even know the stiffs. It's an outing, you know?"

Before Molly could respond, a man patted Bennie on the shoulder and leaned down. "Hey, Bennie." Nodding to Molly, he said, "Sorry to interrupt. I hear the shop over on Dolores is going to be available. I know your dad owns the property, and I'd like to talk to him about it. I need more room, and that place is perfect. Ask him to call me."

After he left, Bennie shook his head. "Man! Talk about small-town grapevine. We just heard Rhonda was leaving yesterday. How the hell did he find out?"

Molly almost choked on her coffee. "Rhonda? I don't think I've met her yet. Is that the woman with the gallery?"

"Yeah. Guess with Dick gone, she needs a change of scene. They were pretty close. I mean, well, hell, it's no secret anymore. They've been seeing each other for a few years. She'll be pulling out end of next month. Her lease was up for renewal, and she told Dad just a few weeks ago she'd sign on for another three years. I can't blame her. Memories, you know?"

"Sure," Molly said. "Guess so." Promising to drop by later, Molly headed back to the shop. Wondering if she should call Randall immediately, or wait until that night, she saw Bitsy standing in front of the door looking like she was about to blow a fuse. "Oversleep?" she asked as she eyed Molly's large to-go cup. "Must have been quite an auction."

Trying hard to be pleasant, Molly shrugged. "The auction was fine, nothing to drool over, and no, I didn't oversleep." She'd be damned if she'd say another word. Bitsy was on her heels, as Molly headed for her desk. "I had a pretty good day yesterday, don't you think?"

Busy moving papers around, Molly avoided eye contact. "Yes, I saw your note."

Bitsy watched her for a moment, then moved to where the red Victorian sofa once rested. "I'm on my way to the hairdresser's. Dick Jacobs's memorial is on for tomorrow at Sunset Center. There'll be hundreds. A girl needs to look her best."

When Molly didn't respond, she added, "I thought I'd stop in and see if you had any questions."

Molly knew it wasn't smart to be acting so rude, but the power of rebellion, and the knowledge that she was leaving were too strong to ignore. "No, but thanks for dumping that red sofa. If I've hated anything here, that was it." Giving her a brief smile, she said, "Max has a truckload coming down again. We'll be able to fill in the gaps now." As an afterthought, she added, "Drop by and take a look. Should be here Wednesday."

Playing with a display Molly had set up earlier, Bitsy stood back, admired her handiwork, and said, "That vase

was off center. I was too busy to move it yesterday."
Turning to smile at Molly, she added, "I'll drop in and
give you a hand." Tossing her a wave, she was headed for
the door, when she stopped. "Oh, forgot to tell you . . .
Pablo's friend? The one who's been storing things in the
garage? He came by yesterday and got all his stuff. He
said to tell Pablo thanks." Giving Molly a smile, she said,
"I told him you'd love to."

Molly thought about throwing something at her before
she made it to the door. Instead, she headed for the
arrangement Bitsy had just changed. Returning it to its
former look, she wondered what Randall was going to
say when he heard Webster and Hubble were history. At
the moment, she didn't care. *Let him worry about it*, she
thought. *It's not my problem any longer.* Staring at the
vase Bitsy had moved, she growled, "I wanted the goddamned vase off center!" Returning to her desk, she had
half a mind to stick some florist's clay under it. Looking
at her list of calls, she remembered the locksmith. While
rummaging in the desk drawer for his card, three women
walked in.

Giving them her shop smile, she said, "Good morning!
If I can be of help, please let me know."

Ignoring her, they split up and began to prowl. She
could hear a few snickers over prices, but that wasn't unusual. Women especially loved to bitch about the cost of
things. When they got bolder, and spoke loud enough for
her to hear, she began to fume. It was when they began to
talk about the *Antiques Roadshow* that her head swung
around. *Not again*, she thought.

When one of the women picked up a Wedgwood vase
and proceeded to tell her friend that it was a fake, Molly
couldn't contain herself. She'd seen one on the show, the
woman said loudly, and the appraiser had warned people

to watch for the way "Wedgwood" was spelled. If it didn't have an "e" in it, it wasn't genuine. "Now," the woman went on, "See? This one is a phony. And they want three hundred for this? She probably bought this at a garage sale for ten bucks. You just can't trust these people. Half of them don't know a thing about antiques."

The two women nodded in agreement. "Well, that's why garage sales have dried up. People are catching on to these crooks. If it wasn't for the *Roadshow*, people wouldn't know what they had."

"Oh, that's true," the third woman offered. "I almost sold my mother's cookie jar collection. You can be sure I'm hanging on to it."

Furious, but smiling, Molly said, "I couldn't help but overhear, and I don't mean to be rude, but you have it backward. Genuine Wedgwood does not have an 'e.' I'm afraid you misunderstood." Taking the vase from her, Molly said, "This particular vase is what is known as Jasperware. It is still Wedgwood, but its manufacture is a bit different. Jasperware vases were made by dipping them into slip." Seeing the confused looks, she happily added, "It's diluted clay." Taking immense joy in their stunned faces, she went on, "This is not an old one, however. The blue is rather darker than the eighteenth century pieces. Three hundred is a fair price, I might add. You'd pay twice that in New York."

"Do you always correct your customers like this? It's a wonder you're still in business."

"Actually"—Molly smiled—"my manners are usually much more evolved. But you were too good to pass up. I suggest you pay more attention next time you watch the show."

"We don't have to listen to this," the short woman snapped.

"Well, then, why don't you leave?" How many years, she'd wondered, had she wanted to say that? Now that she'd decided to leave Carmel, all hell was breaking loose, and it made her feel absolutely grand!

Molly laughed as she watched them scurry out. Nearly on their heels, she quickly locked the door. The day was turning bad. She couldn't afford another outburst. Returning to the desk, she was determined to call the locksmith before she totally lost it. Searching for his card again, she yanked the desk drawer so hard, it nearly fell out. Staring at her like bad mojo was the envelope with Bea's rose petals. She thought about the money upstairs under her mattress. It was almost like a sign from heaven. Take it, and run, a little voice screamed. But her conscience told her otherwise.

With a deep sigh, she hesitated for a moment, then opened the envelope. Gently lifting one of the faded petals, she placed it in the palm of her hand. For all her resolve to walk away, she knew, deep in her heart, that she could not. If Rhonda was pulling out, they didn't have much time.

She took a deep breath and called Randall. When he got on the line, she put last night out of her mind and quickly repeated what Bennie had told her. She had to pull the phone away from her ear. When he finished venting, she said, "I'll come up with an artist for Armand to copy by the time I meet you tonight. By the way, Pablo's friend cleared out the cabinets in the garage yesterday while I was gone. Bitsy gave him the key. Also, I got an interesting fax from Cleo. Somehow, she dug up some facts about Rhonda's last husband. He did a header off the coast in Mendocino a few years ago. Sound familiar?"

The silence on the other end was deafening. "Randall? Hello?"

"I already know about the husband. Now that you know, you might take time out of your busy schedule to listen to me, okay? Maybe you have a better idea what kind of dangerous woman we're dealing with here. I gotta go. Don't forget, Doubletree, eight sharp."

When the phone went dead, Molly was fuming. "Nice talking to you, too."

Driving into Monterey to meet Randall, Molly wondered if Cleo's late-afternoon call was worth mentioning. Evidently, someone in Southern California had tried to unload a few Tobys at Sanford's in Los Angeles. The consignor changed his mind when he felt the low and high estimates were too low. Insisting the pictures were valuable, and the art appraiser was trying to cheat him, he left in a huff. Quickly jotting down the man's name and address, Molly promised to give it to Randall. She spoke with Cleo for almost an hour, and between laughter and a few happy tears, they promised to meet for Christmas. Cleo, it turned out, would be in San Francisco in December. They made plans, and Molly promised to keep her abreast of the investigation.

The information, however, was hardly pertinent, Molly thought. While there were undoubtedly Tobys out in private collections, it probably wasn't vital to the investigation. It did prove, if for no other reason than to shove it in Randall's face, how deep and vast the art and antique underground operated. Unfortunately, since Toby wasn't a well-recognized artist, the accumulation of extensive personal trivia was virtually nil.

Firmly gripping the train auction catalog she'd forgotten to give Randall, she knocked on the hotel door.

Lucero let her in, offered to take her coat, then grandly waved her in. "Champagne? Caviar?"

"Are you kidding?" Molly said.

"Yeah. How's coffee and frozen strawberry short-cake?"

"Just coffee, thanks. Eating at Daria's has added a few pounds I didn't need."

"Coffee it is. Help yourself. Randall and Jackie are on the balcony. Jackie is our undercover. You'll like her. Grab a seat, I'll go get them."

When Randall walked in, she almost spilled her coffee. The woman next to him looked like she'd be more comfortable in a biker bar, than an art gallery, let alone the Doubletree. Unless she was hooking. Ozark skinny, sharp cheekbones, razor back nose, and, across her mouth, a slash of ruby red pretending to be lips. Her flaming red hair hugged her skull like a cap. Her skintight leather pants looked like they'd been put on with Crazy Glue. The short, red jacket with gold epaulets would have looked better on Michael Jackson. Randall had a hard time meeting Molly's eyes when he introduced them. She wasn't sure if it was because of the woman beside him or what had almost transpired between them.

She decided to tell Randall and Lucero about Cleo's call after all. The guy trying to sell some of Toby's works in Los Angeles might be useful. When both Randall and Lucero agreed it might be worth checking out, she handed Randall the catalog. "I forgot to give this to you."

Hovering near, Lucero laughed. "Trains? Oh, man, this is too much. Hard ass L.A. Internal Affairs, and he plays with trains."

Molly knew Randall felt like throttling her. She had to cover her mouth to stop from laughing.

"See this baby on the cover?" Randall sneered. "I've

got two of them. They're worth eight grand each. You got toys worth that?"

Lucero grabbed the catalog and stared at the engine on the cover. "No shit? Hey, is this something I should get into?"

Jackie rapped her knuckles on a table. "Hello? You guys can circle jerk later. I'm gonna be late for a date, okay?"

Lucero looked over at her, then at Molly. It was all too apparent his choice was all wrong. The contrast between the two women, considering the role to be played, was glaring. His discomfort was obvious. He walked to the balcony, jiggling the change in his pockets. Stepping outside, he said, "You know, if you add up all my cousins, aunts, and uncles, my family damn near owned half that wharf over the years. Funny, isn't it?"

"Is this a secret message?" Randall asked. "I mean, what the hell does it have to do with the business at hand?"

"Not a fuckin' thing," Lucero shot out. "Small talk to avoid making myself look like an asshole. I'm pissed, that's all. I screwed up." Looking at Jackie Barnes, he said, "Hey, Jackie, this isn't going to fly."

Molly felt like crawling under the chair. Turning to Jackie, she smiled. "I imagine you just got off . . . uh, an assignment. I love your jacket. Tell me, do you have any art background? I mean, I know you've been to museums, but other than that?"

Jackie looked at Lucero as if she wanted to throw a set of cuffs on him, but decided to play out the role and torment him. Snapping her gum, she laughed. "Sure, I've been to museums. When I was a kid. You been to the aquarium here yet?"

Before Molly could answer, Randall broke in, "I

think . . ." He paused a minute and glared at Lucero to keep quiet. ". . . if you give Jackie a little background on the California artists, and maybe a few buzz words to drop, she'll be able to wing it for the first round with Rhonda. Give her a few books, another meet or two, and she'll handle the rest. A scam's a scam."

Molly knew they were doomed. "How much time do we have?" she asked.

"Two weeks max. We've got to make it worth her while to stick around," Randall said.

Molly shook her head. "It can't be done. No offense, Jackie, but Rhonda will see right through you. I can't teach you enough to—"

"Hold it," Jackie said. "I know what's comin' down here. I've got to act uptown, put on a nice wig, good threads, simple but classy. You give me the lockjaw lingo, I'll do the rest. I'll show her those things you found, and tell her I've got an artist that can take up where—"

"Slow down," Molly interrupted, "just where did you find the watercolors? How did you know they belonged to Dick Jacobs? How did you know she was involved?"

"That's up to Randall and Lucero to figure out." Rolling her eyes, Jackie said, "Look, honey, I don't have to know about art to do this. In fact, I'll tell her flat out that I don't know shit about art. I'm a con with connections, and can deliver. That about wrap it up?"

"She'll smell a phony the minute you walk in the door."

Annoyed her expertise was being questioned, Jackie leaned in toward Molly and snapped, "Where you been, girl? I'm a cop, okay? I've been a hooker, a drug dealer's bitch, a terrorist, and a nun. I fooled them all, and lived to tell the tale." Popping her gum again, she laughed. "Think you can top that?"

Molly saw Randall staring at an unlit cigar. Lucero was pouring enough sugar in his coffee to break out in hives in the morning. Throwing up her hands, Molly said, "Okay, okay! You're the pros here, but keep one thing in mind. Rhonda saw me that morning at Lorna's. Dick must have told her about the artwork, so my showing up with them will make sense. Most importantly, suppose Pablo filled her in on my background in New York? I can talk artists, color, the whole works."

"What the hell does color have to do with anything?" Lucero asked.

"Just about everything!" Molly nearly shouted, "Now all of *you* listen up!" Glaring at Jackie, she said, "The Early California artists at that time developed a look all their own. Color played a vital part in the movement. Because of the light and landscape of Southern California, this group defined themselves with a striking similarity between their works. *Especially with color.* Yellows, for instance, were clearer, paler and lighter, and often tinged with mustard. The grays and greens of cool, floating mists over the ocean were easily identifiable, yet not as translucently poetic as what they painted in Europe. There was a smooth surface Beaux-Arts realism in their works that few artists had captured."

"Molly better do it," Lucero said. "She's right. You know it, Randall."

"And," Molly quickly added, not wanting to lose her momentum, "Toby was not a *plein air* artist!"

"So?" Lucero blurted. "Hey, I'm convinced."

"Too late," Randall said. "She's on a roll. Let her get it off her chest."

Molly knew she had to close this sale. If she could sell six- and eight-figure antiques to jaded tycoons, she ought to be able to sell this group. "Don't you see? I can use that with Rhonda. I mean, to show her what she's doing wrong. Dick was using a technique that is totally wrong. He should have known better, but his own subconscious got in his way."

Not sure if they were still on the same page with her, she quickly added, "The pieces she has in her gallery are too defined. The school her father belonged to—the *plein air* group—worked in the open, at the site, painting what lay before them. Brushwork was looser, almost vigorous, resulting in quick and less-defined images. While the rest of the art world was turning to modernism, this group resisted, and kept the technique sacrosanct. That's where Dick blew it, not to mention not having a flat, opaque look or feel. He was slightly dimensional. I'll point that out. The other thing is, Dick used a bright yellow none of the artists of that time would have used." Looking at Lucero, she added, "Besides using acrylics."

Suddenly interested, Jackie asked, "Uh, excuse me, but who the hell are 'these guys' you keep talking about? Are they famous?" Looking at Lucero, she said, "I mean, if something like this comes up again, maybe I should know?"

Taking a deep breath, Molly pulled what she could from memory, "Oh, Granville Redmond, Franz Bischoff, umm, Edgar Payne. Armin Hansen is my favorite, and Guy Rose is another. Not household names like van Gogh, or Monet."

"I got it," Jackie said.

"Ahh." Molly grinned. *Here comes the final push.* "I've been saving this for last. The men I just mentioned hit their prime in California between 1900 and 1930. Toby's work came after that. Much later. Not only is Rhonda faking pictures, she's lied about her father being a part of that group. Why no one's caught on, I haven't a clue. But then, the average buyer wanting to get in on hot trends doesn't do their homework."

"And," Jackie added, suddenly agreeing with Molly, "who's going to argue with the daughter?"

"Exactly!"

Jackie stood up, and grabbed her bag from the bed. Looking at Randall, she said, "For once, I think the D.A. might be right. Molly brought up some good points. I could pull it off, but hey, who am I to argue? Am I out of here, or what?"

Randall spoke quickly, "It's Jackie, or I can the operation."

"*And let Rhonda get away with murder?*" Molly gasped.

Lucero looked at Randall, then said, "Go ahead, Jackie, I'll call you. We've got to think this out a little more."

About to speak, Jackie hesitated for a moment. Giving Molly a once-over, she sighed. "Maybe Randall's right. Better start packin', honey. I see you as the next vic."

Molly's face fell. Her eyes darted to Randall. She saw the squinty-eyed look, the tight lips. Reality suddenly kicked in. This wasn't an intellectual catch-the-crook game any more. Scared witless now, she forced a tiny smile. "An 'in' joke, I presume?"

"Knock it off, Jackie!" Randall said. "Don't listen to her. She's just trying to spook you. I've had a tail on Rhonda since Dick's funeral. Have one on you, too."

"What?" Molly's face fell. "I'm being watched? You still don't trust me?"

"You wouldn't be here, if I didn't." Turning away

from her, he added, "By the way, close the drapes in your bedroom, or get a robe. Owens wants to know where you got that pink nightgown. He wants to get one for his girlfriend."

Jackie was still at the door. "Owens still with that airhead from Big Sur? Poor jerk, she's a twit."

"Out, Jackie! Out!" Lucero said. Settling down on the bed, his knee bouncing, he said, "Okay, let's get back to basics, here. I opt for Molly doing the trip. With a wire on her, we can be close by if—"

"We?" Randall interrupted. "Stick to the courthouse, Counselor. I'll send you a report." Glancing at Jackie, who couldn't bring herself to leave, he asked, "What do you think? Can she do it?"

Jackie gave Molly another long look. "Guess she'll have to. She's holding a better hand than any of us."

Lucero rose from the bed and jingled the coins in his pocket again. Staring at Randall, he asked, "Well?"

Finally lighting his cigar, Randall used the ritual to think. It was apparent to Molly he didn't want to jump too soon. She knew he had to let them wonder a little; let them think they talked him into it.

"Guess we'll go with Molly," he finally said.

Lucero nodded. "Okay, then." Raising his hand, he added, "Except for one thing. I want you and Molly to see this guy down south and look at his Tobys. I don't want any doubts here. I want the real work examined and compared to what Rhonda's selling. If we go to court on this, I want all our guns loaded, *capisce*? If we can't nail her on murder, we'll get her on fraud. Once I get her in court, I'll break the bitch." Looking at Molly now, he said, "I'd like you to set up a meeting with this guy. If I have to use you as an expert witness, it's important for you to see the real thing. Let's not get hammered on this. Okay?"

"Absolutely," she agreed. "We'll have to go when Bitsy's in the shop." Turning to Randall, she asked, "This Friday soon enough?"

Randall nodded. "Friday it is."

Lucero thought for a moment, then said, "No public flights. I don't want you two seen together. I have a party contributor who's always wanting to fly me somewhere. I'll set you up with him. Randall, you better arrange for an officer's wife to pick up Molly Friday morning and take her to the Monterey Jet Center." To Molly, he said, "You can tell Bitsy you're going somewhere with a decorator you met or something."

Back to Randall now, he asked, "Are we clear now on what we need?"

Taking a deep drag on his cigar, Randall nodded. "Crystal clear, Counselor."

━ 28 ━

$\mathcal{M}$olly's ears were ringing by the time Officer Matthews's wife dropped her off at the Monterey Jet Center on Friday morning. Intent on coming up with a way to ease Randall into the newest developments, Molly only half listened how to can peaches, what tomato varieties not to plant, and which disposable diapers to avoid. She realized the poor woman was nervous. She'd told Molly three times, it wasn't every day that she was able to help in an investigation. Thanking her gracefully for the ride, Molly had to interrupt twice to remind her to be back at seven that evening.

Randall was nowhere in sight. Molly was almost relieved. Being alone with him, even on the plane, made her a little nervous. Glancing around the high-tech interior of the private jet center, she found herself nodding in appreciation. It was perfectly suited for the times and no doubt meant to attract the scores of technocrats that frequented the area. It was the hub, Mrs. Matthews related, for all the high-rolling visitors to Pebble Beach. Finding a plush chair, Molly sank in and waited for Randall. She would have to word her account of the encounter with Pablo carefully. Just because she thought her plan had been brilliant didn't mean Randall wouldn't want to kill her.

* * *

She'd only been open for an hour when an immaculate Pablo sauntered in. Giving Molly an annoyed look, he said, "Max told you we had a full truck. Why haven't you made room?"

Bristling, she answered, "It was nice of you to call and confirm when you'd be down. I didn't think I had to empty the place. I am supposed to be selling this stuff, remember? Besides, where the hell would I put it all?"

Turning away in a huff, he said over his shoulder, "God forbid you should have to think, too. Never mind, I'll have my men set the place up."

His bite this trip wasn't as sharp as usual. The tone of his voice was milder, like this sparring was a common thing between old friends. Was he relaxing his guard around her? Did he no longer consider her a threat? In an instant, she knew the plan she'd been up two nights working out was right. Maybe her brilliance had risen to Olympian heights after all. Scooting into the small storage room, she pulled out the rolled-up watercolors and tucked them under her arm. Randall hadn't wanted to give them back to her, but she told him she needed to study them before their trip to Los Angeles. She made sure to grab Pablo's painting that the previous drivers had mistakenly delivered. Peeking around the door, she could see Pablo standing on the sidewalk with a clipboard in his hands. She took the sketches and painting to her desk. Setting them on her chair, she then turned the painting so it faced the wall. Following the two men carrying in a large Chinese Chow table, Pablo said, "Upstairs, or here?"

"Max said there would be three tables. I'd like to see the others before I decide."

"Don't waste our time. They're dreck, okay? Take my word for it."

Not wanting a fistfight the first ten minutes, she nodded. "I'll do that." Smiling at the two men, she said, "Upstairs. It's unlocked."

At her desk, Pablo set down the clipboard. "Your reports are late." Pulling an envelope from his shirt pocket, he handed it to her. "This week's check. I didn't send it since I was coming down."

Wondering if he thought saving postage was a virtue, she merely said, "Sure, thanks." Praying a little honey would work, she said, "I imagine things are pretty hectic up there now. I mean, getting ready for the Fort Mason show." Not waiting for a reply, she quickly said, "I've always thought San Francisco's fall show was equal to the Armory in New York, don't you?"

Eyeing her, Pablo's smile was almost nice. "That's always been my opinion. But you New Yorkers have your nose so high, I'm surprised to hear it."

"Oh, come on!" She laughed. "Humility does not suit you. Max sent me photos of your last show. You did a top-notch job staging your area. Those faux marble floors and columns were fantastic. And that fountain was to die for! It looked like it came right out of Pompeii." Shaking her head in awe, she said, "Just marvelous."

Smiling slightly, he said, "It *was* nice. But it was a major job, let me tell you. I was up for days doing those floors and columns."

Get a dealer talking about himself, throw a few compliments around—real or not—and you've got him. Giving him her widest eyes, she said, "*You* did those? I had no idea." Before he could respond, she pulled out the painting. Turning it to face him, she said, "I shouldn't be surprised. If you could do this, you could do anything."

The shock on his face was worth the moment. "Where did you get that?"

He was as near to sputtering as she could get him. "It came down with the last load. The driver wanted to take it back, but I just couldn't part with it. I'm surprised you missed it. But then, I guess you've got many of these gems lying around."

Pablo nearly tore it out of her hands. Molly backed away, and laughed. "Hey, I love it! What kind of price do you want to put on it? Two . . . three, maybe four grand? It's a great rendition of Armin Hansen. One of the best I've seen. We could label it 'In the style of.' That way, we really wouldn't be trying to pull a fast one."

"You bitch! It's not for sale. It's . . . it's just a fun thing I do to keep my fingers nimble."

"Like Webster and Hubble? By the way, it was stupid of you to hang a Hubble at Max's apartment. The minute I saw them in the garage . . ." She let that hang, then pulled out the artwork. "Maybe I should get these framed instead." Rolling them out on her desk, she asked, "What do you think? Gold leaf? Or, maybe something a little simpler?"

Clutching his painting, Pablo almost staggered. She swore she could hear his heart beating. The thrill of startling him quickly disappeared when she saw the ice in his eyes. She had a sudden desire to cross herself, when he snapped, "You're in over your head."

Staring back, as bold as she could, Molly gave him a tight smile. "Oh, I don't think so. I *know* this game, sweetie. Better than all of you."

His eyes still narrowed, he half laughed. "You were in with Derek and Greta all along? You played little Ms. Innocent and got away with it? I don't believe you."

"I'm here, aren't I?"

Before Pablo could reply, Bitsy floated in, and grandly said, "Darlings! I do hope I'm not interrupting? I just got off the phone with Max, and he told me about the new merch. I couldn't wait to get over her and see what you two stole at Sanford's."

With her eyes still on Pablo, Molly said, "What timing! Could you help direct placement? Pablo and I have some paperwork to go over."

Setting down her bag, Bitsy fluffed up her hair. "I saw those two hunks unloading the truck. I'd be delighted to give them direction." Her raspy laugh followed her out.

"Set up a meeting with Ms. Martyn," Molly said when Bitsy was outside. "I have a proposal for her."

"I don't know what the hell you're talking about."

"Pablo? I hate people who think I'm stupid. And, I hate people who can't remember their lies. You just told me I was in over my head. Now you don't know what I'm talking about?" Stepping around the desk, she was only inches from his face. "Rule Number One, don't insult my intelligence. I'll be busy Friday with a decorator from The City. You set up a meeting for Sunday."

"I . . ." he began. "I mean, what makes you think Rhonda will even talk to you?"

"She's a greedy bitch, just like me. I need money to get out of this dump. Derek took it all. In sixty days I'll be out of here."

By the time Bitsy left at seven, Molly was a wreck. The fallout from her encounter with Pablo had nearly drained her. She was actually glad Bitsy stayed. Every time a customer walked in, she'd take over and tell Molly to concentrate on placing the new pieces. The few times Molly was able to just sit and rub her aching feet, Bitsy would fix her tea, pat her back, and alternate commiseration with compliments. "You've got to slow down, darling. You look absolutely beat." The compliments, while a tad effusive, were at least welcome. "You've done a fantastic job with this place. One can feel an ambiance of quality. It looks fabulous."

The more time she spent with Bitsy, the more Molly found it difficult to think she could be involved with Rhonda. But then, her own husband of nine years had fooled her. It was just hard to believe this silver-haired dynamo was not all that she claimed. While Max had vouched for Bitsy's relationship with her parents, Molly decided to wait and see.

After Bitsy racked up just under three thousand in sales by four, she preened around a little, then sneaked into the storage room for a smoke. For once, she didn't change the new displays. Nearly falling up the stairs to the apartment, Molly collapsed on the new sofa. She closed her eyes for a moment, then jumped up and hid the watercolors under the mattress next to her New Orleans loot. After a quick dinner, she called Daria. "Can I ask you a favor?"

When Daria got there at ten, Molly hugged her. "I can't thank you enough for taking this stuff off my hands. I'll be back tomorrow at seven. I'll come pick it up then."

"We'll have a bite in the back room," Daria said. "Then I'll walk you back."

When Daria left, she climbed in bed with one of the Westerns Sid loved, and hardly slept all night. She wasn't looking forward to telling Randall what she'd done.

Discarding one approach after another, she didn't see Randall come in the lobby. When he tapped her on the shoulder, she nearly jumped out of the chair. "Let's roll."

"You're late."

"No shit. I do have a town to run, you know."

Running across the tarmac, Molly yelled, "What if someone sees us together?"

Randall's laugh nearly drowned out the jet noise, "I don't think that's much of a problem right now."

In the air, their seat belts unbuckled, Randall said. "Some plane, huh?"

Molly had already taken in the plush appointments. Smiling at the attendant sitting up front, she whispered, "Very impressive. Whose plane, by the way?"

"Some IPO punk who has a weekend house in Pebble. He wants to 'get to know' Lucero. Juvenile King Maker on the prowl. You know the type."

Nodding, Molly finally asked, "You were going to tell me why you were late."

"Oh, that. Yeah, well your tail spotted Pablo following you and Mrs. Matthews. He had to improvise. Max is going to get a body shop repair bill. Jensen had to create a little fender-bender."

Molly felt ill. Her stomach was gurgling and she thought she was going to be sick. "Where did he spot him?"

"On the off-ramp to Salinas. He got to him before Pablo could see you were headed for the airport. Don't worry. He hasn't a clue where you were going."

"Uh, Randall? I've . . . I've got to tell you something."

"Save it. Tell me about this Mr. Hanover we're going to visit."

"Could I have a 7-Up, or something? My stomach is a little upset."

By the time she downed half the soda, she still felt sick. He was definitely going to kill her when she told him about Pablo. "Hanover doesn't own the Tobys. His mother does. She has three. Toby used to rent a studio from her. When he fell behind in the rent, he'd give her a picture."

"Shit. What a life. Poor bastards scrimp all their lives, then die, and some schmuck rakes in the dough. I hear van Gogh only sold one painting in his life."

"His brother sold it to Manet, so the story goes. For today's equivalent of twelve dollars."

"Poor fuck."

"You'd cringe if you knew how many fine artists died paupers. The heartbreak, the frustration, is unbelievable. I had a friend whose child was a gifted painter. He asked a well-known artist what he should do to help his son." She looked at Randall. "The artist told the father to cut off his son's hands."

Randall stared at her, then turned away. He was silent for the rest of the trip. Molly closed her eyes and willed her stomach to behave.

When he nudged her, she was surprised to realize she'd fallen asleep. "We'll be landing in about ten minutes. A detective friend of mine is picking us up."

"Will he turn on his flashing lights?" It was out of her mouth before she could think. His silence was obvious. The story she'd told him about the artist had touched him. She was beginning to see a sensitive side of Randall she hadn't thought possible. "I'm sorry. That was childish."

"Chalk it up to nerves."

The man walking toward them hardly looked like a detective to Molly. Short and round, with a shuffling gait and tilted nose that made him look like a crab sniffing the air for a dead carcass on some lonely beach. He wore a bolo tie with an orange Hawaiian shirt neatly tucked into wide-leg jeans that flapped around his scuffed leather running shoes. Punching Randall in the arm, he said, "How you doin', *Chief*?"

"Cut the crap, Loomis, we've got a schedule to keep." Randall laughed as he gave the man a bear hug. "This is Detective Loomis, Molly. Believe it or not, he's a hotshot in Homicide."

"Hey! Howareya?" Thrusting out his hand, he gripped Molly's so tight she winced. "Nice to see Randall keepin' company with a lady for once."

"And, what a pleasure to meet a gentleman." Glancing at Randall, she added, "For once."

Loomis's roar almost knocked her over. "I like this lady. Can I keep her?"

"Good of you to take the time to play wheel man. Appreciate it."

"Where we headed, Ace?"

Molly's head swung around. "Ace?"

"Shut up, Loomis. I get enough grief from her as it is."

"Oh? Like that?" Loomis winked.

Molly saw Randall's face flush. "No." Randall's bark was almost as loud as Loomis's laugh. "This is business, ya' bum. Let's cut the shit, okay?"

Flinging open the door of a battered brown Camaro, Loomis bowed grandly, "Entreeee, little lady." Smiling, he said, "High-class cop talk. Don't use it much, so don't get excited on me."

Tearing out of the private air strip, Loomis asked, "Where to?"

Holding on to the strap above his head, Randall said, "Cardoza Street in Hermosa Beach."

Molly's nausea on the plane was mild compared to the state of her stomach by the time they reached the small one-story Arts and Crafts bungalow. Why they hadn't been pulled over for speeding was beyond her. Talking nonstop all the way, Randall and Loomis must have forgotten she was along. "Maybe," she broke in, "it might be better if I did this alone. You and Loomis might inhibit Mrs. Hanover. Besides, you two obviously have a lot to catch up on."

Giving her suggestion some thought, he finally nodded. "Just don't stay in there all day." Checking his watch, he added, "Half hour tops. We've got to be back to the airport in four hours."

"Yeah." Loomis laughed. "And we have to schedule lunch yet."

Sliding across the backseat, she nudged aside a bundle of laundry and two empty bags from Burger King. "Half an hour should do it. Just don't take off for coffee and forget me."

Cary Hanover, Mrs. Hanover's son, who Molly figured was pushing sixty, opened the door and gave her a flashing smile. "Oh, Ms. Doyle! We've been so excited about your visit. I can't begin to tell you how much we appreciate your appraising Mother's art collection."

Entering the small foyer, the musty smell of perpetually drawn shades hit Molly like a ton of bricks. Her stomach was ready to explode. Surprised at his change in attitude, and how he'd totally misconstrued her intentions, she frowned. "I think you misunderstood my call. I'm not an appraiser. I explained over the telephone I'm doing a magazine piece on Early California artists."

"Of course you are." He winked. "I know all about museum curator's tricks. I read an article last night about how museums track down a missing masterpiece. They employ appraisers and send them out under false pretenses to feel the owners out." Puffed up by his canny discovery, he said, grinning, "Don't worry, I haven't told Mother. She still thinks you are a writer. Come into the living room. Mother's waiting."

Molly thanked God that Randall agreed to stay in the car. He'd would have been all over this pompous idiot. "Hello, Mrs. Hanover. Thank you for seeing me," Molly said.

Seated in a wheelchair by the front window, Mrs. Hanover waved Molly to a cozy rocker. Moving aside what appeared to be a handmade quilt, Molly said, "I promise not to take up too much time. I've only a few questions about Lawrence Toby."

"Oh, dear, take all the time you need." Patting snowy hair twisted into a haphazard bun, she asked, "Will the photographer be coming along?" Smiling at her son, hovering just behind Molly, she said, "Do fetch the tea, Cary darling."

"I don't have a photographer." Giving her an apologetic smile after seeing her disappointment, Molly added, "I hadn't really thought of it. How careless of me. Maybe after I've seen the Tobys we can arrange another appointment." She hated lying to this sweet old woman, but she saw no way out of it.

"Of course. Another time. Well, then. Turn around. Behind you is *San Pedro Sunrise*. That was the first Larry gave me. In the dining room, just to your right, you'll find the other two."

In the dim room, Molly had hardly noticed it. "May I open the shades?" she asked.

"Oh, yes, of course. I didn't think. I'm so used to this soft light."

Taking a moment to raise the shades, Molly took her time walking to the Toby. She didn't want Mrs. Hanover to see how anxious she was. Standing before the oil, Molly felt her heart lurch. Lawrence Toby was absolutely awful. No wonder he never made the cut. There was no heart in the work. It was as if he was merely going through the motions. Paint-by-numbers had more life than this piece. How Toby managed a listing in Artists of California was beyond her. The colors, however, were of the period. A very mellow mustard was used with more skill than the overall execution.

Stepping into the dining room, she could hear the gentle clatter of teacups being placed on a tray and plastic ripped from a box of cookies. *Oh, God*, she thought, *how the hell am I going to walk out of this gracefully?* The two Tobys in the dining room were slightly better than the first. His brush strokes were surer. It was apparent Rhonda's clients had never seen an original.

Not every work by a famous artist was perfect. Dozens were discarded, done over, thrown in the fire, slashed to pieces in frustration, but these—these were simply not good. She could think of no other explanation. These were not rejects, handed off to pay rent, but finished pieces. Not only did Dick Jacobs use the wrong colors, but he created a better product!

"Tea's ready," Cary Hanover gaily announced. Finding Molly back in the rocker, he said, "Well? What do you think?" Pouring with dexterity, he served Molly first. "Wonderful execution, don't you agree?" Not waiting for an answer, he handed his mother a cup, then settled himself on a camel back sofa. "I knew Larry, too, of course. Fascinating man. Naturally, I was younger, but I do remember him." Taking a quick sip of his tea, he added, "We'd entertain a group price, of course. Low to mid six figures would not be insulting."

Molly's eye began to twitch. Patting it gently, she said, "I don't know how to make myself clearer, Mr. Hanover. I'm not an appraiser from a museum. I have no idea what your pictures are worth."

"Paintings," he corrected with a wink to his mother.

"Pictures," Molly answered. "The correct terminology is pictures."

"Not these. They've been *painted* dear," Cary Hanover snapped back.

Biting her tongue, Molly turned to Mrs. Hanover. "How did you acquire these? I'm not prying, you understand. It's the human interest aspect."

"Of course. You writers love that."

The faint sparkle in her eyes told Molly she hadn't believed her son's fantasy. "Exactly. Were they a gift, or did you buy them?" Besides needing to verify Cleo's source, she loved stories like this. Sometimes the twisty road to acquiring art and antiques was more interesting than the piece or work.

"Hardly a gift," Mrs. Hanover replied. "Larry frequently had difficulty paying rent on the garage I let him use. He didn't sell much, I'm afraid. When he married, and had to support a ready-made family, money became tighter. His job at the refinery was just enough to keep food on the table, let alone cover paints or rent. When he had his accident, well it nearly was the end. He couldn't paint after that." Taking a sip of tea, she paused, then shook her head, "That's really all I can tell you. They left soon after the accident. We never saw them again."

Poor guy, Molly thought. "What happened?"

"Larry was a gambler. He loved playing the horses. Seems the poorer you are, the more you throw money away looking for that sunny Sunday. He got behind with his bookie, you see. When he couldn't pay up, they broke one leg and smashed his knuckles."

Sneaking a look at Cary Hanover, sulking across from her and staring into his tea, Molly decided she'd best ease her way out of there. She could tell he was slowly building up to a boil, and she didn't want to be the focus of his temper. "You've been so kind," Molly said as she rose. "One more question, if you don't mind. Did I hear you say 'ready-made' family?"

"Oh, yes. I never met the woman he married. She had a toddler. A little girl."

29

*R*andall tapped his watch as Molly climbed in the backseat. "Forty-three minutes! You promised a half hour. You should have known we'd be worried. Loomis and I were ready to call for backup."

"Oh, shut up. Let's get out of here. Her son is ready to explode, and I don't want him coming out with a baseball bat. He was convinced I was an undercover appraiser for a museum. He was ready to settle for a low six-figure offer."

Pulling away from the bungalow, Loomis made a sharp U-turn, then let out a whistle. "How much was the stuff really worth?"

"Five bucks," Molly said sadly.

Loomis shook his head. "Hey, the collecting game is a bitch. I've been burned a few times myself. But I'm hooked. Flea markets are my venue. I know 'em all, from Lost Angels to the Mexican border."

"Really?" Molly's eyes brightened. "What's your game?"

Smiling at her through the rearview mirror, he said, "Tortoiseshell tea caddies." Smacking his lips, he laughed. "I got a collection to make the Brits drool. Pallisay is my next love. Hard to find the genuine article, though."

"How the hell can you love a bunch of plates with snakes and crabs stuck on them? Or tea tins made out of dead turtles?" Randall asked. "You know sea turtles were almost driven to extinction because of fucks like you? And stop bullshitting us, you don't find that junk at fleas."

Loomis narrowed his eyes. "You know about these things, huh? I always thought you hated antique talk."

"I do."

"Besides, I didn't say I got them at fleas, did I?"

"Can it and drive."

"Can't. Can't do two things at once. Isn't my nature. Come on, Randall, level with us, how come you know about sea turtles and Pallisay?"

Giving Molly a sidewards glance, he said, "I read, okay? Butt ugly old French dishes with animals and junk on them? You're sick, Loomis. I always said that."

All through lunch, Molly and Loomis talked nonstop about antiques. He was self-taught, but his knowledge was impressive. Randall gave his combination Mexican lunch a lot of attention. Downing two Coronas, he finally said, "Okay, gang. Time to hit the road."

Barely squelching a burp, Loomis asked, "I still wanna know where you read about my dishes."

Randall lowered his head. He reminded Molly of a bull about to charge. Tapping the underside of his chin, with the back of his hand, he said, "I don't remember, okay?"

"You're uncouth, Randall. Always were. Don't do that in front of a lady. You're just jealous." Loomis grinned, then gave Molly a broad wink. "Randall can't stand the fact that women adore me. Don't pay any attention to us. We've been friends for twenty years, we always talk like this." Turning back to Randall, he added, "You're also a cretin. Pallisay plates are works of art. And my tea caddies are antiques! I don't go out and kill turtles."

Blowing out his breath, Randall turned to Molly. "You done? We gotta get smokin'."

When Randall laid out money for lunch, Loomis handed it back. "My pleasure. I miss you, you old dog." Taking Molly's hand in his, he lightly brushed it with his lips. "It's been a pleasure, Molly. Absolutely enlightening. I look forward to continuing our conversation in Carmel."

"Don't make it too soon," Randall retorted.

At the airport, Loomis helped Molly out of the car. "We will meet again, lovely lady. I'll be up for the next Bach Festival."

Grabbing Molly's elbow, Randall said, "You don't need to kiss her hand again, okay? Once is enough."

Loomis laughed. "Oh, am I intruding?"

"Get a life," Randall replied.

The banter, although an obvious routine between close friends, nevertheless made Molly pause. Flattered, she wasn't quite sure what to make of it. Molly laughed about Loomis until they flew over Santa Barbara. "What a surprising man. You must really miss him."

"One in a million," Randall said. "He may head up this way for good soon. His wife died a few years ago. No kids, just two cats. One of the best homicide dicks I ever worked with. His solve rate is one of the highest in the country."

"I'll look forward to that."

"Oh? I thought you were hot to trot for New Orleans?"

"Not yet. I've got a killer to help you nail."

"Okay, let's hear about your visit. I didn't have the heart to interrupt you and Loomis."

"The work is appalling. He mixed color well, but the

rest is simply awful. His perspective is so far off, he—"

"Molly! What the hell did you find out?"

"He had to stop painting when an irate bookie broke his leg and smashed his knuckles. Output is irrelevant now. He wasn't good, so it doesn't matter. Anyway, we know the stuff Rhonda's pushing was done by Dick Jacobs."

"Okay, that it? Was the trip worth it? If we go to court on this, you can swear Rhonda's selling fake art?"

"Absolutely."

He saw the tiny sparkle in her eyes, and he knew she was holding something back.

"By the way, Rhonda Martyn is not his daughter. She came with a new wife."

"I don't see the relevance."

"She may not know it." Giving him a sly smile, she added, "It might be useful."

Randall mulled that over for a moment. "That all of it, then?"

She'd been dreading this all day. She had to tell him about Pablo. Time for truth or consequences. Either way, she was in trouble. She might as well get it over with. "Actually, no."

"Am I gonna like this? Your eye is twitching again."

She spoke so fast, she didn't have time to realize how deadly quiet he was. When she finished relaying her scenario with Pablo, she added, "So I guess we're ready to roll, huh?"

"Oh yeah, right into the morgue."

"That's uncalled for. I think I was brilliant."

"I don't give a damn what you think. It was stupid and dangerous. Now you really got us in a bind."

"Pablo is the best way in to her. He was really spooked."

"Really, now? Listen to me, little girl. Amateurs don't

'spook' criminals, okay? Pros do it. And even then, it's dicey. Did it ever occur to you that you might have opened up the wrong can of worms?"

"Huh?"

"That's exactly what I mean. Don't talk to me. Go to sleep, or something."

Furious, Molly closed her eyes.

Back in the Jet Center lobby, Randall paused to call Lucero. Molly stood a few feet away and didn't speak. When Mrs. Matthews arrived, she started to walk toward her, when Randall grabbed her arm. "Be at Daria's tomorrow night at ten. We gotta fit your wire."

About to speak, she didn't have a chance. He turned away and was heading to the door before she could open her mouth.

Shuffling sideways through the restaurant's kitchen, Molly headed for Daria's retreat. Finding Manuel in the hall, she asked him to let Daria know she was there. Falling into a chair, she lit a cigarette and kicked off her shoes. When Daria came in, she looked up, and said, "If you'll let me pay for once, I'd like a bottle of Gentleman Jack, some soda, and a big dish of pasta. Hold the garlic bread, and forget the wine."

"Bad day?" Daria asked.

"I'm in big trouble with the law."

"Guess I'd better join you. I'm starved anyway."

Filling Daria in, she lost count of the tall tumblers she'd topped off. "And then, he had the nerve to tell me I was on the way to the morgue!" Molly nearly slurred.

"What a hell of a thing to tell you!"

"I'll say. I mean, someone had to get the ball rolling. What did he think I was going to do? Just walk in and say, 'Hello, I have some of your fakes here, can I play, too?' I had to create a plausible entry, didn't I?"

"Makes sense to me. I think you were fantastic. The important thing is, Pablo bought it."

Her head beginning to tilt, Molly nodded. "Thank you. I'm glad someone appreciates what I did."

Daria filled her glass again. "Have a nightcap. I'm going to get the daybed here set up for you. I use it for catnaps when we have a late party. You're in no condition to go home." Watching Molly's drooping eyes, she said, "It might be a little safer, too."

"Not a bad idea," Molly agreed. "Don't fuss. Just throw a blanket over me. I'll be fine."

Daria helped her to the ornate iron bed, then pulled a large quilt from the Brittany chest. Covering her gently, she eased out of the room and headed for the telephone in the kitchen. When Randall came on, she spat, "You insensitive fuck! How could you tell her she was on her way to the morgue! You ought to be thrilled she had the brains and the balls to set the sting up the way she did! You tell your tail she's sleeping here tonight. I'll bunk down in the dining room and have her home before eight." Slamming down the phone, she smiled. *That ought to set his ass straight.*

When Daria woke Molly the next morning, she forcefed her two Cokes. "You won't have a hangover now. Do you want to keep your stash in my safe for the time being?"

"Good idea. They have to go back to Randall anyway." Brushing her hair from her eyes, she said, "You've been a real pal. I can't thank you enough."

"Forget it. You might have to do the same for me sometime."

* * *

By the time she showered, gulped down two coffees from Tosca's, and promised Bennie once again to stop by, it was nearly ten. Opening the shop, she hurried to the storage room, slipped in a few soft classical music CDs, then quickly misted the showroom with a scented spray. When Bitsy hadn't arrived by ten-thirty, she began to worry. As Bitsy was always prompt, and raring to go, her tardiness was a surprise. Not dressed for selling, Molly was about to lock the door and run upstairs, when Bitsy barreled in with Pablo. As she slashed the air with her hand, Bitsy's voice was an octave higher than usual. Her eyes bored into Pablo, as she shouted, "This has got to be sorted out now!" Giving him a swat on the shoulder, she said, "Grab a chair, and don't open your mouth."

Turning to a startled Molly, she commanded, "Lock the door and put the CLOSED sign out. We'll be busy."

Molly almost felt like saluting. Instead, she joined them at the mock living room setup by the fireplace. Pablo was lounging casually, as if he hadn't a care in the world. He stretched his legs out and crossed them at the ankles, while pretending to examine a Chelsea soft-paste porcelain figure Max had sent down. "Up this tag," he said to Molly. "Max priced it too low."

"Didn't I tell you to shut up?" Bitsy growled. Sitting opposite him, she pulled out her ivory cigarette holder, shoved an unfiltered Camel in it, and glared at him as she lit up. Gesturing to Molly to sit beside her, she took a deep drag, then said, "It's time to stop the charade." Turning to Molly, she said, "You know this piece of shit sitting here, as Pablo Evans. My last husband was Rollo Evans. Pablo is my stepson. Unfortunately, I didn't have him around long enough to make a man out of him."

Darting a glance at Pablo, she added, "I don't give a damn that he's gay, I mean fortitude, balls." Seeing the shocked look on Molly's face, she grabbed her hand to stop her from speaking. "Don't faint, dear heart. He's not really dangerous. Only stupid."

Reaching into her pocket for her cigarettes, Molly shook her head. "Good God in heaven, I can't believe this!"

"Believe it. All of it." Still glaring at Pablo, she warned, "And don't you butt in, do you hear me?" When she saw him nod, she went on, "As you have already discovered, this arrogant little bitch is one hell of an artist. Unfortunately, he was too lazy—and too rich—to suffer for his art. He decided the con was more fun. Now, I haven't a problem fudging here and there on a piece." Winking at Molly, she said, "You know the game. Add a few years, make it more rare than it is . . . don't tell the customer the piece is a marriage, create a phony provenance. Many of us dealers get carried away sometimes. Anyway, this little prick decided to stick around Carmel after I sold the shop and complex to Sid. He was a male nurse in Reno before he came of age and collected his inheritance.

"So, when Sid, who was already feeling poorly, needed some help, Pablo here volunteered. While he was here supposedly looking after Sid and the shop, he met Rhonda and Dick. I think you've figured out the rest." Pulling out her silver flask, she said to Pablo, "Get me some tea, shithead."

Molly saw the flush creep up his face. It was all she could do to keep from laughing. It was so wonderful to see the little prince on the wrong end of the stick, she felt like clapping. Instead, she said, "Why are you suddenly telling me all this?"

"I wanted to keep you out of this. I didn't bank on the fact you'd found the watercolors Dick was out of his mind looking for." Her face almost collapsed, and her voice suddenly seemed ancient. "I also believed in you. I'd have sworn on a stack of Bibles that Derek had you fooled. I . . . I didn't want to believe Pablo when he told me you wanted in."

"Are you involved?" Molly asked. "You might as well tell me all the truth."

"No, darling girl, I am not. I've tried my hardest to get Pablo out of Rhonda's clutches. He's afraid she'll turn on him, and he'll end up in jail. She's already threatened to cry fraud and pretend she's the victim."

Returning with Bitsy's tea, Pablo set it down gently on the table between them and settled quietly back on the sofa.

Molly had no choice but to stay with the hand she'd dealt. "I'm sorry I've disappointed you, but I need the money. I haven't a problem selling fake art. If Derek and Greta hadn't run out on me, I'd be somewhere else with my own shop."

Bitsy sighed. "Oh, your mother and father would weep in their graves if they heard you."

Something exploded in Molly's brain. Whirling on Bitsy, she said, "Leave them out of this!" Remembering to stay in control, she prayed God would forgive her. "Daddy Dearest might be having a laugh, or two. Like father, like daughter?"

"Oh, dear Lord," Bitsy said. "I'd have bet on you."

As bad as Molly felt, she wondered if the con was still on? Were Bitsy and Pablo trying to scare her off? Keep the game in the family? Giving her a wide-eyed look, Molly said, "Guess you never know about people, right?"

Snuffing out her cigarette, Bitsy took her time removing it from the holder. "If I can't talk you out of this, then all I can say is, watch your back."

Molly laughed. "Oh, please. I'm not some hick from the boonies."

"I didn't mean that," Bitsy said.

Molly waved her off. "Don't tell me you think Rhonda had anything to do with Lorna's murder. I don't buy that."

"It's hard for me to believe, too, but who knows what people are capable of?"

Pablo finally spoke. "You're both off base. Bea was a nut case, and Dick was a pussy. He was so filled with guilt over Lorna, he couldn't stand himself."

"Guilt?" Molly probed.

"The affair with Rhonda! He told me they had it out the night before she was killed. If they hadn't, she wouldn't have thrown him out and had the garage sale. She'd still be alive, he thought. And then, well . . . I mean, Bea."

Yes, Bea, Molly thought. *But, oh my God, this idiot is either really stupid, scared shitless of Rhonda, or in denial.* She was dying to know why Sid was mentioned only briefly. Didn't Bitsy know he'd been the real brain behind the scheme? Then she wondered if the confession was a fake? Was that why the apartment had been broken into? Had she been wrong to think one of them knew she had the missing watercolors? No, Pablo said Dick was going crazy looking for them. If it was Pablo, and he was only looking for the confession, what about all the money she'd found? He wouldn't leave that if he'd been the one to hide it in the western. No, she'd bet on Sid as the mastermind. Her head was beginning to spin, and she could feel her eye about to take off.

"Look," she said, "this has been loads of fun, but I think the meeting is over." Turning to Pablo, she asked, "Am I on for tomorrow, or not?"

Not daring to look at Bitsy, he said. "Be there at two."

30

"*F*its like a glove," the technician beamed as he made a minor adjustment over her tee shirt. "Just don't jerk around, or touch your . . . uh, chest. These things can get a little ditzy sometimes. Try to keep your shoulders relaxed, and whatever you do, don't sneeze. You'll jerk it out of kilter."

Molly held her breath as they all watched the fitting. She was glad she had time to tell them about her chitchat with Bitsy and Pablo before the tech began fitting the wire. Randall still wasn't cozy with their story, and Lucero didn't believe it at all. Only Daria seemed to think they might have been sincere. Lucero told her she believed in people too much, and that she still hadn't learned a lesson. Wondering what that all meant, Molly pretended not to hear.

Not moving her head, as the tiny wires snaked around her torso, Molly looked at Randall. "Wouldn't bugging Rhonda's place be easier?"

"We'd need a court order," Lucero said. "There's not enough time to set up a bug anyway. This isn't the movies, you know."

"Don't get testy with her, Lucero," Daria said. "You two ought to be on your knees thanking her."

"I hate these militant women, don't you Randall? What about civic duty? We'll give her a watch, don't worry."

"Militant women? Better not let the voters hear that, *paisan*." Daria laughed now.

"Be sure you wear a tee shirt again tomorrow," Randall said. "We don't have a female tech to set you up."

"Come on, this is a new millennium," Molly said. "I do wear a bra, you know." The quick flash of a scowl from Randall surprised her.

Thanking the technician for his help, Lucero told him to be back tomorrow at one. Pulling out a chair, Lucero straddled it and motioned Molly to join him. "There are some legalities I need to run past you. When we do a Fargo, we have certain—"

"A what?" Molly asked.

"It's a term we use. Anyway, it's best to go in with a knowing attitude. Don't be coy and hope she'll spill her guts. It doesn't work that way. You've got to lead her into incriminating herself. I don't want semantics thrown in my face. Her answers have to be vocal, no nodding, no eyes rolling, none of that. I need to *hear* her. Yes, no, whatever. The more you can get her to talk, the better. Now, most important, don't bullshit too much, okay? She'll smell a rat. This woman is sharp. The watercolors are the bait, and your objective is to strike a deal with her. That's all. No . . . did you kill Lorna . . . I saw you there . . . yada, yada, got it? That will blow the whole thing. She'll kick your ass out of there so fast, you won't know what hit you. Worse, she'll be on the first thing smokin' before we know she's gone. For now, we just want her on tape agreeing to fraud." Leaning back, he studied Molly, then said, "Just don't get cute and play Columbo."

"I can hear the butterflies in your stomach," Randall said. "Seasoned cops get 'em all the time. Don't worry about it. I'll be at the other end of the wire in a van parked in front. I'm with you all the way, okay?"

"We'll both be there," Lucero added.

"It's okay. I'm psyched," Molly said, hoping they believed her. "What about Armand?" she asked Randall. "When will he have a sample ready?"

"I was about to get to that. He'll FedEx two pictures in three days. He wasn't thrilled with the artist you selected. He said the artist you chose was too easy for his talents. He wanted a challenge. I reminded him he was to deal with me and not you."

"What a showoff he is," Molly said. "He is brilliant, though. I wanted William Merritt Chase. He's not completely documented yet, and his work is climbing the digits. Rhonda will know of him. I want to show her how good my guy is. Anyway, your idea worked. If he thought he was dealing just with me, he'd pester the hell out of me. He plays nice with the *gendarmes*. By the way, what price did you two settle on?"

Randall's eyes shot to Lucero. "I was meaning to talk to you about that."

Filling their coffee cups, Daria said, "Oh, oh, I can smell it coming! Murphy's Law had to show up sometime."

Molly's eyes narrowed. "How much did that—"

"He wants some teapot you have."

"I'll kill him. I'll break every bone in his body. But first, I'll cut off his hands. He's been after that Napoleonic teapot since I beat him out of it at auction years ago."

When she saw Randall wince, she remembered the story she'd told him on the plane. "I didn't really mean that." Turning away, she folded her arms and stared at one of Daria's French posters. *At least he didn't ask for the miniatures.*

Moving to the table, she licked her lips, then pulled out a cigarette from the pack lying on the table. She watched the smoke billow out before her. She studied the glowing tip, then stubbed it out. "Okay, he can have it. It's at Cleo's with my stuff. He'll have to wait until I can get it to him."

"What's the big deal?" Lucero asked. "You look like you lost your best friend. So he wants a fuckin' teapot."

"About five grand," Molly finally answered. "Depends on who's in the audience at auction. It's rare. It once belonged to James Audubon. Next to Napoleon, and the pirate, Laffite, no one is revered more in New Orleans than Audubon."

Lucero looked at Randall. "You know this guy?"

Randall shook his head, "Get some culture, you jerk. Audubon was the finest ornithology painter in the world. He was from New Orleans."

"Thank you," Molly said.

"Hey, name me every opera Verdi or Puccini wrote, huh? Give me a list of Botticelli's works, what the hell else did Michelangelo do besides the *Pieta*?" Grinning at Daria, he said, "See? He can't do it. Got too much Irish in him." Giving Molly his full attention, he smiled grandly. "Not a problem. I'll fly down tomorrow and set Armand straight. If he's got a jacket, I'll wave it in his face. If he doesn't, I'll make one. Okay?"

The silence, as they waited for Molly to reply, was deafening. Finally, Molly said, "No. We need him. Three people are dead. It's only a teapot."

Daria reached over and squeezed her hand. Lucero was, for once, speechless.

A faint knocking on the door brought Daria to her feet. Manuel was at the door, "For *El Jefe*," he said.

Randall took the envelope and shoved it in his pants pocket. From his jacket, he pulled out a newspaper clipping. Handing it over, he said to Molly, "I wasn't going to show this to you yet, but after what you've just done, I think you deserve it. Like my old Jesuit teachers used to say, 'the end justifies the means.'"

Molly reached for the clipping and unfolded it. She didn't have to read the caption to recognize the woman in the picture. Her hand flew to her mouth, "It's her, the missing woman! Oh, my God . . . even the straw hat!"

"Yep. Guess it's her killing outfit."

"Oh, shit!" Molly mumbled. "No wonder she stared at me that day I went to her gallery." Seeing their confusion, she quickly added, "My baseball hat. I had it on that day. It was the same one I wore to the garage sale. It's dark black with three gold stars on the brim. She must have recognized me." Feeling a cold chill, she shook her head. "She's known all along."

"Probably," Randall said. Turning to Lucero, he added, "Since you didn't read the article, it was taken at the scene of her husband's so-called suicide up by Mendocino. The local paper took it when the rescue crew was trying to hoist his car up out of the ocean." Glancing at Lucero, he added, "Same MO as Dick Jacobs."

"How long have you had this?" Molly demanded.

"A couple of weeks."

Molly stared at him. A surge of rage washed over her. "You could have saved Bea and Dick if you'd shown me this earlier!"

Lucero reached for the clipping and studied it. Looking at Randall, he said, "No, he couldn't have."

"Thanks, Counselor. The picture proves nothing. Even

your description, while it sure as hell fits, only proves she was at the scene. You didn't *see* her stab Lorna."

"But—" Molly began.

"But nothing," Lucero said.

"However," Randall said, "I'd like to think the murderer had a knowledge of anatomy. The entry of Lorna's stab was pretty precise. Bea was knocked out like a pro. How many people know about a carotid artery?"

"Pablo!" Molly shouted.

Randall shook his head. "Doubtful. I'm still betting on Rhonda. I'm thinking it was pure luck both methods appeared to be based on specialized knowledge. Besides, Pablo didn't know about the argument between Dick and Lorna until later. Rhonda would have known right away."

"Is this where *motive, opportunity, and means* comes into play?" Daria asked.

Randall nodded. "You got it." Rising from the table, he stretched and yawned. Turning to Lucero, he asked, "We on track here?"

"*Finito*." Lucero winked.

"Okay, then. Be back here at one, Molly. We'll get you hooked up, you grab the artwork, then stroll around town until it's time. We'll test the wire while you're walking just to be sure." Digging into his pants pocket, he tore open the envelope Manual had delivered and handed her a key. "I figured in case you never got around to calling a locksmith, I'd have one of my guys change your lock. Get a good night's sleep."

31

*M*iracles do happen. She slept like a baby. Awaking at eight, she had a sudden conscience attack and decided today would be the perfect time to start going to Mass. She checked the schedule in the *Monterey Herald* and was pleased to see she'd have enough time to unlock for Bitsy, get to Mass, then head over to Daria's at one.

She chose her favorite outfit for this momentous occasion. The coffee-colored silk tunic she wore over her tee shirt with matching wool slacks gave her the upper crust Manhattan look Rhonda would appreciate. Slipping into alligator loafers, she hooked the clasp on her jade bracelet. When Bitsy arrived promptly at ten, she gave Molly a quick glance, then nodded. "Dressed to kill, are you?" Shaking her head, she added, "I won't wish you luck, you know. In fact, I'm giving my notice. I suddenly find a need for swaying palms and trade winds. I'll be leaving for the Islands in a few days."

Molly was surprised by her disappointment. Was it possible she would actually miss the bossy old bat? "Can't we work something out? I'd hate to have you leave feeling—"

"Ashamed? Disgusted? No, darling, none of the above. Only sad. My debt to your folks has been paid. I did my best to . . ." Turning away, she said, "It doesn't matter. Not anymore."

"What debt?"

"Just a saying. It's nothing. Just a little thing . . . years ago."

God! Molly thought, *is the world comprised of little things?* "Fine. I don't want to hear about it. I've got a few errands before my meeting." Heading for the door, she turned. "What about Max?" she asked.

With her back to Molly, Bitsy fiddled with a French mantel clock. She ran her finger over the bronze figure sitting on top of the clock face. "What about him?"

Hesitating slightly, Molly said, "The art scam. Is he involved?"

Turning to Molly, Bitsy's face was hard. "You should know better."

Leaving the shop feeling better knowing Max wasn't part of the cabal, she wondered if walking to the Mission might diminish the anxiety she was beginning to feel. Realizing she'd be a sweaty mess by the time she returned, she headed for the El Camino.

Carmel was already packed with tourists. It hadn't occurred to her until then that the famous Carmel Mission would be a major stopping point for sightseers, and parking might be a problem. Relieved to find a large lot in the back, she took her time heading for church. Passing the Mission gift shop, she stopped for a moment, then went in. She'd placed her rosary beads in her father's casket and hadn't bought another since. It struck her that she might need new ones before this was over. Selecting a simple crystal set, she was surprised to feel a sense of lightness as she placed it in her pocket. Thanking the clerk for a brochure about the Mission, she checked her watch and noted she had a few minutes before Mass was to begin. Finding a stone bench in the interior garden, she sat down and skimmed over the history of Mission San Carlos Borromeo de Carmelo.

As the bells rang signaling that Mass was about to begin, she headed for the church and was surprised to find she didn't remember it at all. Letting her eyes adjust, she glanced around and nearly held her breath. The Spanish Baroque main altar was riveting. Having just read that the walls were made of crushed seashells, and that the nearby paintings and statues hadn't been moved since the late 1700s, she was filled with a wonderful sense of history.

Dipping her fingers in the Holy Water font, she crossed herself, then headed for a back pew. Her eyes moved to the main altar, where, the brochure proudly stated, Father Serra was buried under a stone slab. Compared to most Catholic churches she'd attended, the mission was relatively simple, but the feeling of comfort she felt was somehow deeper. Kneeling now, she pulled out the new rosary, crossed herself once again, and bowed her head. *I know I'm heavily in debt to Your mercy, but I need a little more credit. I feel responsible for Bea and Dick Jacobs. While there are those who might disagree, and say my inaction was not to blame, I alone am the judge of my soul. I offer my mea culpa, and pray for the strength to face this evil woman. Just please don't get busy around two.*

When Mass was over, Molly felt like raising her hand and requesting a rerun. The safety and comfort she felt was beginning to fade. Standing in the sunlit courtyard, she felt a chill. It was nearly showtime.

Daria handed her a cup of coffee when the tech finished fitting the wire. "I put a little something in it to relax you." Darting a look at Randall, she said, "Just a drop, okay?"

"I'm fine. Really." She lied to a round of worried faces.

"Pretend you're in a school play," Daria offered.

When Randall looked at her and shook his head, Daria said, "Yeah, really." Facing Molly, she went on, "Do like the actors do. Step outside of yourself, be someone else. If it can work for some of those lamebrains, why not you?"

"Slight change of plan," Lucero said. Nodding to Randall, he said, "Give it to her."

Molly held her breath. "Now what?" she blurted.

Handing her a piece of paper, Randall said, "You're not going to show her the watercolors. They don't mean anything. Show her this. She's after the journal."

Taking the paper from him, Molly glanced at the list of titles and figures. "Jesus! What a fool I've been. I'd forgotten all about the journal. Here's two of the titles she has on display."

"It's still not proof of anything," Lucero said. "Any rookie lawyer would argue it was merely an inventory list." Shrugging, he laughed. "But hey, I can blow that to hell in court."

Molly stared at the photocopy. "One page? That's all I'm to show her?"

"For now," Randall replied.

As she stood outside the gallery, it took all of Molly's willpower not to look at the van parked in front. Stepping inside, she saw Rhonda with a young couple examining a bronze sculpture. Dressed in a gorgeous St. John knit, Rhonda presented a sleek look Molly had to admire. Her hair was beautifully cut, her makeup was perfection, and the Manolo Blahnik pumps she wore cost enough to feed a small family for a month. Licking her lips, Molly considered what Daria said about stepping outside herself.

What would Meryl Streep do now? She'd look at artwork, idiot. She forced a studied look on her face, then stepped back to admire a seascape. Rhonda had cleverly added some new artists since the last time she'd been in. After a few more minutes, her nerves began to crackle. If that couple didn't leave pretty soon, she might.

Her mouth was filled with cotton, and her legs felt like Jell-O. Turning away from the seascape, she saw Rhonda staring at her. Giving Molly a quick smile, Rhonda said, "I'll be with you shortly."

Molly smiled back. "Take your time. I'm still browsing."

Moving on, she stopped before a rather large abstract. Molly hated them. She considered them coarse and violent. She almost didn't get her art degree because of her attitude. As far as she was concerned, finger painting had more charm. Finally, she saw the husband shake hands with Rhonda, promise to be back, and trade business cards. As he steered his wife out of the shop, Molly rolled her tongue over her teeth and headed toward Rhonda.

At her desk, Rhonda sat and motioned Molly to take a seat. Playing with a pen, she stared at Molly, then said, "Let's not beat around the bush. I don't have time for preambles or silly games. How much?"

Crossing her legs, Molly said, "I'm not here for blackmail. Is that what Pablo told you?"

"Never mind what Pablo said. I'm asking the questions here. Now, for the last time, how much?"

Setting the copy of the journal page before her, Molly asked, "I guess you're talking about this?"

Rhonda didn't touch it. She merely glanced at it, then nodded.

Shit, Molly thought. *Randall and Lucero want vocals.* "Is it the journal you want, or not?" she demanded.

Rhonda hesitated, then finally said, "Yes."

Molly felt like melting. "You can have it. The water-colors, too."

"Have it?" Rhonda sneered, "*Have it?* Don't fuck with me. What's your price?"

The commitment was made. Molly suddenly felt relief flood through her. It had been easier than she'd imagined. She wondered if she could walk out now. Was it enough? Then, she thought, maybe *too* easy. Finish the script Randall and Lucero had planned. "I want in," Molly said.

"The gig's over," Rhonda replied. "I'm leaving in three weeks."

"Then what's the point in my coming here?"

"I don't want to leave any loose ends."

Molly reached for her bag, flung it over her shoulder, then said, "Too bad. I have two William Merritt Chases coming in a few days I thought you might like. Not to mention a list of prospects that would froth at the mouth for them."

"The real thing?"

Molly laughed. "Of course not."

"Where did you get them?"

Molly knew she had her now. Trust in greed with a dealer, and success was yours. "I've got a genius hidden away who can replicate any artist living or dead. His Boteros are masterpieces. In fact, he's better."

Shifting in her chair, Rhonda fiddled with a letter opener. Molly didn't like her new choice of toys. The long, slender blade was topped with a writhing silver dragon with red eyes. Tearing her eyes away, Molly said, "I can't approach my list. My, uh, little problem in New York is still too fresh. I need a legit gallery to move the stuff. The beauty of Chase is that his auction prices are all over the place. He can go from five to seven figures, and you can justify it."

"I thought you were cleared of those charges?" Rhonda asked.

Reaching into her tote, emptied and cleaned last night, Molly pulled out an envelope and handed it to her. Rhonda took out the newspaper clipping. The *New York Times* had generously splashed Molly's photo over half of the front page. In handcuffs, and surrounded by police, it was not one of her better photos. Rhonda's perfectly arched eyebrows nearly met her hairline as she read the accompanying story.

Setting the clipping back on the desk, Rhonda said, "You had a better hairdresser then."

"I can't afford one now," Molly snapped.

"Why did you lie to Dick about not finding anything in his desk?"

"Insurance."

"Oh, come on! You didn't have a clue to what was going on until Pablo spilled his guts to you."

Molly hadn't been prepared for this. *Help me, Meryl.* "Pablo? Don't be dense. I'm not an idiot. Besides, I've done my research. You need to offer some better-known artists. Take your father up a little slower. Don't flood the market. Someone will catch on." She had to convince her Pablo hadn't said a word. She didn't need another murder on her conscience. "It doesn't take a rocket scientist to know what's going on." She began counting on her fingers, "First my trash is tossed, then the apartment is broken into." She smiled slyly, then added, "I'm a fine arts major, in case you didn't know." She was winging it, and she prayed it was working. "It didn't take long to figure it out. Especially when I saw the similarities between

Dick's work and what you have here. By the way, you better ditch Webster and Hubble. Someone is going to take those to auction and find out they never existed."

When two men entered the gallery, Rhonda rose. "I'll have to think about this."

Thank you, God, for sending them in. This was her cue to leave. She only hoped Randall and Lucero had enough on tape to satisfy them. "I think," Molly said, "it would be worth your while to stick around a little longer. I'm not looking for a long relationship. Just enough to get out of here myself."

Keeping her eye on the two men, Rhonda said, "We'll talk money later. *If* I decide to stay. It will depend on how good your artist is. And how much you plan to hold me up for."

"Ten thousand will do it."

"That's chump change."

"Not for me. Not now, at least," Molly said over her shoulder.

32

She followed the route Randall told her to take to Daria's. It was amazing how much of Carmel she was beginning to have time to see. Her first trip through town, after she'd cleaned the apartment and shop, had been strictly to search for antique shops and check out the competition. Now that her nose wasn't quite so high in the air, she had to admit Carmel proper and the area known as the "mouth of the valley" had at least a half dozen genuine dealers. Her step was a little lighter now that the encounter with Rhonda was over. The prospect of never seeing that woman again was enough to start her humming the rest of the way to Daria's.

She was glad to have the wires removed. Scared to death they might come undone, she'd hardly moved her arms for an hour. "When I reached down to grab my tote," she told Randall and Lucero, "I felt something catch on my bra. Thank God this is over. You got all you need, right?"

Lucero shot a quick glance at Randall. When Molly heard coins jiggling in his pocket again, her heart sank. "What?" she nearly screamed.

Daria excused herself. She'd be back with drinks.

"Only a minor glitch," Randall quickly assured her.

"We didn't get all of it when she said she was leaving for La Jolla." When he saw the blank look on her face, he added, "Bennie told us that was where she said she was moving."

Sinking into a chair, Molly held her head in her hands. "She never mentioned La Jolla. And since when has Bennie been a part of this?"

Lucero pulled up a chair next to her. "I had a little chat with that cousin of mine. When I told him Randall was a half-breed, he decided it was time to do a little reaching out."

"What else did you two miss?" Molly nearly screamed. "You did get her admitting it was the journal she wanted? And that we'd talk money after she saw my samples?"

Lucero looked away. Randall hitched up his pants and took a chair opposite Molly. "There was a little problem with the equipment in the van. We . . . we, ah, didn't get any of it."

Molly remembered the first time she'd met him, and how much she'd wanted to smack him. The feeling returned. "I could be dead, lying on the floor with that treacherous letter opener she kept playing with sticking out of my chest, gasping for my last breath, and you two . . . you two fucking idiots wouldn't have been the wiser."

"Go ahead and yell if it makes you feel better," Randall said rather meekly. "Things like this happen." Shooting an angry look to Lucero, he said, "If this burg had decent equipment, this wouldn't have happened. I've called down to L.A. and pulled a few strings. We'll have a top-of-the-line setup here tomorrow. Loomis is hand-delivering it."

When Molly wouldn't look at him, he added, "You liked Loomis, remember?"

Glaring at him, she snapped, "I love him. So much, I'm willing to let him take my place, okay?"

"Better tell me what happened. We need to know how she reacted, everything she said, body language, the whole nine yards. Have something to drink, a snack maybe, then we'll tape it, and—"

"And what? Tell me what a great job I did, and when I can do it again?" Shaking her head, she said, "Sorry. I . . . I can't do it again."

"You have no choice," Lucero said. "She's expecting you back, isn't she?"

Taking a deep breath, Molly sighed. "Yes, but I didn't think that was for real. I mean, I figured you had enough."

"Sorry," Lucero said. "We need to have money exchange hands to seal it."

"You bastard! You knew that all along."

"When's the next meet?" Randall quickly asked. He didn't need a shouting match between them.

"I don't know. She said she'd have to think about it. I told her my samples would arrive in a few days."

"Okay, then," Lucero said. "That buys us more time. I can get a court order to bug the place now. Maybe sneak in a video camera or two. My uncle can get us in without her knowing we've been there."

Darting an angry look at Randall, she turned back to Lucero. "Then you won't have to wire me again?"

"One more time. The more we have, the better."

"I'm going to look like an idiot if I ask her the same questions again. She'll get wise, won't she?"

"We'll change script."

* * *

A subdued Bitsy greeted her when she got back to the shop. "Slow day. Only four sales. A couple of hundred, that's all. The slips are on your desk. Would you be terribly disappointed if I left early? I seem a bit peaked today."

Not sure if this was a play on her guilt, or if indeed, events had taken their toll on her, Molly quickly agreed. "Go right ahead. I might just close early anyway."

Glancing at her watch, Bitsy said, "The village is packed, but with this beautiful weather, they must all be at the beach. It's close to five. I don't see why you shouldn't lock up around six."

"As long as Pablo doesn't get wind of it, I think I will." Molly could have bitten her tongue.

"I don't think he'll be much of a problem anymore."

"That slipped," Molly said.

"Yes, well, don't get in the habit of doing that around Rhonda. She will let you know soon enough she is queen of all she surveys."

Moving toward her, Molly put out her hand, "Bitsy . . . I . . . I'm sorry I've disappointed you. This business is . . . well . . ."

Turning sideways, as if to forestall any contact, Bitsy said, "*Caveat emptor?* Let the buyer beware? Oh, my dear girl, the temptation finds us all, one time or another. And, I'd have to be the first one to admit, I've been less than honest in my day. But this . . . this is outright criminal. This isn't what your parents wanted for you." Turning to face her now, she quickly said, "I know you don't want to talk about them." Seeing the stubborn lift of Molly's chin, Bitsy drew herself up, and pointed at her. "Sit down. Maybe it's time after all."

Exhausted from her encounter with Rhonda, and nearly dizzy with anger at Randall and Lucero, Molly was surprised to find herself numbly obeying. Dropping to a sofa, she said, "Fine, let's get it over with."

Her energy renewed, Bitsy strode to the door. "We're closing now." Returning with a bottle of Gentleman Jack under her arm, and two mugs from the storage room, Bitsy set them on the coffee table between them. Shoving aside a small stack of leather-bound books, she set down the mugs. Molly's eyes flew open. "Where did you get that?"

Filling their mugs halfway, Bitsy said, "I stashed it here a couple of weeks ago. We'll drink Brit style, no ice, straight up." Eyeing Molly, she added, "You've been around enough, so I won't tell you to sip easy. On the other hand, you might want to take a few good slugs. You'll need a little buzz when you hear what I have to say."

Eyeing her warily, Molly picked up the mug. "Do we need a toast?"

When she raised her mug, Bitsy's eyes were hard. "A eulogy might be more appropriate. I am burying a ghost who has hung around far too long. Time to put it to rest."

Molly wasn't sure how much more she wanted to take today. Captured, she merely shrugged, then said, "Cheers."

"*Salud*," Bitsy mumbled.

Settling back, cradling the mug in her hand, Molly said, "Okay, you're on."

Bitsy pulled her unfiltered Camels from the pocket of her skirt, stuck one between her lips, and over the flame of her lighter said, "I was the woman wearing the bracelet at that fancy party years ago. I'm responsible for your father doing time."

Molly couldn't move. A blowtorch couldn't melt the ice that seemed to fill her. The click of Bitsy's lighter made her blink. Bitsy watched her, then waited for only a short moment. "Your sweet little sister brought it to Max. She sneaked it from your father and tried to hit up Max for a few hundred bucks."

Molly's continued silence worried Bitsy. Whatever the reason for her stoic façade, she had to tell her all of it. "Max often bought estate jewelry from your father. He didn't know it was hot. When your sister showed up with the bracelet, he thought she was playing errand girl. I bought it from Max. When all hell broke loose over the bracelet I was showing off, and your father was hauled off, Max nearly went over the edge."

Finally, Molly raised the mug to her lips and took a long swallow. Setting the mug on the table, she said, "No wonder she refused to come to Dad's funeral. Now I understand a few things." Reaching for one of Bitsy's cigarettes, she lit it and nearly choked. "She left for Seattle with her boyfriend just after Dad was arrested. I haven't seen her since. I had a few postcards, but that was all. I wonder if she ever reads the *New York Times*?"

Dabbing at her mascara, Bitsy sniffed. "If only I hadn't worn that fucking bracelet, none of this would have happened!"

Molly shook her head. "How could you have known?"

"You must really hate me now. I know I've been a pain in the ass, but I loved you as a baby, then you became an obsession with me. I had to keep an eye on you. Max and I swore we'd be there if you needed us."

"Oh, Bitsy," Molly began. "I never hated you. Not even when I wanted to shove you out the door." Despite all she'd just learned, she couldn't help but grin. "You are a bit overbearing, you know. But if you'd only told me right away."

"I wanted to. Max begged me to wait. You had to have time to regroup. Get your sassy act together. He loves you so much." Dabbing at her eyes again, she asked, "Have you read any Westerns lately?"

"No. Oh, no! Don't tell me . . ." Molly had to stop. The room was beginning to spin out of control.

"We know you love books. Max remembered how you wouldn't throw one away. We just didn't know if you liked Westerns."

"You two put that money in the books?"

Bitsy's smile was as close to shy as she could manage. "Every girl needs a little nest egg. We just hoped you wouldn't take it and run to New Orleans too soon."

"But that much?"

"How much did you find?"

"Twenty-three thousand."

Bitsy waved her hand and laughed. "Oh, honey. You've got to keep looking. Check out the atlas. Ever see a movie called *Finnegan Begin Again*?"

Molly held her hands over her mouth, then said, "Yes. I saw it on television with, of all people, Derek and Greta. I'm giving it back. Neither of you owes me a thing."

Bitsy slammed her hand on the table. "Absolutely not! Didn't Max tell you the books were yours?"

"I've been feeling guilty for days about that money. I can't keep it now."

"What the hell kind of dealer are you? You find a treasure, you keep your mouth shut and sell your heart out. Finders keepers, losers weepers. Remember that? It's our motto." Draining her mug, she said, "You needed a stake, you got it. Someday, help someone else out. We'd be tickled pink if you'd stay, but we'd never stand in your way. God knows we've done enough harm as it is. You wouldn't be trucking with that bitch if we hadn't got you here."

The sudden silence between them was interrupted by a knocking on the glass door. Molly looked up, and saw Pablo waving. Heaving a deep sigh, she said, "Now what? I've had it today, I really mean it."

About to rise, Bitsy grabbed her hands. "Don't do this thing with Rhonda. Please, Molly. I'll give you whatever you need. Just don't do it."

Molly was struck by the stark pleading in her eyes. She almost felt like melting and telling her the truth. "I can't back out now." Patting Bitsy's hand, she said, "Trust me a little, okay? I know what I'm doing."

At the door, she let Pablo in. "Why are you closed?" he demanded.

Molly shook her head. Enough was enough. His nerve in scolding her was beyond comprehension. "How about none of your business?" Rushing over to her desk, she grabbed the telephone. "Here . . . want to call Max and tattle? Go ahead, I'll give him an earful too."

In an instant, the immaculate and very haughty man seemed to wither before her eyes. "I . . . I'm sorry. Habit, I guess." Running a perfectly manicured hand through his hundred-dollar haircut, he said, "You've got to convince Rhonda I didn't tell you what was going on. She almost came after me." Joining Bitsy, he threw out his hands. "Can't you make Molly understand what she's getting into?"

"I'm trying. She won't listen." Bitsy was pleading. "There you are. Isn't this proof enough? The woman is ruthless. She'll stop at nothing."

"Even murder?" Molly asked.

Pablo's head snapped around so fast, it was a wonder he didn't fall over. "Don't ask, don't tell. Is the bitch nuts? Yes. Could she kill? Probably. Am I scared shitless? You're damn right I am. Get the picture?"

⌁ 33 ⌁

*B*itsy called and said she wouldn't be in for a few days. Molly couldn't blame her. Too much had passed between them yesterday. They needed a day or two away from each other. When Pablo left them yesterday, he had said he was going back to The City and talk Max into a little trip to Rio. He wished her luck, and said he was sorry for being so rotten to her. He almost made her cry. "I tried to convince Max to sell out, but when he said he was hanging on for you, my heart sank. It was a chance for me to get untangled from Rhonda. Then, when you were the one that found Lorna and bought that evil desk, I really panicked. I figured if I gave you enough heat, you'd leave." He looked over at Bitsy and smiled. "She's a hard old bitch, but she means well. It's a good thing I love her to death. I'd have throttled her by now." Before he had left, he added, "You can still back out, Molly. Call her, tell her you changed your mind. Please."

Oh, Pablo! How I'd love to! But, I'm in too deep now. Besides, they were close to nailing Rhonda. That alone gave her the courage she needed to see it through. When she'd asked Bitsy not to tell Max, the older woman sighed. "I've been enough of a buttinski. You're on your own."

* * *

Busy dusting imaginary motes, and adding fresh water to bouquets she'd picked up at the market, Molly kept herself occupied. When the phone rang, she nearly knocked over a small Rockingham teapot. Delighted at first to hear Angela's voice, she suddenly had a panic attack when Angela breathlessly said, "Now look, sugar, I don't want you to panic, but Armand's a day overdue. I'm sure he'll show up by tonight."

Molly went rigid. "Angela . . . you're not telling me he hasn't completed the commission?"

"Oh, no, he's almost done. I mean, he's got one aging, and the other half-done. But you know Armand! He can whip up a masterpiece overnight. I just thought I'd better call in case he's a day or two late sending them off."

"Is he in jail again?"

"You know what that Cajun blood is like. He just ran over to Puerto Rico. He had a meeting with an old friend."

"I must have those pictures by Wednesday! Call him and tell him . . . tell him I'll . . . oh, shit! Tell him I'll throw in the two Audubon coffee cups and saucers. They match the teapot. If that doesn't get him home, tell him to run as fast as he can. You tell him I'll be after him with such mojo, he won't know what hit him. Tell him that, Angela! Do you hear me?"

"But Molly, there's no phone where he's gone. It's an artist colony out in the boonies."

Molly was glassy eyed. Looking up at the ceiling, she blew out her breath, and mumbled, "I thought we were pals again. I was good at Mass yesterday, wasn't I? I paid attention, and everything!"

"Excuse me, honey . . . I didn't quite get all that."

"I wasn't talking to you. What part of the island? North, south . . . where?"

"Oh, it's near San Juan. Uh, let's see . . . it's . . . ah, Bayamón on the northeast end. But don't fret, he'll be home tonight. I'm sure of it."

"You bet he will!" Molly snapped. "Keep his supper hot, he'll need strength."

The minute Molly managed to get Angela off without hurting her feelings, she punched in Randall's pager number. When he called back almost instantly, she quickly said, "Armand is off on a toot in Puerto Rico. He was due back yesterday, and Angela can't reach him by phone."

"Where in Puerto Rico?"

She spelled out Bayamón, then added, "A little squiggly goes over the o."

"I really don't give a shit, okay? I'll have him home before midnight Louisiana time."

Molly's eyes widened. "You can do that? You know cops in Puerto Rico?"

Randall's laugh was almost scary. "I know cops in places you've never heard of. In fact, I know all kinds of people. Don't panic. You'll have your pictures."

When the telephone woke her just past 3 A.M., Molly's faith in Randall took a giant leap. *"Chère!"* Armand scolded, "It was not necessary for you to call in the fuzz. I was on my way. Your police friend has a very long arm to stretch to Puerto Rico."

"His arm, *mon ami*, is longer than you think. How could you do this to me? You know I have to have—"

"But, my darling, I could not help it. I was on the trail of some very interesting news. And the, the *gendarmes*, they find me and escort me to the airport! This does not look well with my compatriots. But, I shall forgive you. Oh, *chère*, do you have the provenance for the teapot?"

"Are you questioning me? Have I ever been less than honest with you?"

"Do not lose it, *ma petite*. I was only wondering. Do you wish to hear what I have discovered?"

Three in the morning, and he wanted to gossip! "I only want to hear you promise those pictures will be in my hands on Wednesday."

"I am a man of my word. They shall be there. But this gossip . . . it is delicious. You will be eager to hear it."

Molly sighed. "What?"

"Aha, I knew you could not close your ears. We are born *bavaders* you and I, *non*?"

When Molly didn't answer, he hurried on. "*Alors,* I was at Dannerley's the other day, and I came upon him cooking the soup for an order of twenty nineteenth-century gilt frames."

Molly was rubbing her eyes and searching for a cigarette. "And?"

"And, he tells me this order is for his former *patron*, my *ami* from New York who is back in the business. The frames are for English pastorals and hunting scenes. They are to be shipped to Lisbon."

"Go on," Molly said, suddenly interested.

"I only pass this on because—"

"*Je comprends*. I understand. *Merci, mon ami. Merci.*" Molly said.

Molly had a sudden desire to curl up and sleep for days. So, Derek and Greta were back in business, were they? She only hoped they would stay in Portugal. She had enough to contend with at present.

The telephone rang as she was closing on Tuesday. Worn out, she took her time walking to the desk. She really didn't care if she caught it, or not. Whoever it was could wait. She got it on the fifth ring. "This is Treasures. Can I help you?"

"Will your delivery be on time?"

Molly recognized Rhonda's voice immediately. "Yes. It's promised for Wednesday."

"We'll meet Thursday at eight. My place. Grab a pen, I'll give you directions."

Molly's breath caught in her throat. No way was she going to her home. Instead of making excuses, she decided to go on the offense. "Make it your gallery, if you don't mind. Or, here, at the shop. By the way, I'll be expecting a little good faith money. Five grand will do. Cash, and in fifties."

"We'll see," Rhonda said.

"Have it, or you can look elsewhere."

"Is that your final answer?" Rhonda laughed at her little joke. "Never mind. We'll meet at my gallery."

Holding on to the banister, Molly took the stairs one at a time. She wasn't sure if she'd make it to the top. The prospect of fixing dinner was exhausting.

Locking the upper door, she decided she had enough energy to walk the short distance to Daria's. She could call Randall from the back room and tell him about Rhonda's call. She changed her mind. It wasn't worth the effort. Another frozen dinner wouldn't tax her all that much. She could watch a little television. Something simple. A good ole pirate movie would be great. No such luck. It wasn't Saturday. Maybe she'd find something on A&E, or Bravo.

⟫ 34 ⟪

*B*y Thursday, Molly felt as if she'd been sleepwalking the past few days. When Armand's masterpieces arrived, she nearly cried. The man was so talented; it shook her to her core. If only he'd play it straight. But the world knew artists were a strange breed. A persona went a long way in the art world. The crazier you were, the more celebrated you might become.

The new wire fit better. Slowly moving her shoulders, she nodded to the tech. Giving him a nervous smile, she said, "It's better than the last one."

"You're sure? Don't be bashful. If it's constricting, let me know. This is a new model . . . cutting-edge. More delicate than the other one."

Wiggling her hands back and forth to get the blood flowing, she nodded. "With that tape you wrapped me up in, I hardly know it's on. Too bad Loomis couldn't stay."

Randall watched her nervous gestures. It reminded him of a pole-vaulter, ready for the big push into the Olympics. "He's on a case. You sure you're okay? Take some deep breaths. Let's see if it moves."

Daria was leaning against the bookcase, rolling and unrolling the sleeve of her chef's jacket. Lucero was thumbing through cookbooks, his knee jerking under the table. Molly winked at Daria, "This tape makes a hell of a girdle."

"I got the new gear from my DEA buddies in Lost Angels. They swear you can hear heartbeats." Randall boasted.

"Lost what?" Lucero asked.

"It's a joke," Randall said.

Molly's laugh was a little tinny. "I hope I don't blow your eardrums."

Tapping Lucero on the shoulder, Randall said, "Let's roll."

Giving Molly a thoughtful look, he forced a grin. "I told you we changed vans, didn't I?"

"Yes. It's yellow this time."

"Right. And we'll be two parking spaces down."

Molly nodded. "You said that."

"Good. Thought so. The spot's secure. I've got a plain-clothes sittin' in an unmarked holding it for us. Don't forget—"

"I know, don't look at the van. Make sure she doesn't nod, or shrug. Get it vocal. I got it, okay?"

"Yeah, yeah. You're an old pro now. Just don't forget to—"

Lucero yanked his jacket. "Jesus! Randall! Leave her alone, for Chrissake! You're mothering her to death."

The three blocks to Rhonda's gallery felt like the last mile. Her legs weren't shaking this time. They were numb. Remembering the serenity and stillness of the mission, she shifted Armand's samples from one arm to the other and said Hail Marys so fast, her tongue tripped over the words. When her ears began to ring, she stopped before a dress boutique and stared into the window. *Get a grip*, she commanded. *You made it through the first fire dance. You can do it again.* She paused at the corner of the second block. *Okay, look both ways before crossing. Stay in the crosswalk. If you get hit, you can sue. Pedestrians have the right of way in California.*

Standing before Rhonda's gallery, she made sure the van was where Randall had promised. She let out her breath. *Okay, Meryl, let's do it.* Opening the door, she stepped in to the sounds of Mozart. Maybe it was Haydn. She wasn't sure. Her brain was on fire. She didn't remember music last time. She saw Rhonda was dressed to kill again. Molly didn't like that phrase.

"Have a seat. I'll lock up."

She was going to lock the door? Molly hadn't thought about that. Trying to act casual, she slowly moved to Rhonda's desk. Pausing before an abstract, she was surprised it didn't repulse her. In fact, the colors were brilliantly juxtaposed. "Nice," she said as she felt Rhonda standing just behind her.

"It's not bad. He's local with a few out of town followers. He doesn't move fast enough. I had to up my take to 70 percent to justify the space on the wall."

Grateful for an opening to calm her nerves, Molly asked, "What's the going rate here?"

Seated now, Rhonda said, "Anywhere from fifty to seventy. It depends."

Slipping into the chair opposite her, Molly looked around. She remembered her first impression. The gallery was beautifully subdued. And then she noticed that the orchids were gone. In their place, Rhonda had dotted the room with white roses. Stark, but effective. "Get much grumbling over the rates?"

"I give a shit." Pushing aside some paperwork, she said, "Let's take a look at what you've brought."

Molly saw the letter opener on her desk. Looking away, she concentrated on unwrapping Armand's little beauties. "While I unwrap, why don't you show me the money."

Rhonda stared at her for a moment, then opened a drawer. She spread out the money on the desk. "You want to count it?"

"Look," Molly said, "I'm not in the mood for sarcasm. You count it out, nice and loud while I set these up. Indulge me."

"Whatever turns you on."

As she began the count, Molly could feel little rivers of sweat drip down her back. She hoped to hell it didn't short out the equipment. When Rhonda got to five thousand, Molly clenched her teeth. *Gotcha.*

Lucero gave Randall a thumbs-up. "Bingo. Round one to Molly. Coming through nice and clear."

Twisting a rubber band between his fingers, Randall nodded. "So far, so good. This one better not fritz out. I'll go headhunting at DEA."

Lucero pretended to shiver. "Glad it's not my jurisdiction."

Molly set the first picture on the easel Rhonda had ready by her desk. "I don't need to tell you this is William Merritt Chase. With your eye, you can probably see that without looking at the signature. Is this guy fantastic, or what?"

The smile Rhonda's perfectly arched lips managed almost made her look like she had a soul. "Exquisite."

"Wait until you see the other one." Molly preened.

"This isn't the guy that did all those William Aiken Walkers is it? I thought they caught him."

"No, my artist is smarter than that. Infinitely better, I might add. Although, Dick did a pretty good job on your father's style. I was impressed."

"Dick was good. Better than the last one."

Molly laughed. "Really? Where are they now? Not pissed, I hope."

Rhonda waved her off. "Forget it. They won't talk."

Inching away from her, Molly leaned against the desk. Being that close was enough to start her legs wobbling again. "Good. I don't like loose ends."

"You might say they've retired." Pulling the picture down, she leaned it against a chair. "Let's have the other one."

Handing her the next picture, Molly asked, "Will they stay that way? I'd hate to have your past blow this up. I can see some big money coming fast."

"They're dead," Rhonda said calmly.

Pretending to joke, Molly said, "How'd you get so lucky?"

Eyeing the picture, she said, "I make my luck."

"Man, she's a cool bitch," Lucero said. "I can't wait to get her on the stand. I'll make her wish—"

"Will you please shut the fuck up!" the tech said. "Randall, put a muzzle on him, will you?"

Randall snapped the first rubber band. He was working on a second. "Goddamn, but Molly's good. Hang in there, baby! We're comin' out of the turn. The home-stretch is right ahead."

Oh, God! Molly thought. *Is that good enough? Can I leave now?* "I've got a dinner date with a client. If you like the product, tell me now. I'll make a few calls, get a prospect down here by the weekend. He'll probably snap both of them up the minute he sees them."

Rhonda stared at the second picture. "Why are you working so cheap? You know I can get thirty or forty for

each one." Whirling around to face her, she arched an
eyebrow. "I want an answer."

"Let's call them a loss leader. The next ones will be
more expensive."

"Really? Just what did you have in mind for the next
ones? If I want them, that is."

Picking up the money from the desk, Molly stuffed it
in her tote, and turned to Rhonda. "I was thinking a
Charles Rollo Peters, or maybe a Francis McComas."

"They're documented," Rhonda said.

"So?"

"Even if it's fake?"

"He wouldn't have a clue."

"What about Mary DeNeale Morgan?"

"Sounds familiar. Isn't she local?" Molly asked.

"Yes, but she's moving up. Some of her stuff hit high
marks at Sanford's California Art Auction not too long
ago. I have one I can take on consignment. Maybe one of
your buyers might go for it. After that, we'll see."

"I'd rather stay away from local artists. There may be
too many old-timers who would remember output."
Molly began slowly to put distance between them. Inching toward the front of the gallery, she watched Rhonda
return to her desk.

Still on her feet, Rhonda stared at Armand's picture.
Idly picking up the letter opener, she turned it over and
over in her hands. Finally, she slipped into her chair.
"True. Let's just stick with the regulars for now. I'd like
him to do a Toby. I've got a waiting list."

"Oh, come on!" Molly jeered. "No offense, but he really wasn't all that good." Molly could have bitten her
tongue. Pasting on a smile, she quickly added, "Besides,
we can get more money with better-known artists."

Rhonda bolted out of her chair, and was in her face before Molly could exhale. "Wasn't all that good? Wipe that New York smirk off your face. He was the best! Do you hear me? The best!"

That was all Molly needed to hear. "Oh, come off it! I've seen better in high school art classes!"

Not more than two feet separated them. Molly could see the veins in Rhonda's neck pulsing. Pink blotches bled through Rhonda's makeup. Molly jerked back and ran into a small chest. The vase of roses sitting on top, wobbled briefly, then crashed to the floor.

"Back off!" Molly shouted. Her heart began to hammer, and her eyes were locked on the letter opener, but something inside her snapped and she couldn't stop. The memory of Bea and Dick Jacobs overrode her fear. "He was a lightweight, and you know it. You wouldn't have needed Dick if he wasn't. I've seen the work. Too bad his hands weren't smashed sooner; he might have found another hobby."

The letter opener still clutched in her hand, Rhonda's eyes fluttered as she lowered her head. Molly could swear she heard an animal growl rushing up her throat. "My father was . . ."

Molly judged there was about twenty feet separating her from the front door. Two or three seconds at the most, and she could at least throw something through the window. Edging backward, her eyes still on Rhonda, she laughed. "Your *father*? Cut the bullshit. We both know the truth. I did my homework. You were a toddler when your mother married Toby."

Rhonda lifted her head. The fire in her eyes seemed to melt her features into a montage of rage. "You lying bitch! He *was* my father!"

Molly's throat was closing so fast, she could hardly breathe. "You didn't know? You really believed it?"

*   *   *

A pile of broken rubber bands surrounded Randall's feet. Sweat trickled down his face. The van was suddenly sweltering. "She's not sticking to the script." Lucero said, "What the fuck is she trying to do? We've got enough, for Chrissakes! We got the bitch already. Pull her out. I'm satisfied, okay?"

Randall grabbed his arm. "Wait. She's got her unglued now. I'll know when to move. And when I do, I'm the first out the door, got it?"

Molly's first mistake was glancing over her shoulder to see how much ground she'd covered. In a flash, Rhonda was on her. Sharp claws dug into her face then moved to her silk blouse, nearly tearing it off. Although she was shorter than Molly by several inches, the crazed woman's strength was incredible as she spun Molly around like a top. Crashing into the easel holding the abstract Molly had admired earlier, she fell against a marble plinth holding a bronze sculpture. The sharp pain in her back stunned her. Barely managing to get to her knees, she reached for the top of the plinth. Her hands were sweating so badly, they slid down the cold marble. Groping wildly for the bronze sculpture, she suddenly realized greed hadn't been Rhonda's only Achilles' heel. It was Lawrence Toby. It was her identity as his daughter. She had made him into the artist he could never have been.

Wondering where the hell Randall and Lucero were, Molly screamed, "You are so pathetic, I almost feel sorry for you!"

The van door wouldn't open. Randall pulled at the handle, and it wouldn't give. His eyes were popping out of his head. "Who locked this motherfucker?" Leaning into the rear door with his shoulder, he yelled, "Call the medics! They're up the street on standby." Randall and Lucero used their combined body strength and hurled themselves at the door. It flew open, smashing into the grill of a Range Rover parked over its space. Leaping onto the hood of the Rover, Randall swung off easily and ran to the gallery, barreling through tourists like a linebacker. Lucero wasn't as agile. Slipping on the hood of the Rover, he hit the sidewalk like a ton of bricks.

Unable to reach the bronze sculpture in time, Molly threw up her hands as Rhonda pounced on her. The letter opener still in her hand, Rhonda grabbed Molly by the hair, and screamed, "I'll kill you!"

Molly punched Rhonda with her fist. The blow caught her off guard and forced her to roll over. It was all Molly needed to get to her feet. Putting the marble plinth between them, Molly tried to find the sculpture. She saw it out of the corner of her eye. It was wedged under a portable display wall. Creeping toward it, her arms outstretched for balance, she prayed the sharp edges of the winged bird would be enough to stop Rhonda. Where was Randall? "Like you killed Lorna and Bea?" Catching her breath, she added, "And Dick?"

In a deadly crouch, Lorna was moving closer, circling her like a starved coyote. When she stopped in front of the portable wall, Molly knew she'd never make it to the sculpture. "That was business. Killing you will be a pleasure."

Damn Randall! Where is he?

Molly's heart sank. *The wire. It didn't work again. He'd be here by now. He wouldn't put me through this unless something's gone wrong again.* Her knees were wobbling. She had to think of something to slow Rhonda down. "Look . . . ah, can't we talk this out? I'm sorry about what I said."

"I don't think so. You're a nasty little liar. I don't like liars."

"Okay! Maybe I was wrong about your father . . . maybe—"

She didn't have a chance to finish. She only faintly heard the door crashing in. Colors burst and swirled in her head. The sharp pain slicing through her ribs blocked out Rhonda's sickening laugh. The white-hot pain filling her made Randall's face float past her eyes. She opened her mouth to speak, but her tongue wouldn't work. Her eyes began to flutter, and she could almost feel them rolling back.

The letter opener was deep into her chest. Blood quickly began to puddle across the silk of her blouse. In a brief moment of clarity, she touched the dragon head of the opener, then felt the sticky ooze of her blood.

Cradled in Randall's arms, she whispered, "Make . . . it . . . a . . . simple . . . Mass."

The medics had to pull him off. He wouldn't let her go. "Hang on!" he barked at them. Easing her out of his arms, he gently said, "You just hold on, here, Molly. I need merch for my condo, and you're the only dealer I trust."

Rising slowly, he stepped out of the way of the two medics and wiped his eyes.

He found Lucero on his knees, straddling a squirming Rhonda. When she started swearing at him, he banged her head on the carpet. "Molly okay?" he yelled above the din.

Randall lied. "Yeah, just a minor scratch. The medics are on it." Pulling out his cuffs, he threw them at Lucero. "See if you know how to use 'em."

Catching them in midair, Lucero said, "I'm a quick learner."

Randall kept an eye on the medics as Lucero struggled with the cuffs. Jerking his head to one of his uniforms, he said, "Give the DA a hand and read her her rights." To the officer guarding the door, he commanded, "Lead the ambulance out of here." The medics had Molly on the gurney by then, and were briskly heading out the door. In step with them, Randall held his breath, then asked, "She gonna make it?"

The medic shrugged. "The wound's pretty deep. Let's hope the thrust missed her liver." Shaking his head, he said, "I'm not a gambling man, so . . . ?"

Randall stopped dead in his tracks. His feet refused to move. He should have kept her out of this. He knew better. *"Don't take your eyes off her,"* he said.

Running after them, he yelled, "I'm coming with you. You've got an escort . . . get smokin', understand?" Jerking his cell phone out of his jacket, he punched in the number to dispatch, "I've got an ambulance coming out of Dolores onto Ocean. *Clear the fuckin' town, you hear me?"*

*R*andall noticed dust in the front window and wondered if the shop would stay open. He realized he wondered about a lot these days. Maybe coming to Carmel had been a bad idea. He sure as hell hadn't found the peace and quiet he'd expected. But then, he wouldn't have met Molly Doyle.

Through the window, he watched Molly fussing with a bouquet of flowers. Without her, Rhonda Martyn might not be heading to death row. Without her, Dan Lucero might not have found the juice to drum up interest in his upcoming bid for attorney general. He had to hand it to Lucero. Even with the video and tapes, he'd taken jail-house grilling to a higher art.

A lot of people owed Molly Doyle. Even Pablo. Molly never told him Pablo had skipped town before all hell broke loose. When they tried to round him up, he was long gone. Bitsy Morgan finally admitted Pablo would be out of reach for some time. She'd played fairy godmother so he could open an antique shop in carioca land.

Yeah, Randall thought, *I owe Molly, too. I got to know a woman I didn't think existed anymore. A stand-up broad who took her lumps and came back fighting. Sassy enough to make you sit up and take notice. Had her nose in the air when it came to merch, but what the hell, she*

*knew her stuff. And she had heart. She went the extra mile
for people she didn't even know. It was that chin of hers.
I should have remembered. Stubborn to a fault. Knowing
Molly had taught him a lesson he'd never forget. Cop
work was for cops. Period.*

Moving closer to the window, he knocked on the glass,
then opened the door. "Hey! Let's get a move on, okay?"

Grabbing her tote, Molly picked up a fallen petal. With
a tiny smile, she put it in her pocket and headed for the
door. "Chill, okay? I still can't move fast. I'm still so
sore, I have to sit every half hour."

"Stop bitching. You've played the invalid long enough.
So don't get carried away here. Now that you're back on
your feet, I can cut the sensitive guy act. I'm starving.
Daria's got cioppino tonight."

Giving him a look, she said, "Back to square one, huh?
Cioppino is not an Italian dish, you know. It's not from
Italy."

"But it's Italian. It was invented on the wharves in San
Francisco by Italian fishermen."

"I happen to know there were other immigrants fishing
there, too."

Glancing down at her, he gave her his arm for support.
"Yeah, well they sure as hell weren't Irish."

Entering Daria's, Molly laughed. "It just dawned on
me that I've never been in the dining area." As her eyes
took in the room, she smiled. "You were right. It does remind me of the old Russian Tea Room."

Leading her to a round table in the center, he heard
Molly sigh with pleasure as she noted the lush glow of
copper samovars and antique bistro coffeemakers. He
smiled as her eyes darted to silver vases, urns, and serving pieces mixed with huge flower arrangements perched
on the leather dividers separating the banquets.

"Kind of gives you that déjà vu feeling, right?" Randall said.

Nodding in agreement, her eyes were fixed on the exquisite oil paintings in heavy baroque gold leaf frames. Molly immediately recognized it was the style of Daria's friend. She couldn't wait to meet her.

So engrossed in the art, she didn't realize the group at the table was standing. When she heard the boisterous clapping, she tore her eyes from the artwork and nearly fainted.

When nearby diners joined in, she froze. Flustered by the unexpected attention, she almost didn't recognize Bennie without his baseball cap on backward, and nearly let her mouth fall open to see Bitsy standing, like an old friend, next to Daria.

Molly's head was spinning. She stepped back to catch her breath. Turning to Randall, she said, "What is this? Whose idea—"

"You've become a local hero. It'll probably last forever in a place like this."

"Oh my God, I'm so embarrassed."

"Don't fall to pieces on me, okay? Enjoy it, then get over it."

Clutching his arm, Molly flashed a quick, almost shy smile, then waved. Lucero was the first to reach her. Pressing a peck on her cheek, he led her to the table. "I want a moment here for a toast. So shut the hell up everyone. You can do kissy later."

Once the champagne was poured, Lucero took center stage. With most of the diners still watching, he turned on his courtroom voice, raised his glass, and said, "To Molly Doyle." Giving her a wink, his voice up one notch, he continued, "One hell of a job, lady! I'm in your corner for life. Just don't run for DA until I'm gone!" Talking over the laughter, he added, "Got another little bit of news. AP picked up the local story, and the *New York Times* ran it with pictures and all. Way to go, Molly!"

Molly staggered against Randall. Her hands were shaking as they flew to her mouth. "Shit!"

Seeing the horror on her face, Randall couldn't help but laugh. "Hey, you've been vindicated this time. It was a great piece. I saved a copy for you. Even me and Lucero got a mention." Leaning closer, he said, "You're free, Molly. No more hiding."

"No more hiding," she repeated. "God! I didn't know one little stab wound could suddenly feel so good."

Randall's and Lucero's eyes met across the table. They both knew the envelope had been pushed to the edge. Molly's encounter with Rhonda Martyn had been a near disaster, and this gathering might have been a wake.

Between more champagne and dish after dish of Italian delicacies, Molly nudged Randall. "What happened to the cioppino?"

"Save it, okay? I lied. Call a cop, or something."

Trying not to laugh, she said, "By the way, I finally figured out what Lorna Jacobs had been trying to tell me. I guess it was all those good drugs they pumped into me at the hospital." She laughed. "Are you ready for this?"

Rolling his eyes, he said, "You're gonna tell me even if I'm not, so hit it."

"Toby."

Shaking his head, he said, "Fuck. Could have saved us a lot of grief if you'd had your head on straight that day."

"True, but if a certain obnoxious, loudmouthed cop hadn't rattled my cage, I might have remembered."

Randall's smile was almost nice. "Yeah, yeah, touché, okay?"

Until dessert, the talk at the table was nonstop. The excitement of the past weeks had revved them up to near bursting. Now, with Molly back on her feet, they were finally enjoying the winding-down process. Lucero had to tap the edge of his glass twice to get their attention.

"Now that we're all gathered here, I guess I can give you a little insider info. Ms. Rhonda Martyn was arraigned today on five counts of Murder One."

"Five?" Molly asked.

Lucero raised his hand and spread his fingers. "Hubby number one, Sid Wells, Lorna Jacobs, Bea Thompson, and Dick Jacobs." Looking around the table, he raised his eyebrows. "I'd say that adds up to five. Right?"

"How did you get her to do that?" Molly asked, not hiding her admiration.

"I'm good." Lucero grinned. "And when I'm good, I'm very, very good."

"Knock it off, Lucero." Bennie laughed. "Just tell us in as few words as possible." Turning to Daria, he said, "He never changes, same old Lucero."

"I think he's wonderful," Bitsy said, sighing.

Giving Bitsy a perfected deep pocket constituent smile, Lucero said, "By the time I finished with her, she admitted to administering the overdose that killed Sid, wrote the phony confession Molly found, then hid it in one of his books. Bea had to go because her blackmail was cutting too deep into profits. Dick, on the other hand, was just part of the mopping-up process. Lorna was the surprise. She wanted in on the action. Rhonda wasn't about to bow to more demands."

While they digested this latest news, two waiters arrived with silver trays bearing various desserts. After they'd all made their choices, Randall filled Molly's coffee cup, and said, "By the way, your buddy Armand called the other day. He was looking for that stuff you promised him."

"Right. I'll see if Cleo can arrange to have someone send the teapot."

"Don't bother. I told him to get lost."

Touched, Molly was nearly speechless. "I . . . I don't know how to thank you. That was probably the nicest thing you've done since I've been here."

When everyone started to laugh, she added, "I mean, well, you know what I mean."

Randall took the ribbing well. "I figured it was a going-away present."

"What the hell are you talking about?"

Playing with his coffee cup, he looked away. "The Big Easy. I hear that's where you want to be. I figured once you were okay, you'd be catching the first plane to New Orleans."

"Itching to be at Café du Monde sipping café au lait and munching on beignets?"

Brushing imaginary crumbs from the table, Randall said, "Yeah. Something like that."

With a small amount of effort, Molly rose from the table. Easing back her chair, she took in each face, then raised her glass. "My turn for a toast." Waiting for everyone to rise, she saw the disappointment on Bennie's face, the shadow of pain in Bitsy's, a sad smile from Daria, and the look of surprise on Lucero's face. Randall had his head turned, and she couldn't see what might be lurking there.

"If to the victor go the spoils is true"—pausing until Randall looked her way, she smiled—"then look out Carmel! I'm here to stay." When she saw him give her his famous squinty-eyed look, she added, "Probably."